A night in with
Marilyn Monroe
BY LUCY HOLLIDAY

Lucy Holliday's first major work, a four-line poem called 'The Postman is Very Good', was completed shortly before her fifth birthday. It was such an enjoyable experience that she has wanted to be a writer ever since. Lucy is married with a daughter and lives in Wimbledon.

Also by Lucy Holliday

A Night in with Audrey Hepburn

A night in with Marilyn Monroe

BY LUCY HOLLIDAY

HARPER

Harper
An imprint of HarperCollins*Publishers*,
The News Building,
1 London Bridge Street,
London SE1 9GF

www.harpercollins.co.uk

This paperback original 2015

1

First published in Great Britain by Harper 2015

A catalogue record for this book is available from the British Library

ISBN: 978-0-00-758226-6

Typeset in Birka by Palimpsest Book Production Ltd, Falkirk, Stirlingshire

Printed and bound in the United States of America

Find out more about HarperCollins and the environment at
www.harpercollins.co.uk/green

ACKNOWLEDGEMENTS

With colossal thanks to Kate Bradley, Charlottes Brabbin and Ledger, Kate Elton and all at HarperFiction; and to Clare Alexander. Also, just as colossal thanks to my parents and to Josh, without whom this book would just never have ended up written.

PROLOGUE

WhatsApp message 5 Sept 10.17 a.m. To: Nora
Newsagent at Heathrow had copy of You and Your Wedding *magazine!!! Page 84, right? Will look now. L xx*

WhatsApp message 5 Sept 10.19 a.m. To: Nora
Ivory bias-cut one with lace sleeves?

WhatsApp message 5 Sept 10.20 a.m. To: Nora
Love it. Would look perfect on you. Let me know when you want me to come up to Glasgow for bridal shop session. Boarding any minute now. Lx

*

WhatsApp message 5 Sept 10.26 a.m. To: Cass
No, Cass, I can't meet you at Selfridges shoe hall in 5 mins.

WhatsApp message 5 Sept 10.27 a.m. To: Cass
Because am getting on plane to Miami.

WhatsApp message 5 Sept 10.28 a.m. To: Cass
With Dillon.

WhatsApp message 5 Sept 10.29 a.m. To: Cass
Yes, all right, will meet you at Selfridges shoe hall after I get back.

*

WhatsApp message 5 Sept 10.30 a.m. To: Mum
For Christ's sake, Mum, of course am not moving to America to marry Dillon. Cass obv got wrong end of stick as usual. Is just holiday.

WhatsApp message 5 Sept 10.33 a.m. To: Mum
No, Mum, I haven't thought about what I'd say if he asked me because he isn't going to ask me. Has only been 3 months.

WhatsApp message 5 Sept 10.34 a.m. To: Mum
No, Mum, am not worried that he won't buy cow if getting milk for free.

WhatsApp message 5 Sept 10.35 a.m. To: Mum
Also, have to say that is pretty outdated view of relationships.

*

WhatsApp message 6 Sept 13.02 p.m. To: Nora
Idyllic. Lx

WhatsApp message 6 Sept 13.03 p.m. To: Nora
Everything. Hotel. View. Food. Him. Lx

WhatsApp message 6 Sept 13.05 p.m. To: Nora
Appreciate your concern but don't worry. Am not falling in love with him. Even I'm not that much of an idiot. Lx

*

WhatsApp message 7 Sept 18.08 p.m. To: Olly
Hi, Ol, didn't know you knew I was here!! Yep have seen hurricane forecast. But isn't due until day after tomorrow and we're leaving tomorrow morning. Will call when back. Any news on that restaurant lease? Lx

*

WhatsApp message 9 Sept 11.13 a.m. To: Nora

Not home yet no. Couple of slight issues on that front. Just wondering: do you know how easy it is to fly from USA to UK if you don't have your passport?

WhatsApp message 9 Sept 11.18 a.m. To: Nora

That is one of slight issues. Dillon has my passport.

WhatsApp message 9 Sept 11.19 a.m. To: Nora

That is other slight issue. Don't know where Dillon is.

WhatsApp message 9 Sept 11.20 a.m. To: Nora

Because our last night at hotel he bumped into some people he knew and we ended up at random party in Coconut Grove. Had a bit of a row so I left. Forgot he had passports on him.

WhatsApp message 9 Sept 11.21 a.m. To: Nora

Because he didn't come back to the hotel and haven't seen him since.

WhatsApp message 9 Sept 11.22 a.m. To: Nora

He isn't answering his phone.

WhatsApp message 9 Sept 11.23 a.m. To: Nora

No, Nora. I haven't forgotten about hurricane.

*

WhatsApp message 9 Sept 11.27 a.m. To: Olly

Thanks for messaging, Olly. Nora obviously keeping you in the loop. But can't check into another hotel without passport.

WhatsApp message 9 Sept 11.29 a.m. To: Olly

Had already checked out of old one before realized Dillon AWOL. Also minimum room rate there is $800 per night. Also is now fully booked with terrified locals fleeing small houses in advance of hurricane.

*

WhatsApp message 9 Sept 11.42 a.m. To: Cass

No, Cass I can't bring you back bulk order of Kiehls body lotion.

WhatsApp message 9 Sept 11.46 a.m. To: Cass

Yes I do know it's pounds for dollars.

WhatsApp message 9 Sept 11.48 a.m. To: Cass

BECAUSE AM STUCK IN MIAMI WITH NO PASSPORT, NO HOTEL ROOM, 26 QUID IN MY CURRENT ACCOUNT, EXACTLY 17 DOLLARS IN MY WALLET AND HURRICANE APPROACHING.

*

WhatsApp message 9 Sept 6.53 p.m. To: Nora

Crisis averted!!! Am spending night bunking down inside Miami Dolphins Football Stadium.

WhatsApp message 9 Sept 6.55 p.m. To: Nora

Is fine, honestly. Everyone being very friendly. Have met nice family from Arizona who have lent me sleeping bag and are cooking me hot dog on their portable bbq. Is actually all very jolly and Blitz-spirity at moment!

WhatsApp message 9 Sept 6.57 p.m. To: Nora

No. He's still not answering his phone.

WhatsApp message 9 Sept 7.01 p.m. To: Nora

The row? Nothing, really.

WhatsApp message 9 Sept 7.06 p.m. To: Nora

Yes, all right. It was because he was flirting with another girl.

WhatsApp message 9 Sept 7.08 p.m. To: Nora

Norwegian swimsuit model. But not sure that's really important right now.

WhatsApp message 9 Sept 8.44 p.m. To: Nora
OK, am getting small suspicion lovely family from Arizona may belong to fanatical doomsday cult into which they are trying to indoctrinate me.

WhatsApp message 9 Sept 8.56 p.m. To: Nora
Yes, they definitely belong to fanatical doomsday cult into which they are trying to indoctrinate me.

*

WhatsApp message 9 Sept 21.22 p.m. To: Olly
Am OK. Have to admit is getting a tiny bit scary here now. Winds are starting to make a hell of a noise outside stadium. Also might have accidentally joined fanatical Doomsday cult. Seemed like small price to pay for sleeping bag and hot dog at the time, but am starting to have serious regrets.

*

WhatsApp message 9 Sept 22.23 p.m. To: Nora
Shit Nora this is getting scary now. Winds are getting up. People crying. Praying. Not just fanatical Doomsday cult but normal people too. Signal keeps cutting out. Will message as soon as I can. Love you. Sorry about all this. Lx

＊

WhatsApp message 9 Sept 22.26 p.m. To: Cass

Cass. Am slap-bang in middle of worst hurricane to hit Florida in 2 decades. Don't know when, if ever, will be getting out of here. So no. I won't be able to meet you at Selfridges today to go shoe shopping.

WhatsApp message 9 Sept 22.29 p.m. To: Cass

No, Cass. It doesn't even come close to qualifying as a disaster.

＊

WhatsApp message 9 Sept 22.31 p.m. To: Olly

I love you, Olly Lx

＊

It was a big moment, last night, when my grandmother knocked on the door of my hotel room and handed me this box containing about seventeen layers of tissue and, beneath them all, her wedding veil.

A massive moment, actually.

She's not the most warm and fuzzy of grandmothers – nobody on Dad's side is warm and fuzzy; in fact, come to think of it, nobody on Mum's side is all that warm and fuzzy either – but I've always worshipped her a little bit. For her to hand down her wedding veil to me . . . not to any of Dad's brothers' daughters, but *me* . . . well, it makes me feel special. Which is nice, for a change.

And all right, it would have made me feel even more special if she hadn't added, as she watched me open the box, 'I'd give you my wedding dress, too, Libby, darling, but I'm afraid you don't have *quite* the tiny waist I did when I wore it.'

But still. A big moment. A symbol of my super-glamorous grandmother's esteem.

And then there's the fact that it's absolutely stunning.

Seriously, there's no way you could find anything like this in any bridal shop across the land: hand-stitched, palest ivory lace, with a gauzy elbow-length piece to cover your face at the front and an almost ten-foot drop at the back. (Grandmother only got married in a small village church in her native Shropshire, but she was modelling her entire wedding 'look' on her movie idol, Grace Kelly, hence the dramatically long veil, carried up the aisle by her – eight – bridesmaids.) It makes *me* look stunning, and not just because the gauzy lace covering my face is the equivalent of smearing a camera lens with Vaseline to blur out imperfections. Something about the way the veil hangs, the way my hair is half pulled back to accommodate it, the flattering ivory shade, perhaps . . . whatever the reason, I feel a bit ravishing, to be honest with you.

And now, looking soft-focus himself from behind all this lace, here comes Olly, striding towards me. He reaches out with both hands, folds back the veil so that he can see my face, and smiles down at me. His eyes look exceptionally soft, and he doesn't speak for a moment.

'What on earth,' he says, when he finally speaks, 'are you wearing this for?'

'It's Grandmother's. She came round with it last night.' I pull the veil back down, keen to retreat behind the Vaseline blur again, just for one blissful moment. 'Does it suit me?'

'Wonderfully. But – and don't bite my head off here, Libby – don't you think maybe you ought to stick to just a simple hat, or something? It isn't your wedding, after all.'

'I know that,' I sigh. I steal one final glance at myself, a vision of Grace Kelly-esque (well, Grace Kelly-*ish*) bridal loveliness, in the full-length mirror in the corner of my hotel room. 'And obviously I'm not going to wear this to Dad and Phoebe's wedding. Though, to be fair, I don't know if Phoebe could *actually* object – I mean, Grandmother *did* offer it to her for the day, and she turned it down . . .'

This doesn't at all take the shine off Grandmother offering me the veil afterwards, by the way. I mean, all right, she was in a bit of a grump about her soon-to-be new daughter-in-law refusing to wear the veil because it would swamp her rather fabulous figure, but that wasn't why she came to my room late last night and handed it over to me instead. She'd only have let Phoebe borrow it – her Something Borrowed for the day – whereas I've actually been *bequeathed* it . . . if that's the right word to use when Grandmother is still very much alive.

'Still,' says Olly, with a grin, 'I'm not sure if Phoebe would be all that thrilled at a guest turning up in a ten-foot lace veil on her wedding day. Especially not her new stepdaughter.'

I wince.

'Sorry, sorry.' He holds up both hands. 'I know we're not calling her your stepmum. My bad.'

Because it's not as if I don't have enough problems with the one *actual* mum I've already got. Not to mention the fact that Dad has never really been enough of a dad for me to call the woman he's marrying my 'stepmother'. Don't get me wrong: I've got no objection to Phoebe whatsoever, who seemed a pleasant enough woman during the ten-minute chat we had when Olly and I arrived at the hotel last night. But I think we'll all be much more comfortable, once today is over, if we just go back to being polite strangers, exchanging Christmas cards and the occasional text. Which, where Dad is concerned anyway, would be a massive improvement on the last twenty-odd years.

'Anyway, we should probably be heading down to the orangery now, don't you think?' Olly asks as – a little bit reluctantly – I start detaching the veil from my hair and folding it back into its slim cardboard box. 'I know your dad said it's all very informal, but I doubt if that extends to us arriving after the bride and groom.'

'Well, it'd be a bit ironic of Dad to suddenly start deploring lateness right now,' I say, 'given that he only remembered my eighteenth birthday two weeks after the event . . . but, you're right. We should get going.'

I head back over to the mirror and look at our joint reflection. Now that I've taken the veil off, all I'm wearing is a cap-sleeved silk dress and matching suede heels that, both in charcoal grey, feel more wedding-appropriate than my usual head-to-toe black. Olly is looking dapper, and astonishingly different from his normal self, in a dark blue suit, crisp white shirt and striped tie. It's been ages since I've seen him in an outfit that wasn't either chef's whites or, ever since he started doing up his own restaurant a couple of months ago, a paint-spattered T-shirt and baggy jeans, so it's a bit of a surprise to look at him now and remember how well he scrubs up.

'Do we look all right?' I ask, meeting his eyes in the mirror.

Olly studies us both for a moment.

'I think we look pretty bloody good,' he says, meeting my eyes in the mirror, too. 'You in particular. I really like that dress.'

'Thanks, Ol. Oh, and I apologize in advance,' I say, linking my arm through his and starting to head for the door, grabbing my hat and bag and pashmina as we go, 'if any of my relatives mistakenly think we're a couple. I haven't told them we are – I mean, I never see any of them from one decade to the next, obviously – but you know how people jump to conclusions . . .'

'There's no need to apologize.'

'. . . and some of them might even remember you from when you came with me to my granddad's funeral eleven years ago, so they'll probably ask all kinds of questions about why *we're* not married yet . . .'

'Well, it would be a perfectly legitimate question. If we really *had* been together all those years, I mean.'

'. . . but you should be able to fob them off easily enough without even having to tell them we're just best friends. Shove a drink in most of their faces and they'll forget they were even talking to you, anyway.'

'Don't worry, Lib. Fobbing off intrusive lines of questioning from well-meaning relatives is pretty much a speciality of mine.'

And Olly holds open the door, impeccably mannered as always, for me to walk out ahead of him.

*

I'm so, so grateful to Olly for agreeing to be my date for Dad's wedding.

I mean, I know it's just about the last thing he wants to do with his weekend: schlep all the way up here to Ayrshire, where Phoebe originally hails from, just to keep me company at my father's wedding. It's not as if, what with his restaurant opening at the end of this coming week, he doesn't have plenty to be getting on with in his own life.

And I suppose I could always have asked Adam to accompany me. Given that he and I really *are* a couple.

But Adam and I have only been an item for about eight weeks. Yes, things are going terrifically well between us – I mean, *seriously* well – but it still feels a bit soon to be subjecting him to the cauldron of awkward encounters and complicated emotions that are guaranteed to mark Dad's wedding for me. Anyway, Olly agreed to come with me today as soon as I mentioned the surprise (OK, shock) arrival of the invitation, three months ago, and there's not a person in the world I'd rather have as my wingman.

(Not to mention the fact that I've been keeping quiet about the fact that Adam and I are, to put it in nice, clear Facebook terminology that never *quite* translates to real life – not my real life, at any rate – 'in a relationship'. I haven't even mentioned it, yet, to Nora, my other best friend and Olly's sister. As I say, it's still really early days and . . . well, the last relationship I had ended in such unmitigated disaster – quite literally – that I'm a bit wary of announcing that I've headed down that route again, even if it is with a man who's the polar opposite of my ex, Dillon.)

My gratitude to Olly, though, however much I thought I'd already realized it, was made even more obvious to me when Dad walked back down the aisle with his brand-new wife, Phoebe, roughly fifteen minutes ago.

I don't know what came over me, but I suddenly felt this massive lump in my throat, and not in a wedding-y, happy-tears sort of way. So it was lovely to be able to reach to my right-hand side and fumble for Olly's hand to grab on to, and even lovelier to realize that I didn't need to do much fumbling, because he was already reaching for mine.

It's a good thing that Grandmother, who was on my

other side, didn't notice our brief-but-meaningful hand-squeeze, because I'm pretty sure she's already getting all kinds of ideas into her head about me and Olly.

And now I'm *absolutely* sure she's getting all kinds of ideas, because we've all just milled from the orangery, where the ceremony took place, into the sunny-but-chilly grounds of the hotel for an alfresco drinks reception, and she's just this very minute seized my arm and said, 'Libby, darling, your Olly is absolutely *wonderful*.'

'I know.' Thank God Olly has just taken his absolutely wonderful self off to find a glass of champagne for us all, so I don't have to make *I'm really sorry* faces at him and hope Grandmother doesn't see. 'But he's not *my* Olly, in fact, Grandmother. He's just a friend.'

'Oh.' Her face, miraculously unlined for her eighty-odd years (and, fingers crossed, another thing I'll inherit from her apart from her veil) falls slightly. '*That's* a pity. I remember him from your grandfather's funeral. And he wrote me the sweetest condolence letter afterwards. So if he's just a friend, tell me: what's wrong with him?'

'Nothing. God, absolutely nothing at all! He's just . . . we're not together,' I explain. Or, to be more accurate, I *barely* explain. So I go on. 'Do you remember my friend Nora? We came to stay with you for a week one summer when we were fourteen or fifteen? Well, Olly's her brother.'

Grandmother thinks about this for a moment. 'Just because he's somebody's brother,' she replies, tartly, 'doesn't mean he wouldn't make a more-than-acceptable boyfriend.'

Which you can't argue with, I suppose. And certainly I wouldn't dare to argue with Grandmother, who – for all her Grace Kelly wedding attire – is actually a little more along the lines of one of her other screen idols, Katharine Hepburn, when it comes to spikiness. In fact, she's dressed rather like Katharine Hepburn today herself, in splendid cream silk palazzo pants and a black kimono jacket and – I'm touched by this, given that we're not as close as we could be – the beaded lariat necklace I made and sent her for her eighty-fifth birthday a few months ago. (I'm a jewellery designer, I should say, so this isn't as home-crafty as it might sound.)

'Anyhow, he couldn't be any more unsuitable than . . . what was the name of that chap you'd just stopped seeing the last time I spoke to you?' Grandmother asks. 'The one who abandoned you in Mexico in the middle of an earthquake.'

'It was Miami. And it was a hurricane.' I can't, unfortunately, correct her on the 'abandoned' part. 'And his name was Dillon.'

'Yes. Why should this nice Olly be any worse for you than a man who lets you face natural disasters on your own? You wouldn't let Libby face a natural disaster on her own,' she demands, of Olly, who – talk about timing – has just reappeared with three glasses of champagne, two of them impressively balanced in one hand, 'would you?'

'Sorry, Mrs Lomax?'

'You wouldn't leave Libby in Malaysia with a tidal wave approaching.'

'Of course he wouldn't,' I say, hastily, before Olly twigs that we're talking about Dillon. Because Olly and Dillon are not, in any way, shape or form, *simpatico*. 'Thanks for the champagne, Ol. Can he get you anything else, Grandmother?'

'No. But he can dance with me.'

She's pointing an imperious finger in the direction of a very small octagonal dance floor that's been laid down on what must usually be a patio. Music, from three exceptionally bored-looking members of a jazz trio, is emanating from right beside it.

'I don't know if that's a good idea, Grandmother . . .' Because I really don't want her bearding poor Olly in her den and demanding to know exactly why it is that we aren't a couple. He didn't sign up for the third degree when he agreed to be my 'date' today, after all. 'Nobody else has started dancing yet . . . and maybe Dad and Phoebe want to have a dance before anyone else . . .'

'Well, *I* wanted a son who wouldn't put me to shame by neglecting his duties as a father,' Grandmother says, sharply, which is the very closest she ever comes to referencing the Great Unmentionable that is Dad's history with me. 'But we can't always get what we want, Libby, can we?' She hands me her champagne glass and turns to Olly. 'So, shall we dance?'

Olly looks part-amused, part-terrified, but either way he doesn't say no. He puts his own champagne glass down on one of the nearby trestle tables that feature the cold buffet nibbles, shoots me an eyebrow-raise, then extends his arm in a gentlemanly fashion for Grandmother to take as they stroll to the dance floor.

I watch in frozen fascination as they start to put together some surprisingly impressive moves. Surprising because Grandmother is an octogenarian with two artificial knees, and because I literally had no idea Olly could dance 'properly'. The last time I saw him dance at all must have been at his parents' big ruby anniversary party a few years back, but he ended up pretty drunk that night and capable of little more than cheerful bursts of (what I hoped at the time was) Dad Dancing.

Well, look at him go right now, wheeling Grandmother around that dance floor like a cross between Fred Astaire and Patrick Swayze. And, thank God, they're dancing too energetically, by old-age-pensioner standards, anyway, for Grandmother to strike up a conversation, so with any luck I might be able to cut in and insist on a dance with Olly myself before she starts any embarrassing lines of questioning . . .

'Libby.'

A voice, right behind me, makes me turn round.

It's Dad, with one arm around his new wife, Phoebe, and the other arm around the pretty dark-haired girl who acted as the bridesmaid in the ceremony just now: Rosie, Phoebe's seventeen-year-old daughter.

The fact that Phoebe has a daughter was news to me last night. I mean, the first I'd even heard of Phoebe herself was when the wedding e-vite popped up in my inbox back in April. And I've only had the briefest of text-message exchanges with Dad about the wedding since, purely centred on whether or not he might be able to get me the family discount on the room rate at the hotel. (Turns out he could. Which is just about the most family-oriented thing Dad's done for me at any point in the last thirty years.) Any details – how they met, how long they've been together – were a total mystery to me until yesterday. Just for the record, I learned last night that they met last September when Phoebe started teaching speech therapy at the university where Dad lectures in film studies. Which is also when I learned of the existence of Rosie, my – wince alert – brand new stepsister.

'Dad,' I say. 'Phoebe. Congratulations!'

Then, because if I don't do it, he certainly won't, I lean forward and give him a quick hug, and then do the same to Phoebe.

'Aw, thanks, Libby.' Phoebe, a forty-year-old stunner in a wasp-waisted, extremely plunging wedding gown, returns the hug in a nice, if distracted way. 'So good of you to come all this way, love.'

'Oh, that's OK! It was good of you to invite me.'

'Glad you could make it,' says Dad, with one of his rare and extremely fleeting smiles. 'I know you're really busy these days.'

'Honestly, Dad, I wouldn't have missed it.'

And then there's a moment of silence.

This, exactly this, is the reason I didn't bring Adam up here today instead of Olly. This sheer, tooth-clenching awkwardness. And this is better than usual, believe it or not. Up until last summer, it had been years since I'd even spoken to Dad. It took quite a leap of faith, and some gentle pushing from . . . well, from a new friend of mine . . . to break that ice at all last year.

'You should meet your brand-new stepsister!' Phoebe says.

I wince. Thank God, nobody notices.

'Rosie, this is Libby. Libby, this is Rosie.'

'Hi!' I say.

'Hi,' says Rosie.

'Rosie's about to start her final year of college,' Phoebe goes on, 'and she's just starting to think which uni courses she might apply for. And you, Libby . . . you work in a jewellery shop, is that right?'

'Um, well, I sort of design my own jewellery, actually.'

'So you're artistic! That's nice. Rosie's very artistic, too. She's thinking of applying for a fine art degree, or maybe something related to theatre design . . . oh! I'd better just go over and say hi to Jenny and Nick . . . no, no, Eddie, you stay here,' she says, firmly, as Dad does his best to escape after her, 'and catch up with Libby properly. Get the two girls chatting!' she adds, making a sort of criss-cross gesture with her hands at Rosie and me. 'Help them get to know each other!'

This is going to be tricky for Dad, given that he doesn't even know me himself. So – after shooting a slightly panicked look of my own in the direction of the dance floor, where Olly (oh, God) is now being engaged in extremely intense conversation by Grandmother – I take pity on him and decide it's best if I take charge of the conversation myself.

'So! Rosie . . . you're . . . er . . . about to apply to university!'

'Yep.' Rosie nods. Pretty in her pale green bridesmaid's dress, she has a confident look about her that suggests she's one of the popular crowd at school. I don't think her lack of interest in me is anything personal so much as the fact that to her I'm just some boring older person who doesn't know the ins and outs of her social life. 'Just like Mum already told you.'

'Right. So, theatre design, maybe?'

'Not if I have my way,' Dad says. 'You know, this girl here is a contender for a top-notch media and communications course anywhere in the country. I'm trying to persuade her to apply to Kingston, because that's one of the best places for a terrific all-round media education. And she can specialize in film history in her third year.'

'Oh.' I'm slightly startled that Dad is even interested

in Rosie's upcoming choice of tertiary education, let alone quite this invested in it. 'So you're a film fan, then, Rosie?'

'God, yeah, I love movies. Especially all the classics. Eddie's introduced me and Mum to so many of them. We do, like, these old movie nights on Sundays, and I invite my friends over and stuff—'

'And I try not to be too much of an old bore and stop the film every five minutes to lecture them all on the things they should have noticed,' Dad interrupts, with a chuckle.

Yes, that's right: a *chuckle*.

A chuckle isn't something I've ever heard Dad emit before.

'Oh, you're all right, Eddie,' Rosie tells him, with a laugh of her own. 'Anyway, if you do too much of that, we just send you out for more popcorn.'

'So that's what I'm reduced to, is it?' Dad says, with another – *another* – chuckle. 'A PhD, and all my years of experience, and author of a highly regarded book on the history of cinema, and you and your mates just want to send me out for popcorn!'

'Oh, talking of your book,' says Rosie, 'my friend Jasper's been reading it over the holidays, and he said it's amazing. Like, he's learned absolutely loads from it.'

'Well, Jasper is obviously going places!' Dad says. Only semi-jokingly.

But then Dad is always at his most pompous where His Book is concerned. Which I suppose is a good thing in some ways, because it was the writing of His Book that dominated his life and made him such a crappy, absent father to me for over twenty-five years.

Perhaps it's the fact that the book finally came out last year that has enabled him to be (as he so clearly is) a pretty involved stepdad to Rosie.

Just at this moment, I feel a gentle touch to my elbow, and glance around to see that Olly has come over to join us.

I don't *actually* throw myself on him like a drowning woman might throw herself on a passing lifeguard, but it's a pretty close thing.

'Hi,' says Olly, extending a pleasant, if rather chilly, hand to my dad. 'Congratulations, Mr Lomax.'

'Oh, thanks . . . you're . . . uh . . . Oscar, is it?'

'Olly,' I say.

'Are you Libby's *boyfriend?*' Rosie asks, suddenly perking up and showing a bit more interest in me.

Or, to be more specific, in Olly.

At least, I assume this is what all the sudden pouty lips and hair-flicky action are about.

And Olly *is* looking nice today, in his smart suit, and with his sandy hair vaguely tidy for once, so I suppose I can't blame Rosie for all the pouting and flicking, even if it does feel a bit . . . incestuous. Because she's my (wince) new stepsister, and Olly is practically my brother.

'No, no,' I say, hastily, before Olly has to be the one to do so. 'We're just friends.'

'*Oh*,' says Rosie, meaningfully, as if Olly, being helpfully single, might suddenly decide that a seventeen-year-old is a suitable match for him, at thirty-three, and whisk her on to the dance floor for a bit of a smooch.

'I just came over, Libby,' Olly says, tactfully ignoring Rosie's eager body language and turning to me instead, 'to see if you wanted a dance. I think I might have worn your grandmother out, unfortunately, so I'm a partner down. I get the impression the jazz band are keen for some enthusiastic participants, though, so if you're up for cutting a rug . . .?'

'Delighted to,' I say, with abject relief, as I clasp his outstretched hand. 'I'll catch you later, Dad. You probably need to circulate anyway, right?'

'Absolutely,' Dad says, looking pretty abjectly relieved, himself, to be rid of me.

'And great to meet you, Rosie,' I add, with what I hope is a suitably friendly-but-not-overly-intimate stepsisterly wave. 'Maybe we can . . . er . . . keep in touch? I'm sure Dad can give you my email address if you'd like.'

Her eyes boggle at me as though I've just suggested writing each other letters with a quill pen and ink and sending them off by horse-drawn mail coach.

'Anyway, congratulations again,' Olly says, swiftly and smoothly, as he starts to lead me in the direction of the dance floor. 'You're shaking,' he adds, to me, in a low voice. 'Tricky conversation?'

'Not for my dad and his brand-new stepdaughter, no,'

I say, but quietly, because I don't want Grandmother to hear. She's sitting on a chair in the shade of some nearby trees, where Olly must have chivalrously parked her, with a fresh glass of champagne in her hand. 'They seem to be getting on like a house on fire. He's taking an interest in her future . . . introducing her and her friends to all his favourite movies . . . supplying the popcorn . . .'

Olly gives a little wince of his own – amazingly, his first of the trip. 'Sorry, Lib.'

'It's all right.'

It isn't, really. Because although my dad not being bothered about me is something I've come to terms with, it's quite different to see my dad taking such obvious pleasure in building a relationship with a daughter who's come into his life through circumstance, and not biology.

Those cosy-sounding movie nights Rosie mentioned, for example. They were precisely the sort of thing I used to crave – I mean, really *crave* – when I was growing up. I had a few of them when I was eight or nine and still staying over at Dad's for the occasional night (before plans for His Book properly took off, and he lost interest in me entirely). And I can still remember how exciting it was to be treated like a grown-up, and shown Dad's favourite movies until way, way past my bedtime. *Casablanca*, and *The African Queen*, and *Some Like It Hot* . . . with hindsight, of course, not all of them exactly the sort of thing an eight-year-old enjoys. But I enjoyed them with Dad. Despite his stiff, rather formal method of showing them, with frequent breaks for him to point out Meaningful Scenes. A method he seems to have loosened up on where Rosie is concerned.

'Do you want to go?' Olly asks, lowering his voice still further. He has one hand on my waist and one on my shoulder as we dance (or rather, rock aimlessly from side to side; I evidently haven't inherited Grandmother's rug-cutting genes), and he uses the latter hand now to give my shoulder a gentle, comforting squeeze. 'I'm happy to make the excuses if you want. I could say you're feeling ill. Or I could say I'm feeling ill. Or I could say we're *both* feeling ill – blame it all on those mushroom vol-au-vents I've seen doing the rounds, and cause a mass stampede for the exits . . .?'

I laugh. 'Thanks, Olly, but I think I'd be even more unpopular around here if I put the kibosh on Dad and Phoebe's big day.'

'You're not unpopular.' He looks down at me. 'Not with anyone who matters.'

We're interrupted by the sound of his phone ringing, somewhere inside his suit jacket.

'That's Nora's ringtone,' I say, because we've both had her programmed in our phones, ever since she moved up to Glasgow a few years ago, with 'Auld Lang Syne'. 'We should answer. It might be something to do with her flights, or something.'

My mood is lifted, briefly, by this reminder of the fact

that Nora is meeting us at Glasgow Airport later on this evening so that we can all fly back down to London together: she's coming 'home' for the week so that she can help Olly with all the last-minute preparations for his restaurant opening, and come to his opening-night party on Friday evening.

'No, I expect she'll just be calling back to see if I've decided whether or not to take her up on her suggestion about Tash and the motorbike.'

I blink up at him. 'Tash and what motorbike?'

'Er . . . I was telling you about this in the bar last night, Libby.' He looks surprised. 'You weren't *that* drunk, were you?'

No; I wasn't very drunk at all. But there was a full five minutes, possibly even longer, when I got distracted by the sight of the single-malt whisky bottles lined up along the top of the bar. Single-malt whisky bottles make me think of Dillon. And when I think about Dillon, which I very rarely allow myself to do, entire swathes of time can get sucked into this sort of . . . vortex, I suppose you'd have to call it. So Olly could have been sitting in the bar buck-naked with a loaf of bread strapped to his head, talking about the time he was abducted by aliens, and it wouldn't have even registered with me.

'Tash,' Olly re-explains, patiently (more patiently than he'd be doing if he knew it was thoughts of Dillon that had distracted me last night), 'is going to come down to London to stay this week, too. Something about a conference, and apparently she's a dab hand with a hammer and nails . . . she's offering to help out at the restaurant in the evenings . . .'

Tash, one of Nora's closest friends from the hospital they both work at in Glasgow, is almost certainly a dab hand with a hammer and nails. Tash is the sort of person who's a dab hand with everything. A bit like Nora, in fact, capable and unflappable, which is probably why they're such good friends.

I didn't know she was going to be coming down to London with Nora this week.

Not, I should say, that I've got any kind of a problem with Tash, who's seemed really nice every time I've met her.

It's just that I'd been envisaging some lovely quality time spent with Nora over these next few days: helping Olly get the restaurant ready for the Friday opening; chatting late into the night over a bottle of wine; shopping for the last few bits and bobs she might need for her own wedding at the end of July, just over a month away . . .

I mean, obviously we can still do all those things with Tash around, too. From the times I've spent with her whenever I've visited Nora up in Scotland, I know Tash enjoys a drink and a gossip just as much as Nora and I do, and seeing as she's a fellow bridesmaid, it would make perfect sense for her to come on a wedding-shopping expedition.

But still. It's not quite the way I'd fondly imagined this week would go, that's all.

'Anyway,' Olly goes on, 'she's planning on riding down on her motorbike, and Nora wondered if I wanted to hire a bike and go home that way, too.'

'Instead of taking your flight?'

'Yeah. We can do it in eight hours or so, with breaks. I mean, it's not that I think Tash needs the company, or anything – she's always seemed pretty self-sufficient whenever I've met her.'

I don't know why the idea of Olly and Tash riding motorbikes all the way from Glasgow to London should make me feel as antsy as it does. After all, even if I *did* have a problem with Tash (which as I've already said, I absolutely don't), Olly taking the long, uncomfortable route back home with Tash instead of a nice quick flight with me and Nora shouldn't bother me in the slightest. It's just because I've been a bit thrown by the idea that I might not get to spend this week hanging out with Nora in the way I'd envisaged, I decide. And maybe also by the fact that I hate him riding a motorbike, full stop. I watched a terrifying news segment once about a horrific accident caused by a bike skidding under an articulated lorry, and the memory has stayed with me.

'So I was going to say no, but I've been thinking about it, and . . . well, a night-time bike ride . . .' Olly looks wistful for a moment. 'Nora suggested it because she thought I might like to clear my head a bit. What with this big week coming up, and all that, it should be pretty quiet on a Sunday night. And I haven't ridden a bike in so long, I've almost forgotten how peaceful it is.'

'Then you should definitely do it,' I say. Reluctantly, but as enthusiastically as possible. Because I can tell from that wistful expression on his face that he really wants this.

'Really?'

'Absolutely! Just take it carefully, please, please, Olly, and obviously lay off any more champagne for the rest of the afternoon . . .'

'You don't need to worry about me,' says Olly. 'I'm here taking care of you today, remember?'

'I know. And I'll take care of you all next week, Ol, I promise. I mean, I may not be a dab hand with a hammer and nails, but I'll bring coffee, and homemade food . . .'

'There's honestly no need for that,' Olly says, hastily – as well he might, given that he's a bona-fide foodie and I can't cook for toffee. 'Moral support will be fine.'

Which he thoroughly deserves, because he is, indeed, as Grandmother has pointed out, absolutely wonderful.

'Oh, God . . . Grandmother,' I suddenly say. 'Did she go on and on at you about us, Olly? I'm so sorry, she just gets these crazy ideas into her head, and—'

'It's OK, Lib, honestly. I mean, yes, she did *mention* the concept of you and me a few times during our turn about the dance floor . . . you'd make an excellent wife, apparently . . .'

I wince. Not for the first time today and not, I expect, for the last. (I mean, there are still speeches to come, and everything. And if I can get through whatever senti-mental mush Dad will have to say about his ready-made new family, I'm going to need a hell of a lot more cham-pagne than I've drunk so far.) 'Ugh, Olly, I'm sorry.'

'. . . and she wants to live to see at least *one* successful marriage for a member of her family, and to see one bride walking down the aisle in her veil who doesn't make her think the whole thing is doomed from the very start . . .'

It's a fair point. Grandmother's children haven't exactly managed the most successful set of marriages between them, and if the photos of my own mother in the veil are anything to go by, the clock was running out for Mum and Dad pretty much from the very moment they half-heartedly said *I do*.

'. . . and I remind her of her late husband, apparently. And you remind her of herself. And they were blissfully happy for forty-six years. So really,' he finishes, with a strained-sounding laugh, 'what more evidence does anybody need that you and I ought to be together?'

This is mortifying.

I mean, yes, people are always accidentally mistaking me and Olly for a couple: I think both of us are pretty used to that now. But to have it coming from as stern and proper a figure as Grandmother feels, somehow, too real for comfort. It's a bit like the moment we shared our one and only kiss, in Paris – the Mistaken Thing we've never talked about since, after far too much wine and far too intense a conversation about love. I can't quite look Olly in the eye, and I'm certain, from the strain in his voice, that he's just as embarrassed as I am.

'Again,' I say, sounding pretty strained myself, 'I'm really sorry. She's unstoppable when she gets the bit between her teeth. I had no idea she was going to latch on to you like that . . .'

His phone is going: 'Auld Lang Syne' again.

'You really should get that this time,' I say, grateful for the diversion. 'Tell Nora to let Tash know she'll have a companion for the road ahead.'

'All right,' says Olly, taking the phone out of his pocket. 'And then I'll just need five minutes online to pre-order a bike. Promise you'll come and grab me the minute anyone starts speechifying, Lib?'

'I promise.'

I watch him wander away from the noise of the jazz band, putting his phone to his ear as he goes. And then I take a deep, deep breath, and head for the trees, to see if I can persuade Grandmother, politely, to put a sock in it for the rest of the wedding. After all, if I can stand around here on Dad's big day and bottle up all the things I might quite like to blurt out, Grandmother – a fully paid-up member of the Blitz generation – can surely do it too.

Chapter 2

Like I say, it's only been eight weeks. But I really think I might actually be falling in love with Adam already.

In the interests of full disclosure, I should point out that a) I'm an incurable romantic and b) my standards are embarrassingly low. I mean, if you're the sort of girl who's constantly being showered in dozens of red roses just because it's Tuesday, or whisked away to five-star luxury in the Italian lakes before being proposed to on a gondola, in Venice, at sunset, then my reason for suddenly realizing that Adam might be The One is going to seem a bit . . . silly.

But then, they do say that it's the little things that make a relationship go the distance. The offer to dash to the shop at eight a.m. on a drizzly Sunday morning to pick up milk for a cup of tea. The random text message in the middle of a stressful day that tells you how great you make someone feel. The surprise scrawl, at the bottom of the tedious weekly shopping list, that simply announces *Thinking about you.*

My new boyfriend turning up to meet me outside my Very Important Meeting, bringing a Pret espresso and a packet of yogurt-covered raisins, is exactly this sort of 'little thing'.

So yes, it's not red roses, and it's a long way from Venice at sunset, but it's thoughtful, and lovely, and it matters.

'You really, really shouldn't have,' I tell Adam, wrapping my arms round him and giving him a kiss. 'You're so busy. And your flight only got in two hours ago.'

'I slept loads on the plane. I'm fresh as a daisy.' The expression, in his Brooklyn accent, sounds as incongruous as it sounds sweet.

He's probably not fibbing about this: he works for a swanky investment fund, and today's flight, back to London from New York, is bound to have been one of the business-class variety. Unlike my mere hour's flight back from Glasgow last night which, though brief, was of the Ryanair variety: cramped, hectic and a bit like finding yourself in a thirty-five-thousand-feet-high tin of sardines. And Adam does, in fact, look fresh as a daisy: impeccably dressed as ever in his crisp blue shirt and rumple-free grey suit, not a single dark hair out of place. To look at him now, lean and tanned and bright-eyed, you'd think that instead of just stepping off a seven-hour flight, he'd stepped out of a salon.

'Anyway, it's right around the corner from my office,' he goes on.

'Your office is in Mayfair. This – ' I gesture around at the slightly unlovely street we're standing on – 'is Clapham. Now, I know distance is nothing to you Americans, but I wouldn't say this was *just around the corner*.'

'So I'll drop in on Olly while I'm over here. See how everything's going at the restaurant.'

Even though Olly is very definitely the proprietor of his brand-new restaurant, most of the money is being supplied by Adam's investment company. It's how I met Adam, in fact. He was at Olly's brand-new premises, the day after the builders started a little over two months ago, and I dropped in with a bottle of champagne. We got to chatting, and then he walked me to the tube . . . and, eight weeks later, here we are. Proud owners of a fully functioning, mature, adult relationship.

'Anyway,' Adam goes on now, fondly pushing a stray lock of hair behind my ear. (At least, I *think* it's fond. I can't help harbouring the suspicion that my hair, the opposite of his own neat, never-a-strand-out-of-place locks, drives him slightly nuts.) 'I know what a big deal this meeting is for you, Libby. I just wanted you to realize that I'm cheering you on.'

'You're lovely. Thank you.'

'Not to mention that I expect you were up until the small hours polishing up your business plan . . .'

He's half right. I *did* stay up late after I got home last night after the wedding, but that wasn't so much because

I was polishing my business plan as panicking about it.

I mean, this is the first time I've ever done what I'm about to do – go into a meeting with a bank manager and ask him for a small business loan – and I've no idea if what I've produced is even remotely good enough. Professional enough.

But then, perhaps that's the downside of ending up turning a hobby you love into a career you need to make a go of. I started my jewellery design business, Libby Goes To Hollywood, almost a year ago, but I still can't quite shake the sense that it's just a bit, well, *rude* to be walking into a meeting with a perfect stranger and announcing that you'd quite like him to stump up eight thousand pounds – ten if he's feeling really generous – so that you can carry on living your dream of being a jewellery designer, just with a bit more all-important dosh around so that you can buy better equipment, and maybe even employ an intern to come and work for you so that you can keep up with all the orders.

'I *was* up late,' I tell Adam, lifting a hand to waggle the espresso and yogurt-covered raisins at him. 'So these are absolutely perfect.'

Which, of course, they are.

I mean, it's not *Adam's* fault that he thinks I drink espresso, or that I'm a person for whom yogurt-covered raisins are the very acme of pre-meeting treats. I might accidentally have implied, on our second or third date, that I was a go-getting, gym-hitting, green-juice-quaffing sort of girl. Just, you know, to keep up with his own go-getting, gym-hitting, green-juice-quaffing ways.

Obviously in an ideal world, it wouldn't be an espresso, it'd be a cappuccino. And they might be *chocolate*-covered raisins instead.

OK: in a really, *really* ideal world, the snack Adam had so thoughtfully brought me wouldn't have the faintest whiff of raisin about it at all. It'd be those big, chocolate-coated honeycomb bites I've recently developed a slightly worrying addiction to, or a good old Yorkie bar, or – seeing as he's just got off a plane – a massive great Toblerone.

'Well, I know you'll sock it to 'em,' he says, leaning in to give me another big, encouraging squeeze. 'And I can't wait to hear absolutely everything about it – oh, and about your dad's wedding, of course – tomorrow.'

'Tomorrow?'

'Dinner?' he says. 'Tuesday – that Thai place you like?'

'Er . . . sure . . . but I thought we were seeing each other *tonight*. Weren't we?'

'I don't think so, Libby.' Adam shakes his head. 'It's certainly not down in my schedule.'

'Oh. It must be my mistake, then. I just thought we were going to meet at your place, and . . . um . . . you'd said you were going to cook red snapper and kale.'

'That does sound oddly specific . . .' He frowns. 'But I have a work dinner this evening, Lib. And I've asked the Cadwalladrs to keep Fritz for another evening, which

38

you know I'd *never* have done if I'd planned to be home at a normal time. I mean, I've missed him so much . . . Lottie's been sweet, and sent photo messages a few times a day while I've been away, but it's not the same as really *being* with him. Holding him. Smelling him . . .'

Fritz, I should probably explain, is Adam's dog.

A very, very cute dog. And I'm a dog person, through and through, always have been. But still. At the end of the day, just a dog.

It's just about the only thing I'd change about Adam right now, to be honest. This tendency towards ever-so-slight nuttiness about Fritz the German shepherd puppy.

'Though, now I think about it, he's probably missed me horribly . . . I guess I could blow off the work dinner, head home early for some Fritz time . . . And red snapper with you, too, Libby, of course.'

'No, no, don't worry about it. You should go to your dinner. Better not to unsettle Fritz at, er, his bedtime.'

'You're right. He hates that. When I picked him up late from the Cadwalladrs one time after I got back late from Chicago, he was so excited, he didn't sleep all night, and then of course he was grouchy all the next day, and—'

'And you and I can have a nice meal tomorrow evening, like you thought we were doing,' I interrupt, before he can go off on one of his Fritz monologues. Fritz-ologues, I suppose you could call them. 'I can fill you in on all the details of my meeting and my weekend then.' Except, of course, I'm not going to fill him in on all that many of the details of Dad's wedding, because even though we've reached the Possible Love stage, I still think we're a fair way away from me opening up to him about the myriad issues within my family. 'And talking of my meeting . . .'

'You should go, you should go.' He leans in to kiss me on the forehead. 'Go get 'em!'

'Thank you . . . do I look OK?'

'You look fabulous. Very chic.' He casts an admiring glance down at my all-black outfit (cigarette pants, silk top and nipped-in jacket) before reaching up a hand to brush my earrings. 'And I *love* these. Hey, are these brand new? From that little-known but amazing online jewellery store, Libby Goes To Hollywood?'

'They are,' I say, with a little bow. 'From the new Marilyn collection.'

He frowns. 'Named for your *mom?*'

'Named for Marilyn Monroe!'

'Oh. Yeah, that makes a lot more sense.'

The jewellery that I make is Old Hollywood-inspired, you see: a costume version of the sort of thing you might have seen, say, Ava Gardner sporting to the Oscars, or Lauren Bacall wearing in a shoot for *Harper's Bazaar*. It's a Lomax thing, I reluctantly have to admit, this obsession with the movies, whether it's Grandmother with her Grace Kelly wedding or Dad with His Book and his entire university career. My obsession with the movies comes out, these days, in my jewellery line, and since I started Libby Goes To Hollywood, my flat is piled high with endless, and expensive, coffee-table books featuring beautiful posed on- and off-screen photographs of all my favourite stars. These earrings, which as I just said are from my new 'Marilyn collection', were inspired by the glittering chandelier-style ones she wears in that iconic dance scene from *Gentlemen Prefer Blondes*: it's just that in the Libby Goes To Hollywood version they're made from silver and vintage Swarovski crystals, and not the Harry Winston diamonds that Marilyn is singing about.

'I thought I'd better show the bank manager what his money would be going towards,' I go on. 'Which will be a huge mistake if he hates them . . .'

'He won't hate them. They're gorgeous. *You're* gorgeous. And you have to remember, Libby: it's not *his* money, it's the bank's money. And they're not giving it to you as a form of charity, they'll be giving it to you as an *investment*. You don't need to go into this meeting to get him to like you. Just show him your stuff, show him what you've done and what you know you can do, and you won't have a thing to worry about.'

'Thanks, Adam. I . . .' *Can't say I love him, because we haven't said that yet.* '. . . really, really like that you came here today.'

'And I really, really like that you liked it.' He kisses me, swiftly. 'Good luck, sweetheart . . . wait. It's not bad

41

luck to say that, is it? Should I be saying "break a leg", or something?'

'That's only bad luck for actors. And thank God I'm not one of those any more.'

Seriously, thank God. Because if I were still an actress (as I was, shockingly unsuccessfully, until almost a year ago), I wouldn't now be about to walk up these steps and into a meeting with a bank manager to ask for great wodges of cash – sorry, an *investment* – to plough into my very own small business.

It's a big moment.

I watch Adam for a moment or two after he turns away and starts to head towards Olly's new premises, partly for the simple pleasure of watching such a fine figure of a man stroll away from me, and partly to see if he's going to ogle the even finer figure of a hot blonde in a tiny skirt who's just crossed the road to walk ahead of him.

But he doesn't.

Because, as I need to get to grips with remembering, he's Adam. Not Dillon. And I'm not with Dillon any more.

Then I turn away myself and head up these steps, trying to feel as go-getting as Adam thinks I am.

I mean, all his American positivity, it's bound to be rubbing off on me in some way, isn't it? If I just *believe* that the meeting will be a rip-roaring success, then it will be.

*

It wasn't.

A rip-roaring success, that is.

On a sliding scale, with rip-roaring success at one end to abject failure at the other . . . well, that meeting with Jonathan Hedley, Barclays Business Development Manager, Clapham branch, was quite a lot closer to the latter end of the scale than the former.

All right, so he didn't *actually* tell me I wasn't going to get the small business loan I was applying for. But then he didn't actually say, out loud, that there was more chance of his bank investing in a factory that makes inflatable dartboards and chocolate teapots.

It doesn't mean he wasn't thinking it.

I don't know if it was an issue with my business plan, or if he didn't like the Marilyn-inspired earrings, or if he just didn't like *me*, but I certainly didn't walk away from our half-hour meeting with the sense that the eight grand I urgently need will be forthcoming.

And there isn't any time for me to properly take stock (or even to endlessly replay the meeting over and over in my head, torturing myself with the things I must have said and done wrong), because I came out of the meeting to a series of texts from my sister Cass.

Libby where are you?

Libby I need to talk to you

Libby why are you ignoring me?

*Libby this is really unfair, call yourself my big sister,
what a joke, I'm always there for you when you need
me and now when I really need you for like once in
my life you can't even be bothered to pick up the
phone and call me back*

Which did press my guilt button quite a bit because, to
be entirely fair to Cass, she did send me a couple of
really nice supportive text messages while I was on my
way to Dad's wedding (he's not her dad; we have different
fathers).

So of course I picked up the phone and called her
back, only to be directed, through a barrage of incoherent
sobs, to come straight to her flat in Maida Vale, 'because
everything's completely shit, Libby, I can't *do* this any
more!'

I'm not too worried about all the tears and hysterics.
Cass has a tendency to overdramatize things. The last
time I was summoned to hurtle to her flat, after a nerve-
chilling six a.m. phone call, it turned out to be because
she'd stubbed her big toe getting out of bed, wasn't going
to be able to make it to her early morning spinning class,
and could, apparently, literally *feel* the fat blobbing itself
on to her thighs. There's no way of knowing what this

afternoon's crisis has been caused by, but it's not worth ignoring it in the hope that it goes away. It never does. I have a couple of hours before I need to get to my client appointment in Shepherd's Bush, so I may as well use it profitably by ensuring that my client appointment in Shepherd's Bush isn't constantly interrupted by the pinging of my phone, with increasingly furious messages from Cass.

There's another message pinging through now, as I emerge from the tube at Warwick Avenue.

Popped to nail salon. Meet me there?

Oh, and another one, a moment after this.

Bring coffee?

When I stamp into the nail bar around the corner from her flat ten minutes later, with a frappuccino for her and the cappuccino for me that I would have really liked from Adam instead of that espresso, she waves me over, imperiously, from where she's sitting towards the back. Her feet are soaking in one of the foot basins, and a weary-looking Filipina woman is tending to her hands with a cuticle stick.

'Thank God you're here,' Cass announces, which is her way of being grateful, and, 'Thank fuck for this,' as she grabs the frappuccino from me, which is her way of saying thank you. 'You won't believe what's happened, Libby. You literally won't believe it.'

'Tell me.'

'It's all off! The whole thing!'

For a fleeting, thrilled moment, I think she's talking about her relationship with her boyfriend (and manager) Dave. Which, given that he's married to another woman, is about bloody time, too.

'Oh, Cass. Well, I'm really sorry you're upset. But, you know, it was always a terrible idea, and too many people risked being hurt—'

'Who was going to get hurt? Nobody was going to get hurt! It wasn't supposed to be a bloody *stunt* show! It wasn't *Dancing On Ice!*'

I'm confused, until I remember the other thing that could be 'off'.

Her reality TV show, *Considering Cassidy*.

'RealTime Media called Dave this morning and they're pulling the plug,' Cass sniffs. 'Not enough interest from advertisers, apparently.'

'Oh, *Cass.*'

This is genuinely upsetting news for her. *Considering Cassidy* was going to be her very own, eight-part 'scripted reality' show, on the *Bravo* channel, documenting – according to Dave's pitch – 'the crazy, behind-the-scenes dramas of one of the most famous actresses working in Britain today . . . from pampering to premieres, from dating to mating; follow much-loved TV It-Girl Cassidy

Kennedy as she dishes the dirt on Slebsville, her way!'

(And yes, I was a bit surprised they got as far as they did in talks with the production company, RealTime Media, on the basis of that pitch – but, nevertheless, a deal was about to be struck. No matter that Cass *isn't*, by any stretch of the imagination, 'one of the most famous actresses working in Britain today' . . . nor that, thanks to her relationship with Dave, any 'dating and mating' the programme intended to depict was going to have to be far more on the 'scripted' side than the 'reality' side. It was going to be her very own show, her step up from her usual soaps, or her small, regular role in sci-fi drama *Isara 364*. Her springboard, at least the way Cass was looking at it, to Kardashian levels of fame and glory.)

'I'm really sorry,' I begin, only for her to interrupt me.

'I mean, not enough interest from advertisers? Are they *kidding me?* I can be used to sell *anything*, if the angle's right. I mean, your friend Olly wouldn't have invited me to that opening-night party of his this week, would he, if he weren't just using me to get more customers through his doors?'

I'm pretty sure that Olly's invited Cass to his opening-night party because he needs someone there to whom his youngest sister Kitty will deign to talk; she's an MTV presenter now, and a competitor of Cass's from their child-star days, and I very much doubt she'd make a hole in her busy schedule for Olly's big night if it weren't for the opportunity to score points off an old frenemy.

'No, Libby,' Cass is going on, 'it's absolutely nothing to do with the advertisers. It's Tanya, from RealTime. She *hated* me, right from the word go.'

'Um, I'm sure she didn't hate you, whoever she is . . .'

'She's Ned's producing partner. And she did hate me. I mean, not that I give a shit. If I had a tenner for every girl who's ever been jealous of me, I'd have . . .' Her eyes, slightly smudged from all the crying she's been doing, widen as she tries to work out this calculation. 'Well, enough money to start my *own* production company, and produce my own show. And win, like, every single Emmy and Golden Globe I possibly could. And then Tanya could fuck off.'

It's not worth pointing out that scripted reality shows on the Bravo channel aren't all that likely to be in the running for Emmys or Golden Globes. If Cass wants to imagine herself swanning along some red carpet, holding armfuls of awards in one hand and making rude gestures at this Tanya with the other, then it's no skin off my nose.

'Well, look, maybe something good will come out of all this,' I say, as Cass starts to peruse the selection of polish colours the weary nail technician is holding out to her, wrinkling her pretty nose at too-red reds and not-pink-enough pinks. 'After all, you're an actress, Cass. Reality TV would be a bit of a diversion.'

'Yeah. An *amazing* diversion. I mean, we had it all mapped out, Dave and I. *Considering Cassidy* was going to lead to an offer from *Celebrity Masterchef*, and that would lead to an offer from *Strictly*, and then I'd be able to call all the shots with one of the really big TV channels, like *E!*, for an even bigger, better reality show . . . and now I'm going to have to go back to boring old *acting*. And learning *lines*. And, like, pretending to care about character development so the writers don't give all the good storylines to somebody else.'

'I know. It's a tough business,' I say, in the sort of soothing tone that Mum is good at deploying with Cass whenever she's having a meltdown. Which reminds me . . . 'Have you spoken to Mum about it yet?'

'Yeah, and she offered to come back early from the tap festival to come round to mine tonight to cheer me up.'

This isn't the sort of tap you get water from; it's the sort of tap that hordes of star-struck eleven-year-old girls do with their feet. After working as Cass's manager for years (mine too, to be fair; it's just that my own acting career didn't provide her with quite as much work as Cass's did), Mum now owns her own weekend stage-school franchise in Kensal Rise. She's in Cardiff with a posse of those very star-struck eleven-year-old girls now, at the tap festival, and it's heart-warming to hear that she's offered to come back early for Cass's sake. Though it could also be a sign that the reality of spending all day surrounded by star-struck eleven-year-olds, in tap shoes, is starting to get on her nerves.

'That's nice of her.'

'Yeah, but I told her no. She's working over there. I thought you'd cheer me up instead. So, Dave's booked a table for me at Roka tonight, and I'll need you to come with me. I'm going to wear my new cherry-red hot-pants, and Dave's going to let the 3AM Girls know where I'll be . . . I think they might remember you from that time they wrote about you and Dillon.' Cass gives me a quick once-over. 'You'll have to head back to yours and change, obviously . . .'

I can't decide whether to feel truly depressed that Cass is so obviously trying to use me for publicity purposes, to increase the chance of the production company revisiting the idea of her show again, or slightly envious of her ability to pick herself up off the floor and get right back on the horse after a tumble.

Either way, my answer is going to have to be the same.

'Cass, I can't come out with you tonight. I'm . . . busy.'

'Doing what?'

This is an excellent question.

To which the most accurate answer would be, 'With any luck, having mind-blowing sex with my new boyfriend until the small hours of the morning.'

Because having mind-blowing sex with Adam was, in fact, my endgame for this evening. It's an endgame that's been buggered around slightly by him forgetting about our plans to have a cosy night in at his place, and scheduling in that work dinner of his instead, but it's an endgame that I still fully intend to pursue.

50

And if that makes me sound like some sort of nymphomaniac, let me just add that while I was being truthful when I stated earlier that we have a mature, adult relationship, and while I may, let's face it, have fallen in love with him this morning over the whole espresso and yogurt-covered-raisins thing, in eight weeks of dating we still haven't progressed any further than a good old snog on the sofa.

Yes. Eight weeks.

Given that neither of us is Amish, or anything, and given that – as far as it's been possible to tell – we're both in possession of all the necessary working body parts, I can't help but wonder if this is some sort of a record.

There are several perfectly decent explanations. We're both extremely busy. He travels a lot. Fritz needs walking a lot. We have such a good time together that quite often hours of just chatting pass by without either of us noticing that we haven't jumped on each other and started frantically humping.

But still. Eight weeks of snogging on the sofa has left me, at the very least, feeling pretty frustrated. I mean, I fancy the pants off him, and he claims to fancy the pants off me, so I think it's about time we acted on those urges and, well, got our actual pants off.

Hence the sex, sex, and more sex plan that I'd formulated in my head for tonight. And which no inconvenient work dinner is going to prevent. It doesn't need to happen

51

after a candlelit supper of red snapper and super-healthy kale. It just needs to *happen*.

But I'm not going to tell Cass about the (hopefully) mind-blowing sex thing, because that's not the sort of relationship we have. (Or, let's put it this way: if I open the door to frank discussions about sex with Adam, I'm very, very scared that she'll start telling me about sex with Dave. And I value an undisturbed night's sleep. Which I don't think I'd ever have again if I had to think about horrible, cheaty Dave having extramarital relations with my sister.)

So I just say, 'I'm seeing Adam.'

'Adam? Who's Adam?'

'He's . . . well, he's my new boyfriend.'

Cass stares at me.

'You have a *new boyfriend?*'

'I do. Yes.'

'And you're *choosing him?* This *new boyfriend?* Over *me?*'

The nail technician lets out a little wince. It's eerily reminiscent of me at Dad's wedding yesterday.

'No, Cass, I'm not choosing him over you. It's just that, like I said, I have plans with him tonight, and—'

'What plans?' Cass demands, in the tone of voice that implies that any answer other than *sitting by his side in the hospital as he recovers from major neurological surgery* isn't going to be anywhere near reason enough.

'You know . . . plans. Things people make with their boyfriends.'

'Right. *I* get it,' says Cass, with the sort of swoosh of her blonde hair that would say, *Et tu, Brute*, if hair-swooshes could actually talk. 'You're going to swan off and spend all night shagging this *so-called Adam—*'

'He's not *so-called* Adam. He's *actually* called Adam.'

'. . . while your *only sister* sits at home alone, contemplating the *end of her career* at the bottom of a brandy bottle.'

'You don't drink brandy,' I point out. 'And anyway, come to think of it, isn't Monday usually a Dave night?'

'Not today,' Cass scowls. 'His wife's kicking up some sort of fuss about him staying home tonight. For her birthday, or something.'

'How unreasonable of her.'

'Exactly. But only what I've come to expect,' she sniffs, 'from yet another of the people I love in my life. That when the crisps are down . . .'

'The chips.'

'. . . you can't really rely on anyone.'

'Cass.' I allow myself, regretting it the moment I do so, to succumb to the twinge of guilt that's nibbling away at me. 'Look. I've got some time tomorrow, OK? Well, I haven't, really, but I'll *make* some time tomorrow.' All that moral support I promised Olly is going to have to take a temporary second place, until the day after. Still, I'll just redouble my efforts as soon as I can.

'We'll . . . we'll go out for lunch, and then we can go shopping, and I'll even treat you to a . . .' I'm about to say the word 'massage' when I remember that all the places Cass likes to go for a massage charge well over a hundred quid for the privilege. '. . . blow-dry, or something,' I finish, hating the fact I can't be more generous. But if no bank is going to lend me a penny, I'm going to have to use more of my own meagre savings to put into the business. I can't afford to splash out any more than absolutely necessary.

'I don't need a blow-dry.' She muses on my offer for a moment. 'Though I suppose I could do with some eyebrow threading . . . oooh, or a nice collagen facial . . .'

'Threading it is!' I say, gaily, trying to inject the task with a lot more merriment than it's actually going to entail. 'Come on, Cass. It'll be lovely. And you can get a nice early night tonight, and don't even think about any of this production company stuff, and then we can discuss it all in a much more positive frame of mind tomorrow. Over that nice dinner out, if you still want to.'

'We-e-ell . . . I *suppose* so. I mean, just for the record,' she says, never one to end on a peaceable solution where there is drama to be mined, 'I'd never leave *you* alone if you were seriously depressed, Libby. I was There For You right after all that mess with stupid Dillon, wasn't I?'

It's true: she was 'There For Me' right after all that mess with stupid Dillon. Just in her style, which meant hurrying round with a huge carton of homemade (by

54

Harvey Nichols' Food Hall) soup, snuggling up with me on my sofa to tell me what a shit she'd always thought he was, and then getting involved in a FaceTime row with vile Dave and sobbing on *my* shoulder (and guzzling all the soup) until three o'clock in the morning.

'I brought you,' she says, meaningfully, '*homemade soup!*'

'I know, Cass, and it was lovely of you. And I promise I'll be at your beck and call all day tomorrow, OK?'

'All right,' she sniffs. 'I'll just call Stella for the evening, then, and get her to come over for a quiet night in instead. My roots could do with a retouch, anyway.'

I can't fail to feel a fleeting stab of sadness that Cass – partly because she's always accusing other women of being jealous of her, and partly because of her ridiculous habit of sleeping with married men – doesn't really have any good female friends to call upon in her time of crisis. Stella, although a lovely girl who's known Cass ever since they were at stage school together, is less her friend and more her hairdresser.

'OK, good. You do that, and I'll give you a call first thing in the morning to arrange where and when to meet.' I lean across the nail technician, apologizing as I do so, and give Cass a hug. 'But I really do have to go now.'

'To see this Adam?'

'Yes. But I've got a meeting with a client in Shepherd's Bush first.'

'Oh, right.' She's lost interest. 'See you tomorrow then.'

'Sure,' I tell her. 'Love you, Cass.'

'Hmph,' she says, which – and I'm translating again here – is her way of saying she loves me too.

Chapter 3

Lack of sex aside, things are going sufficiently well with Adam that he's let me know the code for his key safe, which is hidden under an artfully disguised fake rock in his tiny front garden. He's told me to let myself into his house on a few occasions since we've been dating, mostly when he was running late and wanted me to go in and tell Fritz he loved him, and missed him, and hadn't forgotten about him. So I'm just sort of hoping he doesn't mind that I'm going to use the key to let myself in this evening, this time without his explicit say-so, to lie in wait for him in absurdly sexy lingerie and give him a wild night of sex that he'll never forget.

Or, that if he *does* mind that I've let myself in without his explicit say-so, that the absurdly sexy lingerie and the wild night of sex will go quite a long way to making him not mind any more.

After a great meeting with a new client (a freelance stylist who's keen to use a few of my pieces in an upcoming shoot with a Sunday supplement; how about *that*, Jonathan Hedley, Barclays Business Development manager, Clapham branch?) I've reached Adam's house, a stunning Edwardian terrace in the middle of a street of stunning Edwardian terraces in Shepherd's Bush. I've just let myself in through the gate, when I hear the front door of the neighbouring house open.

And then I don't hear anything else at all, because there's such a thunderstorm of barking that a small bomb could go off nearby and I don't think I'd notice.

It's Fritz, Adam's German shepherd puppy, who's just on his way out of the house with James Cadwalladr, Adam's next-door neighbour.

I've never actually met James Cadwalladr in person before, and this moment – as Fritz leaps the fence and starts inserting his nose gleefully into my groin – isn't the ideal one for it to happen.

I mean, I'm fairly accustomed to coming face-to-face with very, very handsome actors – I woke up next to Dillon O'Hara several mornings a week for the few short months of our relationship, didn't I? – but James Cadwalladr has that whole arrogant Old Etonian thing going on, which is a lot more intimidating. He's staring at me over the fence now, looking even more icy-cool and unimpressed than he does when you see him as that toff, cricket-loving detective on TV.

'Sorry,' he says, 'but who are you?'

'I'm Libby,' I say, breathlessly, trying to shove Fritz's

nose out of my groin and, when that doesn't work, squatting down to meet him at doggy eye-level, in the hope that he'll nuzzle into my neck instead. He doesn't. He just goes lower and tries desperately to reach my groin again. (I can only hope his owner is equally determined, when he gets home for his surprise sex-fest later.) 'I'm Adam's girlfriend.'

'You're not.'

'I am.'

'You can't be.'

'I . . . er . . . am?'

'You're serious?' He rakes back his posh-boy floppy hair and stares at me some more. 'I didn't know he'd got himself a girlfriend.'

'Well, he has!' I give up fighting Fritz and get back up again, whereupon he instantly loses interest in my groin (hurray!) and starts sniffing round the other side of me – to be precise, my bottom – instead. 'I, um, know your wife, actually.'

Posh James doesn't look that much more interested in this. 'Oh, yeah?'

'Yes. She stocks some of my jewellery in her store.'

I have Adam to thank for this, after he very nicely introduced me to Lottie Cadwalladr when she stopped to make a fuss of Fritz in the street one warm evening. She owns Ariel, an amazing and very hip independent boutique with a branch in Westbourne Grove and a branch in Spitalfields. We got to chatting, and she admired the bracelet I was wearing, and for the past couple of weeks, Ariel has stocked a small selection of my bracelets and earrings in the Westbourne Grove branch. It was a huge coup for me because, even though the orders through my website are nice and steady, it really helps to have a real-life stockist, too. Not to mention that seeing my jewellery in those glass display cases, actually being admired by shoppers the day I went to visit, has given me all sorts of dreams about maybe even managing to open a tiny store of my own one day . . .

'Right.' Posh James slaps his thigh; I'm not quite sure why he's doing that for a moment (pantomime rehearsal?), until I realize he's trying to call Fritz. 'Here, boy! Over here!' He looks irritated when Fritz ignores him. 'He likes you,' he says, in an accusing tone of voice, 'doesn't he?'

'Oh, that's only because I stupidly sneak him tastes of stuff when Adam and I eat together. You know, I don't think he looks at me and sees a human woman. I think he looks at me and sees a walking, talking wodge of chicken liver pâté.'

Posh James doesn't laugh.

'*Here*, boy!' he adds, more commandingly this time, and follows it up with a whistle, which finally persuades Fritz to stop nuzzling my private areas and to jump the fence to join him again. 'Are you going into the house, or something? I thought Adam was still away. I'm not quite sure why Lottie's saddled us with this fur-ball for another night otherwise.'

'Adam's not back until later tonight. I'm just . . . er . . . dropping something off,' I say, because I don't want a complete stranger to realize I'm going into my boyfriend's house to lie in wait for him in my undies. 'I know he's really grateful to you for looking after Fritz.'

'The kids love him,' Posh James says, with a shrug, as he grasps Fritz's collar and clips on a lead. 'Well. Good to meet you, anyway,' he adds, in a voice that implies it wasn't so much *good* as deadly dull and totally tiresome. 'And good luck.'

Which is an odd thing to say.

But I won't ask why he's said it, partly because I don't want to bore him any more than I already have, and partly because Fritz has started barking again, rendering any attempt at further conversation impossible.

They set off along the street for their evening walk, and I crouch down to tap in the code for the key safe, then let myself into Adam's house.

As ever, it's an oasis of tranquillity.

An oasis of ever-so-slightly sterile, obsessive-compulsive neat-freak tranquillity, perhaps, but an oasis nevertheless.

I mean, if I ever ended up living here with Adam, there's so much I'd do to make the place a bit . . . well, a bit less like an absolutely stunning show home, and a bit more like a place to really live in. I'd funk up the cream-and-grey colour scheme for starters, put up a few pictures on the walls in the hallway in place of all the space-enhancing mirrors, make the chrome and grey marble kitchen, where I'm just heading now, a warm and welcoming place to hang out in with our friends, rather than like a photo in a glossy interiors magazine. I'd replace the steel kitchen table with a nice big wooden one, like the one Olly has in his kitchen, and I'd replace the Perspex chairs with mismatched painted chairs, again just like Olly's chairs, and I'd redo the smart, slightly soulless patio area you can see out of the bifold doors at the back; turn it into a proper garden, with grass and flowerbeds and a barbecue . . . The cosiest part of the whole kitchen is Fritz's den, in a little nook on the far side of the range cooker (for maximum warmth), and even this is still stylish enough to feature in a doggy version of *World of Interiors*, with its custom-made safety gate to close him off from any hot-fat-spitting danger when Adam is cooking, and its selection of Kelly Hoppen cushions for him to rest his weary rump on.

But it's not the time to stand here mentally remodelling Adam's beautiful home (not to mention that we're not yet anywhere near the moving-in stage), because I've no idea what sort of time he'll be getting back, and I want to make sure I'm all ready in my sexy lingerie for when he does.

Or rather, my downright slutty lingerie.

Because I'm pulling out all the stops tonight, I'll be

honest. I've already ramped up the raunch factor on the lingerie I've been wearing for most of our snogging-on-the-sofa nights, in the hope that something – the lacy, plunge-front bra; the tactile silken camisole; the wispy, semi-transparent knickers – might get Adam going enough to override all the perfectly good reasons why we haven't done the deed. But none of it has worked, so tonight I'm breaking out the Ribbony Elasticky Thing.

I get it out from the bottom of my bag, now, where it's nestled since I left my flat earlier today.

You know, I'm still none the wiser as to what kind of garment it actually *is*.

I bought it half-price in the Myla sale at the very height of my relationship with Dillon, and though it provided for several extremely pleasant evenings, its precise definition remains a mystery. It's not a basque. It's not a corset. I suppose the most accurate description would be 'playsuit', but I'm not at all sure it contains enough material even to fall into that category. It's just a collection of very, very small pieces of black lacy fabric, held together with strings of black satin ribbon, or lengths of wide black elastic. It requires *either* a degree in mechanical engineering *or* nerves of steel and the patience of a saint to get the thing on – though funnily enough Dillon never had the slightest difficulty in getting it *off* – and tonight, ladies and gentlemen, I shall be hoisting myself into it along with my highest heels, a cheeky smile . . . and *absolutely nothing else*.

Oh, well, obviously the 'Marilyn collection' earrings Adam admired so much earlier. Just in case all the black lace and general sauciness doesn't get him going, my fabulous accessories, with any luck, will do the job.

The only trouble is, as I find when I start to hoick myself into it now, that the last time I wore the Ribbony Elasticky Thing, I was a good half-stone lighter (it's not that Dillon pressured me into losing weight, or anything – in fact, he was always superlatively appreciative of my distinctly non-model-worthy curves – but you try sharing a bathroom mirror with a man as impressively fit as Dillon for more than a couple of occasions, and see if you can resist the temptation to cut out pudding. And bread. And chips. And lunch). The Ribbony Elasticky Thing goes up reasonably smoothly over my thighs, requires a bit of jiggling to get it up over my hips, but when I get to the bit that (barely) covers my stomach, which is where the majority of my regained weight has generously portioned itself, it starts to become a bit of a struggle.

In the war of Libby Lomax versus Ribbony Elasticky Thing, Ribbony Elasticky Thing is definitely winning this particular battle when my phone rings.

When I reach down to grab my phone from my bag, I can see that it's Nora calling.

Well, at least it's a call that's actually *worth* the temporary defeat to a piece of lingerie.

A regular call, not FaceTime, thank God, because long-time best friends as we are, there's no way I'd subject Nora to the sight of me half in, half out of my sluttiest underwear. I know she *probably* sees more disturbing sights on an average shift in her work as an emergency medicine registrar, but I wouldn't actually put money on it, or anything.

'Hi, Nor,' I say, as I answer the phone. 'Everything OK?'

'Is everything OK with *you*?' she replies. 'You're not . . . *exercising*, are you?'

It speaks volumes about my affection for physical exertion that Nora sounds so astonished as she asks this.

'Christ, no. I'm just putting on some . . . er . . . clothes.'

'Full-body armour? A HazMat suit? Because it sounds as if you're getting out of puff there, Lib.'

'I am, a bit. But it's not a suit of armour. The opposite, actually.' I prop the phone between my ear and shoulder, and start again on my attempt to e-a-s-e the Ribbony Elasticky Thing up over my tummy. 'I'm at Adam's. Just getting ready for . . . well, a nice romantic night in.'

'Oh. Right.'

It's ironic – and a bit incomprehensible, really – that Nora, who's spent much of the past few months urging to me to get out there and meet someone so that I can lay the ghost of my failed fling with Dillon O'Hara to rest, is a bit down on the whole idea of Adam. She was excited when I first told her – waiting for our flight last night – that I'd started seeing someone new, but then she seemed to cool off on the news when I explained how I'd met him.

'I forgot to ask yesterday,' she says, now, 'but have you . . . er . . . mentioned anything about this Adam guy to Olly yet? Because if you haven't, don't you think that maybe you should? Given that they work together, and everything.'

'I haven't, yet. But you don't really think he's going to *mind*, do you, Nor? I mean, I know it could be awkward if they worked together properly – like, in the same office, or something – just in case things didn't work out between me and Adam, and Olly ended up having to take a side. But they only meet up every so often, and it'll be even less once the restaurant is actually up and running.'

'True.' Nora clears her throat. 'I wish you'd tell him soon, though, Libby. I'll feel awkward, if I don't mention anything about it the entire time I'm staying here.'

'It's perfectly OK to mention it! It's not a big secret or anything. Besides, I'm sure he'll be pleased. He likes Adam. And it's not like I'm going out with, well, You Know Who, or anything.'

I'm talking about Dillon, not Voldemort, by the way. I just tend to avoid mentioning his actual name to either Nora or Olly, because they still get a bit worked up about him, even all these months on. I mean, I think *I* got over Dillon's shoddy behaviour faster than either Nora or Olly

66

did, and that's saying something. The trouble is that Olly loathed Dillon right from the start – so much so that he resorted to threats of physical violence with kitchen equipment even *before* the Miami hurricane fiasco. There isn't enough kitchen equipment in the world to carry out all the things Olly wanted to do to Dillon *afterwards*.

'Hmm,' Nora replies. 'So. A nice romantic evening, you said.'

'Yes.' I carry on inching the Ribbony Elasticky Thing up over my none-too-perfect stomach. *God*, I wish I hadn't put this half-stone back on. 'At least, I hope so. I mean, I'm here at his house, and I'm going to surprise him when he gets in.'

'Surprise him?' She sounds confused. 'Like a sort of . . . sex ambush?'

'No! It's not a sex ambush! God, Nora, you make it sound like I'm planning to jump out of the wardrobe, knock him out with a tranquillizer dart, manacle him to the radiator and have my wicked way with him for the next three nights.'

There's a short silence.

'That does sound,' Nora says, after a moment, 'worry-ingly *detailed* . . .'

'OK, but it wouldn't be totally incomprehensible if I were to do something of the sort,' I say, finally – *finally!* – managing to edge the Ribbony Elasticky Thing up over my tummy before jiggling the shoulder straps into position. 'I told you on the plane last night. Things are really perfect between us. We just need to work on . . . the sex part.'

'Lib, I do worry a bit when you start using words like *perfect*. I mean, don't get me wrong, Adam does sound lovely. But you know you have a tendency to . . . well, romanticize things.'

'I admit, I might have had that tendency in the past, but not this time. When you meet him, you'll see.' Now that the Ribbony Elasticky Thing is safely (well, safely-ish) on, I can start the complicated process of arranging the lengths of ribbon and elastic so that they cover the parts they're meant to cover. 'He's steady. Dependable. Reliable . . .'

'Well, all right, there's no need to make him sound like the sort of thing my dad might use for weather-proofing his patio furniture.'

'. . . Mature,' I continue. 'Well-rounded.'

'OK, now you're making him sound like one of those mystery cheeses you and Olly are always bleating on about.'

'My point is that I really, truly think this could be it. Adam could be it. I mean, he brought me espresso and yogurt-covered raisins before my big meeting this morning! All the way from his Mayfair office to Clapham!'

'Er, wouldn't you just have preferred a cappuccino and a bag of those honeycomb bite thingies you ploughed your way through at the airport yesterday?'

'Not the point. He really cares, Nora. I really, properly matter to him.'

'Which is great, Lib. And I'm so, so happy for you. I just don't want to see you getting hurt.' There's the briefest of pauses before she adds a light but meaningful, 'again'.

'There's no way, Nora, that I could possibly get hurt.' Though even as I say this, the Ribbony Elasticky thing starts riding, well, *upwards* in a manner that's only going to get more painful if it goes any further. So it's just possible that Nora might have a point, even if it's not quite in the way she was meaning it.

'OK, but after what happened with You Know Who, and all the bloody *chaos* he caused—'

'Talking of chaos,' I say, smoothly interrupting before we get diverted down the Dillon alleyway, from where it's always difficult to escape, 'you spent so long asking me about Dad's wedding yesterday that you didn't actually tell me anything about *your* wedding.' Nora is getting married in five weeks' time, to her lovely fiancé Mark. 'Any news? Any updates? Anything your devoted and dedicated chief bridesmaid can do to help?'

'Actually, that's partly why I'm calling,' Nora says. 'I forgot to ask yesterday, and I know you're really busy these days, Lib . . . but do you think you might be able to spare a couple of hours to go bridesmaid's dress shopping with Tash one day this week?'

Tash, apart from being Olly's motorbike-ride buddy, is going to be Nora's only other non-family bridesmaid.

'I thought maybe you could take along the dress you've

already chosen for yourself, and try to help her find something that would co-ordinate . . . I'll try and come along with you guys too,' she adds, perhaps proving that she's noticed that Tash and I, though perfectly amiable together, haven't quite gelled enough for a girlie shopping trip *à deux*. 'If Olly doesn't need me to run any errands for him at the same time.'

'Happy to, Nora. I'll make a bit of time whenever Tash can do it.'

'Thanks, Lib. And talking of Tash, I'd better get going . . . we're heading into the West End for a bite to eat tonight. Probably the only chance I'll get to show her the bright lights before we become Olly's menials for the next few evenings.'

'Sure, of course. You go.'

'And good luck with Adam tonight!' she adds. 'But you won't need it. I'm sure he won't be able to keep his steady, dependable, teak-garden-furniture-protecting hands off you.'

We can but hope.

And we'll find out sooner than I'd thought, because I've only just slipped my phone back into my bag when I hear a key in the front door.

This isn't a late night! It's barely gone eight! What did they do at this work dinner: sip sparkling water, nibble a small selection of sushi, turn down coffee and then pay the bill?

Well, there's no time to find all this American professionalism and healthy living irritating: thank God, I'm all ready and (barely) dressed, so all I need to do is arrange myself as seductively as possible on one of the uncomfortable chairs, attach what I hope is a come-hither smile, and—

'I don't see why I had to come over and help you find the bloody thing,' comes a voice from the hallway. 'Couldn't you do it on your own?'

It's not Adam.

It's Posh James Cadwalladr.

'OK, OK, but I feel weird about coming into Adam's house all by myself. We don't know him *that* well.'

And this, I recognize straight away, is Lottie Cadwalladr, my brand-new stockist.

Shit.

I can't make a dash for the stairs, because they're out in the hallway, where the Cadwalladrs have just let themselves in. I can't make a dash for the bifold doors that lead into the garden, because they're locked and I don't have time to look for the key. It would be absolutely useless to get on my hands and knees under the table because it's made of bloody Perspex . . .

What the hell am I going to do?

As the kitchen door starts to open, I make the only choice I have available to me: a dash to Fritz's den, where I should be able to hide myself away until the Cadwalladrs have found whatever it is they're looking for, and buggered off back to their own property again.

I jump up from the table, sprinting to the nook by the cooker, and, despite my heels, leap the safety gate in a rather impressive single bound.

'. . . quite sure Adam didn't bring that one over in Fritz's bag of stuff, when he dropped him off?' Posh James is asking, as two pairs of footsteps – one heavy and male, one lighter and ballet-pump-wearing, make their way on to the marble floor. 'Weren't there about half a million squeaky toys in there?'

'Not the green and white one,' says Lottie, before adding, 'Go on, Fritzy! Go find your toy! Go find!'

Hang on: they've brought *Fritz* with them, too?

I don't even need to ask myself the question, because there's a pitter-pattering of doggy feet across the marble floor, and a moment later I'm gazing, from my crouched position behind the safety gate, deep into Fritz's chocolate-brown, adoring, eyes.

He starts – surprise, surprise – barking.

'Fritz, no!' I whisper, flapping my hands at him. 'Go away! I don't have any pâté! *Ich habe,*' I hazard, in desperation, dredging up the German I studied, half-heartedly, when I was fourteen years old, '*kein pâté!*'

Mentioning pâté was, with hindsight, a mistake, in either language.

Fritz goes berserk.

'What the fuck's he barking about now?' I can just about hear Posh James saying over the torrent of noise Fritz is making.

'The toy must be in his den,' I hear Lottie say. 'Clever boy!'

His toy! His green and white squeaky toy! That'll get rid of him. I see it in here, nestling to the side of his (Alessi) bowl, grab it and then, making sure I lean right through the bars of the safety gate for maximum distance, skim the bloody thing as far away across the kitchen floor from the den, and me, as it'll go.

Which makes not the slightest difference. Fritz could no longer care less about his squeaky toy, not when his beloved Bringer Of Pâté is right here before him, cornered behind his safety gate. Besides, now that I've made the mistake of putting my head through the bars to chuck his toy, he's licking my face, practically water-boarding me with meaty-smelling saliva.

It's a bit gross, and I can't pull my head back through the bars fast enough.

Except I can't pull my head back through the bars at all.

I'm serious. I can't get my head out.

It makes no sense . . . I mean, I got my head through them one way, didn't I?

Unless it's the Marilyn Monroe earrings. These great, big, chandelier-style Marilyn Monroe earrings. Jamming up against the outside of the bars, making it impossible for me to squeeze my head back through.

Just as this horrible fact dawns on me, a pair of leopard-print French Sole ballet pumps comes past the range cooker and stops, abruptly, right in front of me.

'Oh, dear God,' says Lottie Cadwalladr, about four feet above my head.

Which sums it up pretty neatly, really.

'*James!*' she goes on, in a horrified voice. 'Come *quick!* Adam's got some woman . . . *imprisoned* back here!'

'Some *woman?*' echoes Posh James.

'No, no, no!' I sound a bit panicked, which is understandable, under the circumstances, but is only going to make me feel more mortified in the long run. I'd prefer to sound more nonchalant, debonair, even, because I've learned from past experience that if you take this sort of appalling humiliation in your stride yourself, other people have no choice but to take it in their stride along with you. 'I'm not a woman,' I go on, in as laid-back a way as I can possibly manage. 'I mean, I'm not just any old woman! It's me, Libby Lomax. Um, Adam's girlfriend? The jewellery designer?'

'*Libby?*' Lottie gasps.

'That's right. Hello!' I add. 'Nice to see you again!'

Posh James's shoes arrive, now, and I hear an appalled, 'For fuck's *sake*,' before he grabs Fritz's collar and – helpfully – puts an end to the water torture by manhandling him back towards the kitchen door and putting him out in the hallway.

'Thanks!' I say, still trying to sound relaxed about all this, in the hope that it convinces them there's really nothing so very extraordinary about finding a virtual stranger with their head wedged between a set of iron bars at the neighbour's house, with only some strands of ribbon and elastic to protect her modesty. 'Much appreciated.'

'But, Libby . . .' Lottie isn't sounding remotely relaxed. 'You have to tell me. Are you . . . in this position . . . *voluntarily?*'

'Adam hasn't fucking imprisoned her in a sex dungeon, or anything,' Posh James says, cuttingly. 'He's not even home. I saw her letting herself in about an hour ago. At least, I *think* it's her . . .' There's a pause. I don't know why, but I get the impression of a neck being craned. 'She looks a bit different from this angle.'

'Then stop looking from that angle!' Lottie snaps. 'Let the poor girl have a shred of dignity, will you?'

What I'd quite like, right now, is for the floor beneath Fritz's den to open up like a large sinkhole, drag me down deep into the earth's crust, and finish me off in a pit of molten lava.

'Anyway, if he's not imprisoned her, what the hell is she *doing* in here?' Lottie demands, before crouching down to meet me at eye level. Her pretty face is creased with genuine concern. 'What are you doing in here?' she repeats the question to me. 'If you're too scared to say anything aloud, just . . . I don't know . . . blink three times . . . or do you have a safe word, or something . . .?'

'No, there's no safe word!' I really, really want my very nice new client to *stop thinking I'm heavily into sadomasochism.* 'This is all just a silly accident. I put my head through the bars, you see,' I go on, cleverly avoiding any mention of why I put on slutty lingerie to do this in the first place. 'I think the problem is my earrings, actually, so perhaps . . .' I reach one hand up to start undoing one of the chandelier earrings on one side and then, the moment it's fallen free, do the same to the other. 'I'm sure I'll be able to get my head out, now.'

Wrong again.

My head, even without the earrings, still won't slide back out through the bars of the safety gate.

'My head hasn't grown, has it?' I'm sounding panicked again. 'Could that have happened? Do heads just spontaneously grow?'

'I don't know about that.' Lottie puts her own head on one side. 'I suppose it could have *expanded* a teeny bit, or something . . . From the friction of you trying to pull it out, maybe?'

'For fuck's sake, the two of you. It isn't amateur physicist week.' Posh James doesn't sound the least bit impressed. 'Obviously what we need is some sort of lubricant.'

'*James!*' Lottie gasps.

'To *rub on the bars,*' he explains. 'To help her slide out. Olive oil, butter . . .'

'Oh. Well, yes, that might be a good idea, actually. I'll go and look in the fridge,' Lottie says, getting to her feet and heading across to the other end of the kitchen. 'Keep talking to her, James!' she calls over one shoulder. 'In case she goes into shock, or something.'

'She's not going to go into bloody shock,' Posh James replies, irritably, before thinking slightly better of this and turning back to ask me, 'are you?'

'No,' I mumble.

'Good. *I* might, though.'

Which I think is just him being rude – *extremely* rude – about the nightmare-inducing sight of my bum, on the other side of the bars from him, until he goes on: 'I mean, I honestly didn't know Adam had it in him. I was pretty sure – a hundred per cent sure, in fact – that Adam batted for the other team.'

'Sorry?'

'Drove on the right-hand side of the road.'

'Um, are you pointing out that he's *American*, because I did already realize—'

'I thought he was gay.'

I blink at Posh James. To be more precise, I blink at his battered Converse.

'Adam's not gay.'

'If you say so.'

'I am saying so.'

'Well, you'd know better than me, obviously. It must just be a very, *very* good male friend of his I see leaving here early in the mornings, when I'm heading home from my run . . . what the hell, Lottie?' he adds, as Lottie's ballet pumps return our way again. 'I suggested olive oil or butter, not half the contents of the store cupboard!'

'Well, *I* don't know what's going to work, do I?' Lottie is crouching back down to my level again, clutching an entire armful of assorted packets and bottles. 'So, which do you think is most slippery? Groundnut oil? Grapeseed oil? Sesame oil? Argan oil . . . oooh, I've never heard of that one before.'

'It's often used in North African cooking,' Posh James says. 'You can use it to make fresh dips, drizzle it on couscous—'

'Oh, was that the thing that made the couscous taste so amazing in Marrakech?' Lottie asks.

'I think it was the cinnamon, actually,' her husband tells her. 'I've started adding it when I make couscous at home, you know, but I don't think the quality of the cinnamon here is as good as it was over there, because—'

'I honestly think any of the oils will be fine,' I say, starting to feel more desperate than ever now that – somehow – we all just seem to be sitting around here swapping recipe tips and reminiscing about couscous. 'Can we just *try* one?'

'Of course. Let's start with the sesame oil!'

So we do. And when that has no effect whatsoever, we try groundnut oil. And when that has no effect whatsoever, we try sunflower oil. And when that has no effect whatsoever (apart from making me smell like some sort of giant Chinese takeaway, that is), Posh James announces, 'Fuck this for a game of soldiers. I'd better call the fire brigade.'

'No!' I moan, gently, because if it's mortifying enough being semi-naked and wedged between two iron bars on my hands and knees in front of Lottie and James Cadwalladr, I can't even begin to imagine the horror of importing half a dozen firemen into this kitchen, too. 'Please . . .'

'Well, I don't see that we have any other option,' he says, irritably. 'I don't own a hacksaw. I suppose I could always go and see if any of the neighbours has a hacksaw—'

'Bogdan!' I suddenly gasp.

I can't believe I didn't think of this before.

'My friend Bogdan – he's a handyman . . . well, and a hairdresser, too, but . . .' Not relevant, Libby! Stick to the important facts! 'He'll have a hacksaw, I'm absolutely sure of it. Look, can you just grab my phone from my bag,' I say, feeling weak with relief, 'and bring it over so I can call him?'

'Absolutely!' Lottie sounds pretty relieved as well, because although this might be the worst evening of my entire life, I don't think it's exactly been a night of unbounded pleasure for her and James, either. 'James, get her phone. I'll just see,' she adds, scrambling to her feet as there's a fresh volley of barking coming from the hallway, 'what Fritz is going nuts about out there.'

I hear the kitchen door open, and then I hear Lottie say, in a startled voice, 'Oh! Adam!'

So he really is back pretty early from his work dinner. Just not early enough, unfortunately, to have prevented me from ending up in my current predicament.

'This probably all looks very strange to you,' Lottie is going on, 'but we have, well, a bit of a situation . . . I don't suppose either of you happens to have a hacksaw on you, by any chance?'

Wait a second: *either* of you?

'I don't have a hacksaw,' comes Adam's voice, sounding bewildered and anxious – unlike him – in equal measure. 'Ben, uh, I'm assuming you don't have one either?'

'No, I didn't bring a hacksaw,' comes another voice. Just like Adam's voice, it's American-accented.

And just like Adam's voice, it's male.

'And I gotta tell you, Ads,' the strange man's voice goes on, with an abrasive chuckle, 'I'm glad we've been dating this long before you asked me that question. I'd be out that door faster than a speeding bullet otherwise.'

I can't move.

I mean, *obviously* I can't move. None of us would be here right now if I could.

Well, Adam and Ben would probably still be here, for their own cosy night in. My boyfriend and . . . *his* boyfriend?

The bars of the safety gate may be gradually cutting off the blood supply to my brain, but even I can put two and two together on this one and make four.

There's the faint squeak of Converse on marble, and then Posh James's face appears in front of me again.

'Here's your phone,' he says, matter-of-factly, as he hands it through the bars to me and folds my frozen fingers around it. And then he adds, equally matter-of-factly, 'I told you he was gay.'

Then he gets to his feet and heads towards the hallway, perhaps to give me a moment of privacy.

With a strength of will I didn't even know I had, I force my fingers to unfreeze so that I can call Bogdan.

He and his hacksaw can't get here fast enough.

Chapter 4

The half-hour after Adam and his date got home turned into a bit of a blur, if I'm honest with you.

Thank God Lottie and James slipped quietly away, and then Adam came (sheepishly) into the kitchen to find me. He didn't say a lot, and I said even less . . . I have a dim memory of being peered at, for a moment, by a very scowly man in a very smart suit, who I can only assume was Ben . . . and then, just as Adam suggested it might be a good idea for me to snack on some edamame beans and a coconut water, to keep my energy levels up, Bogdan arrived.

With Olly.

My second unexpected, unannounced and frankly unwanted visitor of the night.

Don't get me wrong: I'm always happy to see Olly. It's a truly rare situation where I don't want his lovely, friendly face around. I'd hardly have dragged the poor guy up to Dad's wedding this past weekend if I hadn't thought it would make the whole thing better, just having him there.

Tonight, however, was precisely one of those rare situations.

'Am decorating at restaurant,' was Bogdan's explanation, through the noise of the hacksaw, when I asked him, through gritted teeth, why he'd decided to announce my predicament to Olly before the pair of them set out in Olly's van, like cape-less crusaders, to rescue me from Death By Humiliation in Shepherd's Bush. 'Olly is right there beside me when am answering phone. You are expecting me to be lying to him about reason for phone call? When he is currently being my boss? And also, am hoping not to be presuming too much, my friend?'

Well, no, I wasn't expecting him to *lie*.

And given that he blurted, 'Let me be getting this straight, Libby – you are trapped somewhere against your will and only wearing what I am guessing to be some sort of undergarment?' a couple of moments after my terse explanation over the phone, I suppose it's only to be expected that Olly would grab his car keys and hurtle to my assistance.

But it's just one more layer of awkwardness to endure: Olly, who didn't even know I was dating Adam to begin with, coming face to face with me in that terrible, semi-naked, head-wodged predicament.

Quite honestly, the discovery that my new boyfriend, who I really thought might be The One, is in fact gay . . . well, it's almost the least bad thing about the last couple of hours.

I said *almost*.

Olly has insisted on driving me all the way home, which is nice of him, because I'm feeling a bit too bruised – physically and emotionally – for the rough-and-tumble of the tube just now.

The downside, though, is more of that terrible awkwardness.

Even though – obviously – I re-dressed myself as soon as I was free from the bars, the atmosphere between us is so uncomfortable that I might as well be still wearing nothing but the Ribbony Elasticky Thing and a slick of sesame oil. We've sat in embarrassed silence ever since Shepherd's Bush, and we're over the river and stuck in a bottleneck of traffic near Wandsworth Bridge when Olly finally breaks it.

'So. Adam Rosenfeld.'

'Yes.' I swallow, hard. 'Did you know he was gay?'

'Libby, come on. I only work with the guy. And barely even that, really. He dropped into the restaurant this afternoon for the first time in a week. I mean, I don't *remember* pondering, as we pored over some thrilling spreadsheets together, what his sexual orientation might be . . .'

'Fair point.'

'And it's not like I was looking out for anything in particular, one way or the other.' Olly changes gear as we finally move up a little way in the traffic. 'I mean, I didn't even know you were seeing him, Libby. You kept that one pretty close to your chest.'

84

I wince, inwardly, at Olly's mere mention of my chest, given that he's seen more of my chest this evening than I'd have liked him to do in a lifetime.

'It was pretty recent,' I mumble.

'You could have mentioned something over the weekend.'

'I know. I'm sorry. I didn't want to shout it from the rooftops in case . . . well, it didn't work out. Which has turned out to be pretty prophetic of me, really.'

'You're not pathetic.'

'*Prophetic*,' I say.

'Oh . . . well, you might be that.'

'Yeah, except I thought the reasons we might not work out would be because we were both too busy with our jobs, or because we didn't like each other's families . . . I never stopped to think that it might be because he was using me as a beard to hide his true identity from his Orthodox Jewish parents.'

This is based on something that Adam muttered at me, by the way, a few minutes before Bogdan and Olly and the tool kit got there: *I'm really sorry, Libby . . . my mum and dad . . . it's an Orthodox thing . . . they wouldn't approve . . .*

Which, you know, I can sympathize with. I've endured the disapproval of my own mother for the majority of the last thirty years. But I still don't think it's reasonable to drag someone else into the middle of it. Someone unwitting. Someone ignorant.

'I'm just such an *idiot*,' I say, miserably, gazing out of the window as unidentifiable bits of southwest London slide by in the gathering midsummer dusk. 'How did I not realize he was gay? He couldn't have made any more excuses to avoid having sex with me!'

'He made excuses?'

'Dozens of them.' I never usually talk about sex with Olly, but I feel we've crossed that barrier tonight. Actually, not so much crossed as smashed through it. With a ten-tonne truck. 'He was busy with work. He was tired from the gym. He had a headache . . . I don't know. There were a lot of different explanations. And I fell for each and every one of them.'

'So the . . . er . . . dressing up in . . . er . . . sexy lingerie was—'

'My embarrassingly misguided attempt to reverse the situation.'

Olly nods. 'Got it.'

'I mean, what's *wrong* with me,' I go on, 'that I have such crappy awful judgement about the entire male species?'

'There's nothing wrong with you.'

'All right, then, maybe there's just something wrong with *men*.'

'OK, well, that's a bit of an unfair generalization—'

'I don't mean *you*, Ol,' I say. 'I just mean all the others.'

'Come on, Lib, just because it's all gone a bit pear-shaped with Adam, and just because you had a hellish experience with a total wanker like Dillon O'Hara—'

At this moment, there's an angry grunt from the back of the car: it's Bogdan who, I have to confess, I'd completely forgotten was sitting back there.

He looms forward now, to jab Olly in the shoulder with a large and paint-spattered finger.

'Do not be saying the impolite things about Dillon,' he tells Olly. 'Libby is not having the hellish experience with him. Libby is having the heavenly experience with him. And not just in the bedroom.'

'Bogdan!' I turn round and glare at him. 'That's none of anyone's business!'

'Is being the business of mine,' Bogdan mutters, darkly, 'when am hearing the untrue things about the people I am liking.'

(Bogdan is being slightly disingenuous here. He didn't so much *like* Dillon as nurse a colossal, simmering, unrequited passion for him, in a tragic, balalaika-accompanied, Moldovan sort of way. Many was the time, in the course of those few heady months with Dillon, that I half expected to open my suitcase in some glamorous hotel room only to find Bogdan stowed away amongst my shoes and my tops and my sexy underwear, all ready to clamber out and hang on Dillon's every word for the duration of our dirty weekend. I got so paranoid that I even stopped taking the big suitcase, and started cramming everything I might need into the smaller of my two canvas holdalls instead.)

'My mistake, Bogdan,' Olly returns, his voice dripping with sarcasm. 'There's obviously nothing at all hellish about being abandoned in Miami the day before a major hurricane, with no passport and no credit cards.'

'Being abandoned in the Miami the day before the major hurricane with no passport and no credit cards,' Bogdan echoes, '*by Dillon O'Hara.*'

Olly actually takes his eyes off the road for a moment to turn round and stare at Bogdan.

'I'm sorry . . . you're saying that this is some sort of privilege?'

'Am saying,' Bogdan says, in the overly patient tone of one who's decided he's talking to a complete imbecile, 'that Libby is being lucky to be involved with man as handsome and charming and funny and—'

'And coke-addled,' Olly interrupts, 'and woman-izing—'

'OK, that's enough!' I hold up a hand. 'Look, I'm incredibly grateful to you both for coming and getting me out of a tight spot – literally – but can we just *stop talking about Dillon O'Hara* for the rest of the journey?'

'It would make me a happy man,' Olly announces, 'if I never had to so much as hear his name again for the rest of my livelong days.'

Which puts Bogdan into a right old grump, because he inflicts a wounded silence on us all until Olly drops him at the top of his road in Balham a few minutes later. And then thumps on Olly's window just before we drive off and yells, '*Dillon O'Hara!*', petulantly, through the glass.

'Probably not a good idea,' I say, a moment later, 'to have made your painter and decorator *quite* so angry with you four days before your big restaurant opening.'

'Oh, he'll be all right. Besides, everything's on track over there.'

'Really? Because I feel really awful, Ol, about acciden-tally dragging him – and you – away from the place this evening . . .'

'Honestly, Lib, don't worry about it. Like I say, we're right on schedule. And I know you'd do the same for me.'

'If you got your head stuck in between some iron railings at your secretly lesbian girlfriend's house while wearing skimpy undies and having cooking oils rubbed on you by a famous television actor?'

'In that *exact scenario*,' Olly says, solemnly, 'I know you'd leg it across town with your sharpest hacksaw and your trustiest blowtorch.'

'Well, that's what friendship is all about,' I say.

Olly falls silent for a moment, which is a pity as I'd thought we were well on the road to it All Being OK between us again, until he suddenly swerves on to the other side of the road, and into the drive-through McDonald's on the other side of it.

'I don't know about you,' he says, 'but I'm absolutely bloody starving. Would a Big Mac hit the spot?'

Which just begs the eternal question: why in God's name is Olly still single? I mean, this is a man who can seemingly anticipate a woman's desires, and then meet them, before the woman has even had the chance to realize they exist. Apart from those blasted yogurt-covered raisins, I've starved myself all day (in order, pointlessly, to look my best in the Ribbony Elasticky Thing), and a Big Mac would not only hit the spot, it would smack it with a great big thwunking bull's-eye.

And confirmed foodie though he is, Olly has a bit of a habit of taking me for random McDonald's. In fact, this very drive-through is the one we stopped off at several months ago, after he'd picked me up from the Paddington Express on the way home from *that* trip to Miami with Dillon. I think Olly must remember this too, because we've only just driven off from the pick-up window, and I'm only just opening my mouth to wrap it around my burger, when Olly opens *his* mouth to say, 'Thing is, Lib, I thought you'd said you were steering well clear of men for a while. After the way things went with . . .' He stops himself, just in time, to add a Nora-esque, 'you know who.'

'I was,' I say, attractively spraying a bit of gherkin out of my mouth on to the dashboard. 'That was the plan. It honestly, truly was. But then . . .'

'Then what?' Olly takes a bite out of the Quarter Pounder with Cheese I'm holding out for him, so that he can eat without taking his hands off the steering wheel. 'Adam Rosenfeld bowled you over? Lavished you with his beard-seeking attentions? Made you feel like the only woman in the world?'

All of a sudden, I can't swallow my own bite of Big Mac.

Not because it's chewy, and lukewarm, and tastes faintly of marinaded cardboard (though, obviously, it being a Big Mac, it's all of these things). But because Olly has hit a nerve.

A very raw one.

'Yes,' I mumble.

'I . . . oh, Jesus, Libby . . . I was joking! Or *trying* to . . . About Adam, and his being not remotely interested in women, and—'

'Sure. But the awful thing is, it's all true.' I'm making an absolutely colossal effort not to cry and, though I'm succeeding for the moment, it's not looking particularly good for the immediate future. 'I did like the fact that he made me feel so special. After D . . . after You Know Who, and always feeling like just one of many. *So* many. I mean, you know those scenes in horror movies, where all of a sudden the defences break, and all the flesh-eating zombies come flooding over the walls?'

'Er . . . yes . . . I'm just not *quite* sure how that description relates to your romantic life. Unless things were much, much more experimental with Dillon than I'd given him credit for.'

I don't point out that Olly has just used Dillon's name.

'I just felt overrun. Threatened. Engulfed. That one of me was never going to be enough to see off the raging hordes of *them*.'

Because, more than anything else, more than the excessive drinking and the coke habit, more even than the carelessness of abandoning me in Miami as a hurricane approached from across the Gulf of Mexico, this was the reason why it would never have worked out with Dillon: the fact that I was never going to be enough for him; the fact that I was always, always going to play second-best to the excitement of chasing the next woman, and the next woman, and the next.

'And it was nice with Adam,' I go on, 'because I never felt that he was interested in any other woman. But that was because – obviously – he really *was not* interested in any other woman. Not because he was so caught-up-crazy about *me*.'

And then there's a seriously awkward silence, while I gulp back tears, and try not to sniff, and shove the Quarter Pounder in Olly's direction so many times, to give myself something to do, that the poor guy is probably about to choke on the sheer amount of it he's being forced to inhale. He's game enough, though, to keep on manfully chewing his way through the thing until we stop at a long red light just past Tooting Broadway, when he takes the burger from my hand and puts it down on the seat in between us.

'Libby—' he begins.

'So! The restaurant!' I blurt, before he can say anything way, way too nice, too Olly-like, and have me howling all over him before the light has even turned amber. 'Nearly finished, you say? I can't wait to see it! It's been weeks!'

'Yes, but . . . look, I feel awful about upsetting you, and—'

'Now, you must let me know exactly what I can do to help out,' I go on. 'I know Nora and Tash have signed their evenings away for the next week, but I'd really like to do whatever I can, too.'

'That would be fantastic. But Libby—'

'I mean, I may not be a dab hand with a hammer or anything, but if you need boxes unpacked, or waiters' uniforms ironed—'

'Libby. Please. Just let me say this, OK?' Olly takes a deep breath. 'You should never feel like you're being engulfed by flesh-eating zombies. You deserve someone who makes you feel the opposite of that. Whatever that is. Like . . . well, like *you're* the flesh-eating zombie. The *only* flesh-eating zombie.'

It's one of the nicest things anyone has ever said to me.

Which is why it's good timing that we're pulling up outside my building on Colliers Wood High Street, because it's *so* very nice a thing to have said, and in such a gentle, sincere tone, too, that the self-pity is in danger of taking hold again, and I'd much rather hop out of the car while I still have a shred of dignity intact.

'Libby, wait,' Olly says, turning to me as I open the door and start to get out. 'I haven't said . . . quite what I wanted to say.'

'Don't worry, Ol. You've made me feel so much better.'

'But I made you cry.'

'The merest of sniffles. And if it *hadn't* been for you, Olly, I'd have been howling the entire city down by now.'

'Over Adam Rosenfeld? Don't. He's not worth it.'

'Thanks,' I tell him. 'I love you loads. I'll give you a call in the morning, OK? And you can tell me whatever you need me to do for you this week, and I'll be right there.'

'Thanks, Lib. I appreciate that.'

Ever the gentleman, he waits until I've got the door to my building open and am on my way inside before pulling off into the traffic on Colliers Wood High Street.

Chapter 5

Living above one of the takeaways owned by my landlord, Bogdan Senior, has introduced me to some interesting smells over the last year. The muggy pong of frying fish. The eye-watering tang of chicken vindaloo (at least, I can only hope that it was chicken). The greasy miasma of deep-pan, stuffed-crust pizza.

But tonight, as I go up the four flights of stairs to my top-floor flat, the main smell I'm getting is . . . well, I have to be honest, it's a lot more floral than the ones I've endured before.

I didn't notice, as I came in the outer door, if Bogdan Senior has transformed BOGDANZ HOUSE OF PANCAKEZ, as it was when I left home earlier, into another sort of eatery instead; but there's no takeaway food I can think of that smells like a rose garden at midnight. I don't even think it's Moldovan food, which I'm admittedly not all that familiar with, because Bogdan has cooked Moldovan food for me – just once – and as far as I could tell it mostly revolved around doing ingenious things with pork rind and cabbage.

Anyway, I'm too tired to wonder exactly where the smell is coming from. I simply carry on dragging my weary legs up the stairs, put my key in my own front door, and fumble for the light switch as I walk through it.

Oh, Jesus Lord Almighty.

There's a dead polar bear on my Chesterfield sofa.

At least, I can only assume it's dead, because surely otherwise it would have reared its head the moment I put the light on and *roared* at me.

Which probably isn't the thing to be wondering about. Probably the more normal thing to be wondering is: how the hell has a *polar bear* stolen into a fourth-floor flat in Colliers Wood, and come to expire on an over-stuffed sofa?

'Hey . . . who turned that light on?'

I let out a scream. Because the dead polar bear is talking.

And *moving*, and *shifting*, and – oh, God – *shedding its white, furry coat* . . .

. . . to reveal that it isn't, in fact, a polar bear at all.

It's Marilyn Monroe.

Naked – stark naked   now that the white fur coat she was wrapped in has slid all the way down to the floor.

She stares at me.

I stare at her.

And now *she* screams. And draws back her hand, and throws whatever she's holding in it at me.

It's a cocktail shaker. I have previous experience of taking a cocktail shaker to the face, so, despite my shock at what's going on, I somehow manage to leap nimbly to the side. The cocktail shaker zings past me, clatters into the wall and falls at my feet without causing me any damage.

'Who *are* you?' she gasps, reaching down and seizing the white fur coat, and clutching it to herself. (Rather half-heartedly clutching it to herself; I can still see plenty of creamy-white flesh and – even though I'm trying not to stare – more than a hint of nipple.) 'Don't you know it's rude not to *knock*?'

'It's my flat.'

'Huh?'

'My apartment. I live here. I . . . you're Marilyn,' I blurt, blinking my eyes as I truly take in the sight before me. The mussed-up hair; the sleepy eyes; the wide mouth, glossy with exactly the right shade of vermilion lipstick. 'Marilyn Monroe.'

'You know who I am?' Her voice is little-girly, breathy, just the way it sounds in her movies. 'And you know my new name and everything?'

'Yes, obviously, I—'

'Do you think it works?'

'Sorry?'

'The name. Marilyn Monroe.' She's leaning forward

on the sofa, now, eagerly awaiting my opinion. 'I kinda helped them come up with it at the studio, because the boys at school used to call me the *Mmmmm Girl*. And when I told the studio that, they tossed it around a little and came up with *Mmmmarilyn Mmmmmonroe* . . . catchy, don't you think?'

She seems to have completely forgotten that only a few moments ago she thought I was an intruder, and chucked a cocktail shaker at me. But years of living with my sister have helped me spot a narcissist at a hundred paces, so I'm not falling down in shock at this.

Nor am I falling down in shock at the very sight of her, in all her platinum-blonde glory, sprawled on my Chesterfield.

Because this exact thing has happened to me before.

Except last time it was Audrey Hepburn.

Oh, and Audrey wasn't naked. Let's face it, Audrey would no more have been naked in a stranger's flat than Adam Rosenfeld would have come home tonight to the sight of me in the Ribbony Elasticky Thing, had it all gone as planned, and had his wicked way with me on his kitchen table.

'I mean, you'll never guess my *real* name, honey,' Marilyn Monroe is continuing. 'Go on, I dare you! Try and guess!'

'Norma Jeane,' I say, as I shut the front door behind me. 'Norma Jeane Mortenson.'

Her mouth falls open.

'But how could you possibly . . . did you see me in a magazine, or something? That was the name I used back when I was a model . . .'

'No, I just . . . you know what? I need a drink,' I say. 'It's been a strange night already, and it's only getting more strange. If you could just . . . er . . . wait here,' I add – though I'm not sure why, because it's not like there's anywhere else she could go, 'and I'll nip down to the off-licence and get a bottle of wine.'

'Wine?' Marilyn pulls a face. 'Oh, no, honey, we don't need wine. We got cocktails, see?' She gets to her feet, pulling the fur coat on, properly this time, as she does so, and comes to pick up the cocktail shaker from where it fell, next to me. 'Gee, I'm glad this thing's so inde-structible,' she adds, holding it out to show me that the lid is still on. 'Care for a Manhattan, honey?'

I'm honestly finding it hard to form words to reply, because at such close quarters she's absolutely stunning. Much shorter than I'd have thought, and more slender, and not as beautiful as Audrey Hepburn, obviously not, but with such a dazzling glow that it looks as if she's been lit up, by the world's greatest cinematographer, from within. It's Marilyn at her peachiest. She can't be any more than twenty-two or twenty-three; her skin is flawlessly white, her eyes are dazzlingly blue, her hair is softly waved and the colour of a cornfield in July, and her legendary body – at least from the glimpses of it I kept getting before she put the fur coat on properly – is exquisite.

'I'm . . . I'm not wild about Manhattans, actually,' I manage to say.

'Sure you are! You just never tried mine before!' She's setting off for the kitchen, where she opens my one wall-hanging cupboard, and peers inside. 'Where do you keep your cocktail glasses, honey?'

'Ah, well, I don't really have any cocktail glasses.'

She turns to look at me, her blue eyes wide in astonishment. 'You *don't have any cocktail glasses?* But honey, what on earth do you drink out of?'

'Well, I usually just drink wine, you see . . . though I don't even have any proper glasses for that, come to think of it. I break quite a lot of them, so I tend to just drink from a little tumbler.' I go over to her, inhaling her heady, floral scent even more as I get closer, and reach up past her into the cupboard. 'These,' I say, handing over a couple of short glasses. 'Would they do?'

'A Manhattan in a lowball glass?' Marilyn frowns. 'I never heard of that before . . . but hey, what the hell?' She unscrews the cocktail shaker and pours a good slosh of brownish-red liquid into each glass, hands one to me, picks up her own and then chinks it against mine. 'Bottoms up, roomie!' she breathes, with a little wriggle of her fur-clad shoulders.

I gaze at her as she closes her eyes, tilts her glass and takes a long drink from it.

'Sorry . . . er . . . did you just say *roomie?*'

'Sure! Isn't that what you are, honey?' Marilyn opens

her eyes. 'Haven't the studio paired us up to room together?'

'Studio? No, no, that's not what this is . . .'

'So you're *not* an actress?' She nods, her mussed-up curls bouncing as she does so. 'Well, I gotta tell you, honey, that doesn't come as that much of a surprise.'

'Hey!' I'm slightly needled by this. 'I *was* an actress, actually. Admittedly, not a very successful one . . .'

But she isn't listening.

'I think we'll have a swell time rooming together, honey, you and I! Though anyone would be better than the last girl the studio fixed me up with.' Marilyn rolls her eyes. 'She didn't drink, she didn't dance, she didn't know *any* eligible guys . . . say, *you* know some eligible guys, right?' She looks concerned, all of a sudden. 'I mean, you're not dressed like that because . . . well, you prefer girls?'

'No, I don't prefer girls.' I glance down at myself, self-consciously. 'And what's wrong with the way I'm dressed?'

She looks at me.

'*Pants*, honey?' she asks. 'And *black ones* at that?'

'They're chic!'

'Oh, sugar. Who told you that?'

'*Audrey Hepburn*!'

'Well, I never heard of this Audrey gal,' Marilyn says, shimmying back towards the sofa again, 'and I'm sure she's a sweetheart, but I gotta tell you, honey, she doesn't know a whole hell of a lot about style. Ooooh,' she suddenly breathes, as she plops herself back down on the cushions, 'maybe that could be our first proper act, as roommates. We could give each other, whaddyacallit, makeovers! It'll be fun! We'll put on face masks, and paint each other's nails, and then pick out cute new outfits for each other . . . or I could pick out a cute new outfit for you, at least . . . you know, I always wanted to have makeover night with a girlfriend, but for some reason none of them ever wanted to do it with me.'

I don't point out that this was probably because they didn't want to spend too long standing in front of a mirror with her next to them. She's so puppyish with excitement about the prospect of Makeover Night that I don't want to kill the thing stone dead. More to the point, I don't know how to tell her that I probably wouldn't be able to 'make her over' even if I tried. I mean, obviously I don't know for sure, because I never tried this sort of thing with Audrey Hepburn (you don't make-over Audrey; you just *don't*) but these are magical beings we're talking about.

At least, I *think* they're magical.

This is the conclusion I came to, after Audrey Hepburn dropped by to visit me in my flat several times last summer: *that there's something supernatural going on with my Chesterfield sofa.* That – even though I'm painfully aware that it sounds certifiably bonkers to say it – my Chesterfield is enchanted.

I did *say* it sounds certifiably bonkers.

I sit down, rather uncertainly, next to Marilyn now, as she pats the cushion beside her.

'So, honey, before we start all the face masks and the pampering, we should talk a little! Get to know each other. Shall I tell you about myself first?'

'Actually, I already—'

'My real name's Norma Jeane, like you said. I'm nineteen years old . . . OK, I'm twenty-three – ' she gives me a little wink – 'but *officially* I'm nineteen. Anyhow, I'm from California, amongst other places, and I used to model, and now I'm an actress in the movies. I'm sort of doing fine, but . . . well, gee, honey, I just want to become a *huge* movie star!' She wraps her arms around herself, childish in delight for a moment, almost sloshing red Manhattan all over her white mink. 'Like Jean Harlow, only bigger! Can you imagine that?'

I don't know what to reply to this.

Unfortunately she takes my silence for judgement, because she goes on, after an embarrassed little laugh, 'I know that sounds crazy . . . but I always figured, you gotta dream big to make it big, right?'

'It doesn't sound crazy,' I say, 'at all.'

'You think?' She lowers her voice, and leans in towards me. 'Because sometimes I think I want it so badly, I might just *bust*. Go up in smoke, splattering teeny-tiny pieces of Norma Jeane everywhere!' She's solemn, now. Her big blue eyes are wider than ever, like a six-year-old girl's when she's telling you something Important and Secret. 'Did you ever want anything that bad, honey? So much that you thought you might die if you didn't get it?'

It's funny – and in a 'Dr Freud will see you now' way, not in a 'ha-ha' way – that two things pop into my head, simultaneously, when Marilyn Monroe asks me this question. Did I ever want anything so badly that I thought I might die if I didn't get it? Yes, two things in fact: Dad's attention and Dillon's devotion.

Turns out that, in not getting either of these, I haven't actually died. It's just felt like it, a little bit, at times.

'You too, huh?' Marilyn breathes, reaching out to pat my hand in a sympathetic manner. 'So what is it you dream of, if it's not movie stardom? You work at the studio, right? So are you a singer? A dancer?'

'No, no, God, no. And I don't work at the studio. I'm a jewellery designer.'

'Honey! I just adore jewellery!'

'I know. I named my latest collection after . . .' I stop myself, just in time. '. . . er . . . my mother.'

Which is when I notice: I don't have my Marilyn earrings.

Dammit. I must have left them on the kitchen floor at Adam's.

I feel a brief flash of concern that maybe Fritz might end up swallowing them, or something . . .

I'll have to text Adam about it before I go to sleep tonight. Which is incredibly annoying, because the one thing I *did* say to him, while we were all waiting for Bogdan and his hacksaw to turn up, was that I didn't want to have any communication with him ever again. Still, I feel enough fondness for Fritz to temporarily break that vow. After all, he wasn't to know his owner was gay. And, even if he did know, it wasn't as if he could tell me. In German or otherwise.

'That was sweet of you, honey. I don't think my mother would even care if I named my *first child* after her.'

'Me neither,' I blurt.

'But you just said you named your jewellery after her.' Marilyn looks confused. 'So don't you get along with your mother either?'

'It's complicated . . .' I take a large swig from my glass of Manhattan. And have to prevent myself from spraying the entire mouthful back over her.

Christ, it's revolting.

'Isn't that *good?*' Marilyn breathes, with another little wriggle of her shoulders.

'Mmmm,' I say, unconvincingly, but she isn't paying much attention.

'You know, you and me should swap complicated mother stories one day,' she says. 'Now that we're going to be such good friends. I mean, we *are*, aren't we?'

'We are what?'

'Going to be good friends? I don't have a lot of girlfriends, you see.'

I feel a tiny stab of icy sadness for her, right through

the middle of my heart, and I shiver. 'No,' I say, 'I know you don't.'

'Honey, you're cold!' She balances her glass on the Chesterfield's overstuffed arm and starts to peel off the white fur coat. 'Take this! I'm roasting in here, anyhow!'

'No, no!' I yelp, trying to close the coat back around her for a moment before realizing I can't actually bring myself to touch dead mink. 'Honestly, Marilyn, keep it on. I wouldn't even wear it.'

'C'mon, honey, it's real mink.'

'I know. I don't wear fur.'

She stares at me, uncomprehending. 'You don't?'

'I don't.'

'But honey . . . *why?*'

'Well, not to put a terrible downer on the conversation or anything, but I think it's incredibly cruel.'

Marilyn looks even more bewildered for a moment, then she leans over and asks, in a low voice, 'Because you worry that the guy who gave it to you hasn't given as nice a coat to his wife as well?'

'No! That's not why I think it's cruel!'

'Oh . . . then is it some Canadian thing?'

OK, now I'm just plain baffled. 'I'm not from Canada.'

'You're not?'

'Um, no. I'm not.'

She puts her head on one side. 'Then why are you talking in that funny accent?'

'Because I'm British.'

'You're *British*?' Marilyn gasps, delightedly. 'Honey, why didn't you say so? I love British people! Cary Grant, Sir Winston Churchill, oh, and Laurence Olivier! Did you see him in *Hamlet*? Gee, I adore him! You know, I have these silly daydreams, sometimes, that one day we'll star in a movie together . . . and we'll fall in love, and he'll lie with his head in my lap and read me Shakespeare poetry . . .'

'I wouldn't,' I say, hastily, knowing what a disastrous relationship Marilyn had with Olivier, 'waste too much time daydreaming about that, if I were you.'

'Oh!' This time her gasp is dismayed, not delighted. She puts a hand to her cheek, which is turning from alabaster to the faintest pink. 'I thought you said I didn't sound crazy, dreaming about becoming a big movie star!'

'Marilyn, no . . .' I feel as if I've just accidentally trodden on a fluffy baby bunny rabbit. 'That's not what I meant at all! It was a comment about Laurence Olivier, not about you!'

'Because it's kind of mean, honey, one minute to seem like you understand, and then the next minute to sound just like everybody else who's ever told me to stop wasting my time. That I'm not talented enough, pretty enough, good enough . . .'

'Trust me, I don't think you're any of those things.' Shit: that came out wrong. 'What I mean is, I think – no, I *know* – that you're absolutely talented enough and pretty enough and good enough.'

She takes a dejected swig from her cocktail glass, draining it dry. 'How can you possibly know that I'm talented enough?'

OK: we've reached a tricky moment.

I never raised this with Audrey Hepburn, but that's partly because I spent most of the time in Audrey's company convinced she was the result of a brain tumour, or a nervous breakdown. Now that I'm running with this whole Enchanted Sofa angle, maybe it's time to ask the apparition before me what she thinks about it all. It's a thorny etiquette problem, though: working out the correct way to point out to a magical being that she's, well, magical.

Because let's be honest, it's not as if Marilyn seems to realize this in the slightest.

'The thing is, Marilyn,' I begin, nervously, 'I think maybe we should just have a quick chat about why it is you're really here . . .'

'Oh, honey.' She smiles across the sofa at me, heartbreakingly. 'Don't you think it's a little late in the day to start asking big, smart questions like that? I mean, if you stop and think about it, why are *any* of us really here?'

'Yes . . . um, that's not quite what I—'

'Say, can you bring the cocktail shaker over,' she adds, gesturing towards the kitchen worktop, where she left the shaker, 'and give me a little top-up? I sure could use one right about now.'

'Of course.' I get to my feet and go to pick up the silver cocktail shaker.

But it seems to have disappeared.

And when I turn back, Marilyn has disappeared, too.

She's vanished, into thin air, exactly the way Audrey Hepburn did when she was the one materializing through the Chesterfield.

The only part of her that remains is that heady scent of flowers – that rose-garden-at-midnight smell that now, of *course*, I recognize as Chanel No. 5, and a little dent in the cushion of the sofa where her perfectly formed bottom was just sitting.

Chapter 6

I'm woken by the ringing of my phone.

For the third time so far this morning.

Well, if I've ignored it this many times, it can't hurt to ignore it once more.

But this time, I'm awake enough to take a little peek out from beneath my duvet, just to see if, by any chance, Marilyn Monroe has appeared on the Chesterfield again, mink-clad or otherwise.

She hasn't, and the scent of Chanel No. 5 has faded by now too.

I sit up properly, rub my bleary eyes, and then, just to settle something in my own mind, I open the drawer at the bottom of my narrow bedside table. I lift up my vintage-bead box, and my makeup bag, and the pile of bills that I sometimes shove in there when they all arrive at once and get a bit too scary. Then I feel around for the pair of sunglasses that I hope – as I always do when I come back to check on them – will be hidden away there in the back left-hand corner.

They're still there.

I pull them all the way out to have a proper look.

This pair of dark tortoiseshell Oliver Goldsmith sunglasses is the reason why I didn't just assume, when I came upon Marilyn Monroe in my flat yesterday evening, that I was cracking up. Suffering hallucinations. Talking – like some sort of overgrown, Manhattan-swigging toddler – to an imaginary friend.

These are *Audrey Hepburn's sunglasses*. She left them behind the last time she came for a 'visit'. And thanks to the fact that Bogdan has seen them, and that Dillon has seen them, and that half the population of Rome commented on them (*Ciao, Audrey!*) every time I wore them, over there, on the first weekend Dillon and I ever spent together, I know that they're as real as the nose on my face.

I *know* this. I always knew it, even though my faith has occasionally wavered a bit since then.

It didn't help, probably, that in the (thorough, scientific) interests of eliminating any possibility that I was cracking up/suffering hallucinations/talking to an imaginary friend, I shelled out for a couple of terrifyingly expensive sessions with a psychiatrist friend of Nora's, Dr Burnett, a few times last summer. Just to drop in a mention of my encounters with Audrey Hepburn, to see what a professional might say. I don't know what I was expecting, really, but Dr Burnett couldn't have been firmer about the fact that it had all been nothing more than my imagination. *Stress-induced visual and auditory hallucinations*, he mentioned on my second visit. And, as for the sunglasses, well, they must have been an old, forgotten pair of mine, according to him, or even something I'd gone out and bought, in some sort of fugue state, to convince myself that what I'd been seeing and hearing was in fact real.

I never went back for a third session.

Because Dr Burnett was wrong. For all his many degrees, and qualifications, and years of experience, he was, in this case, wrong.

I lean down, again, and hunt in the very back of that same drawer for the other thing I keep tucked away there: a folded-up piece of paper, torn from a copy of *InStyle* magazine, with a picture on it.

It's a picture of Audrey Hepburn, at Pinewood Studios, sitting on my Chesterfield sofa.

What are the odds that Marilyn Monroe, while filming at Pinewood herself, encountered the Chesterfield too?

I mean, she did film whatsit, that film with (ha!) Laurence Olivier over here, didn't she? *The Prince and the Showgirl* . . . I'm not my father's daughter for nothing: some bits of movie history do sink in. That said, I'll just grab my phone and Google it, to be absolutely sure . . .

And of course, the bloody thing starts ringing again, just as I slide out of bed, stagger to the sofa, and pick it out of my handbag.

It's an Unknown number.

The only calls I ever get from an Unknown number are – *were* – Adam, calling from his office.

If it's been him calling three times already this morning, then I guess I'd better get this call out of the way. Accept whatever apology he's offering in a dignified, if chilly fashion, in an attempt to claw my dignity back from where I left it, on his kitchen floor.

Assuming that he *is* offering an apology, and not, I don't know, calling to tell me I owe him for a new safety gate, or doggy post-traumatic-stress sessions for Fritz, or something.

Which reminds me that I do need to tell him about those earrings. I can't have Fritz's choking death on my conscience. Bad enough that I got the poor creature addicted to artery-clogging pâté.

'Hi,' I say, coolly, as I answer. 'Adam?'

'No, sorry,' says a woman's voice. 'Is this Liberty Lomax?'

'Er . . . yes . . .?'

'My name is Erin,' she goes on, in the sort of hushed, oddly reverential tone I've found is always used in spas, or beauty salons. 'I'm calling from the Grove House clinic in west London.'

'Grove House?' The name rings a bell, for some reason, but I can't put my finger on why. 'Sorry, I don't know why you're . . .' Then I remember why I know the name. 'You mean the Grove House *psychiatric* clinic?'

But how can a psychiatric clinic possibly have known about last night . . . and Marilyn?

'We prefer to think of ourselves as a treatment facility,' Erin says, in that same hushed, beauty-salon tone of voice. 'A rehabilitation centre, for anyone suffering from the symptoms of many common substance-abuse disorders.'

'But this thing that happens to me,' I croak, 'it's *real*. I mean, it's not the symptom of a substance-abuse disorder. Famous people really, really *do* pop up out of my magic sofa.'

There's a short silence at the other end of the phone.

'I know, I know,' I go on, 'that sounds crazy . . . but maybe that's just because I shouldn't be using the term *magic*. It's probably a bit off-putting. Would it make me sound any less unhinged if I used the word *enchanted*?'

I really like this, actually, now that I say it out loud: it gives the whole bizarre situation a pleasingly literary flavour, as if my Chesterfield is just part of a great enchanted-furniture heritage that also includes the wardrobe from *The Lion, the Witch and the Wardrobe* and the bed from *Bedknobs and Broomsticks*. Which, OK, I know are both totally made up, but . . .

'Miss Lomax, I think you might have misunderstood the purpose of my phone call.'

'Oh?'

'I'm not calling to discuss . . . sorry, did you say that famous people pop up out of your . . . *magical* sofa?'

'Enchanted,' I correct her, eagerly. 'But yes, I did say that. You're quite right.'

'Ri-i-i-i-ght . . . uh, I'm actually calling to talk about your sister.'

'My *sister?*'

'Yes. Cassidy Kennedy. She was admitted to the clinic last night.'

'I beg your pardon?'

'Cassidy checked herself in,' Erin says, in a voice that's more mellifluous than ever, 'late last night. Seeking the clinic's help to deal with her addiction issues.'

OK, now I really feel like I'm losing the plot.

'But Cass doesn't *have* any addiction issues. Unless . . . well, do you treat *selfie-taking* addiction at your clinic?'

'I'm not really at liberty,' she replies, in the sort of chilly tone that I'd have been using on Adam, if it had been him calling, 'to discuss the precise details of your sister's case. All I will say is that quite often we find that family members are the last ones to notice that there's a problem.'

I'm torn between repeating, again, that Cass *doesn't have* a problem, and allowing myself to give in to the anxiety that's suddenly gnawing away at me.

I mean, Cass is my sister . . . my little sister . . . and now all of a sudden she's taken herself off to a *psychiatric clinic?*

This whole cancelled TV deal must have hit her much worse than I'd thought.

'Anyway, I'm just calling on Cassidy's behalf, because

there are no mobile phones allowed in here, to ask if you might be able to bring a few basic necessities over for her?'

I'm already mentally compiling a list of the things I think Cass might need over there: her childhood blankie that she still likes to snuggle with when she's feeling poorly; her comfiest pair of pyjamas; even a few family photos, perhaps, to make her room feel more homely . . . or, at the very least, a few of the framed selfies that line her living-room walls . . .

'Of course,' I say, casting around my untidy flat for a pen and a piece of scrap paper. 'Hang on a sec, I'm just looking for something to write with . . .'

'Oh, that's OK. Now that we've spoken, I'll send you a text with the list. And I'll let Cassidy know you'll be over to visit her later in the day, shall I?'

'Tell her I'm on my way. I mean, like, right now.'

I hang up, and start pulling on the nearest clothes to hand, which are the black trousers I wore yesterday, and the most beloved of all my grey hoodies that even Audrey Hepburn couldn't persuade me to get rid of, and I've just twisted my hair up into a clip and stuck my feet into a pair of Converse when my phone pings with Erin's text message.

It's not . . . *quite* the sort of thing I was expecting.

No requests for Blankie, or pyjamas, or her framed selfies.

LARGE MAKEUP BOX FROM BEDROOM

MEDIUM MAKEUP BOX FROM BATHROOM

OK, so Cass wants her makeup . . . well, sure, I get that. Every woman knows the power of her favourite lipstick to lift her mood when things are tough.

CURLING TONGS
STRAIGHTENING IRONS
MINI STRAIGHTENING IRONS

Well, her hair *has* always been important to her . . . It's just that I'm surprised that even Cass would have the energy to set about it with curling tongs/straightening irons when she's so depressed about the demise of her TV reality show.

JBRAND SKINNIES
VICTORIA BECKHAM SUPER-SUPER SKINNIES
NEW TAN LOUBOUTIN KNEE-HIGH BOOTS
OLD TAN LOUBOUTIN KNEE-HIGH BOOTS
CHERRY-RED TOPSHOP MICRO-SHORTS
WHITE DENIM CUT-OFF MINI

OK: this Grove House Clinic . . . is it, by any chance, the world's first rehab-facility-slash-nightclub?

Apart from anything else, I'm going to need a massive suitcase to get all this stuff over to Cass, in . . .

Oh, I'd better look up where Grove House is, exactly. Barnes.

Great. So it's all the way up to Cass's flat in Maida Vale in northwest London, and then all the way back across town again to leafy, hard-to-access-by-public-transport Barnes in the south.

But, like I've already said, Cass is my only sister, and I'm not going to think twice about it.

Well, I'm not going to think a *third time* about it.

And, looking on the bright side, at least a schlep across London in the rush hour is going to give me a break from running the whole Marilyn situation through my head again.

*

Three hours, four tubes and a painfully slow bus journey later, and I'm finally approaching the Grove House clinic, a rambling red-brick Victorian mansion overlooking the north side of Barnes Common.

There are tall iron gates (I'll be avoiding putting my head anywhere near *those*, thank you very much) and a large buzzer to press on the wall to the side of them, and . . . oh! A half-dozen or so photographers lurking, right by the wall, who suddenly leap into action as they see me approaching, their cameras at the ready.

There are a couple of bright flashes, dazzling me, until one of them announces, 'She's *no one*,' and they all go back to lurking again.

Which is charming, isn't it, because for all they know, especially given that I'm rocking up here with a large suitcase, I could be here to check into the clinic for serious depression and anxiety, characterized by feelings of low self-esteem and worthlessness.

I give them all a meaningful stare, then stop beside the wall and press the buzzer.

It's not *very* impressive, given the presence of the paparazzi outside, that I'm buzzed through the gates without anyone so much as bothering to ask my name . . . but I try not to take against the place before I've even gone inside. I walk across a gravelled driveway – not easy, with a heavy suitcase to pull – and then reach another buzzer just to the left of the main front door. This time a woman's voice – Erin's? – states a smooth, 'Yes?' out of the speakerphone before I give my name, and am buzzed through here too.

My appointments with Dr Burnett were at his consulting rooms in Marylebone so, despite my own brush with psychiatric treatment, I've never set foot in a psychiatric clinic before. I don't know what I was expecting, really, but if the Grove House clinic has just a touch of Victorian-asylum-chic on the outside, it's not at *all* Victorian-asylum-chic once you're through these doors. If anything, it looks a lot more like a smart new boutique hotel: polished marble floors, stunning floral arrangements and bold expressionist art on the walls.

I feel – in Yesterday's Trousers and my chucked-on hoodie, with my eye makeup still unwashed after last night – way, *way* too grubby and unpolished for a place like this. And I can suddenly see why, after all, Cass might have wanted me to bring half the contents of her wardrobe and all her grooming equipment.

There's a little reception area (leather Eames chairs; a table stocked with glass bottles of mineral water) just inside the main door so, in the absence of a human being to tell me where to go or what to do, I perch in one of the chairs and wait, anxiously, to be summoned.

And then I remember that I was just about to Google 'Marilyn Monroe Pinewood Studios' right before the call from Erin that turned my day into, well, this. So I reach for my phone, my Google finger at the ready, because I may as well at least accomplish something useful while I sit around here.

Yes. Oh, Lord, yes, I was right. If the Gods of Google (and the wise men of Wikipedia) are to be believed, then Marilyn did, indeed, film *The Prince and the Showgirl* at Pinewood, in 1956.

OK, so now I suppose what I'm looking for – if it even exists – is some sort of evidence that she, like Audrey Hepburn before her, came into contact with a battered old Chesterfield sofa during her long days at the studio. I mean, she must have had a dressing room there, right? Somewhere she famously holed up with that intense acting coach of hers to find her motivation for each scene . . .

My train of thought is disturbed by the arrival, on my phone screen, of a brand-new text message.

Hi. We met on Monday night. My boyfriend Adam's house. Call me on this number asap, please? Rgds, Benjamin Milne

Oh, my God.

Ben.

And he wants me to *call him?*

This can't be good news. I mean, he didn't look much of a fluffy bunny of a man when he scowled round the side of the cooker at me. Even factoring in the obvious social awkwardness of arriving in your boyfriend's kitchen to find his secret girlfriend apparently engaged in some sort of solitary bondage experiment there, he could hardly have been *more* irritable-looking.

And now he's suggesting that I *call him?*

I'm not going to call him! Don't I already have enough stress in my life without having to expose myself to the misplaced anger of my ex-boyfriend's boyfriend? If there's anyone he ought to be telling to call him asap so that, presumably, he can have a go at them, it's bloody Adam. Not me.

Adam, I message him, furiously – and fast, because I can already see an ethereal-looking redheaded girl, who must be Erin, appearing as if out of nowhere and heading towards me – *why the hell did you give Ben my number, and why the hell does he think it's OK to use it to harass me???*

I press send.

Then, just as Erin reaches me, I type a follow-up
message.

Btw I think I left my earrings on your kitchen floor.
Please send them back to me by registered post.
Wouldn't want Fritz to choke on them.

'Hello,' says Erin, in that same blandly mellifluous
voice. 'You must be Liberty Lomax? I'm Erin. We spoke
on the phone earlier. You mentioned a magic sofa?'

I laugh, weakly. 'Well, you did catch me only a few
moments after waking up.'

'Of course. Let me just give you this,' she adds,
smoothly, reaching forward to press a glossy brochure
into my hands. 'Just in case you should ever decide that
a short stay with us might be beneficial to you, too.'

'No, no, I'm really not—'

'Cassidy,' Erin interrupts, waving an ethereal hand
towards some huge French windows at the back of the
lobby, 'is in the garden. Her midday yoga workshop
should just about have come to an end. I can keep this
– ' she nods towards Cass's suitcase – 'in the office. We
check our clients' bags when they come to stay with us,
anyway. Not that I'm accusing you of bringing in any
banned substances.'

Well, she pretty much *is* accusing me of bringing in
banned substances, but I'm not about to point that out
to her right now.

Because it's not just Erin's aura of preternatural calm and ever-so-slightly disturbing tranquillity that is sending my heart leaping into my mouth with nerves as I get up and head across the marble floor, and out on to a wide patio. This whole thing is starting to get scarily real, and I'm suddenly anxious about the sort of state I'm going to find Cass in.

In fact, I can see her now, breaking away from a group at the far end of the large, lush lawn to jog across towards me.

I open my arms, eager to sweep her up into a great big, older-sisterly hug, and tell her everything's going to be all right—

'Did you bring my black string bikini?' she asks, the moment she reaches me.

'Erin didn't mention anything about a—'

'No, I know Erin didn't mention it, because I forgot to put it on the list I gave her, but I thought you'd be *bound* to realize it when you got to my apartment.'

'Bound to realize that you needed a *black string bikini?* In a psychiatric clinic?'

'Rehab centre,' Cass corrects me. 'And *duh*, Libby, of *course* I need my black string bikini. I want to sunbathe by the rooftop pool! I'm never going to keep up in here if I just have to sit up there in a pair of shorts and a borrowed bra-top, like I did this morning.'

There's a rooftop pool? For *sunbathing?*

What kind of clinic *is* this, for crying out loud?

And more to the point—

'Keep up with what?' I ask.

'The other patients, of course!'

Cass grabs my arm and leads me to a bench at the edge of the patio, from where we can look out over the entire garden. There are lots of abnormally attractive people hanging out on the lawn: some are busy with yoga, others are drinking coffee and puffing away at cigarettes, and there are several small gatherings of them sitting in circles and engaged in deep-looking conversation. I may not be an expert, but I'd guess they were support groups.

'I mean, you've absolutely no idea how difficult it is to get in with the A list here,' Cass is continuing, as she slumps, exhaustedly, on to the bench.

'There's an *A* list?'

'Of course there is! It's a *celebrity* rehab clinic, Libby! I mean, look around . . . those two girls on that bench over there, with the coffee cups – one of them is in the new M&S lingerie ads, and the other one was on the cover of *Vogue* last November . . . and that guy doing the downward dog in my yoga group – see him? – he's that stand-up comedian Mum likes, the one she went to see at Wembley for her birthday.'

'Right. Well, hard to tell, obviously, from that particular view of him.'

'And there's a tonne of actors, and actresses, and loads of famous musicians that I'd probably know if, like, I gave a shit about music . . . It's why I'm wondering, Lib, if it wasn't the best decision for me to have an alcohol problem.'

'Cass.' I put a hand on top of hers. 'Sweetheart. It's *never* a good decision to develop a problem with alcohol. And I wish you'd *told* me. I had absolutely no idea you've been—'

'No, no, God, no, I don't mean *that*. I mean, maybe it would have been a better decision for me to come in here with a drugs problem. Or – oooh – an eating disorder! Do you think I could have an eating disorder?'

'Er . . . do *you* think you could have an eating disorder?'

'Libby!' She rolls her eyes. 'I'm just asking if you think I'm thin enough! Because obviously if I was going to say I had an eating disorder, I'd have to say it was anorexia . . . bulimia's just *too* gross and totally unglamorous.'

'Right. And anorexia is glitz and glamour personified.'

'Well, I don't know about *that*, Lib.' She's completely missed the sarcasm. 'I mean, sure, you end up really thin and stuff, but if you take it too far your breath starts to smell, and your hair falls out . . . Anyway, I'm only asking because all the really hot models and actresses are either in the eating disorders support groups or the druggie ones, and it would be, like *really* good for me if I could make friends with a few of them before I check out.'

Something is starting to sound more than just a little fishy here.

'Cass. Can you just tell me again why you checked yourself in here?'

'Ooooh, absolutely. I'd love to!'

And suddenly, she's putting on her Acting Face.

If you've ever seen Cass in anything – regional panto, one of her small roles in one of the soaps, her recent role as resident babe in *Isara 364* – you'll recognize her Acting Face: a middle-distance gaze, a half-pouted mouth, and a sucking-in of her cheekbones to make her face look a bit thinner. And she has an Acting Voice to go with it, a way of speaking that makes it sound as if every word she utters has a Capital Letter and is therefore Terribly, Terribly Important.

'The Demon Drink, They Call It,' she's saying, as if she's auditioning for the part of a downtrodden-but-honest gin-soaked prostitute in an especially twee Victorian murder mystery. 'And It's Certainly Brought Out The Demons In Me.'

'Cass—'

'It Started With The Occasional Vodka, At The End Of A Stressful Day. And Then, Before I Knew It, I Was Drinking An Entire Bottle. In One Gulp. And Then Immediately Opening The Next One. It's Why The Time Has Come For Me To Be Honest With Everybody – My Family, My Friends And, Most Importantly Of All, The Great British Public – In The Hope That My Story Can Bring Solstice To Anyone Else In The Same Boat.'

I take a deep breath.

'I think you mean solace.'

'What?'

'Solace. Not Solstice. Solstice is the longest night of the summer. Or winter.'

'No it's not.' Cass shakes her head, irritably. 'It's an ice lollipop.'

I lean forward on the bench and place my head in my hands.

'I mean, I did wonder why I was supposed to start talking about ice lollipops . . . like, why would my story be bringing a Solstice to anyone?' Cass's forehead wrinkles. 'But then I thought maybe it'll be a coupon for a free one with the newspaper on the day my story comes out, or something?' She waves an airy hand. 'Dave'll handle all that side of it.'

I think I'm starting to see the bigger picture here, confusion over ice lollipops notwithstanding.

'Cass. Please – *please* – don't tell me you're faking a serious addiction just to get a story about yourself in the newspapers.'

'Of course I'm not!'

'Oh, thank God, because that would be—'

'*Once* the story's come out in the newspapers, *then* the goal is to convince RealTime Media that they ought to contract me for *Considering Cassidy* after all.'

I take my head out of my hands and stare at her. 'Cassidy Kennedy! You *cannot* pretend to have a drink problem to get yourself a TV show!'

'So *you* think I should go with the drugs angle, too? Or the eating disorder?'

'No! This isn't an American university, for crying out loud! You can't just go around switching your major! Besides, don't you think the clinic is going to find it a bit suspicious that you came in here claiming a drink problem, and then the next day you suddenly say, *Oh, actually, it's turned into an eating disorder instead*?'

'Well, that could happen, couldn't it? I mean, cut off from alcohol, it's perfectly possible you might get so bored that you start obsessively counting calories and become an anorexic? There's not much to do here, Libby. I mean, I've been here less than twenty-four hours, and I'm *already* bored stupid, trying to work out how to fill the time.'

'Well, if you were *actually an addict of some sort*, Cass, I expect that working on kicking your horrible, life-destroying habit would take up a *bit* of the time . . .' Too angry, now, to say any more, I get to my feet. 'I'm going. Seriously, Cass, I'm not going to sit around and . . . *enable* this nonsense.'

'Oh, my God, you're using that word too! What the hell *is* this enabling crap, exactly? They were going on and on about it in my support group this morning, as if it's, like, a *bad* thing. But it just means *helping*, right?'

'No, it bloody doesn't! It means you help people feed their habits, which isn't the same thing. And remember, I know a little bit about all this horrible, *real* addiction stuff, because I was with Dillon O'Hara for three months! Or had you forgotten the miserable mess I got into, getting involved with—'

'Oh, yeah, I almost forgot. He's here.'

'Who?'

'Dillon. He's here. At the clinic.'

I wouldn't have thought it possible to have a bigger shock than encountering Marilyn Monroe in my flat last night.

But apparently it's perfectly possible.

I actually have to sit back down on the bench again, because my legs have turned into trifle.

'Dillon. Is. *Here?*'

Cass nods, not that interested. 'I mean, I haven't seen him or anything, but I had a little chat with that M&S lingerie model while we were eating breakfast this morning – well, *I* was eating breakfast; she was moving a single slice of kiwi fruit from one side of her plate to the other, obviously; God, I only *wish* I had that kind of discipline—'

'Not important.'

'Well, she was saying she'd seen loads of paparazzi gathering outside the gates this morning because apparently –' Cass pulls a disgusted face – 'he's got some kind of discharge . . .'

Years of translating Cass's mis-speaks make this one easy for me to get my head around.

'Do you mean he's *being* discharged?'

'Oh, yeah.' She nods, thoughtfully. 'That might have been it. Though I think he's been in here for his sex addiction, Lib, or at least partly, so it isn't *totally* impossible that he'd have some kind of discharge . . .'

'So he's gone? Or he's still here—?'

'I don't know, Libby! God, it's like you don't think I have anything better to do than to keep an eye on your scuzzy ex-boyfriend's exact whereabouts! I've got a *serious addiction to kick, all right?* Now, just help me decide, once and for all, which one.'

'No. I have to go. I don't want to risk . . . I just don't want to see him.'

'OK, well, if he *is* still around, and if I run into him, I'll say hi to him from you, shall I?'

'No! Don't say anything—'

'Hey, I've had an amazing idea!' Cass's eyes are suddenly very wide and staring, as if she might in fact have a drugs problem after all. 'Maybe I could just hang out with Dillon while we're both in here! That way he'd be able to introduce me to all the really important people – good guest stars for me to line up for the show – and I wouldn't even need to switch to a different support group after all!'

'Cass. If you use my relationship with Dillon to claw your way to the top of the pile in here,' I say, firmly (or as firmly as I can given that my *entire being* has now become the consistency of trifle), 'I will never ever forgive you for it.'

'Hey!' Her eyes narrow. 'Don't you start telling me what I can and cannot do, Libby. *You're* not the one suffering from a Soul-Destroying Alcohol Addiction . . .'

'Neither are you!' I snap, as I turn on my heel (well, the sole of my Converse) and stamp out of the garden and back towards the lobby, leaving my annoying sister and her fabricated drink problem behind me.

I really, really don't want to see Dillon. Today, tomorrow – or, in fact, ever again.

Because I'm not a masochist, all right? I get all stressed out about even having to take off a plaster. I avoid bikini waxes until I'm in danger of being hunted down by torch-wielding villagers. Inflicting pain on myself, of either the physical or emotional kind, is not a thing that is pleasurable to me.

And it would be absolutely sod's law, wouldn't it, if I *did* happen to see him, that I'd do so when I'm unwashed and bed-headed, in boring black trousers and a hoodie with – I've only just noticed this; *how have I only just noticed this?* – a seriously dubious-looking light brown stain right down the front of it. Instead of, say, bumping into him at some miraculous point in the future when I'm two stone lighter, with a glowing summer tan and terrific hair, and while, most importantly of all, I'm sauntering down the street on the arm of, say, Daniel Craig. Or Eddie Redmayne. Or that really dishy one who plays Jon Snow in *Game of Thrones*. Gorgeous, and loved-up, and . . . *sorted*.

Anything, *anything*, rather than seeing him again right now.

Which is why I start to breathe a little easier the minute I've crossed the lobby (without any further pamphlet-eering from eerie Erin, thank God), opened the main lobby door, and made my way at speed across the driveway and towards the iron gates.

The photographers clustered on the other side of the gates all start dancing their paparazzi dance as soon as they see me, and yelling their paparazzi war-cry, and jostling for position, and lifting their Nikons up above their heads to snap pictures, because once again none of them has yet realized that I'm 'nobody'. As soon as I get closer to the gate, they're going to cotton on, and look pretty bloody silly about it.

But they're not stopping. They're just getting more and more agitated, the closer I get.

It's almost as if someone *actually* famous is coming out of the clinic behind me.

I glance over one shoulder, just to see if there's any way I could be right about this.

And yes, someone actually famous *is* coming out of the clinic behind me.

In battered grey jeans and a Run DMC T-shirt, rock-star sunglasses shielding his eyes, it's Dillon O'Hara.

Chapter 7

His mouth forms, just for a second, into a perfect 'O' of surprise when he sees me, stopped up ahead of him.

Then it melts into an all-too-familiar, all-too-wicked grin, and he carries on walking towards me.

'Of all the rehab clinics,' he says, as he reaches me, 'in all the world . . .'

He puts one hand on my shoulder and leans down to kiss me, softly, on the cheek.

At which point, obviously, the photographers all go berserk.

And at which point, also, the gates start to swing open, and a sleek black Audi starts to pull through them. Or, rather, it tries to pull through them, but it's not the easiest job for the driver to do without accidentally bringing the sleek black bumper into contact with some of the paparazzi.

'Now, I'm *fairly* sure I asked the car company to send a driver who was OK with mowing photographers down,'

Dillon says, conversationally, as we watch the Audi edge forward, centimetre by centimetre. 'But perhaps I needed to be more specific. Ask for someone who's actually *keen* to do it.'

I'm still too stunned to say anything.

'Ah, now we're getting somewhere,' he's saying, as the Audi finally manages to get sufficiently far on to the driveway to leave the photographers – who are presumably worried about trespass charges – still snapping forlornly a few feet behind it. 'Libby, my darling. Would you care to join me in my transport of delight?'

'Actually, I was just going to walk to the train . . .'

'Yeah . . . that can't happen now. They'll hound you every step of the way there. And I don't know if you remember being hounded by tabloid scum while we were together at all, Libby, but it's not the most joyous experience you'll have had, I'll bet you.'

Actually we weren't hounded much while we were together (largely, I suspect, because I was nowhere near a titillating enough romantic interest for the tabloids to get invested in), but there was one incident, on our way through Gatwick Airport, that was sufficiently invasive and unpleasant for me, right now, to choose the lesser of two evils.

Dillon is holding one car door open for me.

I slide through it, then sit, facing rigidly forwards, as he gets into the car himself.

'Onwards!' he declares, dramatically, to the driver,

who's looking as if he wishes he'd never agreed to this job in the first place.

And anyway, saying 'onwards' doesn't *quite* hit the spot, because obviously the Audi has to do a careful three-point turn in the driveway, and once that's been accomplished, run the gamut of the photographers again, all crowding at the rear of the car to take pictures through the (thankfully tinted) passenger windows, and risking broken feet from the car's wheels with every jostle they make.

'I don't know what your hourly rate is, mate,' Dillon says, leaning forward to speak to the driver, 'but I'll tell you what: I'll triple it, and add another tenner for luck, if you just put your foot down and get us the fuck away from these goons.'

This was all it needed – who knew? – because the driver does exactly as asked, puts his foot down with little-to-no regard for the feet of the paparazzi, and has us leaving the gates behind and out on the open road before Dillon can offer to 'quadruple' his hourly rate and stump up a fifty-quid bonus into the bargain.

It's my turn to lean forward now. 'Could you drop me,' I ask the driver, 'at Barnes mainline station?'

'Libby. Come on.' Dillon looks at me. 'Let's drop you home. It's still Colliers Wood, right?'

'I'd rather take public transport.'

'And I'd rather stop off and have a pint at my favourite new local by the river in Barnes village. Colliers Wood, please, mate,' he tells the driver, before turning back to me again. 'But we can't all have everything we want, Libby. If there's one thing I've learned these past few weeks in rehab, it's that.'

My plan, to sit primly facing forwards, making as little eye contact as possible and with my hands locked defensively around my knees, falls at literally the first hurdle, because at this comment, I can't help but glance across the back seat at him.

'You have to be kidding me. While you were in rehab, you tracked down a *new local?*'

'You know me, Libby.'

'Yes. I do know you. But I'd have thought the clinic might have slightly more stringent standards.'

Though *why* I'd have thought this, I don't quite know, seeing as they've managed to let my sister check herself in despite displaying no signs of addiction at all.

'Oh, no, no, Libby, they didn't give me permission to go or anything.' He lowers his voice. 'There were a few of us, from my alcohol support group, who sort of banded together . . . I mean, we initially came from all these different backgrounds – lots of Brits, a couple of Americans, even an Aussie or two – and there wasn't much holding us together. But then we started to dig this tunnel out from under one of the clinic rooms, in the direction of the Hand and Flowers in Barnes village . . . we hid the excavated dirt underneath our trouser legs, then we'd wander out to the organic herb garden and let the mud out from our trousers with these sort of pulley things . . .' He lets out a long sigh. 'One of the guys went blind, tragically, from all the work in the dark tunnel, but he thought it was worth it, for the chance of a sly pint or two; another bloke suddenly started suffering from the most terrible claustrophobia, but luckily he had a good buddy who rallied round to help him through . . .'

OK, so now I know he is, in fact, kidding me.

'That's the plot of *The Great Escape*.'

'No!' His brow furrows. 'Are you *sure* about that, now, Libby? I mean, I don't remember a nice local pub in *The Great Escape*. By the river or otherwise . . .'

'You're not funny.'

'I'm a little bit funny.' He sits back and grins at me. 'Come on, Libby. Aren't I allowed to joke about any of this? Of course I haven't been to any fucking pub. I'm a changed man. Seriously. Do you think they'd be letting me out if they thought I was in any danger of hitting the booze again?'

'How should I know? They let my sister *in*, and she's . . .' I pause. I don't want to be the one to blow open the fraud behind Cass's entry to the clinic. Appalled as I am by the whole endeavour, she's still my sister. 'Well, she's not got *that* much of a problem with drink.'

'Oh, so it was your sister you were there to visit?'

'Yes. She checked herself in last night.' I glance at him. 'Did you think I was there to see *you*, or something?'

'Well, it was the most logical explanation when I first saw you, Libby McLibster. I mean, I didn't know your sister had any kind of a problem with alcohol—'

'Nor did I.'

'And then there's the fact that I'm, obviously, irresistible.'

'Are you?' I say, coldly.

'Well, the proof of the pudding is in the eating, I'd have thought. I mean, I was an out-and-out bastard to you, Libby, and yet there you were, standing on the driveway as I left rehab, coming back for more.'

I don't know which part of this statement to tackle first.

Obviously the most important thing to lay to rest is *any suggestion whatsoever* that I was coming back for more, but the first thing that pops out of my mouth deals with something else he said instead.

'So you've finally realized that you were an out-and-out bastard, then?'

'Libby. Be fair to me. I realized that I was an out-and-out bastard the moment I woke up in LA, surrounded by scantily clad strangers, and saw the messages from you on my phone. And my brand-new opinion on my character – or lack of it, to be honest with you – was confirmed when I was too much of a coward to even message you back.'

I'm a tiny bit astounded by the frankness of all this. Even from Dillon, who was never one for missing an opportunity to laugh at himself (which was, let's face it, always one of the many extremely attractive things about him), it's self-deprecation of the highest degree.

'You did,' I mumble, 'in all fairness, message me back.'

He raises a faintly astonished eyebrow. '*Did* I?'

I nod. 'So.'

'Huh?'

'*So*. That's what you messaged me. I mean, obviously when you drink, you tend to get even more incredibly Irish, and use the word *so* every time you finish a sentence. But I gave you the benefit of the doubt and assumed you'd started typing the word *sorry* but then . . . well, I don't know, Dillon. Maybe you passed out in yet another alcoholic stupor; maybe you found yourself unable to fight the need to snort another line of yummy cocaine from between the magnificent breasts of a naked Norwegian . . .'

Dillon winces. 'She was Finnish, actually. But, nevertheless. I deserve that.'

'You do.'

'And I had no idea I'd messaged you. Even something as pathetic as that. I just felt so unbelievably shit about myself, Lib, when I came out the other side of . . . well, that whole episode. I pretty much just wanted to forget you even existed.'

'Well, congratulations, then. Job done.'

'Hey.' He reaches over and, briefly, touches my shoulder. 'I said I wanted to. I didn't say I managed.'

My shoulder, beneath my stained hoodie, tingles where he's just put his hand on it.

Which is the first moment, since we met outside the clinic five minutes ago, that I actually *remember* that I'm wearing a stained hoodie. And yesterday's trousers. With my hair uncombed, and my face still coated in yesterday's makeup, and with the puffy dinginess to my skin that comes from a hangover brought about by drinking too many Manhattans with Marilyn Monroe. (It does give me a bit of a kick, though, that my hangover is the result of late-night drinks with Marilyn. Because for all Dillon's absurd antics with hot blondes, he's never managed to match drinks with a blonde quite as hot as *that*.)

I mean, this is a long way from the Best Case Scenario in which I might ever have idly imagined reacquainting myself with Dillon. You know, the one where I've miraculously *lost* two stone (from my hips and thighs) and *gained* thirteen stone (in the form of Daniel Craig, looking tasty, on my arm).

And here's Dillon, sitting beside me, looking, himself, like an insanely buff and particularly sexy Greek God.

Let's face it, I was disposable enough to Dillon when I was actually making the best of myself. After seeing me today, he's going to forget I even exist, again, the moment he's dropped me at my front door.

Well, sod him. I'm going to forget about him, too. Not quite so easily, perhaps, and with quite a lot more drink involved. But I'm not going to give him the satisfaction

140

of just cruising back into my life, pulling his I'm-too-charming-for-my-pants routine, and then cruising right off back out of it. Changed man or no changed man: he's not going to take up a single iota of my head-space again.

'It's pretty great, actually, that I bumped into you right as I was leaving today,' he's going on. 'Because you've been right at the very top of my list.'

This throws me. 'Your . . . list?'

He nods. 'People I seriously need to apologize to. I mean, I don't know if you know anything about drink and drugs rehab, Lib, but if you're doing it at all properly, you end up with a list of friends and family who you finally realize you've shafted, or screwed over, or fucked about with in some way. People you've really upset, and pissed off, and rightly won't even speak to you again unless you make some proper amends. And maybe not, in some cases, even then.'

'You want to make amends to me?'

'Christ, woman, of course I fucking do! I'd have given you a call, once I'd worked my nerve up – a lot harder without a drink to help you out – and asked you out for a bite to eat.'

'It would have to have been a bloody expensive meal,' I retort, 'if it was going to make amends. Somewhere with three Michelin stars, and vintage champagne, and oysters, and . . . and foie gras,' I add, before remembering that I don't actually eat foie gras, that oysters make me

141

physically ill and that Dillon can't drink champagne anyway, vintage or otherwise.

'Libby, darling, the meal isn't the part that's meant to make amends. It's just the *setting* for me to do it in.'

'I see. Then I've saved you a pretty penny,' I say, frostily, 'by conveniently bumping into you and allowing you to do the whole thing in a minicab, haven't I?'

'Licensed private hire vehicle,' the driver mutters from the front seat. 'Not a minicab. Actually.'

Oh, for Christ's sake – how could I have forgotten, *again*, that there's someone else in the car when I'm having a private conversation about my disastrous love life? And this time not even Bogdan, who is at least a friend of mine, but a perfect stranger.

It's all a cue for me to sit more primly than ever, staring out of my window like Miss Jean Brodie, and willing the traffic to ease up so that this journey can come to a merciful end, so that Dillon can go back to forgetting about me (but more happily than ever, in the knowledge that he's finally Done The Right Thing by ticking me off his apology list), and so that I can stagger up the stairs to my flat with the hope, at the back of my mind, that Marilyn Monroe might turn up again. Because I could murder another one of her revolting Manhattans, apart from anything else.

'You know what?' Dillon is saying, as if fully aware that his 'making amends' conversation hasn't gone terribly well, 'let's not keep talking about me and all my stupid mistakes any more. I've had six weeks of rehab to blether on about myself to anyone who'd fucking listen. Tell me all about what's happening with you.'

'Just the usual stuff,' I say, trying to look Extremely Interested in Wimbledon Common as we sail on by.

'Oh, now, come on. Running your own successful jewellery business isn't "just the usual stuff". I can't open a newspaper without reading about you.'

'I've done one interview.' And I am *not* going to react to the fact that he's just admitted he read it. 'With the *Evening Standard*'s Friday supplement.'

'Well, I read that interview. And I thought about giving you a call then, too, to say how proud I was of you, but that was right at the start of the weekend that sort of precipitated my trip to rehab . . . You see, I was at this party in Soho that Friday night, and the next thing I knew it was Tuesday morning, and I was in—'

'I thought,' I mutter, 'you were tired of blethering on about yourself.'

He grins, sheepishly. 'All I'm trying to say, Libby, is that I heard that things were going really well for you on the professional front, and I was dead pleased. Am I allowed to say that?'

'You're allowed to say whatever you want,' I say, coolly. 'It's a free country.'

'So it is. So it is.' He looks out of his own window for a couple of minutes, drumming his fingers, casually, on the door handle. 'And personally?'

'Personally what?'

'On the personal front. How are things going there?'

'Fine, Dillon. Thank you.'

'Any family news? Apart from your sister's drink problem, that is.'

'No family news, no.' I'm not going to get into all the stuff about Dad's wedding, and my new stepfamily, because that was never the kind of stuff I talked about with Dillon.

'That nice-sounding friend of yours had her wedding yet?'

'Late July.'

'Good for her. And is her brother still a massive wanker?'

'Olly's incredibly well,' I say, fiercely, 'and opening up his own restaurant in Clapham any day now, in fact.'

'Jesus. Well, tell me the name of the place so I can avoid it like the plague. I'm not keeling over dead just because Olly fucking Walker has taken it upon himself to put rat poison in my poncey white truffle ravioli.'

'There won't be any white truffle ravioli. Or any ponciness,' I say, trying not to look surprised that Dillon actually remembered Olly's full name. 'Anyway, rat poison isn't his style. He's more likely to clobber you with a cast-iron crepe pan.'

'And finish me off with a squeeze of lemon to the head? Either way,' Dillon drawls. 'I'll still steer clear.'

We're on our way down through Wimbledon now,

and we're just passing the old Edwardian theatre, where I once narrowly avoided an audition for *The Sound of Music* many years ago, and where I first met Olly and Nora, in fact, when Dillon speaks again.

'And are you seeing anyone?'

I'd love to be able to report that there's an edge to his voice; something that hints at a *soupçon* of seething jealousy. But I can't. Because there isn't. He's just asked this question in the same polite tone that he was using when we talked about my success with work, and Nora's wedding.

Which is the only reason I say, 'Yes, as a matter of fact, I am.'

Just to see if there's any other reaction. Because I'm suddenly feeling so desperately frustrated, and sad, and angry, that I can't seem to inspire a single feeling in him except . . . well, what? A slightly sheepish brother-liness, as if he's a particularly trying younger sibling who's left my Barbie doll out in the rain one time too many.

I know it sounds ridiculous, given that I've been *craving* some sort of apology from him for so many months, but right now I'd rather hand back the apology and have it replaced with something deeply unapologetic but also deeply . . . passionate.

'Well, that's terrific news, Libs! Good for you!' If Dillon were the high-fiving sort, I think he might actually high-five me. 'Who's the lucky fellow?'

'His name's Adam.' (It's not a *lie*. We haven't actually *broken up*. Not officially.) 'He works in private equity, and he lives in Shepherd's Bush, and he's a really, really great guy.'

None of which, again, is actually untrue.

Well, apart from the bit about him being a really, really great guy, that is. I just think this whole thing won't have quite the same ring about it if I were to say, *He's a really, really pathological liar.*

'Private equity? So he's a rich fellow as well as a lucky one!'

'He does OK,' I mumble, not quite able to look Dillon in the eye, and feeling that I might have lost my unassailable position up on the moral high ground, just a smidgen.

'I'll bet he does. Ah, I think we're here,' Dillon says, as we pass Colliers Wood tube station. 'Somewhere you can stop for a minute, please, mate,' he tells the driver. 'I'm just going to see my friend here up to her flat, and then I'll be right back down.'

'No!' I yelp.

Dillon stares at me. So, I can't help but notice, does the driver, in his rear-view mirror.

'I mean, there's no need to see me up!' I know the Marilyn incident might have been a one-off, and I know nobody else ever had even a hint of a sighting of Audrey, but somehow I still don't want to take the risk. 'The place is a tip, and I've got . . . er . . . valuable bits of jewellery lying around on the floor with glue drying, and stuff . . .'

'All right,' Dillon says, but he still gets out of his side and walks round to my door to open it for me.

Which I refuse to let him do, because I won't let myself be *remotely* charmed by any of his easy displays of chivalry, so I'm already opening my own door out on to the pavement when he reaches it.

'Well,' I say, 'thanks for the lift, Dillon. And . . . congratulations. Genuinely. On rehab, I mean. I know how hard it must have been for you.'

'I appreciate that, Libby. I really do.'

'OK.'

'And congratulations to you, too, sweetheart. On the career thing, and the Adam thing . . . I can't tell you how happy I am that you're doing so well. And not being dragged down by an eejit like me.'

'I appreciate that, Dillon.' I know I'm echoing what he's just said, but I'd rather play it safe right now; stick to something that I already know sounds mature and polite and well adjusted. Just in case, you know, I accidentally start screaming at him that his apology felt meaningless, that I still think he's a selfish, arrogant shit, and that I was obviously never any more special to him than sitting down to . . . to a pleasant cup of tea and a digestive biscuit. 'I really do.'

He smiles at me, and leans down to give me another of those soft kisses on the cheek.

This time, without the distraction of a dozen photographers going wild with their flashes, I'm able to notice that he smells his usual citrusy, musky, cigarette smokey smell, just without the additional aroma of forty per cent proof alcohol.

I don't know if anyone else has ever had a heart-stoppingly sexual moment on Colliers Wood High Street before, but I'm willing to bet that, even if they have, the one I've just experienced would knock it into a cocked hat.

'I'm really, really, *really* sorry,' he murmurs, into my right ear, 'about it all. About Miami, and the hurricane, and the Finnish model . . .'

'It's all right, Dillon,' I reply, wearily. 'I mean, you weren't actually responsible for the hurricane. Even you can't possibly think you're quite as God-like as that. And, let's face it, there was always bound to be a Finnish model. Or a Swedish one, or a Dutch one, or a Venezuelan one.'

'Oh, now, be fair. I don't think there was ever a Venezuelan model.'

'It was only,' I tell him, pulling away, 'a matter of time.'

Then I turn and walk, quickly, towards my building, hoping that he isn't going to follow me.

And hoping, illogically, stupidly, *dangerously*, that he *will* follow me, at the same time.

Chapter 8

He hasn't followed me.

So I'm taking the stairs up to my flat as quickly as I can, because now that I'm home, I desperately want to know if Marilyn is back for another visit. From the pervading smell of Chanel No. 5, I'm thinking she has to be . . .

. . . but as I open my front door, I can see, straight away, that Marilyn isn't here.

Nor, I'm alarmed to notice, are my TV, my coffee table or my Chesterfield sofa.

It would have to be an *extremely* strong and equally determined burglar – or, more to the point, two or three of them – to have got the Chesterfield out of my flat in the first place.

Or . . .

. . . is that the sound of my TV that I can hear coming through the partition door?

I should explain: this minuscule flat started out life as a slightly larger flat, until my landlord Bogdan (Senior) decided, a couple of days before I moved in, to put up a plasterboard wall and turn the slightly larger flat into two minuscule ones instead, to double his opportunities for rent. But the flat is so very small, and the amount he insists on asking for the rental of it so very large, that nobody has yet expressed the slightest interest in coming to live there. These days, hoping against hope that Bogdan Senior never bothers to drop round to check the place out, I quite often use it as a sort of unofficial work studio, because the light is better in there than in my flat, and because there's no furniture in it to take up space that I can use to spread all my bits and bobs out in.

Oh, and it's no longer a plasterboard wall dividing the two flats, but a flimsy wooden door. Because Bogdan Junior took it upon himself, one day last year, to smash his way through the plasterboard with a sledgehammer. I honestly can't remember why: I think it was some peculiar attempt to stand up to his father. But eventually he did pop round to make good the hole in the wall, and decided it would be 'more stylish, Libby, less Soviet-era utilitarianism' to replace the hole with a door instead of a wall.

Either way, wall or door, there's the sound of a television blaring out, loudly, from behind it.

I'm pretty sure I know what – or rather, *who* – else is on the other side of that door with it.

'Marilyn,' I say, a moment later, as I open the door.

She's sprawled on the Chesterfield, this time mink-less

but wearing a fluffy white bathrobe and a turban-style towel on her head, and she's gazing at my TV.

'Hi!' Marilyn turns her head as she hears me come in: beneath the towelling turban, she's still fully made-up and as glowing as ever. There's a cocktail shaker and an empty glass perched precariously on the coffee table, and she's holding, in one perfectly manicured hand, a glass of her own, filled with noxious-looking amber-coloured liquid. 'You're just in time, honey! There's going to be a *wedding*!'

I glance at the TV screen in front of her. Kim Kardashian is trying on a huge white wedding dress, while all around her a selection of Kardashian sisters weeps, photogenically.

'You're watching *Keeping Up with the Kardashians*?'

'I sure am, and you gotta sit down and watch it with me on this amazing television set! Did you notice, honey, that the picture's *in colour*?'

'Yes, but . . .'

'Incredible.' Barely tearing her eyes off the screen for even a moment, she leans over to the coffee table, picks up the cocktail shaker, pours it into the empty glass and hands it to me. 'Have some ice tea,' she adds, 'and tell me what you think of the guy who plays the fiancé. I think he's kinda cute, but I think the writers made a mistake when they picked out a job for him to do. I mean, wrapping gifts in a department store? I don't think it'll make for a *very* exciting storyline. Couldn't they have made him, like, an African prince, or something?'

I've absolutely no idea what she's talking about. Until there's a fleeting glimpse of Kanye West on the screen, and I remember that he's a *rapper*, and instantly see where the confusion is coming from.

'And isn't it amazing, honey, how they managed to find so many actresses that looked so similar, to play the sisters?' Marilyn takes a sip of her iced tea. 'They coulda done a better job with the one playing Khloe, though.'

'No, no, Marilyn, they're not actresses.'

'Well, they're sure not very *good* actresses . . . I mean, don't get me wrong, honey, it's absolutely gripping, but I've seen better acting from a barn door!'

'No, I mean, they're not actresses in any way, shape or form. They're real people. It's a show about their lives.' I sink down on to the sofa with my iced tea. 'So, er, when – no, *how*, more to the point – did you manage to move my stuff through?'

'While you were out, of course. I mean, I'd no idea, when I first got here, that there were *two* rooms in this apartment! It's gonna be nice for us not to be living so much on top of each other, isn't it? But honey, I don't understand what you just said.' She gestures with her glass at the TV screen, where the closing credits are showing. 'This *isn't* a serial? It's . . . a *documentary?*'

'It's reality TV, that's all.'

'What TV?'

'Reality. They're a real family. Well, real-ish. They

actually are all sisters, and the bride really is getting married . . . But Marilyn, you still haven't told me how you got the sofa in here.'

'Oh, this incredibly sweet homo helped me with it. At least, I think he was a homo, because when he showed up, I accidentally answered the door in my birthday suit, and he couldn't have been less interested in, well, any of *that*. All he wanted to talk about was my hair.'

I stare at her. 'You answered the door to . . . a *gay man?* Who wanted to talk about your hair?'

'Oh, Lord, no, honey, he really wasn't all that gay! I mean, he was sweet, and all that, but he was sort of gloomy, to be honest with you. But I guess Russians are often like that, right? Or he coulda been one of those Bulgarians, or a Polack, or—'

'Moldovan.'

Because it was Bogdan who helped her move the Chesterfield, wasn't it?

Magical Marilyn has met Bogdan.

And, more to the point, Bogdan has met her.

'Ooooh, another episode!' Marilyn suddenly shrieks with excitement as *Keeping Up with the Kardashians* starts up again on the TV screen. 'I just can't believe this is *real*, honey. I mean, isn't that a clever idea? To just film people going about their everyday lives, and all?'

I'm not paying much attention; I pull out my phone and go, hastily, to my messages.

OK, so Bogdan hasn't sent a message. There are no

missed calls from him, no voicemails asking why a naked girl looking exactly like Marilyn Monroe – and, I presume, *calling* herself Marilyn Monroe – invited him into the flat this afternoon to help her move my sofa.

'Did you tell him who you were?' I ask, taking a sip from my iced-tea glass to steady my nerves, and then promptly spitting it straight back into the glass again. It's just as revolting as the Manhattans she made yesterday. 'Jesus! What's *in* that?'

'Just a splash or two of vodka, honey.' Marilyn gives me a little wink, steadying her turban for a moment as she does so. 'Iced tea is awful *dull* otherwise, don't you think? And I told him my name was Marilyn, if that's what you're asking. Hey, what's that you're holding?'

'My phone.'

'Gee, you Canadians sure have funny-looking phones!'

'It's a mobile phone. It means I can take calls when I'm out.' I shove my phone back into the pocket of my hoodie. 'Well, I suppose I'll just have to ask him about it the next time I see him,' I mutter. 'Maybe he thought you were a lookalike, or something.'

After all, it's what I thought when I first met Audrey.

And it *is* – just – possible that Bogdan was so interested in Marilyn's hair that he didn't think twice about who she might really be.

'Now,' says Marilyn, 'can we stop talking about the gloomy homo for a moment?'

'Marilyn, just while we're at it, you really can't say—'

'And you can tell me, honey – ' she turns her attention back to the TV screen – 'how I can get myself on to a show like this one.'

'You … want to go on *Keeping Up with the Kardashians*?' Her eyes widen. 'Oh! Do you think they'd *have* me?'

'That's not what I meant.'

'No, no, honey, it's a *great* idea! I just need to know how I go about it: You say this is their real lives, right? So, would I have to *meet* them somehow? Make *friends* with them? Because I think I could get along real well with Khloe. I'm not too sure if Kim would like me all that much, though—'

I'm distracted, momentarily, by a ping from my phone in my pocket.

It's Mum.

JUST HAD CALL FROM DAVE RE CASS'S INCARCERATION IN MENTAL INSTITUTION.

Oh, God. I know what's coming next.

DID YOU NOT THINK IT REMOTELY IMPORTANT TO TELL ME, LIBBY??????!!!!!!

I begin to type a reply when a third message appears.

COMING HOME TOMORROW. MEET ME 4.45 PADDINGTON STATION.

'. . . and the mother seems a little scary.'

'She's not scary. She's just a massive pain in the back-side,' I say, before realizing that Marilyn is still staring at the screen, and that she's talking about the Kardashians' mother, and not my own. 'But, Marilyn, trust me: you have bigger and better things in your future than trying to get a guest spot on a reality TV show. I mean, I know I put it badly when we talked about it the other day, but you mustn't get it into your head that you're not talented enough to become a huge movie star. One of the biggest the world has ever seen, in fact.'

'Gee, honey.' This gets Marilyn's attention off the TV. So much so, in fact, that she actually picks up the remote control and deftly switches it off. She stares at me now, instead of Kim, Kourtney and Khloe. 'You really believe in me, don't you?'

'Yes. I do.'

'Well, that's just about the nicest thing anyone has ever said to me.'

Her wide-eyed gaze, not unlike the way Fritz looked at me right after I handed him a morsel of pâté, is actually making me a little bit uncomfortable. 'I'm only telling you because it's a fact.'

'You're swell, honey,' she goes on, 'did anyone ever tell you that?'

'Don't be silly,' I say, awkwardly.

'But you *are*. And you know, while we're on the subject of believing in yourself, maybe you should try it, too.'

'Oh, don't worry. I'm fine.'

By which all I'm trying to say is that I'm not plagued by the sort of crippling self-doubt that afflicted Marilyn Monroe.

'I mean,' I go on, without quite meaning to, 'obviously I do have the occasional wobble on the whole self-belief front. Mostly down to the fact that no matter what I do, I can't seem to stop being a human digestive—'

'Huh?'

'Oh, you might call it a graham cracker, I suppose? I mean the really boring, pointless biscuits that everybody overlooks on their way to grabbing the more exciting, chocolately, delicious ones.'

'You're saying you feel like the cookie nobody wants?'

'Yes!' I stare at her. 'You get it.'

'Well, of course I get it, honey. I spent my *entire life* being the graham cracker. Mousy little Norma Jeane, with her no-good family and her no-hope future. She got over-looked by everybody, all the time. But then . . . well, I don't know what happened.' Marilyn shrugs. 'I guess my figure got a little more womanly, and the boys seemed to like that . . . say, is it a boy you're talking about?' she adds, suddenly. 'The one who thinks you're a graham cracker?'

'Amongst others.' I take another gulp of vodka-laced iced tea. 'His name's Dillon.'

'And he doesn't know you exist?'

'No, that's not quite it. He knows I exist; he just knows a lot of other women exist as well.'

'Oh, honey, I can help you with that!' she gasps. 'Men always seem to notice me in a crowd of other girls!' She tilts her turbaned head slightly. 'Though, you know, I never stopped to think exactly *why* . . .'

This is so surprisingly sweet and naïve of her that I forget to feel miserable about Dillon for a second.

'. . . but maybe I could think about it right now and see if there's anything I do that you could do, too!' She beams at me. 'Passing on tips, kind of like we're sisters!'

'That's really, really nice of you, Marilyn, but I don't think there's *anything* you do that I could do. I mean, for starters, I don't have your figure.'

'Oh, just stuff your bra with pantyhose, honey.' Marilyn waves a dismissive hand. 'Even I do that. It never hurts to enhance what Mother Nature gave you! And you know the other thing you could do right away? Lose the black pants.'

'It's got nothing to do with the black pants!' I say, defensively. 'I used to wear nothing, absolutely *nothing*, for Dillon, except a cheeky smile and a pair of high heels. It still didn't stop him ditching me for a Norwegian lingerie model the moment he met one, and forgetting I even existed.'

'Oh, honey, that's—'

'Sorry, Finnish.'

'Well, I would have, honey, but you just interrupted me.'

'No, I meant the *model* was Finnish. From Finland.'

'Oh, I get it,' says Marilyn, in the sort of voice that implies she doesn't get it at all, before she goes on, 'Ooooh, and maybe you oughta think about lightening your hair. My modelling agency nagged at me to do it for ages and ages and ages, and then when I finally did . . .' She snaps her fingers together. 'Bam! It was like I was suddenly walking around with my own little spotlight above me.'

'I don't know. I'm quite happy with brown hair, really.'

'And another thing! You should start wearing makeup.'

'I do wear makeup!'

'Then wear a *lot more* makeup. And wear a *lot tighter* clothes. A whole size smaller,' she goes on; 'at least, that's what I always do. Nothing a man likes more than looking at a woman who seems as if she might fall out of her clothes any minute! Now, if you wore a nice pencil skirt, a low-cut blouse, a little belt to cinch your waist in, some cute peep-toe heels . . .

'Marilyn . . . er, look, I'm grateful for the advice – really grateful – but it all just seems a bit . . . surface.'

'Well, of course it is, honey.' She reaches out a hand and touches me, lightly, on my shoulder for a moment. 'You seem like a real sweet person on the inside. It's just your outside that could do with a little work.'

I take this in the spirit in which I'm sure it was intended.

And I don't say – because she's been so enthusiastic about all this that I don't want to bring her down – that, actually, sweet person or not, I'm pretty sure my inside could do with a little work, too. After all, even if blonde hair and tight clothes worked like a charm with Dillon, they wouldn't have the slightest impact on the other significant people in my life to whom I'm usually an afterthought: my family.

'Oh, and I just thought of one more thing I do!'

'You shave down the heel on one of your shoes?' I ask.

She blinks at me. 'Why on God's green earth would I do that, honey?'

'I thought I read, once, that it was something you . . . er, I mean, that *people* do, to give them a sexy wiggle when they walk.'

'*That* would give you a sexy wiggle when you walk?' She frowns. 'Wouldn't it just put you in the hospital with acute lumbago?'

'Probably. Look, I don't know, OK . . . It was just a thought.'

'Oh, don't get me wrong, honey, I'm not saying I won't try it! But that isn't what I was about to say.' Marilyn reaches down into the pocket of her dressing gown and pulls out a little vial of perfume. 'Chanel Number Five,' she breathes, holding it up as if it's some sort of elixir of life. 'I'm telling you, honey, no man I've ever met has been able to resist it. You know, one time, I told this guy it was *all* I wore in bed . . . and whaddya know,' her eyes widen, 'the next thing, he's buying me that beautiful mink!' She takes the lid off the vial, picks up my hand and spritzes a cloud of Chanel No. 5 on to my wrist. 'Isn't that good? Doesn't it make you feel prettier, just wearing that alone?'

'It does,' I assure her, because she seems so excited. 'And I appreciate all the suggestions, Marilyn, I really do.'

'Oh, honey, I'm happy to help! And trust me, if you do all that stuff, this beau of yours will only have eyes for you! You'll be his snickerdoodle.'

'Sorry?'

'Instead of his graham cracker . . . oh, maybe you don't get snickerdoodles in Canada . . . they're these little sugar cookies, honey, rolled in cinnamon. One of my foster mothers used to bake the most delicious snicker-doodles I ever tasted – warm from the oven, crisp on the outside and melting on the inside.'

'Ah. Right. Got it. But remember, I'm not from—'

'Good!' She lets go of my hand, reaches for the remote control, and – rather niftily, for a woman who's just here on loan from the early 1950s – gets the TV started again. 'Now, let's get on with the really important stuff, honey, and carry on with this . . . what did you just call it? *Say Hello to the Keshishians?*'

'*Keeping Up with the Kardashians.*'

'Isn't that what I said? Anyway, it's the big wedding coming up in this episode, and I can't *wait* to see whether the brother turns up or not!'

So we settle in for a night of vodka-laced iced tea and Armenian-American high drama.

Which, I suppose, is as good a way to spend an evening with Marilyn Monroe as any.

And, if nothing else, it might stop me thinking about Dillon.

Chapter 9

I don't need to be at Paddington to meet Mum until mid-afternoon. So, although it's a golden opportunity to stay at home, put on the kettle and catch up on the mammoth amount of jewellery orders I've neglected, horribly, for the last few days, I'm not going to do this.

One, because Marilyn Monroe is still, when I glanced through the partition door this morning, asleep in front of the TV in the room where I'd normally be getting on with making my designs.

And two, because I've decided to go to the restaurant premises in Clapham, just like I promised Olly I would, and do whatever I can to help out.

It doesn't hurt that, with any luck, Bogdan will be working on-site there, and I can take the opportunity to ask him about his encounter with my brand-new roomie.

I did try texting him late last night, but in the end I gave up because I wasn't sure how to word it. I couldn't just write, *Hi, B, hope all OK with you, btw I gather you met Marilyn Monroe at my flat y'day? Do you think this is something we should talk about?*

You see my difficulty.

It'll be much easier – if not *actually* all that easy – to discuss it face to face.

And, talking of difficult text messages, here's another one in Mum's latest series, showing up on my phone as I get off the tube at Clapham North.

STORY ABOUT CASS ON HEATWORLD AND POPBITCH THIS MORNING!!! I TOLD YOU ONLY MATTER OF TIME BEFORE PRESS GET HOLD OF IT.

A second text, sent only a couple of minutes later, follows.

SUGGEST YOU COME TO STATION IN DISGUISE. PAPARAZZI WILL BE WATCHING.

Which would sound sinister if it didn't sound so ridiculous.

I text back: *OK, will come in disguise. What do you suggest? False moustache and glasses? Richard Nixon mask? Pantomime horse (back or front)?*

Mum replies a moment later.

DON'T BE RIDICULOUS LIBBY. SUGGEST SIMPLE BUT EFFECTIVE COMBINATION OF BASEBALL CAP

AND LARGE PASHMINA. MAYBE HUGE BLUE 100%
CASHMERE BRORA ONE I GAVE YOU FOR B'DAY?

Mum didn't give me a huge blue Brora cashmere pashmina for my birthday; she gave me a gift set of Space
NK body lotion and shower gel.

OH HANG ON, another message comes through,
PASHMINA WAS CASS'S B'DAY PRESENT NOT YOURS
SORRY

A gift set of body lotion and shower gel I was perfectly
happy with (despite the full knowledge that Mum only
buys me stuff from Space NK so she can get the extra
reward points on her store card) until learning, right
this minute, that Cass's birthday gift was a rather snazzy-
sounding huge cashmere pashmina instead.

Anyway, it's convenient that Mum has asked me to
come in disguise, because I already feel as if I've come
out in some sort of costume this morning.

I might have taken some of Marilyn's advice a bit
more seriously than I thought I was going to.

I haven't exactly gone totally off-piste, given that pretty
much everything in my wardrobe these days, post-Audrey,
tends towards the blacker end of the spectrum. But still,
after my shower this morning, I dug out a pencil skirt,
a white blouse and – just for kicks – my highest pair of
nude-tone heels as well. I think I must have bought them

when I was trying to channel Kate Middleton, right before the royal wedding a few years ago. Anyway, the pencil skirt, although still in the dreaded black, conforms neatly to Marilyn's diktat about wearing clothes a size too small, because I last wore this when I was that good half-stone lighter, last autumn. It was a squeeze to get the zip done up, and I certainly won't be able to actually *eat* anything while I'm wearing it . . . but I can't deny that it does give a certain wiggle to the hips, wearing a skirt so tight that I can only take extremely small steps in it. And it's a refreshing change to wear a smart white blouse, even if I do worry that Olly is going to think that, rather that coming to help out for free, I'm in fact hoping for a part-time job as a waitress.

I have unbuttoned an extra button on it, too.

Though I haven't – I couldn't – go as far as stuffing my bra with old tights. No amount of feeling sidelined could possibly make me go that far.

The main trouble with Marilyn's outfit advice is that it isn't all that conducive to getting anywhere very fast, and it takes me fifteen minutes to make the three-minute walk to Olly's restaurant-to-be.

It's just off the main Clapham High Road, overlooking the wide green space of the common, and sandwiched between a posh French patisserie on one side and a newsagent's/mini-mart on the other.

And I have to say, as I approach it (slowly), I'm already wildly impressed by how it's looking on the outside.

Last time I was here, for example, there weren't even any windows: just a big wooden hoarding that had been unattractively fly-posted with adverts for an upcoming family fair on the common. But now the hoarding and its unattractive adverts have gone, replaced by large plate-glass windows that, as soon as the builders' dust is cleaned off them, are going to look fabulously shiny and . . . professional-looking.

I know it sounds stupid, but seeing just these windows, and not even the rest of the place inside yet, is giving me a bit of a lump in my throat.

I mean, how well has Olly done, to be opening up his *own restaurant* with his *own windows?* Olly who, on our very first evening out together over a decade and a half ago, borrowed a biro from my rucksack and wrote out, on a napkin at the Chinese restaurant we were eating at, the entire menu he planned, one day, to serve at his very own place. I can't remember all the details of it, because Nora and I were far more inter-ested in 'helping' him come up with ever-more ridiculous restaurant names, but unless he's intending to serve up retro-late-Nineties cuisine, with truffle oil in abundance, and prosciutto wrapped around abso-lutely everything, I expect the napkin menu will have been long forgotten.

I wish one of us had kept it, though, just to remind Olly of how far he's come.

But I can't just stand around out here waxing lyrical

about plate-glass windows – I need to go inside and have a proper look at the place.

I can hear all kinds of banging and drilling and wood-planing sounds coming out of the open door, so either Nora and Tash are even more competent at DIY than I thought, or it's Bogdan, labouring away with whatever Moldovan colleague he's called in to help for the day.

I'm wrong about this, though, because just as I'm about to head through the door, I see Bogdan coming out of the newsagent's next door, a newspaper in one hand and a packet of Frazzles in the other.

He raises a dusty hand in greeting and heads over to me.

'Libby,' he says, portentously, 'you are having something to be telling me?'

'Yes. I suppose I am.' I take a deep breath. 'First things first, you need to tell me exactly what *you* think is going on.'

'Who am I to be saying this, Libby?' Bogdan tucks his newspaper under one arm, opens the Frazzles and, mournfully, offers me one. 'Is not up to me to be commentating on such a surprising turn of the events.'

'No, OK, I get that. Obviously you might be having difficulty . . . *processing* what you saw.'

'Not half,' says Bogdan, extracting a solitary Frazzle for himself, putting it into his mouth and chewing, rumi-natively. 'Is not a thing that I am expecting to be encountering.'

'Oh, trust me, it wasn't a thing that I was expecting to be encountering either.' I take a deep breath. 'Though . . . well, it has happened before.'

'This is the common knowledge.'

'But last time, it was . . .' I stop. 'Sorry?'

'The common knowledge. Is this not a phrase? Is my English being incorrect?'

'No, no . . . I mean, occasionally your English is a *bit* wonky, yes, but—'

'And how,' Bogdan asks, pointedly, 'are you progressing with the speaking of the Moldovan?'

'I just don't understand,' I continue, 'why you said it was common knowledge. What you saw, I mean.'

'Because we are all knowing about this.' For a moment he stares deeply into his Frazzles packet, as if he secretly hopes the meaning of life, and not bacon-flavoured snacks, might be concealed in there. 'Is not exactly the big state secret, Libby. Is not the sort of thing that is popping up on the WikiLeak.'

'Well, OK, OK, maybe it's not WikiLeaks worthy,' I say, feeling slightly shirty all of a sudden. 'But are you seriously telling me that my friends have all known about this . . . phenomenon? And not bothered to even *ask* me about it?'

'Libby!' Bogdan looks rather shocked. 'Of course we are not asking you about this! This is being your own private business.' He takes a second Frazzle from the packet, then lowers his voice and says, 'But am pleased

169

to be hearing that is phenomenal, Libby. To be honestly with you, am never thinking it could be anything else. Not when it is Dillon O'Hara that we are talking about.'

OK. We don't seem to be on *quite* the same page here.

'*Is* it Dillon O'Hara that we . . . well, that *you*, anyway . . . are talking about?'

Bogdan nods.

'And *why*,' I go on, 'are we talking about him?'

'Because of pictures in paper.'

'What pictures? What paper?'

'*Daily Mail*,' he says, pulling his newspaper out from under his arm. 'And I think also *Mirror*. Am not being sure about *Sun*. Am assuming not *Telegraph*. Or *Guardian*. And am thinking definitely not *Independent*. Or *Financial Times*. Though am happy to be going back into news agency and looking inside these papers, Libby. Man behind counter is not liking the people who are looking and not buying, but am thinking that if we are getting another packet of the Frazzles . . . perhaps two . . .'

I take the copy of the *Daily Mail* that he's holding out to me, opened about halfway through, and look down to see . . .

Photographs of me and Dillon, outside Grove House yesterday.

Terrific photos of Dillon, to be accurate, looking even more buff and lean and chiselled than he did in real

170

life. And atrocious photos of me, of course. Looking even more drab and scruffy and in need of a full hair- and body-makeover than *I* do in real life.

And I'll be honest: I think Marilyn might have a point about the black trousers.

BAD BOY ACTOR LEAVES REHAB, screams the headline.

Troubled Irish star Dillon O'Hara was discharged from a west London rehabilitation centre yesterday afternoon, the story continues, *after treatment for drink and drugs addiction. He was greeted by a woman in her 40s—*

'Forties?' I yelp. 'I'm not even thirty-bloody-one!'

. . . who, it was last night claimed by sources close to the actor, might have been his housekeeper.

Great. Just bloody great.

I mean, it's not like I wanted the papers to print these wretched pictures of us in the first place, but if they were going to do it, couldn't they at least have made me sound exotic and exciting? *A mystery brunette . . . a former flame . . .?*

Still, I suppose they've called it as they've seen it. And I do look bloody awful in those trousers, with that stained hoodie, and with my hair all sort of grungily pulled into a messy, grubby-looking bun.

'Dillon is looking in the tiptop shape,' Bogdan observes, coming round behind me to look at the newspaper, and crunch Frazzles, over my shoulder. 'Am thinking that the prefab has been good for him.'

'Rehab. But yes,' I murmur, 'he does look good.'

'And you are looking . . .' He pauses for a moment, perhaps trying to work out the kindest way of saying something. 'Tired.'

Which is kind, I suppose.

'And little bit flabby.'

Which isn't quite so kind.

'And in urgent need of doing something with the dull-as-dishcloth hair—'

'The expression,' I snap, 'is dull as dish*water*.'

'Ah.' Bogdan nods. 'Am preferring this. Also is more accurate to describe particular problem with your hair. Cloth that is used for washing of the dishes might be bright and colourful shade of blue or green. Whereas *water* that has been used for washing of the dishes is dirty-looking, and sludgy-brown . . .'

'Yes, all right, thank you. Point taken. Dillon looks like a Greek God and I look like a—'

'Greek salad,' Bogdan supplies, helpfully. 'By which am meaning, a bit of a mess. And suffering the effects of too much of the cheese.'

I'm just about to come up with a withering reply when there's a loud engine very nearby, and a motorbike pulls up to the pavement right beside us.

It's a sleek, super-fast-looking black Yamaha, with one person driving it and a passenger, riding pillion.

The passenger gets off the back of the bike, pulls off his helmet, and grins at me.

It's Olly.

Which means, I assume, that it's Tash's bike, and that she's the person at the handlebars.

And I'm right about this, because a moment after Olly's removed his helmet, the driver does the same, to reveal a bouncy, honey-blonde ponytail, and Tash's pretty, smiling face.

She waves at me. 'Libby! Hello!

'Hello!' I say, trying to sound as perky as she does. 'I love your bike.'

'Ancient and slow, compared to the one I hired,' Olly says, in a teasing tone of voice.

'Yeah?' Tash raises her eyebrows at him as she swings long, leather-clad legs off the bike. 'Well, at least it's an ancient and slow bike that's *actually mine*. Not some poncey rented thing I had to drop off at Superbikes as soon as I got to London.'

Olly laughs, good-naturedly, before breaking off from all the banter with Tash to come across the pavement and give me a hug. 'Hi, Lib. You look . . . wow.' He blinks. 'You look . . . great.'

'*Thank you*,' I say pointedly, with a glare in Bogdan's direction. 'That's nice to hear.'

I close the *Daily Mail* hastily, and shove it back at Bogdan with a warning look, because from Olly's cheery demeanour I assume he hasn't seen the pictures of me and Dillon yet.

And I'd like to keep it that way.

Anyway, Tash is striding over to join us, and leans down (she seems taller than I remember, but perhaps it's just the sexy, Emma Peel-type boots she's wearing with all her leather bike gear) to give me a kiss on either cheek. 'Bogdan, good to see you this morning. And it's *so* great to see you again, Libby! It's been ages!'

'Great to see you, too,' I say. And then feel bad that I don't mean it. Because she's really, really nice, Tash: friendly, and warm, and good for a laugh.

Honestly, I don't have a single bad thing to say about her.

Or to think about her! I mean, I just don't. You'd have to be some kind of seriously sour-faced cow to find Tash anything other than delightful.

I like to think I'm not a sour-faced cow.

And, more importantly, I realize that if it is a *tiny* bit annoying that Tash is so eternally upbeat, and naturally pretty, with all the glowing good health that comes from her ever-so-slightly galling habit of running half-marathons and – when she's not being all boyishly sexy on her motorbike – taking hearty cycling holidays across her native Northumberland . . . not to mention the fact that she's got an even more impressively grown-up and serious job than Nora, administering specialist care to tiny pre-term newborns at a world-class neo-natal unit . . .

Well, if the combination of all these things is, just occasionally, a little bit irritating, I'm fully aware that most of the problem is my own. That I'm guilty of a touch of the green-eyed monster. It's not Tash's fault that she's so sorted, and confident, and not remotely the sort of person who'd accidentally date a closeted gay man, get her head stuck in his puppy's safety gate and have to be cut out with a hacksaw.

'So, Nora said you've got a conference down here?' I go on.

'Yeah, but only tomorrow and Friday morning. The rest of the time I'm at Olly's beck and call. Oh, that reminds me,' she says, turning to Olly, 'did you want me to call your mum and tell her to expect me and not Nora this morning? I don't want to just turn up and interrupt your parents doing anything, you know, private, that they wouldn't want an outsider to see.'

'My parents are incapable of doing anything private,' Olly says. 'If you're really unlucky, Dad will probably even show you the jar with his gallstones. Anyway, you're not an outsider. And all Mum will need is five minutes' notice to get the kettle on and whip up a batch of flap-jacks to pop in the oven.'

'Oooh, I love a good flapjack,' says Tash.

'Then you're in luck. Mum's are the best in the whole of Chiswick. Isn't that right, Libby?'

It's been a long time since I've had one of Olly's mum's flapjacks; in fact, it's been a long time since I've gone and hung out there, full stop. I used to spend vast tracts of time at the Walker house at weekends, and during the holidays; even after Nora moved up to Scotland three years ago, in fact, I'd still pop round there with Olly pretty often for a cup of tea and something home-baked to eat. And to enjoy the experience of feeling like part of a proper family for a change. But this past year or so, everything has been so busy, and sort of . . . in flux, that months and months have, I realize, gone by without me managing to get over to Chiswick to see them at all.

'I could go,' I say, which isn't an answer to Olly's question. 'Out to your parents' house, I mean. Do whatever it is Nora was meant to be doing over there.'

'Oh, I'm just picking up the cushion covers Olly's mum has made for the booth seating areas,' Tash says. 'Nora's stayed back at Olly's. She's got a bit of a stomach upset.'

'Ha!' says Olly. 'Too much sampling of the menu when you were here last night, more like.'

So they were all here tasting the food last night, while I was in my flat alone? Or, OK, in my flat with Marilyn.

I know it's pathetic; I know I sound like a whiny seven-year-old. But why wasn't I invited?

I mean, I've told Olly how keen I am to help with anything at all regarding the restaurant this week, and I'm pretty sure he'd have known menu-sampling would have been a forte of mine.

I guess I should have called him at some point yesterday, really, to ask what I could do to help . . . but what with schlepping all over London with Cass's belongings, and then, yes, getting a bit side-tracked by Dillon, I suppose I forgot.

'Honestly,' I say, to Olly, now, 'let me go to your mum and dad's and get the curtains—'

'Cushion covers,' says Tash, brightly.

'Cushion covers,' I repeat. 'Of course. It's silly for Tash to go all the way, when she . . . when *you*,' I go on, turning to Tash, so I can address her directly, 'could be taking advantage of a conference-free day to do anything else you might want to do while you're down here – some shopping, sight-seeing, a matinee . . . I hear *The Lion King* always has seats available, and the puppetry is meant to be spectacular.'

Tash laughs, heartily. 'Thanks, Libby, but no thanks! I took my goddaughters the last time I was down here and it took me six months to recover from all the Hakuna flipping Matata-ing! Anyway, it's just the day for a nice ride over to west London. Not to mention I've been promised flapjack now. And trust me when I say you don't mess with a northern lass and her flap-jack.'

Olly laughs. 'I don't think any of us would dare, Tash.'

'Too right.' Tash grins at him, then at me, then at Bogdan.

'Trust me,' Bogdan says, in a rather scared tone of voice. 'Am not planning on coming anywhere near your flapjack.' Then he turns to me, and hisses, in an all-too-audible tone of voice: 'What is this flapjack, Libby? Is slang word for lady parts?'

There's a moment of silence.

'Aaaaanyway,' Tash says, 'talking of shopping, I think you and I are meant to be finding the time this week for a quick bridesmaid's dress sesh, aren't we, Lib?'

I'm too taken aback at her confident use of the short-ened 'Lib' to reply for a moment, but when I do, I say, 'Yes, absolutely. When's good for you?'

'Well, I'm going to say Friday, seeing as I expect Olly will have all the staff in place that day getting everything ready for the opening party, and he won't want too many cooks spoiling the broth?' Tash glances over at Olly, who shoots her a casual thumbs-up. 'Great! Does Friday work for you, too, Lib? My conference should finish before lunchtime.'

'That's fine. Terrific,' I add, in an attempt to inject my reply with the same levels of enthusiasm as she greets everything she does.

Though I can't help noticing she seems most enthu-siastic of all when she's talking to Olly.

Or, if we're being honest here, *flirting* with Olly. Which I'm pretty sure is what she's doing.

I'm just not absolutely certain, yet, whether Olly is definitely flirting back.

'Perfect!' Tash says, going one better than my 'terrific', and then starts to fold her perky blonde ponytail up into her helmet like some kind of glam, karate-kicking

Charlie's Angel. 'So I'll call your mum when I'm a few minutes away, OK?' she tells Olly.

'Great, thanks, Tash. And while you're there, maybe ask Dad if he's had the time to go up into the attic yet and get down any of those old picture frames he was telling me about. I'll need something to frame those pictures you and Nora unearthed at Spitalfields Market yesterday.'

Bloody hell, they went *art shopping*, as well as did food tasting?

'Sure. Will do!' Tash is striding back to her bike and throwing a sexy leather-clad leg over the saddle. 'Good to see you, Libby . . . Bogdan . . . See you at home later, Ol,' she adds, before revving up the bike and roaring off towards the traffic lights.

'Force of nature, that one,' says Olly, cheerfully, before turning and heading for the restaurant doors.

'Absolutely!' I say.

'She is definitely,' Bogdan mutters, as he follows us, 'force of *something*.'

I hate myself for the tiny little kick of pleasure I get from the fact that Bogdan, it appears, finds Tash almost as much of a trial as I do. But there's not much time to delve any deeper into my pool of guilt, because I'm distracted, immediately, by the sight before me as we walk through the doors.

It's a hell of a lot less like a building site than it was the last time I was here.

The floor, which was concrete only a few weeks ago, has been laid with huge, charcoal-coloured slate tiles; the ceiling, which didn't really *exist* a few weeks ago, is now securely in place and has been hung with dramatic movie-set-style lights. There's a discernible bar area towards the back, near the swing door that leads to the kitchen, which is currently being finished off by a (presumably) Moldovan carpenter, almost as huge and tragic-looking as Bogdan. There's evidence of actual tables and chairs, neatly and carefully stacked away under huge dustsheets near one of the windows. And – most excitingly of all – there's a completed reception area, with a wooden lectern and a small leather sofa, which Olly heads for right away and pulls the dustsheets off.

'Well?' he asks, after he's given me a moment to take it all in. He looks nervous. 'What do you think?'

'Olly, it's . . . I can't believe it.'

'I can't believe it *good?*' he asks, in the neurotic, self-critical tone of a man who's been spending far too long with Bogdan, 'or I can't believe it *bad?*'

'Good! Very, very good!'

'You like the floors?'

'I love the floors!'

'The lighting?'

'The lighting's amazing.'

'The colour of the walls?'

'I love the colour of the walls,' I say, but not quite

loudly enough for Bogdan, who's just climbing up a stepladder with a tray of paint and a roller in his hand, to hear me. (I'm still pissed off about the Greek salad comment, and I don't want him to accidentally mistake a compliment about Olly's choice of paint to be mistaken for a compliment about his decorating skills.) 'Seriously, Ol, it's looking fantastic. It looks like you're pretty much all there for Friday night.'

'Fingers crossed.' He actually holds up two crossed fingers. It makes him look like a little boy; an even younger version of the teenage Olly who wrote that menu on the back of the napkin all those years ago. 'The kitchen's all up and running now, which is a bloody great relief, I can tell you . . . the chefs are starting to get things going in there right now, if you want to come and take a look?'

'I'd love to! But, Olly, I don't want to get in the way, or anything.'

'You couldn't if you tried. Follow me,' he says, putting a hand, briefly, into the small of my back as he guides me, in my too-tight skirt and tippy-tappy heels, towards the swing door right at the back of the room. 'I've got the waiting staff coming in later to start getting to grips with the ordering system,' he goes on, sounding more like he's running through a check-list to reassure himself than actually communicating all this stuff to me, 'and hopefully they'll all get the chance to sit down and try as much as possible from the menu so they know what they're talking about when they take the orders from the customers.'

I'm suddenly hit by noise and heat as we head into the kitchen: it's pretty small in here, and there are five young, male chefs crammed in behind the newly fitted range, clattering pans and stirring things, and talking loudly over each other.

'Don't let us stop you, guys,' Olly tells them. 'I'm just bringing my friend Libby in for a sneak peek, to see where all the magic is going to happen.'

The clattering, and the stirring, and the talking-over-each-other stop.

I mean, they grind to a halt. Instantly.

The five chefs have stopped what they're doing and they're staring at us.

Correction: I don't think they're staring at Olly. They're staring at me.

My first thought is that more of my shirt buttons must have popped open . . . or that I've got a huge morsel of Frazzle stuck between my front teeth . . . or that during the ten seconds it's taken us to walk back here from the front of house, I've unintentionally grown an extra head.

'Oi,' says Olly, with a bit of an edge to his voice, to the staring chefs. 'I brought Libby back here so she could have a good look at the kitchen. Not so that you lot could all have a good look at her.'

There are a few mutterings of 'yes, chef', 'sorry, chef',

before the clattering and the stirring all start up again.

'Sorry,' Olly says to me, as we head back out through the swing door. 'I didn't mean to subject you to that.'

'To – er – what?'

'A bunch of sex-starved chefs lusting over you.'

'*Were* they?'

'Well, it was either that, or I *really* need to stop wearing this aftershave.'

I laugh.

'Of course they were lusting over you,' he goes on. 'You look . . . well, you look really great today, Lib.'

'Thank you,' I say, suddenly feeling embarrassed.

Because it all feels a bit silly. I'm exactly the same person as I was yesterday – exactly the same person recently mistaken, by a national newspaper, for a house-keeper in her mid-forties. And now . . . what? A skirt a size too small, a pair of impractical shoes, oh, and a solid half-hour in front of the makeup mirror before I left the flat, and suddenly an entire kitchen full of chefs is rendered silent by my allure?

Looks like Marilyn actually *does* know exactly what she's talking about, after all.

And really, when it comes to Marilyn Monroe, why on earth did I ever doubt it?

'I mean, don't get me wrong, you always look great.' Olly isn't actually looking at me as he says this; he's busying himself with a nearby dustpan and brush, stooping down to sweep up a pile of sawdust from near the bar. Which seems a bit of a pointless task to me, given that the carpenter is still creating sawdust like it's going out of fashion, and that someone's going to have to do a pretty mammoth job with a Hoover at some point later today. 'Are you off somewhere smart?' he adds. 'After here, I mean.'

'Smart? Well, that depends what you mean by smart. I've got to meet Mum at Paddington this afternoon, and take her to visit my sister. In her rehab clinic.'

Now Olly looks at me again. 'Your sister's gone to *rehab?*'

'Yep. To misquote Amy Winehouse, nobody tried to make her go to rehab – because she didn't really have an addiction problem – but she said yes, yes, yes anyway.'

'Right . . .' He's looking a bit confused. 'I'm not sure that would have been *quite* as catchy a hook if Amy Winehouse had written it that way.'

'It wouldn't.'

'But Cass is OK?'

'Well, that might depend on your definition of OK. If it includes the category of "entirely morally bankrupt and without shame or scruple", then yes, she's absolutely fine.'

Olly nods, appearing to Get It without me having to say much more. Which is, to be honest, the main reason I can tell him these kinds of things in the first place.

'I'll just put her down as an unlikely,' he says, 'for the party on Friday, shall I?'

'I think that would be best, Olly, yes.'

'And you're OK?' he adds. 'I mean, I haven't really seen you since . . . er . . . the other night.'

'Let's not speak of that,' I say, hastily, 'ever again.'

'Right. OK. Just so long as you're all right.'

'I'm fine. And, like I told you at Dad's wedding, I'm here for you this week, Olly, not the other way around.' I clear my throat. 'I mean, you have to tell me what I can do to help, whether it's picking stuff up from your parents, or choosing art for the walls . . .'

'Sure, Lib.' He chews his lip for a moment, as if he's debating whether to say anything or not. Then he says, 'It's just that you did say you'd call me and find out what I needed you to do. So when you didn't call, I thought probably you'd just ended up too busy with work, and stuff. And your sister and this rehab stuff – I know, now. Obviously.'

And Dillon.

And Marilyn Monroe.

'I'm really sorry. And you're right. And that's why I'm here, now, this morning. To help. I'll do anything you want me to do, Olly. Anything at all.'

'I wouldn't go around offering that, Lib,' he says, lightly.

'I'm serious. I've got two whole hours before I need to go to meet Mum.'

'I know. But honestly, today's a quiet day. Tash is picking up the stuff from my parents. Everything's under control in the kitchen. Bogdan's finishing up in the dining room itself, so it's a bit too crowded for anyone to do anything practical in there . . . I tell you what, if you come over tomorrow, I could use your expert eye for hanging those pictures, and your expert tastebuds to help me settle on a house cocktail?'

I shudder, inwardly, at the mere mention of the word 'cocktail'. But obviously I'm not going to let Olly see this.

'I'd love to.' I reach out and squeeze his arm. 'I'm just really proud of you, Olly. I mean, after all these years that you dreamed about your own place . . . Oh, that reminds me! You haven't told me what it's going to be called yet.'

'I haven't.'

It's a statement, not a question.

'So . . . er . . . you're planning some sort of big reveal on Friday night?'

'I am.'

'Wow. That's a bit of a risk, isn't it?'

He shrugs. 'I hope not.'

'Well, *I* hope not. Oh, God, it's not going to be one of the names Nora and I used to come up with for a laugh, is it? Like . . . The Ravishing Radish?'

'I mostly remember The Amorous Aubergine. Or . . . what was that really ridiculous one about Stroganoff?'

'BOGOF Stroganoff?'

'That was the one!'

'Nora's favourite,' I say. 'I'd better give her a call, see how she's feeling.'

'Trust me, she's fine. Anyway, she's got Tash round mine to look after her.'

'Of course. A fully qualified doctor.'

'Exactly . . . oh, hang on a minute, mate,' he's suddenly saying, to Bogdan, who's just moved his ladder over to the bar area in a purposeful manner and is about to set about the still-unpainted section of wall behind it. 'I think I've changed my mind about the colour on that particular section of wall. Can you do it in the pure brilliant white you used on the walls in the loos, and not the jasmine white we've used everywhere else?'

'If this is what you are wanting,' Bogdan says, mutinously. 'Is not what I would be doing. But is your memorial service.'

'I think he means it's your funeral,' I translate, in a whisper, as I go up on tiptoe to give Olly a kiss on the cheek. 'Thanks for inviting me, Ol. I'll see you tomorrow. Oh, and Bogdan,' I call over to him, 'give me a quick call if you're in Colliers Wood later on today, will you? There's . . . something very important that we need to talk about.'

His eyes light up. 'You are finally deciding that is time to do something drastical with your hair?'

I'm about to say no when I realize that it would be simpler all round for me to just say yes. Partly because it will stop Bogdan from asking if the important thing to talk about is in fact the situation with Dillon. And partly because he could be right. Maybe I *am* finally

187

deciding that is time to do something drastical with my hair.

'Yes, Bogdan. That's it.'

'Is excellent news, Libby. I will be dropping everything for this.'

'Yeah . . . could you maybe *not* drop everything,' Olly asks, 'until you've actually finished painting the restaurant that's due to have its big opening party on Friday night?'

Bogdan scowls at Olly but returns, mutinously, to his painting.

And I totter out of the mystery-name restaurant, and head towards the High Street.

Chapter 10

Bogdan is going to kill me when he finds out what I've done.

And I don't use the phrase lightly: his father is a successful organized-crime overlord. Bogdan, I'm fairly sure, Knows People. It's probably only a matter of a single phone call, and I'll be found a few days from now, my legs encased in concrete, washed up on the banks of the River Wandle.

Still, at least my hair will look good when they find me. Even if nothing else does.

That is, I *hope* it will look good. It's hard to believe it right now, what with all these bits of foil that are being folded into my hair, but Daisy, the very nice colourist at the Clapham branch of Headmasters, has assured me that she's opting for nice subtle shades of honey and caramel, which are exactly what I requested when I walked in off the street and asked for a full head of highlights almost an hour ago.

'I can't believe you've never changed your hair colour

before!' Daisy is saying now, as she paints another section of my virgin hair with her pungent-smelling brush. 'And then made a snap decision to go blonde like this! What made you suddenly take the plunge?'

I'm not quite sure how to answer this. Because it's not *just* that I can't tell her that my new flatmate, who is none other than Marilyn Monroe, has strongly counselled me to do it.

It's also that I don't quite know what suddenly made my mind up either.

Because it isn't just Marilyn. It isn't just Bogdan, who's been urging me to do this for months.

It's a lot to do with those photos, I suppose, in the *Mail.* They were a bit of a nasty wake-up call.

And . . . well, it's no more than that. At least, I don't think it is.

'It was just time for a change,' I tell Daisy, before adding, nervously, 'but you're not going to make me look *completely* different, are you?'

'Relax,' Daisy says. 'I know what I'm doing here. And we're going for a very natural blonde. Sunkissed, that's all. I'm not going to turn you into Marilyn Monroe or anything.'

'Ha, ha!' I laugh, noisily. 'Of course not.'

She puts her hands on my shoulders, and says, 'I'm just going to get a few more foils. Be back with you in a minute. And you're sure you don't want tea, a coffee?'

'I'm fine,' I say. 'Thank you.'

Anyway, my phone has just started to ring, so I'll use the couple of minutes she's gone to answer it. It's probably Mum, announcing that her train has been delayed, or—

Oh, hang on. It's Bogdan.

I toy with not answering, fearful that he'll have some sort of hairdressing sixth sense and be able to tell, from the precise decibel-level and pitch of the background noise, that a BaByliss is blowing out somebody's hair a few feet away from me. But actually, I think I should take this minute risk and answer the call, just in case he's calling to tell me Olly's seen those pictures in the *Mail*, or something.

'Bogdan, hi, I'm just—'

'Oh, hi, there, honey! I wasn't sure if you'd pick up.'

'*Marilyn?*'

It's so much of a shock to hear her voice like this that I actually drop my iPhone, which falls with a clatter on to the floor beneath my swivel chair.

'Whoops!' says Daisy, coming back over with her foils and crouching down to get my phone for me. 'Here you go, darling. I hope you didn't lose your call!'

I take the phone and hold it to my ear.

'How on earth,' I whisper into it, 'are you calling me?'

'Oh, well, honey, I don't know how it works in Canada, but in America we have these things called *phone lines* . . . now, I couldn't tell you how they work *exactly*, because I'm not all that bright, but I think it's something to do with—'

'That's not what I mean,' I hiss, furtively, while Daisy gives me a slightly strange look in the mirror. 'Are you using Bogdan's mobile?'

'You mean this little-bitty phone that looks like the one you were using last night? I sure am, honey! I guess he must have dropped it when he was helping me move the furniture.' Her voice fades out for a moment, before coming back in at normal volume. 'It says Samsung on the top, I don't know if that's his surname or something?'

'No, it's not . . . did you scroll through and find my number?'

'Scroll? I don't know about that, honey, I just jabbed the little screen a few times with my finger and your name came up . . . say, is there a little *TV set* on this thing, too? Because I thought this enormous TV set in the apartment was incredible enough . . . now you're telling me there's a TV set as small as the palm of my hand, too?'

'Yes, it's . . . sort of a TV set. But, Marilyn,' I lower my voice, 'is everything OK? Why are you calling?'

'For a little chat, of course, honey!'

'A chat?'

'Well, honey, you were gone when I woke up this morning. Which was sort of a shame, because I had this *real* romantic dream about Burt Lancaster that I wanted to tell you all about . . . well, not *all* about,' she giggles, breathlessly. 'I mean, a girl's gotta have some secrets, doesn't she? Anyway, then I got up and went to look for some way to make a cup of coffee, but all I could find was this funny-looking machine, and I didn't know how to work it . . .'

'I really wouldn't worry about getting that started,' I say, hastily, because the last thing I need is Marilyn getting as obsessed with the Nespresso machine as Audrey Hepburn did. 'There should be a jar of instant in one of the cupboards.'

'Oh, I already found that, honey! And I found your secret stash of cookies, too, and now I'm just all stretched out on the couch and I'm watching this terrific show about being a housewife in Beverly Hills, or something?'

'*Real Housewives of Beverly Hills?*'

'That's the one! It looks like another of those reality TV shows you were telling me about, honey, is that right? I mean, it's kind of hard to tell if they're acting or not because their faces don't seem to move.'

'Ooooh, tell your friend to watch the Miami version,' Daisy whispers, joining in the half of the conversation she can actually hear. 'That's the best one. I could spend my whole day off watching back-to-back episodes of that.'

'Anyhow,' Marilyn is continuing, 'the woman with the huge house and the little dog is mad at the woman with the handsome husband and the drunk sister, because the woman with the handsome husband and the drunk sister didn't invite the woman with the huge house to the cocktail party she was throwing. And then the woman with the famous actor husband started a fight with the woman with the—'

'OK, OK, I get it. They're all fighting.'

'Of course they're all fighting!' Daisy tells me, excitedly. 'That's the *whole point* of the show!'

'Oooh, who's that you're with, honey?' Marilyn asks. 'She sounds a fun gal! Maybe you should invite her over tonight!'

'Tonight?'

'Yeah, honey, I was thinking we could have another girls' night in! But a proper one this time, something we plan in advance. I could make us some cocktails—'

'No!' I yelp. 'I mean . . . let's have a bit of a break from cocktails tonight, shall we?'

'And drink champagne, you mean?'

'Er, I suppose so.'

'Because I just adore champagne. It'll be perfect! You, me, and . . . what's that other girl's name, the one you're inviting over?'

'Daisy?'

'Yes?' Daisy says.

'No, no, sorry,' I tell her, 'I didn't mean—'

'She sounds swell!' Marilyn says, breathily. 'And maybe she'll want to watch some more of this *Housewives* stuff. I mean, it's giving me all kinds of ideas for my own show. I think I just need to find a few more friends I can fall out with . . . preferably ones with little dogs . . . Daisy doesn't have a little dog, does she?'

'No, I don't think so.'

'Oh, well, nobody's perfect. And what shall we eat? I don't cook much, but I can put Velveeta on top of saltines, or make it kinda continental with a little piece of olive . . .'

'No, no, don't worry about food,' I say, hastily, because if her cocktails are anything to go by, I dread to think what magical snacks will materialize themselves. 'I'll pick up a pizza on my way home later.'

'Pizza's good, honey! Isn't this exciting? Is Daisy excited, too? You know what, honey, put her on the phone, I want to get to know her a little before she comes over tonight.'

'I can't,' I say, firmly, 'she's busy right now.' It's neither the time nor place to get into a long explanation of why I won't, in fact, be inviting Daisy round for pizza and a *Real Housewives* marathon tonight. 'But I'll see you later, OK?'

'Sure thing, honey! Toodle-oo,' Marilyn breathes, before hanging up.

Daisy smiles at me as I slide the phone back into my bag.

'I once had a flatmate a bit like that,' she says, with an affectionate eye-roll.

I seriously doubt this.

But I nod and smile anyway.

'It used to drive me nuts,' she goes on. 'All the long, pointless phone calls, and constantly badgering me to make plans with her . . . but then I realized one day, she was just sort of looking for a family.'

'Sorry?'

'My old flatmate. She didn't really have a family. And she had a hard time making friends. I think it was why she kind of latched on to me so strongly. Is that the same way with your flatmate?' Daisy asks.

'Oh . . . er, yes. Yes, I suppose it is.' I think about this for a moment. 'I mean, she never really knew her father – didn't know who he *was*, even – and her mum left her with a tonne of different foster families and then ended her days in a lunatic asylum.'

Daisy is staring at me. 'Oh, my God. That sounds awful.'

'And she ended her own days,' I go on, gazing at my foil-covered-hedgehog reflection in the mirror, 'dying alone from a possibly deliberate overdose at the age of thirty-six after tragic affairs with all sorts of unsuitable men.'

Now Daisy is looking at me in a manner that implies she's seriously wondering about calling her manager over and saying she doesn't want to finish my highlights any more.

'Sorry,' I say, stopping myself just in time. My face is flaring. 'I'm just . . . er . . . trying out the plot of a novel.'

'Right.' Daisy nods. 'Er . . . OK! So, we'll just get you finished up as soon as possible, shall we?'

'Thank you. Yes, please. Great.'

We don't talk much more while she finishes off covering me with foils, right up until the last one, when she suddenly says, 'Marilyn Monroe.'

I jolt in my seat and cast a sharp glance over each shoulder. 'Where?'

'No, I mean, that plot you were trying out. For your, er, novel. That sounded a lot like the life of Marilyn Monroe, didn't it?'

'Oh! Yes, silly me! So it did!'

'Poor thing,' Daisy sighs. 'What a terrible waste of such a spectacular life.'

There's a sudden, extremely hard lump in my throat.

Poor Marilyn and her inescapable demons.

I mean, here's me letting my own family make me feel rubbish – Dad with his shiny new stepdaughter; Mum with her flagrant favouritism – but I can't possibly imagine how much Marilyn's own hopeless excuse for a family must have dragged her down over the years. It's small wonder, really, that she's the needy, desperate-to-be-loved soul that she is. I think, while she's here, that I should probably be taking care of her a bit more. Because she's no Audrey Hepburn, floating through life with a steel backbone beneath all that grace and charm. To quote (sort of) Marilyn's rumoured lover John F. Kennedy, I think I need to ask not what my magical Hollywood legend can do for me, but what I can do for my magical Hollywood legend.

I'll try to do just this when I go home for pizza and

Real Housewives tonight. Return a bit of the advice Marilyn was giving me yesterday. Be a good friend to her the way she so clearly wants and needs.

'Anyway!' Dasiy adds, brightly. 'Talking of hot blondes, let me leave you here for a bit with a pile of magazines, and then we can get you all washed out and blow-dried . . . and fabulous!'

*

Well, I don't know about fabulous. But it certainly looks . . . good.

I mean, it suits me far more than I thought it would. And luckily Daisy was telling the truth when she re-assured me that she wasn't turning me into a peroxide blonde: the highlights she's given me are actually pretty natural-looking, and span the spectrum of flattering tones from warm honey to light caramel. It seems to have brought a bit more softness to my face – and, we can but hope, knocked a few of those forty-odd years off me without the need to resort to plastic surgery and/ or a paper bag over my head – and it doesn't hurt, either, that Daisy finished it all off with a swishy, glamorous blow-dry that makes me feel as if I've lost that wretched half-stone in sheer weight of limp hair alone.

And here's a thing that I've noticed only twenty minutes into being blonde: men are suddenly an awful lot friendlier to you. Pathetic and cliché-ridden, yep. But from my (admittedly limited) findings, I can definitely confirm that this is the case. Two separate men stood up on the tube to offer me their seat on the way from Clapham North to Paddington, and I'm *ninety* per cent sure it wasn't because they thought I was pregnant. Or, I suppose, an old-aged pensioner. And since I've been waiting at Paddington for Mum's train to pull in, I've been smiled at by a passing policeman, winked at by a man driving one of those floor cleaners from one side of the station to the other, and sexually propositioned by a man selling copies of the *Big Issue*.

Which was the only moment, so far, that I wished I'd stayed as a brunette, to be honest with you.

I've still got ten minutes to kill before Mum's train gets here, so I'm just wandering over to the AMT bar to get a coffee (and, in all honesty, to avoid the lurking *Big Issue* man, who looks as if he might be headed my way again) when a FaceTime call starts to ring on my phone.

I know that Bogdan's phone doesn't do FaceTime, so this definitely can't be Marilyn.

I get almost as big a shock when I see who it actually is, though.

It's Dillon.

For a split second, I think about not answering. To keep at least *one* of my Communications Bans alive, just to prove to myself, if nothing else, that I do have a fraction of steel in me.

But then I remember the terrible pictures of me in

the paper, looking like a 45-year-old housekeeper – pictures that I assume Dillon has seen, this morning, over his breakfast tea and toast – and the prospect of being able to undo a bit of that, by answering his FaceTime call with my glossy new hairdo . . .

So nope. No steel. Just a big, fat, bottomless pit of neediness worthy of Marilyn Monroe herself.

I slide the bar on the screen to take the call.

And at least have the gratification, even if I am a spineless jellyfish, of seeing Dillon's eyes widen in astonishment when he sees my face pop up on his screen.

'Jesus, Mary and Joseph,' he says.

He's looking as fresh-faced as he was when he left the clinic, wearing a blue T-shirt and, I can't help but notice, the little plaited leather-cord necklace I made him after a random scavenge around my handbag while we watched, of all things, *Some Like It Hot* at his flat one evening.

'Not Jesus, Mary or Joseph, I'm afraid,' I reply. 'Just me. Libby.'

'Well, now, I'm not sure about that. The last time I saw Libby she was a very attractive brunette. Whereas the person I see on my screen before me is a stunning blonde.'

I refuse to let myself get remotely excited by the fact that, in one breath, he's just called me both *very attractive* and *stunning*. After all, this is Dillon we're talking about. He's such an inveterate charmer that he probably compliments his kettle before he puts water into it, and butters up his favourite Manchester United coffee mug before taking a swig. Besides, I've never quite been able to shake the opinion that Dillon's compliments are just as much about making *him* feel good (about being so goddamn charismatic and delightful) as they are about improving the day of the person (or kettle, or coffee mug) on the receiving end of them.

'Oh, yes,' I say, as airily as possible. 'I just fancied a bit of a change, that's all.'

'Well, it's a bloody good change. Not that I didn't think you looked fantastic before. But there's just one thing I'm worried about . . .'

'Yes?'

'Well, it looks like it might be quite an expensive style to keep up. And I've already budgeted for my housekeeper's salary for the year, and I'm afraid I can't add any extra for a personal hairdressing allowance.'

'You've seen the pictures, then?' I sigh.

'I have indeed.' He grins. 'Cheer up, Lib. I think we both look pretty spectacular.'

'No, Dillon. You look spectacular. I look *exactly* like I've spent the majority of my forty-plus years down on my hands and knees scrubbing your grouting.'

'Don't be like that. Besides, if you were going to go down on your hands and knees, Libby, I can think of a lot more enjoyable ways for you to do so than scrubbing my grouting.'

I must look a bit shocked, because he adds, hastily, 'Sorry. You set that one up. I couldn't resist.'

'It's all right.'

'Adam's not with you, is he? I don't want to make your boyfriend angry with me.'

'Er . . . no. He's not with me. I'm just waiting for my mum, actually.' In fact, I can see the Cardiff train pulling in at the platform ahead of me. 'She'll be here any minute, in fact, Dillon, so if there was something specific you wanted . . .?'

'Oh, yeah. There was. Sorry, I just got sidetracked by your phenomenal new look there for a moment.' He smiles at me again, a smile that wobbles ever so slightly when I don't return it. 'I was just wondering if you might happen to be free tonight.'

'Tonight?'

'Yeah. For dinner.'

'Dinner?'

'Yes, it's this meal people eat in the evenings, usually—'

'Let's not do all that again, Dillon,' I say, because even though I might have found his stock-in-trade joke charming at first, it doesn't stay quite so charming when you've been so badly let down by the person doing the joking. 'Let's just stipulate that I know what dinner is. And that I'm only expressing surprise because I don't really know why you're inviting me to eat it with you.'

'Because I owe it to you. Remember? That posh meal you said you wanted?'

'Er . . . I don't think I said I wanted a posh meal.'

'I said I'd planned to take you out for dinner, and a proper apology, and you said only a three-Michelin-star meal at the most expensive restaurant in town would do. With oysters, and foie gras, and vintage champagne. Well, I tried calling the most expensive restaurant in town, name-dropping as if it was going out of fashion, and still the bastards wouldn't give me a table until three weeks on Tuesday—'

'That must've made you feel good.'

'And then I got my agent to call them, tell them they were calling on behalf of George and Amal Clooney, and – lo and behold – a table magically materialized for tonight . . .'

'Dillon, my mum's getting off the train. I really need to go.'

'. . . and then I decided that any restaurant with that kind of shitty attitude didn't deserve our custom. So I booked a table at a nice little Italian instead.' He clears his throat. 'Please, Libby. Will you let me take you there?'

I don't know what to say to this.

Or rather, I know what I *should* say – *thanks, Dillon, but no thanks* – and what I *want* to say – *tell me what time and I'll meet you there.*

It's just that the two things are totally incompatible with each other.

Which, ironically, is pretty much the way it was for me and Dillon.

'We'll drink some wine . . . or rather, *you'll* drink some wine . . . we'll eat calamari . . . or rather, *I'll* eat calamari, I know you're always creeped out by the wierdy tentacles—'

'Dillon. I need to go.'

'Then just say yes. Just say you'll meet me there. I can text you the address. I can send a taxi to pick you up. I can come in a taxi myself and pick you up. I can send a helicopter. I can *fly* a helicopter—'

'OK, OK, OK. I'll come and have dinner with you.'

'Ace.' He grins. 'Calamari and a hot blonde Libby Lomax. All the ingredients for a magical evening.'

I don't point out that if it's a *magical* evening he's after, he could always just pop round to my flat. Because I'm pretty sure he'd get the wrong idea.

'And just in case Adam's worried about anything,' Dillon goes on, 'just assure him we're only doing this as friends, yeah? So that I can give his girlfriend the proper apology she deserves.'

'I don't think Adam will be worried.'

'Well, maybe Adam needs to develop a bit more of an imagination,' Dillon says. Lightly, but with the merest hint of an edge. 'Seven thirty this evening, then, darling, OK? I'll send you the address.'

'OK. I'll see you there.'

And then I end the call, because Mum is coming through the barriers towards me.

At least, I think it's Mum. She's shrouded in a huge

black scarf and wearing enormous bug-eyed sunglasses, and looking fitfully around the station as if she's expecting three dozen photographers to leap up from behind the Paddington Bear stall and start snapping her picture with huge Nikons.

'*Libby?*' she hisses, as she reaches me, in a tone of surprise and wonderment.

'Yes, Mum. It's me.'

'You look very . . . *glamorous*.'

It's a bit of an accusation, so I'm not really sure how to respond, except to say, 'Well, you did tell me to disguise myself.'

'True, darling, but I'm not sure you needed to take it *quite* this far. I mean, who are you meant to be? Grace Kelly? Doris Day?'

'I'm . . . er . . . meant to be me. I'm just trying out a different look for myself.'

'Was this something you did for your father's wedding?' She pulls off her sunglasses, her eyes narrowing. 'Because I'll tell you, Libby, you could have turned up in a Ku Klux Klan robe with a burning cross in your hand, and he wouldn't have paid you any more attention than he has for the last twenty-odd years.'

'Mum. Leave it.'

'How was the wedding, anyway?' she asks, curiously. 'What's the new wife like? Young? Pretty? A glutton for punishment?'

'She seemed fine,' I say, shortly, because I don't discuss

Dad with Mum. Ever. (My inner eight-year-old can't take the emotional battering.) 'Anyway, I just did my hair this afternoon. Not for the wedding.'

'Well, I don't know if this is the most sensitive time to have done it. What with poor Cassidy being such a wreck, and all.'

I take a deep breath. 'Let's just go and get a taxi, Mum, shall we?'

'All right.' She puts the handle of her wheelie suitcase into my hand, takes her heavy canvas bag off one shoulder and puts it over mine, and starts to lead the way towards the exit and taxi rank. 'Anyway, I *was* right to tell you to disguise yourself, because they're all over this story already! Heatworld, Popbitch, the 3AM Girls . . . I haven't had the chance to look at any of the other newspapers, or their bloody websites, because my phone battery cut out on the train. Oh, maybe we can stop into WHSmith and get a few of the tabloids now!'

'No, no,' I say, firmly (while steering clear of the *Big Issue* man, who's leering at me on our way out to the taxi rank). Because even though it's inevitable that Mum *will* find out about the paparazzi pictures of me in the *Mail* (or maybe not, if she takes it at face value that the person who looks an awful lot like me is, in fact, Dillon's middle-aged housekeeper), I'd rather not be in her orbit when she does so. 'Time for all that sort of thing later.'

'I suppose . . .'

We reach the front taxi in the rank, into which I'm

all ready to start hauling Mum's heavy bags until the driver leaps out and starts to do it for me.

'Where to, darling?' he asks.

'Just Baker Street—' I begin, before Mum interrupts me.

'Actually we're heading to Maida Vale instead.'

I look at her. 'We are?'

'Cassidy's left the clinic, darling. She sent me a message telling me so before my phone conked out. She wants us to meet her at her flat instead.'

'She's left the clinic? Already?'

Mum nods, as the taxi starts to move off. 'And I can't tell you what a relief it is, darling, that I don't have to go and visit her in that *dreadful* place.'

'You mean the celebrity rehab clinic that was more like a five-star spa hotel?'

'Oh, I don't care how *comfortable* it was!' Mum reaches into her handbag and pulls out a little packet of the nuts and raisins she always buys when she travels, to prevent herself from buying, and snarfing, a family-sized bag of giant chocolate buttons instead. 'I was a total nervous wreck about having to set foot in there. Facing down all the judgement, the disapproval . . .'

'From who?'

'The doctors,' she spits, inadvertently sending a cashew nut ricocheting off the plastic dividing window, and making the driver glance round in alarm. 'It all ends up being the mother's fault, you know.'

'*What* all ends up being the mother's fault?'

'Mental problems,' Mum says, airily, in an un-PC fashion that might put even her namesake, the other Marilyn, to shame. 'Anxiety. Depression. Addiction. I dread to think what sort of poison they were pouring in poor Cass's ear while she was there. *Were you breast-fed or bottle-fed? What age were you potty-trained?*'

'Er . . . sorry, are you asking *me* those questions . . .?'

'No! For heaven's sake, Liberty! I'm doing an impression of the doctors at the clinic!' She looks annoyed that I didn't get this. 'It's exactly the sort of thing they'll be asking her. Trying to imply it was something *I* did. Especially if Cass told them that I'm in show business, too. There's nothing more fascinating to a psychiatrist,' she declaims, 'than a mother who's put her daughters on to the stage. It's the sort of thing they write their doctoral theses about, you know.'

'I think it's more the sort of thing *Noël Coward* wrote *light-hearted songs* about, actually . . .'

But she's not listening.

'I'm quite sure they tried to tell her that I was living through both of you. Which is obviously a pile of steaming horse-manure, because if I'd been wanting to fulfil my ambitions through *you*, Libby, I'd have been much better off steering you away from a career in the theatre altogether! I mean, you were hopeless at it!'

'Thanks, Mum.'

'You couldn't sing, you couldn't dance—'

'No need to hammer it home.'

'And really, if it was either of you who was going to succumb to depression and addiction, I'd have put my money on it being you, not your sister. After all, she was the one with the looks and the talent, and you were always in her shadow—'

'*Mum*. Can you stop slating me for a second and *listen?* Cass is fine, OK? She hasn't . . . *succumbed* to anything.'

'Well, of course she hasn't, darling.' There's a dramatic wobble to Mum's voice, and she clasps a hand to her chest. 'She's a fighter, your baby sister; always has been, always will be.'

'Sure. But she's not fighting depression. Or addiction.' We're pulling up outside Cass's block now, so I stop talking for a moment as I haul Mum's bags out of the taxi and – oh, so this is how it's going to be, is it? – have to root around in my purse for a tenner to pay the driver because Mum claims her own purse is packed deep down at the very bottom of her huge suitcase. 'Look, I'll let her explain it to you all herself,' I add, as I push the buzzer to Cass's ground-floor flat and almost immediately hear the clack-clack of heels on the other side of the door. 'I think that would probably be best.'

The door opens and Cass is standing on the other side of it.

She looks absolutely sensational.

She's wearing the cherry-red micro-shorts I packed in her suitcase to take to the clinic, a sexy off-the-shoulder sloppy sweatshirt, and strappy tan-coloured sandals with a five-inch heel.

There's a split second in which she looks, first, incredibly smug about her own appearance, and then, just for a flash, incredibly annoyed about my own appearance, and then she flings her arms around Mum's neck, bursts into the noisiest sobs I've ever heard, and cries, 'Oh! My Mummy, my Mummy!' exactly like she's auditioning for *The Railway Children* at the Swan Theatre in High Wycombe – like she did, unsuccessfully I might add, when she was eleven years old.

It's only then that I notice the man with the film camera in the hallway behind her.

Actually, the man with the film camera looming out of the hallway, over Cass's shoulder, to perfectly capture mine and Mum's stunned reactions.

At least, I'm looking stunned; I can tell, because my mouth has dropped open like a goldfish and I seem to have forgotten how to close it.

Mum, on the other hand, has adapted to this astounding turn of events like the seasoned professional actress she always wanted to be.

'There, there, my darling,' she says, in a rich, warm, motherly tone of voice that I've never heard her use before in my life, *ever*. (I've never heard her use the phrase 'there, there', either, so it's a double-whammy of weirdness.) 'I'm here now. Let it all out. Everything is going to be all right.'

To which Cass lets out a fresh round of sobbing for the cameraman to linger on for another few moments, until she decides that this has been quite long enough for the camera not to have a view of her face. She pulls away from Mum's embrace and starts to lead the way inside.

And I'm still standing here, staring like a goldfish.

An expression that's captured perfectly by the cameraman, who turns his lens on me for a moment, obviously assuming that I'll do or say something interesting.

'Er,' I say, which isn't very interesting. 'What's going on?'

'Just keep going, keep being normal!' a man's voice calls from just inside the hallway, just before he emerges, himself, to chivvy the cameraman through to follow Mum and Cass. He's got pale ginger hair, and designer stubble, and an air of high importance. '*Hiiiii*,' he says, to me, in a meaningful tone, sticking out a hand and walking towards me. 'I'm Ned, from RealTime Media. I . . . assume you're the older sister?'

'Yes . . .?'

'Right! Well, this is good. This is great, actually.' He's staring at me. 'Cassidy had led us to believe that you were a lot less . . . telegenic.'

'Than who?'

'Than her. Than you actually are . . .' He laughs, nervously. 'So . . .'

And then he stops talking.

'So?' I ask.

'I just . . . sorry, I forgot what I was saying there for a moment! You're very . . . ah . . . distracting.'

'I'm not doing anything.'

'No, you're . . . ah . . . so, are you an actress too?'

'No. Look, Ned, can you just tell me what's going on? I mean, obviously you guys have had a miraculous change of heart about giving my sister her own show . . . but are you *really* already filming it?'

'Yeah, of course.' He seems to pull himself together. 'We wanted to get the whole thing from the very moment of her leaving rehab this morning . . . God, she's really suffered,' he adds, rather falsely, 'hasn't she?'

'During her two-night stint in celebrity rehab? Yes,' I say. 'The sort of suffering that is known to only an unfortunate few.'

'And it must have been really, really hard for you, too,' Ned goes on, sliding one hand under one of my elbows and starting to manoeuvre me through Cass's front door. 'I expect you'll need to off-load about it.'

'To your camera crew?'

'Well, that's the obvious place to start,' he says, smoothly, as we reach the living room.

Here, Cass is slumped on the sofa, prettily dabbing her tears, while Mum sits beside her, mopping her brow with a portion of her huge black pashmina. Mum is murmuring to the looming camera about the terrible guilt she feels, As A Mother, that she was away working with her successful stage-school franchise, Gonna Make U A Star, while her only daughter was 'trapped in a loony bin'.

'We'll need to edit some of this footage, obviously,' Ned murmurs to me, although he's just given an excited thumbs-up to a woman with a clipboard and an in-charge air on the other side of the living room. She must be Tanya, the incredibly jealous one that Cass was moaning about before her 'breakdown'. 'But obviously we want to keep it all as real as possible.'

'Do you, now?'

'For sure. So whether it's comedy gold from your mum, or . . . I don't know, maybe a few on-camera tears from you . . . we really just want to get your family on to the screen as raw and as authentic as we possibly can.'

'Right.' I take a deep breath. 'Sorry, has Cass *told you* we'd all participate in this?'

'Well, it's understood. I mean, it's a show about Cassidy's life . . . sorry, I don't think I caught your name.'

'Libby.'

'Libby. Beautiful name.' He's gazing at me again. 'Is that short for Elizabeth, or . . . er—'

'Liberty.'

'Like the statue. Well, that fits. You're very statuesque, obviously . . .'

'Look, could I just have a moment to speak to my sister, do you think, *without* the camera on?'

'Oh . . . I don't know about that, actually, Liberty.' He

places slightly too much emphasis on the full use of my name, and looks seriously pleased with himself for doing so. 'We really want absolutely unrestricted access to your sister.'

'And, just at this moment, *I* want absolutely unrestricted access to my sister.'

'OK . . .' he says. It's the OK of a person who's about to refuse to do whatever it is you've just asked. 'But I'm sure there's absolutely nothing you could say to her that she wouldn't want the viewers to hear.'

'I wouldn't be so sure about that.'

'We-e-e-ll . . .' Ned mouths something over to Clipboard Woman, and she pulls a face and shakes her head. 'Yeah . . . um . . . no, I don't think we're going to be able to turn off the cameras until the end of today's session, actually, Liberty.'

'I see. Well, I suppose we wouldn't want to anger the gods of reality TV.'

'Exactly,' he agrees, earnestly. 'So, where did we land on the whole off-loading thing? I don't know if you'd prefer to do a piece straight to camera, talking all about what it's like to hear your sister has gone into rehab, or if you'd prefer just to sit down and have a chat with Cassidy about it face to face, and we'll use the footage from that?'

'You know, if it's all the same to you, I think I'll take option C,' I say, turning for the door.

'Libby! Wait!'

I glance back to see Cass getting to her feet and pushing past Mum (who's still dabbing her with the pashmina and wittering on about Regrets) to come over to me.

'I Suppose You Thought I Wouldn't Notice,' she says.

It's her Acting Voice. Saints preserve us: it's her Acting Voice.

I would ask 'notice what?' But whatever it is, I know full well it's only Cass's way of trying to drag me into her narrative. Lord only knows who she wants to cast me as – Boring But Likable Older Sis, perhaps, or maybe Bitter And Jealous Sibling From Hell . . . Whatever her plans for me, I'm in no mood to just accept them.

'I have to go, Cass,' I say, quietly, and hoping the camera won't hear even this. After all, I'm not miked up or anything. But as soon as I think this, an extremely tattooed man appears as if from nowhere and hovers a bloody great boom over our heads, anticipating High Drama, no doubt, and Great Television. 'Glad you're home,' I mutter, out of the side of my mouth.

'Off To See Dillon?' Cass asks.

Oh, for crying out loud.

Mum, still sitting on the sofa, emits a dramatic gasp.

You know, I actually have to take my hat off to her; she's taking this ball and running with it.

'I Saw The Photo Of You Two In The Paper,' Cass goes on. 'Don't You Think It Was A Bit Inappropriate To Use

215

Your Visit To See Your Sister In Rehab To Kick-Start Your Relationship With That Man Again?'

'Inappropriate?' I arch an eyebrow. 'Really, Cass?'

To give her credit, she doesn't so much as flinch.

'I Just Don't Need The Headache Of Worrying About You And Your Disastrous Love Life, Libby, On Top Of The Long, Hard Road To Recovery.'

Behind her, I can see Ned, and Clipboard Woman, and a couple of other randoms standing around holding cans of Coke Zero, all starting to mouth things to each other in a great frenzy: *Dillon who?* I expect they're asking, with visions of their reality TV show turning out even more thrilling than they thought it would be, and possibly even rivalling Marilyn's beloved Kardashians for A-list intrigue. *Dillon O'Hara? The sister's got a disastrous love life going on with* Dillon O'Hara?

'I'm fine,' I say, keeping it as brief as possible, because I'm damned if I'm going to fan this ridiculous flame with the slightest puff of oxygen. 'No need to worry. We'll talk soon, Cass, OK?'

'Libby, No! Don't Walk Out That Door . . .'

But I do. And I close it firmly behind me.

I mean, for fuck's *sake*.

I'll be having serious words with Cass about this ludicrous three-ring circus, when – *if* – I can be sure she's not got a camera crew at the ready to burst in and film the whole 'authentic' thing.

But, ghastly as the whole spectacle is, I can't totally

deny the smallest, sneakiest hint of pride in Cass's sheer, unbridled chutzpah. I mean, here's a girl who knows what she wants and isn't afraid to lower her (already shaky) moral standards to get it.

Which – if nothing else – makes me feel marginally less of a sell-out for agreeing to dinner with Dillon this evening.

Chapter 11

There was no time to get home to change before meeting Dillon, so after I left Cass's flat in Maida Vale, I just nipped to the MAC counter at Selfridges, where a very talented transvestite with extremely delicate hands has given me a fresh face of makeup for the price of a new kohl eyeliner. He was very complimentary about my new hair colour, and suggested all kinds of makeup tweaks to help make the most of it, and even though I might *feel* a little bit like I'm wearing enough on my face to sink a medium-sized battleship, I don't actually look like it.

Then I made my way to the Chanel concession and spritzed on my first-ever puff of Chanel No. 5.

Then I undid one more button on my shirt.

And now, on the dot of seven thirty, here I am arriving at the restaurant.

It isn't *exactly* the simple little calamari-serving Italian trattoria Dillon made it out to be.

I mean, I listen to enough of Olly's talk about the

restaurant business to know that this place, Sapori, on Chiltern Street, is the very latest venture from some super-successful restaurant group, and therefore The Place to eat, drink and – most of all – be seen.

I don't know if Dillon's heart-warming tale about spurning the snooty three-Michelin-starred place for their inegalitarian bookings policy is *quite* so heroic now. I mean, I assume he must have pulled a string or two of his own to get a reservation here at such short notice.

Unless, of course, he's just had a table booked here every night for the next three weeks ever since he first went into rehab, just to cover all the Big Apologies he knew he was going to have to do.

Anyway, now that I know it's this place, I really wish I'd done the whole schlep home to get changed. It's all a bit painfully hip here, and I'm not sure my super-tight skirt, womanly blouse and nude heels are going to cut the mustard.

Still, it's too late to do anything about it now.

Really, *really* too late, because I've already told the hostess who I'm here to meet, and she's already leading me across the restaurant towards a booth table where Dillon is waiting.

Sitting there, by himself, not knowing that I can see him and so not putting on any of his usual easy swagger and charm, he looks softer, and younger, and more vulnerable than I've ever seen before.

It hurts my heart, just for a moment.

And then he sees me, and his face breaks out into that familiar devilish grin, and my heart isn't the part of my body that I can feel any more.

Dillon gets to his feet.

'Hey, blondie.' He leans down to brush my cheek with his lips. 'You look sensational.'

'Good to see you,' I say, primly. 'Nice restaurant.'

'Well, we won't know that for sure until I get my hands on that calamari,' Dillon says, ushering me into my seat. 'So, I'll get the waiter, will I, and you can order something to drink?'

'Yes, please. I mean, that is, if you don't mind me drinking . . . I don't know how it works . . .'

'Well, what you do is, you lift your glass, and you take a sip . . .'

'No, really. I don't want a drink if it makes you uncomfortable.'

'The only way you ordering a drink could make me uncomfortable, Lib, is if your sister turns up with it in a massive cocktail shaker and chucks it over us.'

He's talking about this incident that happened – the first night we slept together, in fact – when Cass threw a cocktail in my face at a nightclub in Shoreditch.

'So please,' he goes on. 'Order the biggest, booziest cocktail on the menu, and don't waste a single moment of good drinking time worrying about me. I'm perfectly content over here with this delicious glass of sparkling mineral water. I mean, it's got a *lime wedge* in it, would you believe?'

'Well, I don't suppose anyone needs alcohol when they've got a lime wedge instead.'

'You said it, sister.' He gestures to the nearest waiter, who hurries over to our table. 'My friend would like the biggest, booziest cocktail,' he tells him, 'on the menu.'

'That's not quite true,' I say. 'Could I just have a nice red wine, please?'

'Of course.' The waiter nods. But he doesn't actually leave the side of the table to go and place the order. He just stands there a moment longer, and then he says, 'Would you like Chardonnay?'

I hesitate for a moment, because I have to admit my knowledge of wine isn't exactly encyclopaedic, and I don't want to make an idiot of myself. 'Um . . . I think I'd said . . . red?'

'Sorry, sorry . . . my mistake . . .' The waiter clears his throat. 'We have some very nice Chianti, if that's the sort of thing that gets you in the mood?'

I blink at him.

'I mean,' he falters, 'if that's the sort of thing you're in the mood for . . .'

'Yes, Chianti would be lovely. Thank you.'

'I'll bring a bottle.'

'No! No, no, just a glass.'

'Right. One glass of Cabernet coming up.'

'But I thought you said . . .'

The waiter has shot off, deaf to my confusion behind him.

I glance over the table at Dillon, who's looking slightly amused.

'OK, well, the service isn't all that promising,' I say.

'Ah, give the kid a break. It's not his fault he's just fallen hopelessly in lust with you.'

'He kept getting his wines in a muddle. I don't think it was anything to do with lust.'

'Course it was! He couldn't take his eyes off you, poor lad.' Dillon has his own eyes fixed pretty firmly on me as well. 'So,' he goes on, 'Libby à la blonde.'

'Yes. I don't want to spend the *entire* evening talking about my new hair colour . . .'

'We won't. I just wanted to say, again, that I really, really like it.'

'OK, but just so we're absolutely clear about this, I didn't change my hair colour for you.'

'*Didn't* you?' he asks, with a cheeky eyebrow-raise. 'Are you sure about that?'

'Quite sure, Dillon, thanks for asking.'

'Because if there's one thing I learned in rehab, it's that most of our actions are guided by our subconscious . . . so although you may *think* you weren't changing your hair colour to impress me, in actual fact—'

'Save me,' I say, as witheringly as I know how, 'the amateur psychology.'

'All right, then. Why *did* you change your hair colour all of a sudden? When the closest you've ever come to dyeing your hair before now was wearing a bright red wig to your sister's Disney Princess sixteenth birthday party, which you attended in the guise of Ariel from *The Little Mermaid*, because she was the only Disney Princess who didn't make you want to throw up?'

I'm so astounded by this revelation that all I can do is blink at him for a moment. 'You . . . really remember me telling you about that?'

He shrugs. 'I wasn't in an altered state for the *entire* relationship, darling.'

Thank God the hopeless waiter is returning now, with my wine, because it's a welcome distraction at an uncomfortable moment.

This is the Dillon I struggle to be around, you see. The debonair, cocky, laugh-a-minute Dillon isn't the problem. It's this one, the one who lobs out these occasional glimpses of the real, lasting feelings he might actually have for me . . . this is the one that should have a sign around his neck, warning: *HAZARDOUS TO HEALTH. DO NOT TOUCH WITH TEN-FOOT BARGEPOLE.*

'Here's your champagne,' the waiter says, rather breathlessly, putting a chilled glass of the stuff down on the table in front of me.

I gaze at the champagne, and then up at the waiter, in astonishment.

'Please,' he says, fervently, 'let me know if there's *anything else* you want.'

And then he's gone again, before I can say that,

actually, I'd quite like that glass of red wine we'd talked about.

'Told you,' says Dillon, 'Junior's got the hots for you. It's making me a bit jealous, actually, Fire Girl.'

'Fire Girl' is what he sometimes used to call me, because of the fact that I set my hair on fire the first time he met me.

To be more accurate, Fire Girl is what he used to call me when he was flirting with me.

Fire Girl is what he always, always called me when we were in bed together.

And, right at this moment, a couple walks past our table and then stops beside us.

'Jesus Christ,' says Posh James Cadwalladr, looking down at us, 'look who's here.'

Except he isn't talking to me, he's talking to Dillon.

'Jamie fucking Cadwalladr,' says Dillon, with a grin, as he gets to his feet and pulls Posh James in for a brief, manly hug. 'And Lottie. Sweetheart.'

'Dillon! How lovely to see you!' Lottie gives him a kiss on either cheek before turning to me. 'Hi, nice to meet you, I'm . . .' She peers at me, then does (I've never seen one of these before in my life) an actual double-take. '*Libby?*'

'Hi,' I wave a sheepish hand. 'Yep. It's me.'

'Oh, my God! You look . . . wow. I love the hair.'

'You know each other?' Dillon asks.

Whichever way you look at this, my attempt to make

Dillon think I'm still with Adam is a bit buggered, isn't it?

'I stock some of Libby's jewellery,' Lottie says, and then, just when I think I might have got away with it, she adds, 'and of course we live next door to her . . . well, I presume, now, er, *ex*-boyfriend.'

'Do we?' Posh James is looking confused. And a bit bug-eyed, too, for some reason, because he's staring at me in that exact same way that the hopeless waiter was just doing. And that Ned from Cass's TV show was doing too, come to think of it. 'Hi,' he says, to me, leaning around Lottie and extending a hand. 'I don't think we've met . . .'

'James, you bloody idiot! Of course you've met her! It's Libby! From . . . the other night.' Tactfully, presumably because she doesn't know the status between me and Dillon, Lottie doesn't mention the whole nearly-nude-and-stuck-in-a-dog's-den thing. 'You know. Adam's house.'

Posh James's eyes practically launch themselves off his forehead. '*You're* that chick who got her kit off and got her head stuck in Fritz's safety gate?' he blurts, nowhere near as tactfully.

I sneak a glance at Dillon across the table; he's got one eyebrow raised himself.

'Um, yes,' I say. 'I'm that chick. Girl. *Woman*, in fact,' I add, drawing myself up, as if trying to make a feminist case of this is going to draw Posh James into all the embarrassment, so that I'm not the only one dying here. 'Good to see you again.'

But Posh James doesn't look embarrassed. He just carries on staring, those eyebrows still stuck up near his hairline, and murmurs, almost to himself, 'The one we rubbed with argan oil . . .'

'This is a story I have to hear,' says Dillon, lightly.

'Oh, I think it was sesame oil in the end, actually,' I say, jovially, to try to bring about an end to the awkwardness. 'I still wake up in a cold sweat dreaming that I'm being stir-fried!'

Lottie laughs. 'Well, we should leave you two to your . . . romantic dinner.'

'It's not romantic,' I say, just as Dillon says, 'Thanks, Lottie. We hear the calamari is spectacular.'

'Do we?' I ask, pointedly.

'We certainly do. And Jamie, buddy – we should get together soon, yeah? I mean, obviously my hell-raising days are over . . .'

'Oh, don't worry about that,' says Lottie, putting her arm through Posh James's. 'His hell-raising days are pretty much behind him, too.'

'I can still raise hell,' he replies, irritably, finally taking his eyes off me and looking at Lottie. 'For Christ's sake, I'm thirty-nine, not ninety-nine. I'm not completely past it.'

'Well, you know what,' Dillon says, clapping him on the shoulder, rather harder than when he greeted him, 'we can compromise. We'll go out, you can pick hell up with your little finger and then put it straight back down again. How's about that?'

Posh James doesn't laugh. 'It'd be good to catch up properly,' he says, ungraciously, before starting to steer Lottie in the direction of their table, further along the restaurant. 'Have a good night.'

The moment they're gone, I reach for my champagne glass and take a big, steadying gulp.

Dillon sits back down again.

'That guy,' he says, in a voice that isn't *quite* quiet enough, 'is such a fucking tosspot.'

I take another sip of champagne. 'It looked like he was a friend of yours.'

'We were at drama college together. Stayed friends for a few years afterwards. Christ knows why. Him a toffee-nosed git from Eton and me a simple Irish country boy . . .'

'Spare me,' I say, 'the quaint fictionalization. There'll be leprechauns joining us at the table before we know it.'

'And very welcome they'd be, too. Besides, they could be an audience for you when you tell this story about . . . what was it again? Getting your kit off and letting James Cadwalladr rub you with olive oil?'

'Sesame oil,' I snap.

'I stand corrected.'

'And it wasn't *remotely* like he made it sound. It was just this . . . *incident*.'

227

'At Adam's house?'

'Yes.'

'Your *ex*-boyfriend Adam's house?'

'Mm.'

'So you're not actually with him any more?'

'No,' I admit. 'Not really.'

'Right.' Dillon takes a sip of his sparkling water. 'He fancies you, you know.'

'Who, *Adam?*' I stare at him. 'Er, no, which was precisely the—'

'Jamie Cadwalladr.'

'Oh, for Christ's sake! According to you, everyone fancies me. James Cadwalladr, the waiter . . .'

'Me.'

He's put his glass down, and is looking at me across the table. He isn't wearing that devilish smile any more.

'Dillon,' I begin.

'Fire Girl,' he says.

'I thought this dinner was just meant to be an apology.'

'It was.' His knee brushes mine. 'Until you turned up looking like that.'

I take a deep breath. 'It's the blonde hair,' I say. 'That's what it is. You've always had a thing for blonde hair.'

'It's not just the blonde hair. It's something else about you, Libby. You look like a proper . . . *woman*. Yeah, not now, mate,' he adds, rather sharply, to the waiter, who has reappeared at the side of the table with a notepad and a hopeful expression. 'Can you give us a minute?'

'Look,' I say, as the waiter slinks off again. 'Whether or not you fancy me . . .'

'I do fancy you.'

'. . . isn't really the point. The point is that obviously we can't actually be together.'

'Says who?'

'Says me. Because clearly I'm the only one of the two of us sensible enough to do so.'

'And what if I were to ask you for a second chance?'

I stare at him.

For a split second, it feels like it's Christmas morning. And I've just opened the curtains to a winter wonderland of snow. And decent Christmas presents are waiting under the tree for me, not just box sets from Space NK that get Mum extra points on her reward card. And Dad has remembered to send me a text wishing me a Happy Christmas for once.

But, thank God, that split second passes, and level-headedness (just) prevails.

'No.'

'Not even if I take some sort of lie-detector test to prove that I don't plan to drink another drink, or do another line of coke?'

'No.'

'Not even if I promise to never leave you stranded in the path of a hurricane with no passport ever again?'

'Dillon, come on. It wasn't the drink or the drugs. It wasn't even the hurricane . . .'

'It was the women, wasn't it?'

I shrug, as casually as possible. 'That certainly played its part.'

He thinks for a moment. 'Would it convince you at all if I were to become a monk, say?'

'Well, that would still be a barrier to us getting back together again,' I say, 'because I don't think monks are allowed to have sex with women. Or, come to think of it, with men.'

'Ah. So even the other monks would be off-limits, then.'

'I think that's probably down to the discretion of the individual monastery.'

'And to the proclivities of the individual monk?'

'Exactly.'

He laughs. 'God, Fire Girl. I've missed you.'

I don't stop myself from saying, 'Me too.'

'But you still don't believe that I've changed?'

'It's not that I don't believe that you've changed, Dillon. It's that I'll never believe you won't change back. I mean, can you *really* see yourself settling down with just one woman? Having a few children . . .'

'I love children. And children love me.'

'. . . and staying up all night burping them instead of staying up all night knocking back vodka?'

'Hold the phone. Children need *burping?* Oh, now, come on, Libby – next thing you'll be telling me they're incontinent, too.'

I finish my glass of champagne.

'I only wish someone had *told* me this,' he goes on, 'before I turned over a new leaf. I mean, if I'd known the lifestyle adjustments that come from deciding to settle down and start a family, I'd never have touched rehab with a bargepole.'

I stare at him. '*Have* you decided to settle down and start a family?'

'Well, one step at a time. Let's just focus on the settling-down part first.'

'Dillon. You've only been out of rehab for about twenty minutes. I think it's probably a bit too soon to start making any major life decisions.'

He leans across the table, picks up my hand, and holds it, gently, in his own.

'If there's one thing I learned in that place,' he says, 'it's that the thing I've always been looking for is an anchor. Something to keep me rooted.'

'Something,' I say, 'to weigh you down.'

He shakes his head. 'It wouldn't be like that. I keep telling you, Libby, I've changed. I've grown up. I've done all the messing around that I'll ever want to do. And quite a lot of messing around that I wish I'd never done in the first place. You're the only girl I've ever met who's ever meant more to me than that.'

'That's because you have terrible taste in girls.'

'True. But it's also,' he says, 'because it took me a very long time to find *you*.'

All of a sudden, I feel like I can't breathe.

And not in a giddy, heady, sexy way, either. It feels a lot more like the time I got trapped between two very, very overweight men in a crush to get on a bus in Palermo. If it hadn't been for Olly, who was there on holiday with me, practically crowd-surfing his way towards me to haul me out with his bare hands and a smattering of negligible Italian, I'm honestly pretty sure I'd never have made it out of there alive. Death by paunch.

I can still remember, eight years on, the mushrooming sense of panic.

'You can't . . . *say* things like that,' I croak.

'I'm just trying to be honest, Libby. To explain. To let you know how I feel.'

'Dillon, for fuck's sake. This isn't a therapy session at bloody rehab. You can't just be honest, and explain, and let people know how you feel when you risk . . . hurting them. Again.'

'I know how much I hurt you . . .'

'No, you don't. You don't know what you did—'

My phone is ringing.

Saved – hallelujah – by the bell.

Really, really saved, because I'm in danger of either bursting into tears all over Dillon and telling him just how hard I fell for him the first time, or in the even greater danger of flinging myself across the table and into his lap, kissing him until neither of us can breathe, then gasping that I'll agree to any of his absurd suggestions if he just takes me back to his place right this minute and has wild, mind-blowing sex with me until the sun comes up.

'I need to get this,' I mumble.

'Fine.' Dillon is getting up out of the booth. 'I think I need a breath of fresh air, anyway. I'll give you a moment.'

It's so unlike him to walk off in what looks remarkably like a huff that I'm almost too surprised to actually pick up my phone for a moment.

When I do, I don't even have time to say the second syllable of the word 'hello' before an American man's voice on the other end of the phone says, 'Hallelujah! So there is life out there after all.'

I know, without needing to ask, that it's Ben. Adam's boyfriend.

I could – maybe should – hang up. But instead, I'm going to stand up for myself.

'All right,' I begin, 'first off, I had absolutely no idea that Adam had a boyfriend. By which I mean that I had no idea that he was attached, *and* no idea that he was gay. Because if I'd known either of those things, I can assure you I would never—'

'It's Libby, right?' he interrupts, brusquely. 'I mean, that is your name, right?'

'Yes . . .'

'Libby. You've got the wrong end of the stick. This is nothing to do with, well, you having the wrong end of my boyfriend's stick.'

'Actually, I never *did* have his stick, wrong end or . . .'

Not the time, Libby. Not the time.

'So what *is* it to do with?' I ask, cautiously.

'I found your earrings on the floor in Adam's kitchen,' Ben says, 'and I really liked them.'

'Right . . . er . . . well, I could make you a pair . . .?'

'Jesus Christ, Libby, I'm a gay man, not a transvestite! And more than a gay man, I'm an investor. I put money into small businesses, in the hope that they'll turn into bigger businesses. And quite a lot of them are fashion-based. I've had a look on your website, bought some things from those little boutiques you supply to . . . it's good stuff. Original. Different.'

'Thank you.'

'Well, don't thank me yet. I haven't decided whether or not I'm going to invest in you yet. So, look. I need to see a business plan.'

'I . . . er – ' *haven't got a very good business plan* – 'can work something up for you, if you like . . .?'

'That'd be a good place to start. Can you email something over by the weekend?'

'Yes.' *If I spend the next forty-eight hours doing nothing but working on it.* 'I can do that.'

'And please, don't write me any long, teenage essays about your ideal customer, and how fulfilling you find your career, and where you see yourself in ten years. I just need the basics. Current profits. Turnover. Projected financials. Sales pipeline.'

'Right. Yes. Sure. Absolutely.'

'Good. I'll have my assistant call with the email address.'

'Thank you so much, Ben, I really appreciate . . .'

'Good to finally talk to you,' he says.

And that's the end of the call.

Bloody hell.

Given that, only a few days ago, I was being sneered at by a bank manager in Clapham for asking for a small-business loan, the possibility that an investor wants to put money into Libby Goes To Hollywood is quite astounding.

I don't have more than a few seconds to sit and savour this turn of events, though, before my phone rings again.

Bogdan.

Or, rather, given that she's using his phone: Marilyn.

Which is the first time, since we spoke earlier, that I remember the plans I made with her for this evening. Our girls' night in.

Shit.

I answer the call.

'Marilyn, I'm so, *so* sorry.'

There's silence for a moment.

'Did you forget about me?'

'No! Of course not. I didn't forget about you. I just . . . didn't remember.'

'Coming from someone who says she's tired of always feeling second best,' Marilyn says, softly, 'it's sort of ironic. Don't you think?'

'Yes. I know. You're right. But look, I can explain. I've sort of ended up coming out for dinner with that guy I was telling you about . . .'

'Oh, I get it, honey. You're giving me a taste of my own medicine.'

'What?'

'Well, I guess I deserve it. It's exactly what I've done in the past. Gone out dancing and drinking champagne with some fellow who's only going to break my heart, leaving a girlfriend sitting at home all on her own, with nothing but a pitcher of Manhattans and . . . say, did you ever see a show called *The Only Way Is Essex*?'

I swallow. 'I feel terrible.'

Which I do. And not just because she's had to endure multiple episodes of *TOWIE*.

It's absurd, I know, because obviously it would have made no logical sense to have turned down an evening with real, live Dillon O'Hara just to hang out at my flat with a magical Marilyn Monroe. But didn't I just tell myself, earlier today, that Marilyn needs a friend? A proper friend, the kind of friend I've always tried to be, who would never ditch her flatmate – not even if that flatmate didn't really, anything more than metaphorically speaking, exist – for a man. After all, she's right: I know only too well how it feels to be unimportant to a person that matters to you. And if there's anyone likely to suffer, terribly, from a sense of abandonment, it's Marilyn Monroe.

'Don't feel terrible,' she says, now, in her little-girl voice. '*I* don't. Well, not any more. That second pitcher of Manhattans probably helped . . .'

'OK,' I say. I've heard enough. 'I'm coming back. Just hold tight, and I'll be there in under an hour.'

'Honey, it's all right, you stay out and enjoy your evening with your beau. Did you take my advice? Did you stuff your bra with pantyhose?'

I ignore the question. 'I'm on my way. And . . . don't drink any more, Marilyn, all right?'

'I don't think I could if I tried, honey,' she says, sadly. 'I seem to have drunk it all.'

I end the call, slide out of the booth and head for the exit.

Bumping into Dillon – literally – as I open the door and step on to the street.

'You're ditching me?' he asks, lightly but pointedly. 'Way to make a guy feel good, Libs.'

'No, I'm not ditching you.'

God, he really does look unnaturally gorgeous tonight.

And as for all those things he's been saying about how much he fancies me, and how he'd like a second chance . . .

Not to mention that cheeky, throwaway comment he made earlier, that I can't *quite* seem to shake from my mind, about being able to think of a few better ways for me to spend time on my hands and knees than scrubbing his floors.

I so, so want to go home with him tonight.

'But I have to go,' I tell him. 'Something's happened. I need to help . . . a friend.'

'Oh. Well, let me come with you . . .'

'You can't.'

'Is it Olly Walker?'

I blink at him. What an odd thing to say.

'No. I just need to go. God, sorry, I should have left some cash for the drink . . .'

'Don't be ridiculous. I can pay for your drink.'

He's being sharp, which is unlike him.

'I'm sorry,' I say.

'For what? Abandoning me at dinner or turning down my advances?'

'I haven't turned down your advances.' I look up at him. His eyes are fixed on mine. 'I just need a bit of time to think about all the things you've said.'

'Sure. That's fair enough. But, Libby . . .'

'Yes?'

He puts his hands on my waist, and pulls me ever-so-gently towards him.

'Don't just think about all the things I've said. Think about the things I've done, too. Or rather, the thing I'm about to do.'

The thing he's about to do being to lean down, put his lips tantalizingly close to mine, and then, when I move closer, start to kiss me.

It's just as wonderful as it was the last time I kissed him, in our hotel room in Miami.

No: it's more wonderful. Because that time I wouldn't have been able to shake off the bad feeling about him smiling a little too wickedly at the pretty pool attendant, or the weary sense that he was bound to be up for yet another big night of cocktails, cocaine, and chatting up the bar staff.

This time it feels as if I'm the only thing that matters to him in the world.

Ironically, it's absolutely intoxicating.

I give into it for as long as I can possibly handle, and then I turn away and start to hurry towards the tube.

But when I get back home to my flat, Marilyn has gone.

Chapter 12

S he still hasn't returned.

It's four o'clock in the afternoon now, and there's been absolutely no sign of her since I got back last night.

No cocktail shaker, no white mink coat, no scent of Chanel No. 5.

The only signs she was ever here at all are the Chesterfield and the TV, which are still on the other side of the partition door. Leaving me with the colossal headache of how to get them back to this side again.

Which is a neat addition to the *actual* colossal headache I've had all day, to be honest with you.

I shouldn't have a headache at all, given that I only drank one glass of champagne last night, and given that I got into bed (my own) at a perfectly respectable hour.

But I couldn't sleep a wink for worrying about Marilyn.

And rerunning that kiss with Dillon.

And then there's the fact that I have spent all day cooped up indoors working on this business plan for Ben.

Or Benjamin Milne, CEO of Milne Equity Partners, as I need to start thinking of him. Head of a private equity fund that might be able to plough some much-needed capital into my business, rather than the man who's ploughing my ex-boyfriend. Because I've Googled him (more than once) in the off-moments when I wasn't getting on with work (and when I was trying to distract myself, last night, from the emptiness of the flat without Marilyn in it, and the horrible, stomach-churning guilt of knowing I'd let her down), and it turns out that he's a bit of a big shot. Personally worth millions – and fond of giving those millions to all sorts of annoyingly good causes – things like dog shelters, and equine hospitals and, I don't know, beauty salons for underappreciated cats; he also runs this investment fund that cherry-picks small, often fashion-related businesses, sets them up with capital and some specialist mentoring, and then watches them grow into . . . well, bigger, significantly more successful fashion-related businesses. He's invested in these two shoemaking sisters from Utah, for example, who started out with $165 and the family shed as their workroom, and who now employ fifteen staff and have recently featured in a six-page spread in American *Vogue*. He's invested in a tiny, family-run cashmere company based on the Isle of Arran, which now supplies fabric to the likes of Vivienne Westwood and Stella McCartney. He's invested in another jewellery designer, some young guy from Brooklyn, whose website had 300,000 visitors last year, and who has now closed that website down because he's been appointed head of design for Net-a-Porter's new own-brand jewellery 'department'.

Basically, you get the picture. A bit of a big shot, like I've already said.

So the fact that he's even *interested* in me submitting a business plan is seriously, seriously exciting news.

Whether or not he's going to want to take it any further . . . well, that's up to me now, isn't it?

Me, who's spent most of the afternoon creating a neater, more professional-looking spreadsheet of the last six months' net profit than I presented to the Clapham bank manager, and who is now trying to craft a short, succinct memo all about my sales pipeline.

Which is doubly tricky because I'm still not a hundred per cent sure what a sales pipeline actually *is*.

I really, really wish that Marilyn was still here.

Not that I expect she knows the first thing about sales pipelines, either. And I'm fairly sure that if she *were* here, I wouldn't be getting anywhere near as much done, with the TV blaring and with her near-constant stream of chatter, and with the pitchers of foul-tasting cocktails she'd probably keep producing for us to drink . . .

But I'd probably be able to focus better if I weren't still feeling so bad about last night. And I'd have had the chance to explain more about the Dillon thing – not to mention to tell her how we'd ended up kissing. And

I'd have liked her to see my new hair colour, to let her know I'd taken some of her advice to heart. It would have been . . . well, 'swell', as she'd have put it, to see what she thought.

Not to mention the fact that I can't shake the feeling of unease that she left when she was annoyed with me. At least when Audrey Hepburn disappeared from my life, everything was good between us.

I've no idea if I'll ever see Marilyn again. And the last thing I did, like everyone else she ever had in her life, was to let her down.

And now my buzzer's going, so I'm going to have to haul myself up from in amongst my laptop and this scattered pile of invoices, and go and see who it is.

'Hello?' I say, into the entry phone.

'Libby?'

'Yes?'

'It's James Cadwalladr.'

'Huh?'

'Sorry to bother you. I hope it isn't an inconvenient time. Can you buzz me up?'

'Um . . . sure.'

Which I regret doing the moment I've done it. Because actually, it *is* an inconvenient time. Bloody inconvenient, what with the fact that I've got paperwork everywhere, and absolutely no refreshment to offer him apart from the half-drunk can of warmish Diet Coke that I've been using to sustain me all day, and the leftover crusts of the pizza I picked up on my way back last night, just in case Marilyn still wanted it . . .

And, anyway, convenient time or inconvenient time, what the fuck is he *doing here?*

It's a question I ask, though a bit more politely than this, as soon as I open my front door and see him jogging round the last of the four landings with a broad smile on his abnormally handsome face.

'James, hi. Er . . . this is a bit far from your neck of the woods, isn't it?'

'Well, I wasn't exactly just passing, no!' He leans in and kisses me on either cheek then, in an over-familiar fashion that I've often noticed in posh men who went to posh boarding schools, closes my front door behind him. 'Lottie gave me your address. Or, rather, I found your address in Lottie's records. I didn't want her to know I was coming here.'

This is a bit . . . alarming.

Was Dillon right about him fancying me, after all?

'I want to commission you to make something for her,' he goes on. 'It's her fortieth next month and I'd love to give her a really special necklace, or some earrings . . .'

'Oh!' I'm relieved. 'Of course! I'd love to do that.'

'Good.' He's looking around my flat with interest. (Or possibly superciliousness and condescension: it can be hard to tell from a face like his.) 'Nice place you've got here.'

(It can also be hard to tell, with the über-toff accent, if he's being genuinely pleasant or downright sarcastic.)

'Thanks. So, what sort of thing were you thinking, exactly?'

'Sorry?'

'For Lottie's birthday. I mean, you said a necklace, or earrings, but can you be any more specific . . .? Is it something to wear for going out, or something a bit more ordinary, for everyday . . .?'

'Oh, I haven't really thought about any of that, yet.'

'Right. Um, because it might help, if I had more to go on.'

'I mean, my head's off in the clouds half the time, Libby, what with thinking about the kids, and work . . . I've got this really exciting new project in the pipeline at the moment, actually. I'm in talks with Sam Mendes to play Hamlet at the National Theatre.'

He waits for my response to this earth-shattering piece of information.

Unfortunately the only reply I can think of is: 'Talking of pipelines, you wouldn't happen to know anything about the sales kind, would you?'

But he's an actor, not a business-school graduate, so I stop myself.

'Wow,' I manage to muster, instead. 'Hamlet. At the National Theatre. With Sam Mendes. Amazing.'

It's pretty much just parroting back the bare bones of the information he's just given me about it, but it seems to satisfy him as a response, because he preens, visibly, just for a moment, leaning back against the kitchen counter.

'Well, people have been going on and on about me playing Hamlet for so long now that eventually you feel almost a *social obligation* to do it, you know?'

'Absolutely.' I'm not really paying attention; all I'm trying to work out is how to persuade him to bugger off and leave me in peace to get on with my work. 'A social obligation. Yes.'

'I mean, don't get me wrong, I'm not saying it's up there with providing clean drinking water!'

'Oh, I don't know about that . . .'

'*Thank you.*' He suddenly leans forward, from the counter, and seizes my hands. 'Thank you for saying that, Libby. You're one of the people who really *gets it*, aren't you?'

'Er . . . am I?'

'Gets how important the arts really are? Gets that acting isn't just a job, it's a way to *speak directly to the people?* Of course you are, Libby. I could tell that right away about you, the very first time we met.'

I don't want to say that the very first time we met the only way he could have shown less interest in me is if I'd been a lone and greying sock.

'So, please,' he goes on, not letting go of my hands. 'Would you tell me more about performances of mine that you've enjoyed, Libby? I'd really love to get some feedback . . . hey, do you have a bottle of wine lurking around the place anywhere? It's always a lot more enjoyable to hear excoriating reviews of my less-than-stellar performances when I'm getting pleasantly pissed!'

Now I'm getting confused (and my hands, still swaddled in his, are getting warm and a little bit sweaty).

I mean, he started out saying he wanted to order a piece of jewellery for his wife, and now he's asking me to tell him what I think of his acting, and using words like 'excoriating', and suggesting a bottle of wine . . .

'No, I don't have any wine, actually. In fact, James, I was just—'

'Oh! Fucking idiot that I am!' He's sliding his canvas backpack off his shoulder. 'I totally forgot, I stopped off at Waitrose on my way over here and picked up a few things for cooking later . . . I've got a nice bottle of red right here. Two of them, in fact!'

Oh, *has* he?

I may be a bit slow to get these things. But I'm not actually stupid.

'I'm fine without any wine,' I say, firmly. 'And in fact, James, I think it would be better if you . . .'

I stop talking. Because I've just heard a noise from the other side of the partition door.

It's the sound of the opening credits of *Geordie Shore*.

And it can only mean one thing: Marilyn is back.

'. . . leave,' I go on, more firmly even than before. 'Right away.'

'Do you have a flatmate or something?' Posh James asks, obviously having heard the TV himself. 'Because there's plenty of wine to go round, if she'd like to join us . . . It *is* a she, right?'

'Don't go near that door!' I yelp, as he takes a step towards it.

'Oh, come on. I'm only being friendly.'

'Well, I'd prefer it if you were friendly elsewhere. From the carriage of a northbound Northern Line train. Or the back of a taxi.'

'Your flatmate doesn't seem to agree.'

'What?' I jerk my head round just in time to see that the partition door, behind me, is opening a crack. 'Stay there!' I bark at Posh James, before grabbing the door handle, opening it a little more (though still by as narrow a margin as I think I'll be able to get through), squeezing myself through the gap and then closing it behind me.

I stand with my back pressed against it, just in case the deceitful philandering bastard on the other side of it can't be trusted.

Marilyn is standing right in front of me, wearing – again – nothing but her white mink coat and an excited expression on her pretty, alabaster-white face.

'Honey!' she whispers. 'Is that a *man* I heard on the other side of . . . oh! You went blonde!'

'Yes,' I hiss, 'but Marilyn . . . look, I'm really glad you're back, but actually this isn't the time to . . .'

'It looks swell, honey. And I was right, wasn't I? I

mean, here you are, a brand-new blonde, and lo and behold you've suddenly got a man back to the apartment! So is he the one?' she goes on, gleefully. 'You know, that made you feel like a graham cracker?'

'No, he's not. And I didn't "get him back here" at all. He just turned up. And he's married, and he's a total creep.'

'Oh.' Her face falls for a moment. 'Say, if you need me to take care of him, I'll do that for you, honey. I mean, creepy married guys always seem to like me, for some reason. In fact, sometimes it seems like every man I ever meet is the creepy married sort.'

'No! I don't need you to take care of him, Marilyn . . . and anyway,' I add, remembering my promise to myself that I'd try to be more of a friend to her, and relieved she's back again for me to get a second chance to do so, 'you're worth more than just some creepy married guy, you know. Now, just let me get rid of this one, and then we can . . .'

'Everything OK in there?' comes Posh James's voice through the door; worryingly *close* to the door, in fact.

'Fine,' I snap, 'and, by the way, if you open this door, I will get on the phone to Lottie so fast . . .'

'OK, OK, OK,' he says, his voice moving away from the door. 'No need to get all militant on me now.'

'I know you say he's creepy and married, but he *sounds* just *wonderful*,' Marilyn breathes, with her customary shoulder-wriggle. 'And what's that accent? Is he Canadian, too?'

'*No!* Now, look. Can you just stay on this side of the door while I go and get rid of him properly?'

'Sure!' Marilyn performs an adorable little military salute, which causes her mink to swing open. 'Whoops!' she giggles, half-heartedly clutching the revolting thing round her again, before turning back to the TV where – I was right – half a dozen drunk-looking Geordies are falling out of a nightclub and screaming at each other. 'I Sky-Plussed a whole load of this show last night. Everyone's kind of orange-coloured, and there's a lot of yelling, but I don't really understand what it is they're yelling *about* . . . or why they're all orange-coloured, for that matter.'

It's not the moment to ask how the hell she knows about Sky Plus.

I open the partition door, slide back through it, and close it firmly behind me.

Posh James isn't anywhere near the partition door any more, thank goodness; he's over by the entry phone instead. 'Uh, sure, I guess,' he's saying into it. 'Come on up.'

'Who are you telling,' I demand, more annoyed with him than ever, 'to come on up? This is my bloody flat! You can't just invite people in!'

'Calm down,' he tells me, with an eye-roll. 'It was someone saying she was your sister. Well, she's got a couple of other people with her. One of them might be called Ned?'

'Oh, for the love of God . . .' I run to the entry phone and start yelling, 'No! No! Take your fucking camera crew somewhere else, Cass!'

But it's too late. I can already hear footsteps, several sets of them, coming up the stairs.

'Camera crew?' James is staring at me. 'Why the hell would anyone's sister turn up with a camera crew?'

'Because she's got her own reality TV show,' I snap at him. 'That's why!'

'But . . . I can't . . .' He's turned extremely pale. 'I can't be found up here by a TV crew. I'm . . . married.'

'A fact that probably ought to have occurred to you,' I say, 'before you turned up here with conveniently purchased wine and some pile of utter bollocks about ordering your wife a necklace.'

'I'm serious! I don't want footage of me in here! I'll get a super-injunction! A brand-new one, I mean . . .'

'Well, if you don't want footage, I suggest you do what I've been trying to get you to do for the last five minutes . . .'

'OK, OK, I'm on my way.' He opens the front door, looking more stressed when he hears voices on their way up the stairs. 'You don't have another way out,' he asks, 'do you?'

'Unless you count a freefall jump from a fourth-floor window?'

'No. Right.'

'Just pull your hood up,' I suggest, suddenly taking

251

pity on him, grabbing the empty pizza box and handing it over, 'and take this. Keep your head down and they'll think you've just delivered me a pizza.'

He looks perturbed by this. 'But why would I be taking a pizza box away? And to be honest with you, I don't know if I can actually project a delivery guy kind of air . . .'

'It's an emergency,' I tell him, 'not an opportunity for Method Acting. Besides, if you can do Hamlet at the National Theatre with Sam Mendes, you can do anything.'

'You're right,' he says, pulling his shoulders back – and then, conversely, hunching his shoulders forward to give himself a sort of stoop, pulling his hood up and starting to limp out of the door.

I've no time to wonder why he's made the creative decision to make his pizza delivery guy a dead ringer for the Hunchback of Notre Dame, because he's only just set off down the stairs when Cass, Ned, Clipboard Woman, Boom Man and – of course – the man with the camera all pass him and begin to troop into my flat.

It's quite a slow troop, thanks to the fact that my flat, even without the Chesterfield in it, is so short on space. Cass, who has flown through the door first, all lip gloss and legs and tan knee-high Louboutins, has to pause in whatever dramatic opening line she was about to deliver because the man with the camera is stuck in the queue, and the heavily tattooed man with the boom is stuck in the *door* . . .

'Did anyone else,' Ned asks, filling Cass's pause, 'think that pizza delivery guy looked just like that posh actor from that detective show?'

Which doesn't bode all that well for Posh James's performance as Hamlet at the National.

'Because if the sister knows him, too, as well as Dillon O'Hara—'

'Cass,' I interrupt Ned, before he's worked up a whole plot-line about me and my intimate knowledge of famous actors, 'what the hell do you think you're doing, bringing a camera crew to my flat without my permission?'

'Oh, well!' Cass tosses her hair. 'If we're talking about *permission*, why don't you tell me why you thought it was OK to go blonde without asking me first?'

'Why on earth would I have to ask you first?'

'Because *I'm* the only blonde in this family!'

'Mum's a blonde.'

'Well, that doesn't fucking count!' she storms. 'Mum's fifty-nine! She's past it!'

'She's fifty-seven.'

'Potato, tomato.'

'What?'

'It's what you *fucking say*,' she snaps, 'when the silly cow you're talking to wants to correct every little thing you say all the fucking time!'

I think I see the confusion.

'I think you mean potay-to, potah-to.'

'Don't be ridiculous. Potah-to isn't even a fucking *word*.'

'Oh, this is *good*,' I hear Ned breathe, as reverentially as a devout Catholic who's just caught a glimpse of the Pope on a tour round the Vatican. 'Are we getting this, guys?'

'Anyway,' Cass goes on, after a quick glance round to check that both the cameraman and the boom guy are now squeezed into the room, 'that's not really what I wanted to talk to you about. I mean,' she shakes back her hair, gazes into the middle distance and repeats, in her Acting Voice, 'That's Not Really What I Wanted To Talk To You About.'

'Cass. I'm not doing this.'

'I'm Really Worried About You, Sis.'

'Sis? You never call me sis.'

'After Everything You Put Me Through When Your Fling With Dillon Ended, Do You Really Want To Cause Me All That Stress Again?'

'Everything I put you through?' For a moment I forget that my only priority ought to be to get Cass and the crew out as fast as possible. 'Seriously, Cass – *what?*'

'The Endless Sobbing Phone Calls At Four In The Morning . . .'

'Not one time did I call you at four in the morning, sobbing or otherwise. I might have texted you, once, at around six, asking when you were free for a chat.'

'The Weight Gain . . . that's *you* gaining weight,' she adds, hastily, 'not me.'

254

'Heaven forbid. But Cass. Why on earth are you here to talk to me – with this delightful camera crew or otherwise – about Dillon? I'm not . . . *seeing him* again.'

Cass lets out a gasp. (In fact, so does Ned, and so does Clipboard Woman, and even Boom Guy.)

'Now You're *Lying* About Him, Libby?' She claps a hand to her mouth. 'It's Worse Than I Thought.'

'Right, look, it's really, really not a good time for any of this – ' it wouldn't be, even if I weren't conscious of the fact that Marilyn Monroe is still on the other side of that partition door – 'and I haven't actually agreed to be in this reality show at all, so if you could all just get your things and—'

'*I've Seen The Footage.*'

'Footage? What footage?'

'You And Dillon. Outside That New Italian Restaurant Last Night. Kissing.'

My mouth falls open.

'How did you . . . sorry, you say there's *footage* of this?'

Cass nods, reaches into her shoulder bag (a brand-new *actual* Chanel 2.55 that I've never seen before; possibly her treat to herself for surviving her long and arduous stay in rehab, or possibly just a new wardrobe 'essential' for the show) and pulls out her phone.

'Here!' she declares, holding it up and pressing the screen.

It is, indeed, slightly shaky, blurry video of (a very blonde-looking) me and Dillon standing outside the restaurant last night. Dillon is sliding his arms round my waist, and then leaning down, and I can actually feel the same wave of overwhelming desire wash over me once again as I watch him kiss me . . . and me kiss him back . . .

And then I remember where I am, and that this is all an appalling violation of my privacy.

'Was this these guys?' I demand, jabbing a finger in the direction of Ned and co. 'I never gave permission for them to stalk me like that!'

'Nobody Stalked You, Libby. People Are Just Concerned For You. Me, Most Of All. And I Think You Need To Know,' Cass adds, choking back an impressively convincing sob, 'That This Is A Very Bad Time For Me To Be Dealing With Too Much Drama. What With Me Being In Recovery And All.'

I take a very, very deep breath, willing myself to grip on to the last remaining threads of loyalty I might still retain for my sister, and *not* blurt out *YOU'VE GOT NOTHING TO BE IN RECOVERY FROM, YOU SILLY COW* in front of Ned and the crew.

But before I can say anything at all, I hear a tap-tap-tap on the other side of the partition door.

This is very, very ominous indeed.

'Look, just give me a minute,' I say, pulling open the door, darting through it and shutting it behind me.

Marilyn is standing right beside the door, her blue eyes wide open and staring at me.

'Honey, did I *hear* right?'

'Did you hear what right?'

'The TV was a little loud, but . . . well, I swear I heard you say something about a reality TV show being filmed in our apartment.'

'Er . . .'

'And I can hear a girl doing that terrible, stilted, kind-of acting . . .'

'Yes. OK. It's a reality TV show.'

Marilyn gasps.

'But look, it's nothing to do with me. It's just my sister. And I'm trying to get them to leave.'

'*Leave?*' she hisses. 'Honey, why on earth would you . . .?'

'Libby?' This is Cass now, shouting through the closed partition door. 'What the fuck are you doing through there?'

'I'm just dealing with something!' I yell back.

'Can we come through?' comes Ned's smooth, insistent voice. 'Film whatever it is you're dealing with?'

'No, you fucking can't,' I say. 'I'm . . . er . . . changing. I'm naked, in fact. So you can't come in.'

There's a brief silence.

'OK,' I hear Ned say, sounding disappointed, though whether this is because he has to stop getting awesome footage for a minute, or because he doesn't get to burst in and see me naked, I couldn't say for sure. 'Let's do a piece to camera while we wait, Cassidy, shall we? Just tell us more about how worried you are for your sister and her tumultuous love life.'

'OK, you gotta help me fix my hair, honey!' Marilyn is saying, hurrying over to the Chesterfield, picking up the cocktail shaker, and holding it up to check out her reflection in its shiny chrome. 'And tell me more about the show. Are there housewives? Orange people? Do I need to get in a fight with anybody?'

'You can't go through there.'

'Oh! Should I try to get hold of a little dog from somewhere? You know, I think I'd feel a lot more confident if I had a little dog . . .'

'Marilyn. I'm serious. You can't be in the show.'

'But honey, you *know* how much I want to be a reality TV star.' She stops sorting out her hair in the shiny surface of the cocktail shaker, reaches into the pocket of her mink for a little bottle of Chanel No. 5, and spritzes it on. 'This could be my big chance!'

'I promise you, this isn't your big chance.'

'Don't tell me things you don't know!'

'But I *do* know.'

She ignores this and starts to push past me.

I've honestly no idea what would happen if she opened that door. I'm nowhere near enough of an expert on metaphysical manifestations to be able to work it out. All I know is that, what with there being a fully operational camera crew on the other side, I don't want to risk it.

'Marilyn,' I hiss, 'I'm serious. I *do* know. I know for

one hundred per cent certain. And if you do what I say, and stay right here for the next three minutes, I'll tell you exactly how I know.'

This, thank *Christ*, stops her in her tracks.

She stares at me.

'Three minutes?' she asks.

'Three minutes. While I get rid of them. And then I'll tell you how I know this isn't your big break. And if you don't like my answer,' I add, 'I promise you, I'll call my sister and her blasted crew right back and you can join in the show to your heart's content. I'll even pop down to the pet shop two blocks away and see if I can borrow you a little dog, all right?'

Marilyn thinks about this for a moment. Really, really thinks, with her pretty nose slightly screwed up and a frown etched into her smooth forehead.

'All right,' she concedes. 'I guess three minutes isn't too much to ask.'

'Good. I'll be right back.'

I open the partition door again, hurry through, and close it smartly behind me.

Cass is perched on my minuscule kitchen counter, tanned legs sexily crossed in her mini-skirt and boots, intoning earnestly into the camera.

'I Mean, Obviously I've Made A Few Mistakes In My Own Love Life, But It's Just Really, Really Hard For Me To Watch My Sister Do Something As Silly As Start Shagging Dillon O'Hara All Over Again . . .'

'OK. That's enough,' I say, briskly. 'You all have to leave.'

'I thought you were getting changed,' says Ned, looking slightly disheartened that I've re-emerged wearing the same shorts and vest top as before, instead of whatever fabulous outfit he might have imagined I'd appear in. 'Can we film the two of you having that chat now?'

'No. I've already told you. I'm not participating in this. Or rather,' I go on, suddenly seeing the golden opportunity to get them to bugger off, 'I *might* participate another day, *if* you all go away now and leave me to get on with some very important work. Oh, and as long as you never, ever film me like that without my consent again. Whether I'm having dinner with Dillon O'Hara or . . . or George and Amal Clooney, OK?'

Ned is staring at me in that Pope-spotting way again. '*Do you know George and Amal Clooney?*'

'Of course she fucking doesn't,' says Cass, sliding down off the kitchen counter and starting to head for the door. 'Let's go and leave Miss Boring-Pants to her work.'

'Well, do you think *they* might agree to appear on the show?' Ned is asking, as Clipboard Woman, thankfully retaining possession of her brain cells, takes his arm and hauls him after Cass. 'Actually, not him maybe. I'm not sure he's our target demographic. *She's* great, though . . .'

Boom Guy and Cameraman follow them, wordless as

ever, until Boom Guy, who's the last out, looks at me before he pulls the door shut behind them all.

'For what it's worth,' he says, in a surprisingly soft voice for such a large and scarily tattooed man, 'I've worked on a few shows with Dillon O'Hara in my time. Nicest guy in the world.'

'Oh! Right. Er . . .'

'But if he ever came after any daughter of mine, I'd castrate him first and ask questions later.'

'Well, that's good to know. I mean, we're not dating, as I've already tried to say. But . . . thank you.'

'You're welcome,' he says, and closes the door just as softly as he's spoken.

Which just leaves me and Marilyn. Alone again, thank heavens.

I pick up one of the bottles of wine that posh James left behind – because my God, after the last fifteen minutes, I think I need it – and grab a couple of glasses from the cupboard. Then I open the partition door again.

Marilyn is sitting on the Chesterfield, gazing at the television screen.

Which is no longer showing shouting, orange Geordies, but the polar opposite of that, in fact. The polar opposite being Audrey Hepburn.

It's the opening credits of *Breakfast at Tiffany's*, and Audrey-as-Holly-Golightly, in a scene I know all too well, is gliding along Fifth Avenue sipping a coffee and nibbling a Danish pastry.

261

'I got kinda tired of all those orange people, honey,' Marilyn says, rather dreamily, 'so I had a look at the movies you had on Sky Plus instead . . . Gee,' she goes on, before I can express my renewed astonishment at how well she knows her way around my TV controls already, 'the girl in the black dress is real pretty, isn't she?'

'Yes. She is.' I go and sit down on the sofa beside her, open the wine and pour each of us a glass. 'In fact, she's the one I've mentioned a few times. Audrey Hepburn.'

'You *know* her?' She turns to look at me. 'Well, I wish you'd invite her to one of our girls' nights. I'd love to get her to do that eye makeup on me.'

'Well, she is a bit of a style icon . . .'

'And then *I'd* persuade *her* to put some pantyhose down her bra,' Marilyn goes on. 'I mean, sure, she's just about the prettiest girl I've ever seen, but she could use a little help in the chest department.'

Part of me would almost like to be around if that conversation ever happened; part of me would run like the wind.

Either way, this isn't the important thing right now.

'The thing is, Marilyn,' I say, 'that my knowing Audrey Hepburn . . . well, it's related to what I was going to talk to you about. You know: how I know for sure that everything turns out OK for you in the future. I mean,' I correct myself, a little too late, 'that *your career* all turns out OK for you in the future.'

Marilyn draws her knees up to her chest, tucking her mink coat cosily around herself, and gives me one of her most excitable smiles. 'I think I might have an idea how you know, actually.'

'You do?'

'Sure! You're psychic, right?'

I blink at her.

'Oh, it's OK, honey. You don't have to feel embarrassed or anything! I've known psychic people before. One of my foster mothers was psychic, in fact. And she was into runestones, too, and tea leaves . . . say, you don't work with tea leaves, do you? Because they were never very reliable with me in the past. The ones my foster mother kept reading for me were always saying I was going to marry a man who worked the land and have nine children.' She pulls a face. 'I mean, I *guess* I could still meet a farmer, but there aren't all that many of them living in Hollywood, and as for the thought of nine children . . .'

'No. No, I don't work with tea leaves. And actually, Marilyn, it isn't so much a *psychic* thing as . . .' I take a deep breath. 'Do you believe in magic?'

'Sure I do, honey! You mean, like princesses in towers, and fairy godmothers, and that kind of stuff?'

'Um, not really. Those are more, well, fairy tales.'

'Oh. Because I sure believe in those! You have to, don't you, when you grow up the way we do?'

'The way *we* do?'

263

'Well, you already told me you had a difficult mother, honey. And I may not be the psychic one around here, but it doesn't take extrasensory powers to work out that you might have a little daddy trouble, too. I mean, never feeling good enough for a guy . . . wanting this man you like to pay you more attention . . .' She shrugs, but with a heartbreakingly sweet smile. 'It takes one to know one, honey. Besides, there's nothing so very wrong with liking fairy tales.'

The wind has been sucked out of my sails here for a moment.

'I'm . . . er . . . not quite sure,' I croak, when I can speak, 'how we've ended up talking about fairy tales?'

'Honey, you were the first one to mention fairy tales! I'm still waiting to hear what you've got to tell me about my future! From your rune stones, or your tea leaves, or your visions, or however else it is you do your psychic thing.' Marilyn takes a sip from her wine glass and – outrageous, given the cocktails she's inflicted on me for the past few nights – pulls a face. 'I don't have to drink much more of this stuff in my future, do I? Because, I gotta tell you, that would finish me off even more than the nine kids!' She laughs, then stops abruptly. 'You're not gonna tell me I really *will* have nine kids, are you?'

'No. And again, Marilyn, I'm really not . . .'

You know what? Screw it. If she thinks my knowledge of her future comes from me being psychic, let her. I just want to let her know that her dreams are going to come true: as long as she believes what I'm telling her, and stops being so down on herself for not 'Making It' yet, what does it really matter?

'You have an amazing future ahead of you,' I say, in a voice that – I hope – sounds portentous enough to keep up the whole 'psychic' thing. 'You're going to become an even bigger movie star than you could possibly imagine. You're going to star in movies with Jane Russell, and Betty Grable, and Tony Curtis, and, yes, Sir Laurence Olivier . . .'

'Oh!' Marilyn gasps, her hands flying to her mouth. 'And Tim Holt?'

'Er . . . Tim who?'

'Tim Holt. From *Treasure of the Sierra Madre*. Oh, honey, I have such a crush on him! If you could tell me I'll be in a movie with him one day, I'll be just about the happiest girl in the whole of Hollywood!'

'Or Colliers Wood.'

'Huh?'

'Never mind. Well, I don't know for sure if you're in a movie with this Tim Holt or not, Marilyn . . . but aren't the others I just mentioned enough for you?'

'Sorry, honey, of course they are. More than enough! And you really mean that I'll be the *star* in these movies? And that people will recognize me wherever I go?'

'I really mean that. You're going to be more than famous, Marilyn. You're going to be legendary.'

She sinks back into the Chesterfield with a happy . . . no, a *relieved* sigh.

'It just helps,' she says, in a little-bitty voice, so soft that I can hardly hear, 'to know that, for once in my life, I won't be getting the fuzzy end of the lollipop.'

'I'm glad.'

'And do you know anything else about me?'

'Sorry?'

'My future.' She smiles, wistfully. 'I mean, obviously I don't want the nine kids my foster mother was always threatening me with, but I always did think three or four might be kinda nice.'

I swallow.

'And a man? Do I end up with a good husband? Someone who treats me nice, and stays faithful, and makes me . . . happy?'

I'm still unable to find the words to reply.

Because, honestly, what am I going to tell her? That she died naked and alone, at thirty-six? That there weren't any children at all, and that even though there were a couple of husbands, they certainly don't qualify for the whole 'treating her nice and making her happy' thing she's fondly imagining.

'Honey?' Her blue eyes blink at me, wide and trusting. 'You've gone awful quiet.'

'Yes . . .' My throat is dry. 'Uh, sorry, I was just . . .'

'Well, now you're scaring me a little, here! Do you know something about my future that's . . . *bad?*' She reaches for my arm. 'Oh, for God's sakes, honey, do I get *fat*, or something?'

'No, no! No need to worry about that!' I'm relieved that it's such a silly question – and even more so when I hear the front-door buzzer going. I get to my feet. 'I'd better get that,' I say. 'You just sit back and enjoy your wine . . .'

'No chance of that, honey,' she says, pulling a face.

'. . . and watch the movie,' I finish, closing the door behind me. 'I'll just be a minute.'

I'm blinking back tears, I realize, as I head for the entry phone and pick it up. 'Hello?' I sniffle into it, hoping to God it's not Cass and Ned, back for a second bite of the cherry.

'Libby?' says Bogdan's voice when I pick up the entry phone. 'Is yours truly. Bogdan. Am able to be up and coming?'

'Yes, Bogdan.' I don't think I've ever been so happy to welcome one of his unannounced visits in my life. '*Please.* Come up.'

He's the only other person who's seen Marilyn. And I desperately want to be able to talk to someone about this whole bizarre situation.

'Am needing,' he declares, in an out-of-puff manner, as he pushes open my front door a couple of moments later, 'to be dispensing with more of the pounds. Those stairs will be the dying of me.'

Obviously, it would be nice to talk about the situation

to someone who had a *marginally* less mangled command of English . . .

And now he's staring at me.

'Joseph, Mary and the Baby Jesus,' he says, using an expression he's picked up, obviously, from Dillon. 'You are highlighting the hair.'

'Oh.' My hand flies to it; I'd completely forgotten, what with everything else going on, that this is something I'm going to have to explain to him. 'Yes . . . It was on a whim, really, Bogdan.'

'Whim?'

'I mean, I just decided to do it on the spur of the moment.'

'Spur?'

'I didn't plan it,' I finally say, keeping it as simple as possible. 'It was a last-minute decision.'

'But I am telling you to do this for the longest time.'

'I know. And I'm sorry. I don't know what suddenly made me do it. But I'm really glad you're here now, Bogdan, because I need your professional feedback. Did the colourist do an OK job?'

Marginally mollified, he reaches out a hand to ruffle through my hair. He pulls an iffy face.

'Is not *total* zone of disaster.'

'OK! Good to hear!'

'If am being given honour of doing it myself, am choosing more ash tones, fewer caramel ones.'

'Sure. But it's basically OK? I mean, it looks all right?'

'Is suiting you, Libby, yes,' he sniffs. 'But this is not making me fall down in the surprise. Am the one who is always saying this. Am lone voice in wilderness. Am only surprised that you are not trusting opinion and skill of *good friend* and are putting your hair in hands of stranger instead.'

'I know. And I'm sorry. I'll never do it again.' I take both of his huge, surprisingly soft hands in mine. 'But Bogdan, look. I need to talk to you about something other than my hair. *Not about Dillon*,' I interrupt myself, because he's got that look about him that suggests this is precisely the topic of conversation he's assuming I'll bring up. 'About something much more important.'

'*Is* anything being more important?'

'I think there is, Bogdan, yes.' I take a deep breath. 'OK, we haven't had the chance to talk about this yet, but . . . well, you met a girl in my flat the other day, right?'

He nods. 'Am helping her to be moving hideous orange sofa.'

'Right. Which was very nice of you. And as you can probably see through the crack in that door,' I wave a hand in the direction of the partition door, 'she's still here, sitting on it.'

'I am seeing this, yes.' He starts towards the door. 'Is OK if am going to say hello?'

'Wait! This is exactly what we need to talk about!

Now, look, I don't know how much she said to you, or what you made of the whole situation, but . . .'

'She is Marilyn Monroe,' Bogdan says, 'yes?'

I stare at him.

A strange croaking sound comes out of my mouth.

'Libby?'

'Yes,' I say, trying to speak again, and just about managing this time. 'She is.'

'OK. This is what I am assuming.'

'But . . . don't you . . . didn't you think it was *strange?* I mean, surely you assumed she was a lookalike, or a kissagram, or . . .'

'Kissagram? What is this kissagram?'

'Oh, it's just this silly thing,' I say, faintly, 'where people dress up as someone famous and show up at parties to kiss the birthday girl or birthday boy. Marilyn Monroe, quite often, or Tarzan, or James Bond . . . that sort of thing.'

'Am never hearing of this thing before.'

'No, of course, but I'd rather we stayed with the main issue here—'

'Tarzan, you are saying?' His eyebrows have knitted together. 'There is good money to be made by becoming this kissing-a-gram, Libby?'

'I've absolutely no idea. Maybe look it up on Google or something. Right now, I'd really like to talk about the fact that . . .'

'You are thinking I am making the more convincing Tarzan or the more convincing Bond?'

'*Bogdan!*' I yell. 'For crying out loud! Can we *please* talk about the fact that Marilyn Monroe is in my flat? And that you don't seem to think there's anything odd about that? Anything *magical?*'

There's silence for a moment.

'But of course,' Bogdan says, calmly, 'is being magical. Am not questioning this for solitary minute.'

'But . . . *shouldn't* you be?'

'What are other explanations?' he asks, with a shrug. 'That am becoming insane? That am seeing the ghosts? These are not the convincing explanations, Libby.'

'And the fact that she might be magical; that I might own a magical sofa from Pinewood Studios: this *is* a convincing explanation?'

Bogdan takes a step towards the partition doors, then stops and looks at me.

'In Moldova,' he says, slowly and rather wisely, 'we are having saying.'

He mumbles something at high speed in his own language, then looks at me for a reaction.

'Er . . . as you know, Bogdan, my Moldovan isn't exactly conversational . . .'

'Is translating something like . . .' He thinks for a moment. His eyes are half closed. 'When you are eliminating what is impossible, whatever is remaining, however improbable, must be truth.'

I think about this.

'Hang on,' I say, after a moment, 'isn't that from Sherlock Holmes?'

'Is not mattering where it is originating from!' Bogdan looks irritated. 'What am trying to be saying is that in my home country, we are accepting the magic as part of the everyday life. My great-uncle Viktor is having the magical well on his farmland. It is producing the water even in the middle of Great Drought of fifty-five. My grandmother is having the magical grandfather clock. It is always stopping at exact second of death of major world leader: Josef Stalin, President Kennedy, Mahatma Gandhi . . .'

'That sounds very . . . all-inclusive of it,' I say, faintly.

'And you are having magical sofa.' Bogdan shrugs. 'Is not being the big deal to me.'

'It's *not?*'

He shakes his head. 'Besides, am knowing about this before. Am overhearing you chatting with Audrey Hepburn when she is the one who is popping out of it.'

Which leaves me standing, motionless with amazement, in my half of the flat, as Bogdan wanders through the partition door and towards the Chesterfield.

'Good evening,' I hear him saying to Marilyn. 'Is very pleasant to be greeting you again.'

'Oh! It's real pleasant,' Marilyn breathes, gazing up at him with those wide blue eyes, 'to be greeting you again, too.'

272

'Let me be giving you some more of the wine,' he goes on, sitting down on the Chesterfield beside her, 'and we can be having some chat.' There's a short pause, filled only with the clink of bottle on glass, before he goes on. 'Am just wondering, Miss Monroe, are you ever thinking how you might be looking as brunette . . .?'

Chapter 13

Today's the day I've agreed to go bridesmaid's dress shopping with Tash and Nora.

At least, I hope Nora will be coming, too. I had a message from her yesterday morning saying she was still feeling a bit ropey, but I haven't had a reply, yet, to my message this morning asking her if she's feeling recovered enough to come along today. Because, lovely though Tash is, obviously, I don't think she and I gel well enough to get through an entire lunch and shopping session, just the two of us. We're meeting – Tash's suggestion – at the second-floor restaurant, near the shoe department, in Selfridges, which is a much more formal setting than I'd have chosen (I'd thought that we were just going to grab a quick sandwich before the shopping action began), so maybe she has a long lunch in mind, with the booze flowing, while we talk about . . .

. . . Well, this is what's making me desperately hope that Nora's coming, too.

Apart from our friendship with Nora, I don't think Tash and I have an awful lot in common.

Anyway, I'm the first to arrive at the second-floor restaurant, so I ask the head waiter for a table for three (I'm keeping my fingers crossed) and sit down, giving my tired feet a rest, just as my phone chimes with a message.

Lunch? D x

So we're back here again.

Back here being the place where my heart starts to thud and my hands start to sweat at the slightest contact from him.

Can't L x, I reply. Because it's better to keep these things short and sweet. Not get sucked into anything that could become flirty.

His reply comes a moment later: *Shame Dx*

I type back: *Yes L x*

Dinner? D x

Can't L x

There's a brief pause in our one-word tennis. Then another message comes through.

Date? D x

Is he *asking me* on a date, or *interested to know* if I'm going on a date?

Party L x, I reply.

Whose? D x

Friend L x

Another, brief pause.

Olly? D x

Yep L x

Ah D x

To which I'm not sure what to reply. I mean, 'ah' doesn't give me much to go on, does it? But I'm getting such a thrill from this little game that, childish though it sounds, I don't want it to end.

I haven't worked out what cute little witticism I can message back, though, and I can see that the head waiter is showing someone towards the table . . .

Thank God, it's Nora.

'Wow,' she says, open mouthed, before she's even sat down at the table. 'When did this happen?'

'Oh, the hair, you mean?' I touch it, self-consciously. 'Just a couple of days ago. Do you like it?'

'I really like it . . . I mean, it's very different, Lib, don't get me wrong . . . but I like it. And I like this whole sex-kitten thing you've got going on with your outfit, too.' She sketches a hand in the direction of my pencil skirt and – today's fresh foray into the world of Marilyn-wear – twinset.

Well, it's a black short-sleeved sweater beneath a black cotton cardigan. Not an *actual* twinset, but my version of it.

I'd have asked Marilyn's opinion this morning before I left, but she was fast asleep beneath her white mink on the Chesterfield, and I didn't want to disturb her. She was up even later than I was last night, drinking cocktails and chatting to Bogdan while I tried to get on with my business plan for Benjamin Milne. I did double-check, I'll be honest, that she hadn't allowed Bogdan to transform her into a brunette or anything, even though this involved me lifting up a corner of the disgusting mink, as most of her head was covered by it. But no: she was still as platinum-blonde as ever. And as naked as ever; if she stays very much longer, I'm going to have to see if I can persuade her to borrow some of my clothes, or possibly even order her a few things as cheaply as I can on ASOS, or something.

'Lib?'

'Huh?'

'You're miles away.'

'Sorry . . . I was just . . . you look great, too,' I say, as Nora sits down opposite me. (This is a tiny bit of a fib, because she looks rather pale and shadowy under the eyes, but I'm not about to point this out.) 'Are you feeling better?'

'Yes. Better-ish, anyway.' She glances down at her hands for a moment. 'I didn't know if you knew I was feeling rubbish. I mean, apart from that message you sent this morning asking if I was coming today, you haven't called or messaged since we last spoke on Monday . . .'

'Oh, God, Nora, you're right. I'm really sorry. I've just been so busy.'

'It's OK. And I meant to reply to your message this morning, but I was over at the restaurant helping Olly hang pictures on the walls, and I didn't get the chance.'

My heart plummets into my stomach.

Because not only have I forgotten about Nora while she's been staying down in London and feeling poorly, I've also forgotten about Olly.

'*Shit.* I was supposed to go over to the restaurant yesterday and help with that!'

'Ah.' Nora reaches for the bread basket and delves for a chunk of focaccia. 'That might be why Olly seemed in a bit of a mood this morning.'

'Oh, God.'

'Well, he's been a bit stressed about the whole opening thing for the past couple of days, so maybe it was just that.'

'He's been stressed?' I stare at her. 'I thought he was taking it all in his stride.'

'Lib, come on. You know Olly. He isn't going to *admit* if he's stressed. You just have to sort of . . . work it out.'

'But I told him he should call me if he needed any moral support at all . . .'

'OK. But maybe,' Nora says, lightly but pointedly, 'he thought it was best not to bother you. If you were doing something so important you'd forgotten to go round there when you'd promised to, that is.'

Guilt, white-hot, sears through me.

'I wasn't doing anything important,' I mumble. 'I mean, I was, in a way – it was a business plan for this possible investor – but it could have waited a day.'

'Oooh, that sounds exciting! But you should probably

tell Olly, just so that he knows why you've been a bit . . . unreliable . . .'

This stings.

'I'm not unreliable! I'm always there for people if they need me! My sister . . . you . . . OK, admittedly I've let Olly down a bit, recently . . . and of course I should have called you when I knew you were ill . . .' I tail off, then gaze across the table at Nora, feeling a bit stricken. 'Is he OK? Is everything ready at the restaurant? Do you think,' I add, anxiously, 'he'll forgive me?'

'I'm sure he will. You know how he feels about you, Libby.' Nora busies herself with the bread basket and grabs another chunk of focaccia. 'Hey, that reminds me. I never found out how it went with Adam the other night.'

Why talking about mine and Olly's friendship should remind her of Adam, I don't know.

'Was he completely stunned when he saw you?' she goes on.

'Er . . . yes, in a way . . .'

This isn't quite the same thing as the little fib about her looking great, when in fact she looks pale and tired. I mean, I can't sit here with my best friend and *not* mention, in the course of updating her on my relation-ship statues with Adam, that I might accidentally have started having feelings for Dillon O'Hara again.

Dillon O'Hara who, incidentally, has just texted another one-word message to my phone.

This time there's no *x*

Has he *forgotten* the *x?*

Or deliberately left it off, because . . . why? He's pissed off that I can't make lunch *or* dinner?

Well, that would be childish of him. Even more childish than this silly, one-word text game we've been playing together, which suddenly seems silly, now, in the wrong way.

'Libby?' Nora looks irritated. 'You're miles away again!'

'Sorry . . .'

But Nora's own attention is suddenly diverted from our conversation as she starts waving over my shoulder. 'Tash!' she calls out. 'Tash, over here!'

Because Tash has arrived, looking smart-but-summery in knee-length navy shorts, a crisp shirt and some gorgeous espadrille wedges, her swingy blonde hair twisted up at the back of her head.

'Girls!' she says, giving each of us a kiss on both cheeks as she reaches the table. 'How are we all this fine day?'

How, *how* does she manage to be so upbeat all the time? It's almost as if she has literally no worries in her life; no gnawing anxieties about relationships, or friendships, or letting people down . . . Which is probably because she *doesn't* let people down, to be fair. I don't imagine that Tash is at all the sort of person to promise

280

someone she'll do something and then fail to do it. Let's face it, she's helped out Olly more this week than I have, and she's not even one of his oldest friends.

'Nora?' she adds. 'You feeling OK?'

'Yes. How was the conference this morning?'

'Oh, *God.*' Tash sits down, heavily, in the chair beside mine. 'Callum Sutherland insisted on sitting next to me.'

'*No.*' Nora lets out a groan. 'You poor, poor thing. Did he say anything gross?'

'No, but he did sit uncomfortably close, and kept accidentally-on-purpose shifting in his seat so our knees were touching. I suddenly realized what it must have been like for you that time he cornered you at the Christmas party. And I couldn't even flash an engagement ring at him, surreptitiously, or drop 'my fiancé' into the conversation every now and then, just to remind him to back off a bit.'

'Callum Sutherland is one of the senior consultants in Tash's department,' Nora tells me, in case I'm feeling left out of the conversation, I suppose. 'And a total pervert.'

'With a thing for blondes,' Tash sighs, before adding, 'oh, my God! I've only just noticed you've gone blonde, Lib!'

'Doesn't it look fab?' Nora says.

'It does! Wow! What made you suddenly decide to do it? Oh, no . . .' Tash glances across the table, theatrically, at Nora. 'It wasn't Bridezilla over there, was it?

Laying down a decree that all her bridesmaids have to have the same hair colour?'

Nora laughs.

'It's pretty different from your shade, though,' I say to Tash.

'Actually, I think it looks pretty similar.' Tash peers at me, more closely. 'Don't you, Nor?'

'Well, yes, now you mention it, it's actually pretty identical. Good call, Lib. Thanks for fulfilling my secret Bridezilla wish to have matching bridesmaids.'

'Oh, now, talking of matching bridesmaids,' Tash says, leaning down and reaching into her handbag, 'I've seen a couple of Reiss dresses I really like the look of in this magazine, so it might make sense to head straight to that section of the store after we've had lunch . . .'

The two of them start leafing through the copy of *Grazia* she's just pulled out, which gives me a moment to ponder what they've both just said about my hair.

I mean, it *isn't* identical to Tash's.

And, if it is, that's obviously a coincidence. I don't want to copy Tash. Yes, she's really pretty, and, as I keep saying, she's obviously really nice, so you could do far worse than to copy her, if that's what you were doing . . . But I wasn't. I have no reason to copy Tash. The fact that I now have very similar hair is merely a quirk of the colourist's brush. I mean, really, how many different shades of blonde *are* there, at the end of the day? You're basically a sophisticated dark blonde, like Jennifer Aniston, a sexy platinum blonde, like my own dear Marilyn, or a pleasant, everyday, butter-and-honey blonde like Tash.

And now, well, me.

'I really like the look of this blue one,' Nora is saying, pointing at a picture in the magazine. 'You'd look great in it, Tash.'

'Really? You're sure it's not a bit too sexy, with that split in the skirt? For a bridesmaid's dress, I mean?'

'Who says I don't want sexy bridesmaids?' Nora says with a grin. 'I've already got newly hot blonde Libby over here, who I'm fairly sure Mark is going to ditch me for at some point during the course of the evening. I might as well persuade you to rock up in a thigh-split frock, so you can end up with one of the ushers. I'm just going to nip to the loo,' she adds, in a non sequitur, getting up with sudden haste that makes me think she's not quite as over her stomach trouble as she's claimed. 'Order some sparkling water, would you, and I'll be back in just a minute.'

Tash, in typically organized fashion, summons a waitress, orders a bottle of sparkling water, 'and a glass of champagne for you and me, Libby, yeah?' and then turns to me, as soon as the waitress has gone, to say, 'Well, if we're bagsying ushers already, you have to let me have first dibs on Nora's big brother.'

'Olly?'

'That's the one!'

I blink at her. 'Sorry . . . you fancy . . . Olly?'

'*God*, yes. He's gorgeous. Don't you think he's gorgeous?'

'Er . . . I suppose so . . .'

'I fancied him the first time I met him, to be honest with you. It's partly why I jumped at the chance to stay at his and help him out this week, when I knew I'd be down here at the same time for the conference.' Her eyes go a bit dreamy for a moment. 'I mean, he's so tall, and so handsome . . . and he can cook! My mum's always said to me: make sure you choose a man who can cook. My dad can't boil an egg – I mean, he *literally* can't boil an egg; the only time he ever tried, he put them in the kettle, and an empty kettle, at that . . . Which reminds me,' she goes on, reaching for the bread basket that Nora's pretty much decimated, 'talking of food, you and I should start talking about where to go for Nora's hen-night dinner.'

'Oh!' I'm still a bit too dazed by the fact she's set her sights on Olly. 'Er . . .' I try to gather myself. 'I had a few ideas already about the hen do, actually . . .'

And what I'd been thinking about the hen do – she fancies *Olly? Seriously?* – was something along the lines of this: a lovely picnic lunch in Kensington Gardens, where Nora and Mark went for a walk on their first official date ten years ago; over to Nora's mum and dad's house in Chiswick, for a homemade afternoon tea with lashings of champagne, in the garden where Mark asked her to marry him; everyone getting ready together in Nora's old bedroom with cheesy pop blasting out from her beloved old CD-player, and then a fleet of taxis over to Clapham for a big, boozy, chilled-out dinner at a huge table at Olly's mystery-name restaurant, before hitting one of the bars on Clapham High Street. A bar at which, I decided in a moment of inspiration a few weeks ago, I'll have prearranged with the staff to bring over round after round of a brand-new cocktail called 'The Flaming Nora', in honour of the nights Nora and I once spent on a holiday in Greece, drinking dodgy, on-fire cocktails and getting chatted up by the locals in an otherwise sedate fishing village.

Olly?

'Great!' Tash beams at me. 'Because I'd been thinking that I could put together a shortlist of a few options and email you all the details so you can see what you think. Nora was hoping for the third Saturday in July, if you think that's enough notice to get everyone together? Most of her friends are up in Glasgow, obviously, but you'll need to book a flight up from London, and then there are her sisters, too . . . OK, Nor?' she suddenly asks, as Nora reappears at our table and sinks into her seat.

'Yes. Fine. Don't tell me – you two were discussing the hen do.'

I wouldn't call it so much a discussion as a monologue, I think, but don't say.

Which I know is mean-spirited to even think, let alone blurt out over a pre-wedding girlie lunch with our mutual friend, the bride.

But I'll admit it: my nose is feeling quite seriously out of joint now. Because OK, maybe it's a more practical (albeit less personal and romantic) solution to have the hen do up in Scotland rather than down here in London. But wouldn't it have been nice to have come to this conclusion at the end of an actual conversation? Or, more to the point, for Nora to have mentioned to me, at some point, that she'd asked Tash to get in on the hen-do planning with me?

And it's not even like Nora has the excuse that she thinks I'm too disorganized and faffy to do a decent job. The surprise twenty-first that Olly and I threw for her at her parents' house was a triumph . . . Then there was the graduation celebration Olly and I put together for her at last-minute notice, the evening of the day she found out she'd got a first, at her then-favourite bar in Soho . . . Not to mention the super-elegant engagement dinner that (again) Olly and I co-hosted for her and Mark at his flat . . .

Olly who – sorry, but I still can't quite digest this – Tash is saying she *fancies?*

It's all just . . . well, it's a bit much.

Which, it's suddenly occurring to me, is the problem I have with Tash: that she's just a bit *much*.

Because I'll admit it: I suppose I do have a little bit of a problem with her. One that I'm not having quite so much trouble admitting to, in the light of these latest developments. Yes, she's lovely, and fun, and pretty, and smart, and all the bloody things that fairy godmothers bless their godchildren with in fairy tales. But all this hen-do-appropriating, and chief-bridesmaids-jobs-usurping and . . . and *Olly-fancying* . . . it's a bit much. A bit overwhelming.

And it all makes me feel like the third wheel. On a regular two-wheel bike.

I'm used to feeling like this in my romantic life. But it isn't something I'm accustomed to experiencing with Nora.

'Don't worry,' Tash is telling Nora now. 'We'll keep it calm and very low-key.'

'Sure, but we don't want to go *too* low-key,' I say. 'I mean, several of your sisters are going to feel seriously short-changed if we don't end up face down in the gutter at *some* point in the evening, aren't they?'

'Oh, I don't know, Lib. I'd rather not do anything too rowdy. Not so close to the wedding.'

'Well, sure. I mean, I'm not suggesting we all fly to Prague, drink our body weight in beer and end up getting arrested for weeing all over a statue of some great revolutionary leader.' (This springs to mind because of a stag do that Dillon went on, during the course of our relationship.) 'I just think it'd be nice to let our hair down a bit.'

'Hair!' Nora suddenly stares across the table at Tash. 'Shit, that reminds me! I've got to change my flight to tomorrow morning!'

'I thought you weren't leaving until Saturday afternoon,' I say.

'I wasn't, but I've had to move my wedding-hair trial appointment to tomorrow evening instead of next Friday. I need a three-hour appointment instead of two hours now that the hairdresser has to work in the veil as well, and tomorrow is the only time she has that block available.'

'Veil?' I'm confused. 'I thought you'd decided against a veil ages ago, because you thought it'd swamp the dress?'

'Yes. But . . . well, I've bought a different dress now, Lib. Didn't I tell you?'

'What?'

'Oh, don't worry, I've already managed to return the original one. Luckily I hadn't had the hem taken up yet, or the sleeves shortened . . .'

'But that dress was stunning on you!' I stare at her. 'Why did you change your mind?'

'The new dress is stunning, too, though,' Tash says.

'You've seen it?' I say, more sharply than I intended.

'Well, yes, I mean, I helped her choose it.' Tash pauses for a second, because the waitress has just brought over the drinks she ordered. 'It's just as gorgeous as that first one you helped her choose, honestly, Libby . . . ivory lace, and a lovely Empire waist . . .'

'Empire waist? But you wanted bias cut,' I say to Nora. 'All the dresses you tried on in the first place were bias cut! I even tried to get you to try on an Empire waist one, and you wouldn't, because you said people might think you were . . .'

I stop talking.

Nora is turning pink.

'You're *not*,' I say.

Nora is turning more pink. She clears her throat.

'Nine weeks,' she says.

'Almost ten,' Tash says, 'isn't it?'

Hold on: *Tash knew?* And I didn't?

No, no, no, Libby. *No.* That's not – not *remotely* – what's important right now.

'Nora! That's *amazing!*'

I get up, go round to her, and pull her in for a tight, rather fierce hug.

'How are you? I mean, how are you feeling? And, oh my God, that's why you're only drinking sparkling water, isn't it? And you haven't had a stomach bug all week . . .'

'I'm quite tired, mostly, is all. But I'm fine. As long as I'm not getting myself in a panic about it all, that is.'

I pull back and stare at her. 'You're not happy about it?'

'No. I mean, yes, I am happy! Really happy! It's just lousy timing, is the trouble . . . I mean, work is even more mental than usual, and . . . well, we haven't told either of our families yet, actually, but you know how traditional Mark's family is. I mean, I'm going to be fifteen weeks pregnant at the actual wedding!'

'You'll barely show,' Tash says. 'Especially now you've ditched the clingy dress.'

'And swathed myself in whatever massive veil I can find,' Nora adds. 'In fact, maybe when we've finished with your dress, Tash, we could pop along to some of the bridal shops on Chiltern Street and see if they've got any reasonably cheap veils for sale that I can take back home with me tomorrow.'

'You could borrow Grandmother's veil,' I blurt.

Nora blinks at me. 'Your Granny Judith?'

'No. Grandmother. Dad's mum. She's given me her wedding veil, for me to use one day . . .' *When I marry Olly*, I almost add, just because I'm feeling so thoroughly fed up with Tash now, after this secret pregnancy revelation that wasn't a secret to her. But I don't say this, because it would sound weird, and potentially freak out Nora, and I don't want to freak her out. 'It's stunning,' I go on, 'and absolutely massive, so it'd do a great job covering anything you want covered.'

'Oh, wow, Lib, that would be amazing . . . but if it's a family heirloom . . .'

'You're family,' I say, more awkwardly than I'd normally say this. 'Besides, it can be your Something Borrowed. Unless – ' I glance over at Tash as I ask this – 'you've already got your Something Borrowed all sorted out and ready to roll, of course.'

'Of course I haven't. Libby, that sounds fantastic!' Nora reaches up to give me a return hug.

'I can bring it to the party tonight,' I say, 'or you could drop round tomorrow to collect it, depending on what time your flight home is.'

'God, no, Lib, don't bring it to the party. There'll be red wine and fruity cocktails all over the place! I'll come and collect it tomorrow, first thing. I can't wait to see it! I bet it's beautiful, if it's your grandmother's. Libby's grandmother is *so* stylish,' she tells Tash. 'We went to stay with her for a week when we'd both just finished our GCSEs, and she's just the most incredible woman . . .'

I go back to my seat, pick up my menu and start to study it intently, while Tash, to be fair to her, sits and listens, with her usual enthusiasm, to Nora's long description of that summer, and Grandmother's treasure-trove of movie-star-worthy outfits she let us try on, and the glasses of pink champagne she'd offer us to drink before 'going down to dinner'.

But then, of course she does, because Tash is the sort of ideal friend who shows a real interest in everything you have to tell her.

Pregnancy and all.

But of course, if everything goes to plan for Tash, as I've no doubt it will, she won't just end up being the friend who was chosen as the first to learn Nora's baby news. She'll also end up being its auntie.

Chapter 14

It turned into a long – very, very long – afternoon of bridesmaid's dress shopping.

Tash seemed to want to do such a thorough job that only trying on three dresses from every concession in Selfridges would suffice, and Nora claimed that the distraction was making her feel better than she had in days, and even once Tash had settled on a dark blue prom-style dress from LK Bennett (that she looked absolutely stunning in, by the way), there were matching shoes to be sought . . .

By the time I get home, it's six o'clock, and I need to get a move on if I'm going to be on time for Olly's party at . . . well, at his mystery-name restaurant.

'Marilyn?' I call as I shut the front door behind me. 'Are you here? I need some . . .'

The words *help getting ready* fade on my lips.

The Chesterfield is back in my own flat. And Marilyn Monroe is sitting on it.

And even though this doesn't sound that much of a

surprise, believe me, it is. Because she's no longer wrapped up in her white mink coat, or a towelling robe with a matching turban.

She's wearing her shocking-pink satin dress, complete with matching gloves, from *Gentlemen Prefer Blondes*, with a glittering rhinestone choker, bracelets and – bringing back memories of Fritz's safety gate – chandelier earrings. Her hair, if it were possible, is blonder than ever, and fluffed in a platinum cloud around her head, and her makeup – glossy red lips, thick eyelashes – has a professional-looking sheen to it, as if it's taken a good while in front of a makeup-artist's mirror to get it just so.

She stands up as soon as she sees me, her face breaking into one of her dazzling smiles.

'*Honey*,' she breathes. 'Gee, am I glad to see you!'

'Marilyn, you look . . .'

'How long has it even *been*? Three years? Four?'

'Er.' I blink at her. 'Sorry?'

'Well, however long it's actually been, it feels just like yesterday, doesn't it?'

'That's because . . . it *was* yesterday.'

'Oh, honey. You always were funny!' She sits back down on the Chesterfield, neatly folding the huge bow on the back of the dress beneath her as she does so, and pats a cushion for me to come and sit down next to her. 'I know I've been lousy at keeping in touch, but I missed you, you know. And I want to hear all about how you've been, and how it's going with that jewellery career of

293

yours . . . oooh, and most important of all, what happened with that man you liked! The one who thought you were a Ritz cracker.'

'Graham.'

'Oh, was that his name? I totally forgot!'

'No, I just meant . . . Marilyn, look, you are aware that it really was just yesterday that we last saw each other? You watched *Breakfast at Tiffany's* on my sofa? Bogdan came and chatted to you about your hair?'

'Bogdan! I'd forgotten all about him, too! He was your fruity friend, right? Only you didn't like me calling him fruity, did you . . .? Gee, it's all coming back to me, now! Your funny Canadian ways, and all those swell times we had in this teeny-tiny apartment . . . You know, I live in a much bigger apartment now, obviously, but I don't think I've ever liked a place I lived in more than I liked this one.' Marilyn gazes around, fondly, at the tired-looking walls, and the cramped bedroom area, and the one-cupboard-and-two-gas-rings zone that passes for the kitchen.

'Good . . . good,' I murmur.

I mean, I'm still trying to get my head around the fact she seems absolutely convinced it's years since we met, while I'm equally convinced that the last time I saw her she was asleep on this very sofa when I left this morning.

Though, come to think of it, I'm not really sure why this should bother me any more than her appearing on my sofa in the first place. Given that she's about as real

294

as a unicorn being ridden by a flower-fairy, that is. I suppose there's no reason whatsoever that she can't materialize from the Chesterfield from pretty much any life-stage she likes. (It does make me a tiny bit concerned, though, that I might end up with barbiturate-filled, chronically neurotic Marilyn from her later years the next time she visits. If I've been worried about her fragility up until now, I don't quite know how I'd cope with that.) Either way, I think the best thing right now is just to Go With It. I mean, I *could* sit around here trying to insist it's barely even been twenty-four hours since the last time we spoke, but based on the past few conversations I've attempted with Marilyn about the peculiarity of this situation, I don't think I'll get very far.

'So! You've . . . er . . . made it?' I go on, sketching a hand in the direction of her shocking-pink outfit. 'In Hollywood, I mean. That's a costume from one of your movies, right? With Jane Russell?'

'That's right, honey!' She beams at me. '*Gentlemen Prefer Blondes*! Did you see it yet? I've had a few pretty decent reviews, and people in Hollywood are being real nice about it, and all, but I still haven't dared ask anyone who really knows me what they think of it.' She bats her long lashes, looking shy all of a sudden. 'Did you think I was any good?'

'You were terrific, Marilyn.'

'Really?'

'*Really.*'

'Oh, honey. You don't know how much that means to me.' Her blue eyes fill with tears. 'It's just nice to hear it from someone who knew me before all this craziness began. Because things really *are* crazy for me these days, you know. I mean, that's partly why I've been wanting to come back and see you for so long – to tell you that you were right!'

'Right?'

'Your predictions, honey! All that psychic stuff! I've made movies with all the people you said I would: Jane Russell, obviously, and I just finished shooting this little comedy with Lauren Bacall and Betty Grable, of all people . . .! It's all turned out positively uncanny!'

'Oh, er, well, you know. I always knew you had it in you, Marilyn.'

'Honey, there's no need to be all Canadian and modest about it! You have an incredible gift. In fact, if I were you, I'd be thinking about giving up the jewellery making, and concentrating on a full-time career as a psychic. I mean, no offence, honey, but if you're still living in this little place three years on, cute as it is, I don't imagine the jewellery making is going all that well.'

'Actually . . .'

'And you could charge anything you liked as a bona fide psychic, honey! I have a tonne of friends in Hollywood these days who'd give their right arm to know what's going to happen to them in the future . . .

well,' she adds, as a fleeting expression of sadness passes across her face, 'I don't know if I can call them *friends*, necessarily. I mean, sure, people are all super-nice to me these days, but it can be hard to tell if they're being nice to me for me, or if it's just because they want to be friends with, you know, *Her*. Marilyn Monroe.'

'No. I get that.' I reach over to pat her hand but, suddenly feeling uncomfortable about touching such a dazzling screen icon, settle for sort of rubbing the seam of her glove instead. 'I'm sure they like you for you, though, Marilyn. Just be yourself, and I can't imagine who wouldn't.'

She doesn't say anything in reply for a moment. Then she takes a breath, shakes her shoulders, and smiles again. 'Just one aspect of those psychic skills I think you need to work on, though, honey, and that's the ones to do with romance. Didn't you predict I was going to marry a farmer, or something?'

'No, I think that was your foster mother.'

But she isn't listening. Her eyes have lit up, and her body language has become coy. 'Because I met someone, honey, and he sure as hell isn't a farmer! Now, I'd better not go into *too* much detail, because he sort of likes to keep himself to himself, and he doesn't like the whole three-ring circus that comes from being with me . . . but he's a *very, very famous sports star indeed*.'

'Joe DiMaggio,' I blurt, before I can stop myself.

'Oh! You've seen a photograph of us together, then?'

'That's right. A photograph.'

'Those darn newspaper men! They drive poor Joe absolutely crazy. I don't mind so much, for myself – if they want a picture of me, I'm not gonna deny them – but Joe says it isn't what he signed up for. And you have to keep a man happy, right? Otherwise they don't stick around.'

'Er . . .'

'And trust me, honey, this man is worth the sacrifice! If we get married – I mean, he hasn't asked me yet, of course – I think I'd be absolutely fine about giving up the whole Hollywood thing. After a couple more years, that is. Get it all out of my system and then just settle down with my man and those kids I used to talk about . . . do you remember?'

'Yes, I remember. But, Marilyn, don't you think—'

'I'd love for you to meet him one day real soon,' she goes on, 'so you can see what I'm talking about. I've told him a lot about you, too.'

The thought of Marilyn Monroe filling in some spectral Joe DiMaggio on all the gossip about me is just too weird to get my head around, to be honest.

'I mean, you're still the best girlfriend I ever had,' Marilyn adds, almost shyly. 'I really felt like you cared about me, while we were rooming together.'

'I did,' I say, with surprise – because I'm feeling like a pretty shit friend right now, and it's unexpected to hear that Marilyn feels differently, even if her standards of female friendship are admittedly pretty low. 'I'm really glad you thought that,' I go on. 'I was actually worried I was too distracted to be a decent friend to you. I mean, I stood you up the other . . . er, I mean, *one night*, to go out with the guy I liked. And I left you alone here a lot of the time while I ran around town doing other stuff . . .'

'Honey, are you kidding me?' she breathes. 'The time I spent living here were some of the happiest days of my life!'

I don't point out that, from my point of view, it was, quite literally, *days*, because she's continuing.

'I mean, I had a really lousy childhood, you know? I moved around like a hobo, and nowhere ever felt like home to me. But this funny little place *did* feel like home. And most of that was down to you. I liked that you listened to me. I liked that you took me seriously. I liked that you seemed to think I mattered.'

This should be lovely to hear. But it isn't. It's just making me realize how very, very far away I've ended up – since Dillon first came into my life – from the person I used to be.

Because it isn't just this past week, since Dillon's reappearance, that I've let down Olly: I've been so busy trying to *keep myself busy* these last few painful months, that I've not been anywhere near as involved in the restaurant as I should have been. I mean, even that first time I visited the place, two months ago, with my congratulatory bottle of champagne, I ended up leaving with Adam and throwing myself into a relationship with him for the next few weeks. I wasn't there for Olly right from the word go. And I've not exactly been the greatest friend to Nora, either. I should have taken the reins of her hen night weeks before now; I should have been calling her more often, just to check in. And while she's been down here in London, for all my pie-in-the-sky plans about us having a proper chance to catch up over bottles of wine (or even sparkling mineral water, given her current state), I didn't even get round to texting her until I wanted to find out if she was leaving me alone with Tash or not.

I've not just been a bad friend. I've been a nonexistent one.

After all these years of having a nonexistent family, I've somehow ended up pulling exactly the same shit on the very people who've really been my family all along. The people whose good opinion actually matters to me.

'Honey? Did I say something wrong?'

'No . . . you didn't say anything wrong, Marilyn.' I get to my feet. 'I'm really glad you said what you did. And I'd love to sit here much longer and chat, but I absolutely can't risk being late for this party I'm going to tonight.'

'Oooh, a party!' Marilyn gives that familiar little shoulder-wriggle. 'Is Graham going to be there?'

'Graham . . .? Oh, you mean Dillon! God, no. This is

my best friend Olly's party, for the opening of his new restaurant . . . at least, I hope he's still my best friend,' I mutter, as I head for my wardrobe, open the door and pull down a couple of hangers. 'It would serve me right if he barred me from the door, to be honest.'

'Well, I gotta tell you, honey, if you turned up to a party of mine wearing one of those outfits, *I'd* bar you from the door.' Marilyn gets to her feet and, with a rustle of pink satin, shimmies her way over to me. 'I mean, gee, it's a restaurant opening, right, not a wake?'

'Yes. His first-ever restaurant. His dream for the last twenty years.'

'Then for Pete's sake, honey, don't wear black pants,' Marilyn says, taking one of the hangers that does, indeed, hold my very smartest and most chic pair of black trousers, and casting it on to the futon behind her. 'And don't wear a black *dress*, either!' she gasps, grabbing the second hanger from my hand, the one that's holding my favourite, figure-flattering Little Black Dress. 'Don't you have a nice *white* dress you could wear? Everybody always pays attention to you if you wear a white dress.'

'That's usually because it's a wedding, and the one in the white dress is the bride.'

'So you *don't* own a white dress?'

'I don't. No.'

'Well,' she replies, rather snippily, 'all you had to do was say so, honey. Oh! This is pretty! How about this?'

She's reached into the wardrobe and taken down the

blue silk dress I'm going to wear to Nora's wedding, as her chief bridesmaid.

'I mean, if you dress it up a little with a nice fur jacket . . . stuff your brassiere with pantyhose, so that neckline doesn't look so empty . . .'

'Marilyn, for the last time: I don't wear fur! And it's a bridesmaid's dress, anyway.'

'Honey! Who's getting married?'

'My best friend Nora.'

She frowns. 'I thought you said your best friend was this Olly, with the restaurant.'

'Yes. He is. They both are. They're . . .' I sit down on the futon, on top of my nicest trousers, and my favourite LBD, and stare, miserably, down at the floor. 'They're sort of my family, really. More than my actual family has ever been to me. But I've screwed up with returning the privilege to them myself, recently. Especially with Olly. He's always been like a . . .'

I'm about to say the words *big brother*, but find that I can't. I mean, I can't get those words out of my mouth. They're sort of lodged, somewhere, at the back of my throat, like a particularly troublesome fishbone.

Which is odd, because I've described Olly as my de facto big brother for years, and never had the words turn into a fishbone in my mouth before.

'Oh, honey, you don't have to tell me about friends being better than family. And if this Olly is as good a friend as you say he is, he'll forgive you. I mean, you've

302

forgiven *me* for not keeping in better contact with you for the last three years, haven't you? We're right back to the way things always were between us, just like that!' Marilyn snaps two be-gloved fingers. 'It's just like the two of us only spoke yesterday!'

'It's exactly like that, Marilyn, yes.' I get up and start to rifle through my wardrobe again, only to be stopped by an excited gasp from Marilyn as she seizes a hanger from the end of the rail.

'This looks perfect!'

She's pulled down a pale yellow sundress that I last wore when . . . yep, now I think about it, I was actually wearing this in Miami when the hurricane started rolling in.

I'm not sure I'd fit into it now, or that it would even look OK without a tan: it has a halter neck and a flippy, just-above-the-knee hemline, and it might just feel too revealing in warmish Clapham rather than sweltering Miami. But this doesn't seem to concern Marilyn, who's holding it out and gazing at it approvingly.

'This will look swell on you, honey. Far better than all that gloomy black!'

'I suppose . . .'

'Don't suppose it, honey! *Do* it! I mean, not that I'm criticizing, but you haven't changed at all since the last time I saw you, and . . . well, look at me!' She strikes an eerily recognizable little pose, hip jutted out, arms aloft. 'I doll up real nice, don't I?'

'You certainly do.'

'In fact, you know what, honey . . .' She notices one of her rhinestone bracelets dropping down to her elbow, and lowers her arm. 'Take one of these. It'll really jazz up that dress for an evening occasion.'

'Oh, that's sweet of you, Marilyn, but I can't possibly.' I gaze down at the heavy bracelet she's just handed me. 'These are incredibly valuable.'

'They're not real diamonds, honey! Just paste.'

'I know, but that's not why they're valuable.'

She looks confused, and slightly hurt. 'Honey, I'd really like you to have one. It could be . . . well, would it sound funny if I called it a friendship bracelet?'

It's a far cry from the sort of woven-thread friendship bracelets I used to make for Nora and Cass and my other friends back in the day, which were the things that kick-started my interest in jewellery making in the first place.

But times have moved on, and I'm a retro Hollywood jewellery designer now, and this piece I'm holding is pretty much the Holy Grail of all Golden Age Hollywood jewellery.

I mean, it feels like my fingers might actually be glowing, Ready-Brek style, where they're touching it.

'See, honey? You know you want it!'

'Well . . . if you're really sure.'

'I'm sure. It'll be something to remember me by! You know, if I don't make it back to visit for a while.' Another of those fleeting expressions of sadness washes across her face. 'I'm just awful busy for the next few months . . .

I'm going to be shooting a movie with Robert Mitchum next, would you believe, and I have publicity to do for that little comedy I told you about, the one with Betty Grable. And I really need to be sure to spend more time with Joe, because he gets terribly jealous if I'm gallivanting all the time . . .'

'Marilyn, it's fine. I know you have a lot going on.'

'Really? I mean, you'll be OK? Can I lend you any money, or help you find somewhere a little bigger to live . . .? Or you could come and stay in a room near me at the Beverly Hills Hotel? You wouldn't need to worry about the bill or anything – I could handle that.'

My heart melts, a little bit.

'Thank you, Marilyn. And the Beverly Hills Hotel sounds wonderful. But I'm really perfectly OK here. Or rather, I *will* be, once I sort my life out a bit.'

'That's the spirit, honey! I can't tell you how much better *I* feel, now that I'm exactly where I always wanted to be. I mean, sure, I still sometimes feel blue about a lot of stuff . . . but everybody feels that way, right? And once I've finished shooting this next movie, I'm going to take a little time off, take a holiday with Joe, maybe try and see the world a little . . . oh, honey, did you think about what kind of shoe you're gonna wear with the dress?' she adds, meandering off the subject of her near future. 'A cute peep-toe would be perfect, in white or yellow if you have them.'

'No, I don't think I own any white or yellow peep-toes,'

I say, tactfully. 'But I think I might have a nice strappy sandal at the back here somewhere . . .'

I delve to the very back of my tiny wardrobe, rifling through my (mostly black) shoe collection, until I eventually dig out the light tan sandals I'm thinking about.

'What do you think of . . .?'

But she's pulled that disappearing act again. Where she was just occupying a Marilyn-shaped section of hot-pink coloured, Chanel-scented space, now she's left it empty again.

I've no idea whether this means she'll be back, another day, in her *Some Like It Hot* sequin gown, or her *Seven Year Itch* white halterneck dress, or whether I'll ever, in fact, see her again at all.

But there isn't time to dwell, or wonder, or hope. Because I'm not going to add insult to injury by being shamefully late for Olly's all-important opening-night party.

Chapter 15

The sign above the restaurant door says *Nibbles*.
This is what Olly has ended up calling it?

It's . . . not great.

I mean, I know it's a tapas place, so the precise idea *is* that you sit and nibble . . . but still, I sort of had in mind something a bit more exciting than that.

I'm not going to say anything, though; I'm not going to *be* anything other than a hundred per cent positive about the entire evening.

Which, to be fair, I don't think is going to be a very difficult task. It's all looking absolutely terrific. The plate-glass doors are all open on to the street, and there's music filtering out, and there's a (rather pretty) waitress standing by the main entrance with a plate of delicious-looking *arancini*-type things, offering them to interested passers-by. And if this weren't enticing enough, there are all kinds of amazing aromas wafting out: fresh herbs, and grilling meat, and something sweet underlying it all that smells like peaches baking with vanilla . . .

'Welcome to Libby's!' the waitress says.

I must have misheard this; she must have said, *Welcome, Libby.* Though it's a bit of a mystery how she knows my name.

'Sorry!' she goes on, screwing up her face and looking annoyed with herself. 'Welcome to *Nibbles.* The name got changed at the last minute, and I keep saying the wrong one!'

'You mean . . . the name *was* Libby's?'

She nods. 'Right up until this afternoon. Such a last-minute thing, and he had to get the decorator to redo half the sign, and the manager had to run to the copy shop and reprint all the menus . . .' She lowers her voice. 'And don't tell anyone I said so, but I quite liked the name before.'

'Libby's?' I repeat. 'That was what it was?'

'Yeah. I liked that better. Still, Nibbles is good, too. Talking of which, would you like one?'

'Sorry?'

'A nibble! These are deep-fried rice balls, and they're great. Some of them are stuffed with mozzarella, and some of them are filled with fresh peas . . . um . . . I've forgotten which are which, to be honest with you . . .'

'That's OK. I'll have something in a bit.'

'Good plan. Get yourself a drink first, I would. The bar is serving Aperol spritzers, or there's some pretty nice wine being circulated by my lovely colleagues.'

'Wine,' I blurt, clumsily. 'God, yes.'

'Er – right. Well, enjoy!'

It's all a bit of a blur as I walk past her and into the crowded restaurant, and not just because it's filled with noise and people.

Olly *named the restaurant after me?*

And then . . . *un-named* it again?

He must be even angrier with me than I thought.

I can see him, over in the corner near the bar, chatting animatedly to Jesse, his former assistant chef, who is now in charge of all Olly's location catering operations.

Just for a moment, our eyes meet.

He doesn't smile.

He simply waves, mouths a 'Hello', and performs a quick mime that I think means *do you have a drink?*

He doesn't wait for my response before he re-enters his animated conversation with Jesse.

I need to go and talk to him, and apologize, profusely, for not turning up yesterday when I said I would. And then apologize even more profusely for not being around as much as I should have been for moral support these last few months. Apologize, frankly, as much as I need to. Because seriously: how pissed off with me must he have been to . . . remove my name from his restaurant?

I mean, obviously there's the other fact that I'm pretty much astounded he'd even have chosen me to name the restaurant after in the first place . . .

I need to find Nora, somewhere in this crowd, and

see if she knows anything about this. She'll be tricky to locate, being so tiny, but I'm quite sure if I can spot Tash's tall, blonde head, Nora won't be too far behind.

I'm just setting forth through the sea of people, eyes peeled, when I feel a hand on my shoulder.

It's Adam. Yep, my secretly gay ex-boyfriend.

I suppose I should have realized that, as Olly's major investor, he'd probably be invited tonight.

'Adam,' I say.

'Libby!' he replies, with a lot more enthusiasm, and leans in to kiss me on either cheek. 'So good to see you . . . if it really *is* you under that blonde hair?'

'Yes. It's me.'

'Well, it suits you! You look terrific. That dress,' he sketches a hand at the pale yellow sundress I eventually decided to risk wearing, 'is fabulous. And have you lost weight?'

'Thank you, Adam.'

'No, no, I'm not saying you were overweight before . . . you absolutely weren't. Certainly not that I ever noticed, anyway. And before you accuse me of not paying attention, let me just say, Libby, that I always found you very attractive, even though . . .'

'Even though you prefer men?'

'Well, it's not just about *preferring* . . . I mean, I'm not *bi*, if that's what you were wondering. I don't fancy women in the slightest.'

'And yet,' I point out, 'you didn't feel the need to

310

mention that to me at all during the course of our two-month relationship.'

'No.' He looks a bit sheepish. 'I get that I screwed up. But I'm trying to be nice here, Libby. I'm saying that *even though* I don't find women attractive, I always thought that *you* were.'

My head is reeling with all this. 'Are you saying I look like a man?'

'No! Christ, no. I'm just saying . . . look, you have a nice personality, Libby, OK? I found you an appealing person to be around. And just so you know, I really did see us having a future together!'

'As what?' I stare at him. 'A future based on me making myself available for jaunts across the Atlantic whenever you had a family wedding or bar mitzvah to go to, and didn't want to leap out of the closet just yet?'

Adam turns rather pink. 'I wouldn't put it *exactly* like that, Libby, no . . . anyway, I'd have told you the truth eventually.'

'I doubt that. Ben might have, though.'

'Oh, yes, Ben.' Adam looks relieved to be able to latch on to a way out of this uncomfortable conversation and, to be quite honest, I'm perfectly happy to give it to him. 'He mentioned that he'd finally managed to speak to you. I'm telling you, Libby, he really loves your stuff. Wouldn't it be terrific if he does decide to invest in Libby Goes To Hollywood? I mean, I'd just feel really good about bringing the two of you together . . .'

You know what: I can't be angry with him any longer.

For one thing, I'm *not* really angry with him any more. (I'm even, sort of, glad to see him, with his abnormally healthy complexion and his uncomfortable-looking casual wear.) But for another, I don't really have the time to carry on the conversation, because I really, really want to go and find Nora.

'Yes,' I begin, distractedly, 'and it's been good to catch up, but actually, I should go and say hi to . . .'

'Oh, now, *that* is a tall drink of water,' Adam suddenly says, his attention already wandering off me and over my shoulder.

I glance round to see who it is he's talking about.

It's Bogdan, who's just walked in through the door. When he sees me, he raises a huge hand in greeting, and then starts heading our way.

'Isn't he the one who came to cut you out of the gate the other night?' Adam is hissing, in my ear. 'You have to introduce me properly!'

'You're serious?' I stare at him. Then I stare at Bogdan, who's looking, well, unique this evening in (why?) pale orange denim dungarees that have more than just a hint of Guantanamo about them, and a *Keep Calm And Love Harry Styles* T-shirt. 'Adam, you have a boyfriend!'

'I'm not asking you for his inside-leg measurement!' Adam squeaks. 'I'd just like a chat . . . Adam Rosenfeld,' he's saying, extending a hand to Bogdan before I can even say anything. 'We met the other evening. I don't know if you remember . . .?'

'Of course am remembering this. Am not being able to forget.'

'Oh, well, you're very kind . . .'

'Image of Libby with head between iron bars and bum in air is grilling itself on brain for whole of eternity.'

'I think you mean *searing*, Bogdan,' I say. 'But thanks for reminding us all about it, either way.'

'Is no problem,' Bogdan replies, affably. 'Is good to be seeing you again, too,' he tells Adam. 'Am thinking about you a lot since first meeting.'

'What an incredibly sweet thing to say,' Adam breathes. 'And in such an attractive accent, too . . . what *is* that? Russian? Hungarian?'

'Am raining from Moldova.'

'He means hailing,' I translate, starting to feel a bit like one of those simultaneous interpreters at the UN. 'Not raining.'

'Am apologies,' Bogdan hangs his head, humbly, 'for bad English.'

'Don't be ridiculous!' says Adam. 'Your English is a heck of a lot better than my Moldovan!'

'Is nice,' Bogdan says, shooting me a pointed look, 'to hear somebody saying this.'

'I mean, I do speak a few words of Russian; I don't know if that's similar at all . . .?' And to prove a point, Adam drops into rather fluent-sounding Russian, ending whatever it is he's said with a raised eyebrow in Bogdan's direction.

'Am very much liking you to be doing this for me,' says Bogdan.

Which is a little bit worrying (I mean, what has Adam actually *said?*), until Adam turns and heads off towards the bar. So I'm assuming that what Adam was suggesting, in Russian, is that he fetch Bogdan a drink.

'This is very charming gentleman,' Bogdan observes, the moment Adam's out of earshot. 'Is pleasurable treat for me to be treated like king for change.'

'I'm happy for you, Bogdan, but you do remember that he has a boyfriend, don't you?'

'Am not assuming he is giving me measurement of the inner part of thigh,' Bogdan says, rather primly. 'Am just enjoying the conversing.'

'Yes, well, I really need to converse with you, as it happens.' I take a deep breath. 'Did Olly really get you to change the restaurant sign at the last minute? To Nibbles instead of Libby's?'

'Ah.' He nods. 'Yes. This is what Olly is having me to do.'

I feel something sag, somewhere inside me.

'Wow,' I manage to say, after a moment. 'He really must think I'm the shittiest friend in the world.'

'Am not thinking is to do with your shitness as friend, Libby. Is more to do with the snogging of Dillon.'

Hang on . . .

'*My* snogging of Dillon?' I ask, in far too loud a voice, before going on, in a more discreet tone, 'Sorry, how does Olly even *know* about the snogging of . . . about me kissing Dillon?'

'Am here earlier when your sister is calling him . . .'

'When Cass called Olly?' I'm confused. 'Why on earth would she do that?'

'She is letting him know that she is not making it for his big opening night party. She is on speakerphone. She has a bit of the nose of toffee, your sister. Am not sure why she is assuming is big deal whether she is coming to party or not.'

'She is a bit toffee-nosed at times, yes,' I say, 'but her calling to bow out of the party still doesn't explain how—'

'Because she is telling Olly that if you are turning up to the party with Dillon as your date, he must be calling her and letting her know. This would be good reason for her to come to party after all, apparently.'

'With her TV crew in tow,' I murmur, the penny not just dropping, but thwunking down for a crash-landing, 'for a ready-made moment of high drama.'

'And Olly is looking a bit – how am I saying this? – blue in the fins?'

'Green about the gills?'

'This is how he is looking,' Bogdan confirms. 'And he is asking Cass why you would be bringing Dillon to the party when you are breaking up eight months ago. And Cass is telling him—'

'That she has footage of me kissing Dillon from the other night.'

'Something like this. Olly is going outside at this point, so am not being able to drop the eaves any longer.'

Right. Well, this all makes perfect sense, now.

I needn't have worried about adding insult to injury by being late for Olly's party: I've already added plenty of insult to injury by appearing to get involved, again, with the ex that Olly loathed.

Still . . . to actually go to the lengths of taking my name off the restaurant . . .

'Is making me feel bit worried,' Bogdan is going on, 'about Dillon coming to party this evening.'

'Why on earth,' I ask, 'would Dillon be coming to the party this evening?'

'Because I am mentioning this to him.'

'Because you are mentioning *what* to him?' I gaze at Bogdan, ominous dread spreading over me. 'And when? I didn't know you were . . . in touch with Dillon.'

'He is dropping into salon for trim this afternoon,' Bogdan says, rather proudly. 'He is still liking the way am doing his fringe.'

'OK, this all stops, right now.' If I had sleeves, I'd roll them up. 'All this Chinese whispers, and people talking about me behind my back . . . I'm going to go and find Olly and tell him there's nothing going on between me and Dillon, and that actually, it's not really any of his concern whether there's anything going on between me and Dillon . . .' Because he can be as angry as he likes with me about being a rubbish friend: I'll totally accept that. But to extend that same anger to the choices I make in my romantic life . . . now, that doesn't seem completely fair. Does it? 'And while I'm doing that, you're going to *call Dillon right now*,' I shove my phone at him, 'and tell him *under no circumstance* is he to come here tonight.'

(I might be a bit pissed off with Olly for his high-handed disapproval, but I'm not about to have his big night ruined by Dillon swanning in. Not to mention that we're only feet away from a fully stocked professional kitchen, laden with more meat cleavers and cast-iron cookware than you can shake a stick at. I can't let Dillon put himself in that sort of danger.)

'Please,' Bogdan says, in a low voice, as I start to walk away from him, 'be taking your time with Olly. Am wanting opportunity for private chat with Adam . . . and tell him I am being single,' he hisses, realizing I'm about to walk right past Adam on my way to the bar, which is where Olly is still standing. 'And ready to be mingling . . .'

I do nothing of the sort, because I honestly don't think that either Adam or Bogdan need my help matchmaking the two of them tonight, and because I don't want to be remotely complicit in any infidelity that Adam might be about to inflict on my (possible) investor.

When I reach Olly, he's just finished up his conversation with Jesse, and is going behind the bar to grab a couple of bottles of wine that the barman is opening up for him.

I clear my throat. 'Olly.'

He glances over at me. 'Oh, Libby. Hi.'

Not the most prepossessing start, what with him talking in this strange, coolly pleasant manner.

'Everything seems to be going really well!' I say.

'It does, yeah.'

'Great! Um, actually, I wanted to have a quick word with you, Olly . . .'

'Right. Now's not really the time, Libby, to be honest with you.' He holds up the bottles of wine. 'I need to make sure everyone's got plenty of this.'

'Of course. Sorry. I don't want to stop you, I know you're working. It's just . . .'

The first, the most important thing I'd intended to do was offer that massive apology.

But this isn't what comes out of my mouth, as I'd been assuming it would.

'Why are you so angry,' I hear myself asking, 'that I had dinner with Dillon?'

He flinches. It's slight, but visible.

'It doesn't sound,' he says, quietly, 'like it was just dinner.'

'OK, so let's say it wasn't just dinner.' (Where the hell has my planned apology gone? Why am I getting side-tracked by all this ridiculous Dillon stuff, for crying out loud?) 'Let's say it wasn't even just kissing. Let's say I

318

went back to his flat with him and had torrid sex all night . . . I didn't, by the way,' I add, hastily. 'But why do you have to end up so furious with me about it that you . . . take my name off your restaurant?'

He looks right at me, properly, for the first time in this conversation. 'Who told you about . . .? Oh. Bogdan.' He sighs. 'I thought I'd sworn him to secrecy.'

'Olly, this is Bogdan we're talking about. He doesn't do secrecy.'

'He's kept his own bloody sexuality secret from his father for God knows how many years,' Olly says, irritably. 'Though quite *how* he's managed that,' he goes on, gazing over to where Bogdan, in his Harry Styles T-shirt, is coyly sipping wine and letting Adam (oh, for heaven's sake) feel his biceps, 'remains a total mystery to me.'

'Agreed. But that's not what I want to talk about.'

'Fine. But *I* don't want to talk about any of this at all.' Olly puts one of his bottles down on the bar, picks up a clean white napkin and starts to wrap it, expertly, around the bottle to prevent leaks while pouring. 'What you do with Dillon O'Hara is your lookout, Libby.'

'Look. If you're annoyed because you think I should have told you I'd seen him again . . .'

'That's not why I'm annoyed.'

'. . . then you're right. I should have told you. The only reason I didn't is because you've had such a lot on your plate at the moment, and I know how much even the mere mention of him winds you up. And I know

319

you wouldn't have been prepared to hear how much he's changed . . .'

'Bollocks.'

'He has, actually. A lot.'

'Leopards,' says Olly, scathingly, 'don't change their spots.'

'OK, well, I always think that's a ridiculous thing to say.' I'm feeling pretty irritated now myself. 'I mean, it's just pointing out the fucking obvious. You might as well say tigers don't change their stripes, or penguins don't change their beaks, or elephants don't change their trunks . . .'

'They probably do,' mutters Olly, 'if the ones they're wearing need a wash.'

I glare at him. It's not a time for levity.

'My point is that just *randomly observing* that living creatures don't change their essential physical character-istics is no proof at all that people can't change! I mean, if people couldn't change, what would be the point of an organization like Alcoholics Anonymous? What would be the point of people going to therapy . . .?'

'Libby, sweetheart, I wouldn't pull on that thread, if I were you,' says Dillon, who's just strolled over to the bar to join us.

Oh, dear Lord.

If we all come out of this alive, I'm going to kill Bogdan.

'Hope you don't mind the gatecrash, mate,' Dillon goes

on, leaning down to give me a kiss – a rather slow, deliberate one – on the cheek, before reaching over to hand a bottle of whisky to Olly. 'Just something to say congratulations, about the new place.'

'Thank you,' says Olly, accepting the whisky in the sort of way a disgruntled footballer accepts being sent off by the referee.

'It's looking good,' Dillon goes on. 'Nice décor.'

Olly merely grunts.

'Decent-looking paintwork,' Dillon adds, in a tone of deliberately pleasant surprise.

'You know a lot about paintwork, then, do you?'

'Sure do. Worked as an apprentice to a painter and decorator for two summers when I was a lad.'

'Well, the decorating world's loss is the acting world's gain—'

'OK!' I interrupt, brightly, all ready to lead Dillon firmly away from the bar and out of the restaurant (and, ideally, as far from Clapham as he'll let me take him), but he's rooted to the spot.

'So what did you use on these walls, then?' he asks. 'Looks like that overpriced slop from Farrow and Ball. What's this one called? Dowager's Tipple? Weasel's Belch?'

'It's Dulux, actually,' Olly says. 'Jasmine White.'

'This is never Jasmine White,' Dillon scoffs. 'I did a whole house in Jasmine White back in Clondalkin. Jasmine White's got a more buttery undertone. This is Natural Calico, not a shadow of a doubt.'

'It's Jasmine White.'

'I'm telling you, mate, it's Natural Calico. Less creamy, more peachy.'

'It isn't peachy.'

'Apricoty, then.'

'*Or* apricoty.'

'Jesus, mate, have you never seen the colour of an apricot?'

'There's more than one sort,' Olly says, 'of fucking apricot.'

Oh, God. Here we go.

'Have *you* never seen a Moorpark apricot?' Olly goes on, eyeballing Dillon as if his life depends on it. 'They're fucking *green*. Or the Red Velvet apricot . . .'

'OK, well now you're just making up apricots.'

'. . . which is the colour of a fucking plum.' Olly shoves a hand in his pocket and pulls out his phone. 'I'll Google it for you,' he says, stabbing at his phone screen, 'and then you can cast your expert painter-decorator's eye over my walls again, and tell me they're apricot coloured.'

'Hey, look, it's no skin off my nose what fucking colour walls you have.' Dillon's smile has faded. 'You can paint them in all the colours of the fucking green-grocer's, for all I care—'

'Dillon, look,' I say, stepping in front of him before the apricot paint wars start to become physical. 'Maybe it's a better idea for you to head off and get a drink somewhere else . . .'

322

'He can't have a *drink*,' Olly observes, savagely, 'he's a *recovering alcoholic*.'

'Better a recovering alcoholic,' Dillon says, 'than a smug, self-satisfied, apricot-obsessed . . .'

And now, all of a sudden, Tash appears, like a good fairy in a fairy tale, all blondeness and good health and looking lovely in (damn her) exactly the sort of all-black outfit I'd have probably felt more comfortable in if I'd worn it tonight: a black cotton broderie anglaise sundress, with her hair in two annoyingly cute farm-girl braids.

She puts a hand on Olly's shoulder.

This is it. This is all she does.

But I can see, immediately, what it does to Olly.

He cools down.

And then he gives Tash a brief touch of his own: just one hand, cupping the small of her back.

It feels like the temperature, just around me, has dropped by about fifteen degrees. While over in the Tash and Olly corner, it's pleasant weather: idyllic, in fact.

I may not know much about relationships. I may not even know much about men in general.

But I know Olly.

Something has started to happen between him and Tash. It's as clear as day.

'Everything OK?' she asks him.

'Everything's fine,' Olly tells her.

'I'm Tash,' she goes on, in her smiley, confident way,

extending a hand to Dillon. 'And don't worry, I know who you are, I've seen you in loads of stuff on TV!'

'Don't stoke his ego any more than he already does himself,' I mutter, as I grasp Dillon firmly by the elbow and finally – *finally* – succeed in manoeuvring him away from the bar, through the throng, and out on to the street.

'What the *fuck*,' I say, 'are you doing here?'

Dillon opens his mouth.

'And don't give me some crap,' I go on, 'about Bogdan mentioning the party and you *just thinking* it might be lovely to pop along and give your old pal Olly a nice bottle of whisky you can't drink any more.'

'Who says he's not my old pal?'

'*Everyone on the entire planet.* Especially if they'd just heard the two of you bickering like schoolboys over shades of apricot, for Christ's sake. And *were* you ever a painter and decorator in Clondalkin, by the way, or is this just another of your many fantasies about your old life back there?'

'Hey.' He's serious again, now, in the blink of an eyelid. 'I don't lie, Libby. I never lie. Not about stuff that matters.'

'Oh, so deliberately coming all the way here to wind up Olly doesn't *matter*?'

'That's not why I came here. I came to see you.'

'You could have called and asked me to meet you after the party.'

'I didn't want to wait until after the party.' He reaches

out a hand and touches my face, with a hand that feels light as a feather. 'I wanted to see you now.'

'Dillon . . .' I take a small step away. A very, very small step. OK: so small a step that his hand is still touching my cheek. But still. It's the principle of the thing. 'We agreed we couldn't make it work between us.'

'You said that. I never agreed it.'

'Point taken.'

'Great. Now all I have to do is persuade you to be.'

I blink at him. 'Me to be what?'

'Taken.'

The pavement feels as if it actually just shifted under me. Which could mean that Clapham has just been the epicentre of a small earthquake. But, more likely, means that Dillon, and my all-consuming, unstoppable desire for him, has just made my legs turn to trifle again.

'Can I hope that your silence,' Dillon says, with one of his most devilish grins, 'means that you're at least thinking about it?' He lowers his voice. 'And the fact you've turned shocking pink and look as if you're about to expire . . .?'

'No.' Arrogant bastard. I swallow, very hard indeed. 'Or rather, yes, OK? I am thinking about it. But thinking doesn't have to equate to doing. Now,' I go on, 'I need to go back inside and apologize to Olly, on your behalf, for all that apricot nonsense a few minutes ago.'

And, way more important even than that, I need to go and make that hugely important apology I got sidetracked out of doing earlier. If I can get Olly alone for a moment to do so. If I can disentangle him from Tash . . .

'I don't think Olly gives two shits right now whether you apologize to him or not.' Dillon pulls his hand away from my face. 'Or didn't you notice that he and Blondie are seriously into each other?'

So Dillon spotted it too.

'Anyway, I'll get out of your hair,' he goes on. 'Get a cab home. I'm sorry I can't persuade you that my intentions towards you are . . . well, not honourable, obviously. I can't possibly claim that. But they're genuine. And I'm sorry, Libby, but where you're concerned, I just can't help myself. I'll never be able to help myself.'

He turns away and starts to walk in the direction of Clapham High Street.

And I turn the other way and – on legs that are still pretty trifle-like – head back into the restaurant.

Olly and Tash are still standing over by the bar.

They're talking, and smiling. Their heads are very, very close together; her hands are resting on his arms; one of his hands is resting on her waist.

I think it's best if I just leave them to it.

Best, in fact, if I just leave the party altogether.

Though what part of me it is that thinks it's also best to leg it out of the front door, out on to the street and after the retreating back of Dillon in such a hurry . . .

The stupid primitive part, I'll wager.

I catch up with Dillon just as he reaches the corner with the High Street, and holds his arm out for an oncoming taxi. When I reach for his other hand, he turns round.

'Fire Girl,' he says, looking surprised for a moment. 'I thought you said . . .'

The taxi's not even pulled up to the pavement before we start kissing.

Chapter 16

So I'm here. Back where it all started.
Dillon's flat.

To be, in fact, more specific, Dillon's bed.

But things haven't moved quite as fast as all *that*, OK? We're both still fully clothed.

Well, *I'm* still fully clothed. Dillon has just this very minute pulled off his T-shirt, and is now displaying an upper body even more impressively defined than I remember.

'Rehab,' he says, when he catches me looking.

'Sorry?'

'Responsible for this.' He gestures down at his abdominal muscles. 'When you give up drinking, and you can't have sex, and all there is to do all day is sit around gazing at your navel, there's quite a lot of time – and incentive – to make sure it's an extremely attractive navel.'

'Oh, right, of course.'

'And talking of extremely attractive navels . . .'

He lies back down on top of the duvet and pulls me towards him.

Which just goes to show that love – or lust, or whatever it is he's feeling for me at the moment – really *is* blind, and with an appalling memory, because my navel *isn't* what anyone would call extremely attractive. At best, on a very, very good day, and by nice, dim candlelight, it can be described as serviceable.

'And I'm absolutely loving this dress,' he murmurs, nuzzling into my neck and using the fingers of one hand to touch, gently, the halterneck strap and the skin underneath it. 'What with the blonde hair, it makes you look a bit like Marilyn Monroe.'

'Oh, trust me, I don't look anything like Marilyn Monroe.'

'You're right,' he says. 'You're even more gorgeous.'

I'd point out that this is even more inaccurate than his compliments about my belly button, but there's no opportunity to say anything at all. He rolls sideways, pulling me with him, so that I end up lying on top of him, his arms around me, as he starts to kiss me again. His hands are in my hair, and his body feels warm against mine, and it's all just as incredibly wonderful as it was the first time we did this, and the last time we did this, and all the times in between.

So it makes no sense whatsoever that I suddenly roll away, lie on my back and stare at the ceiling for a moment, and then say, 'So *you* think Tash and Olly are into each other, too?'

'What?'

'You said something earlier, outside the restaurant . . . I'm just asking if you definitely think Tash and Olly like each other.'

'Uh . . . is this really the time to be talking about other couples, Libby?' Dillon rolls over to face me and props himself up on his elbow. 'I mean, far be it from me to quash any desires of yours, if that's what's tickling your fancy . . . I can nip out and get a nice big goldfish bowl in the morning, we can all chuck our keys in it and re-enact something that might have happened in the suburbs in the Seventies . . .'

'You think they're actually a *couple?* Already?'

'Because that was the most shocking aspect of what I just said,' Dillon observes. 'Of course.'

'Well, obviously you were joking about the wife-swapping . . .'

'I never joke,' he says, 'about wife-swapping.'

'. . . but you didn't seem to be joking when you called them a couple.'

'Yes. No. I don't know . . . Look, Libby, in all serious-ness, can we just get back to what we were doing?' He edges closer, puts an arm around my waist and fixes his eyes on mine. 'I mean, you're driving me insane, Fire Girl. I can't think about anything else but you. Your gorgeous, soft body, and how great you are in bed, and your goofy smile when you wake up next to me in the morning . . . I haven't slept a wink the last few nights, thinking about it all, and all the stuff I want to do with you, and to you, and adjacent to you . . .'

'And perpendicular?' I ask, with a smile, because I sense we're both trying to find our way back to the flirtatious banter we were engaged in before I brought up the topic of Olly.

'Oh, Christ, yes.' He lets out a theatrical groan. 'Perpendicular. Please, please, Libby, don't deny me the pleasure of doing anything perpendicular.'

'I won't,' I say.

And we start to kiss again.

Until I pull back, a moment later.

'When you say you *can't think about anything else* but me . . .?'

'Oh, Jesus.' He rolls onto his back. 'You're not going to make this easy, are you?'

'I just think that's something we should talk about.'

'You think the cure for me not being able to think about anything else but you is to *talk* about it?' He stares at me, deadpan. 'It's like being in a therapy session all over again. Only with a really hot therapist. That I can't keep my hands off.' He thinks about this for a moment. 'In fact, if you were up for any role-play . . .'

'Not right now.'

'. . . I could be the lapsed drunk . . .'

'Because that's really sexy.'

'. . . and you could be the head of the Institute of

Really Hot Therapists . . . where they all wear mind-blowingly sexy uniforms, with, like, really small white doctors' coats, and heels, and nothing underneath . . .'

'Wouldn't be terribly practical, for a therapy session.'

'Ah, well, that might depend on the sort of therapy the Institute of Really Hot Therapists offered . . .'

'Dillon. Come on. Don't you think it's even a *little* bit important that within hours of coming out of rehab, never planning to touch a drink or a drug again in your life, you're suddenly . . . fixating on our relationship?'

'Who says I'm fixating?'

'You! You said you can't think about anything else!'

'It's a figure of speech.' But he's frowning, and not meeting my eye any more. 'And I don't appreciate the amateur psychoanalysis.'

'Fair enough. But I don't appreciate being used as some sort of a crutch. If that's what you're doing.'

'I'm not just using you for your crotch . . .'

'Very funny.'

'. . . and I don't know how many times I have to tell you this, Libby. I want to give us another chance. Not because I'm using you to replace the drink or the drugs. Just because I prefer my life when you're in it. Is that such a bizarre thing?'

'It is, actually. I mean, you're pretty much the only one who does.'

'The only one who does what?'

'Prefers their life with me in it.' I laugh, to take the

edge off what I've just said, but this is a mistake, because the laugh just comes out sounding a bit embittered. 'Nobody else I know feels that way about me, Dillon, OK, so it's just a little hard to believe that you might.'

'You're kidding me, right?'

'No.' I can feel a wave of self-pity wash over me. It's not a feeling I care to indulge at any time, in any place, so it's certainly a bad idea to give into it here, when there are so many better things I could be doing. So I'm really pissed off with myself when I hear myself blurting out, 'I mean, obviously I've always been peripheral to my family, but I never thought I'd end up screwing up so much I'd be peripheral to my oldest friends, too.'

'What on God's green earth,' Dillon asks, 'are you talking about?'

'Well, there's Nora,' I tell him, 'who's slowly but surely replacing me with a shinier, newer, better-all-round best friend . . . and then there's . . .' My voice catches in my throat. 'Olly.'

'Who's finally put down the torch he's been holding for you for the past decade and a half and settled for a replacement instead.' Dillon makes a scoffing noise. 'Come on, Libby. You can't honestly claim you'll ever be peripheral to Olly.'

I stare across the bed at him.

'Why are you looking at me like that?' he asks. 'Are you about to claim you didn't *know* he's head over heels in love with you?'

333

I open my mouth. No sound comes out.

'Oh, Jesus.' Dillon half sits up, looking dismayed. 'You *didn't* know he's head over heels in love with you.'

I'm immobile.

I mean, it's possible that I've just turned into one of those iPhone emojis that are only capable of one facial expression at a time.

'Shit,' says Dillon. 'I just thought . . . well, I thought you just didn't like to openly talk about it. I didn't think . . . I mean, I honestly didn't think you wouldn't know.'

'I . . . but . . . Tash.' I manage to utter three syllables. 'He likes *her*.'

'Yeah, I'm not really in a position to discuss anything else going on in Olly Walker's life right now . . . but if he does like her, I'm pretty sure that's only because he's just got sick of waiting for you.'

Talking of sick . . . I have to hunch myself up into a sitting position at the side of the bed, doubled over, just in case the nausea welling inside me accidentally spills outside me instead.

Is this actually happening? Is Dillon even *right* about this? That all these years – closer to two decades, in fact, than one – Olly has been harbouring these . . . *feelings* for me?

My mind is racing, giddily, back to the Mistaken Thing that happened between us in Paris, many years ago, when we suddenly found ourselves in the middle of a drunken kiss as we sat in a bar on the Left Bank. Olly had been telling me about some girl he was in love with, some girl I just assumed – and he didn't correct me – was an old friend of his from college, and he was looking so vulnerable, and it was such an intense discussion that it felt only right and natural that I lean in as he leaned in—

'Hey . . .' Dillon jumps up and comes round to squat beside me. 'Don't throw up. Much as I'd like to think that someone hearing Olly Walker is in love with them is the sort of news worthy of vomit, I've got my posh bed linen to think about.'

He grins at me, his handsome face displaying kindness and frustration in equal measure. 'I honestly,' he says, softly, 'didn't know you didn't know.'

'But . . . do other people? Know about this, I mean?'

'You mean, is everybody who knows you and Olly aware of the unrequited passion he's nursed all these years? Well, I can't speak for all of them, given that I don't *know* that many of them . . .'

'Nora,' I say. 'Nora must know.'

'. . . but yes, I'd have to assume Nora knows. And Bogdan certainly knows. I mean, why do you think I even came to that party in the first place? Bogdan was the one who told me that Olly was planning on saying something to you tonight.'

'*Saying something?*'

'Yes. You were going to turn up to find the restaurant

named after you and then he was going to take you off somewhere quiet and tell you he can't live without you, or hire a fucking violin quartet to serenade you while he warbled "I Will Always Love You", or dig William fucking Shakespeare up from his grave to write a sonnet about your eyes . . . I don't know exactly what he was planning, the tosser, but tonight was going to be the night.'

'Then what happened?' I gaze at Dillon, but rather blindly. I think I might actually be seeing Olly's face superimposed on his, for a moment or two. 'All these years, and he just chucks in the towel at the eleventh hour?'

'That's Olly Walker for you. No balls.' Then Dillon peers at me. 'You don't . . . *mind*, do you? I mean, the fact that he chucked in the towel – that bothers you?'

'Well, of course it fucking bothers me!'

'Because you like him.'

'Yes, I like him, Dillon, he's my oldest—'

'You like him,' Dillon repeats. It's a statement, not a question. 'Not in an oldest friend way. In the same way he likes you.'

'How can I possibly know that?' I say. 'I've had precisely three minutes to get used to the information that he's wildly in love with me. Not seventeen years. I don't know if I like him or not! I mean, I actually really *don't* like him very much just now, to be perfectly frank . . .'

'Here,' says Dillon, reaching behind me and grabbing the shirt he discarded when we first got up to the bedroom. He dabs my eyes with it, which is the first time I realize – though I couldn't say why – I'm crying. 'And keep going with that last bit,' he goes on, 'you know, about how you don't like him. I was enjoying that part. More of that, please.'

I blink at him, making more tears spill out on to my cheeks as I do so. 'Is that why he hates you so much?' I sniff. 'Not because he thinks you're a bit of a toe-rag, but because of . . . me?'

'Oh, I'm quite sure he thinks I'm a toe-rag, too.' Dillon grins at me. 'And it's a tiny bit the reason I can't stand the sight of him, either. It's nothing personal to him, in one sense. I just really don't like having competition.'

Despite everything I'm trying to process through my addled synapses at the moment, something is suddenly dawning on me.

'Dillon. Be completely honest with me.' I dab away what I hope is the last of the tears. 'Actually, be completely honest with yourself. Are you only as obsessed with me as you currently claim you are because you know some-body else likes me too?'

'Hey! Five minutes ago it was because I'm a hopeless addict.'

'I'm not saying it's not because of that, too.'

'Well, you're wrong. On both counts.' He looks a bit sheepish, though. 'I mean, I won't deny I'm the jealous type. And obviously it's a bit of a motivator when suddenly you have all these men dropping like flies at your feet, Libby . . . nobody could notice that and *not* want to step up their game . . .'

'Oh, Dillon.'

'But I'd still like you just as much as I do even if it weren't for the Olly Walkers and the Jamie Cadwalladrs and the gooey-eyed waiters. They just pile on a bit of pressure, that's all. Because I want to make sure I'm the one who . . .' He stops himself.

'Wins?' I ask.

'All right,' he says. 'Maybe.'

'So maybe you're not so much addicted to me as addicted to the chase.'

He doesn't say anything for a moment.

This being Dillon, of course, who seems to have a ready quip for every occasion, his silence speaks volumes.

Then he says, 'You know what I really want right now? More than anything?'

'Oh, God, Dillon,' I say, 'I don't think we should do that now.'

'Well, I don't know what you had in mind, but I was just going to suggest that I put the kettle on and we can have a nice cup of tea.'

'Tea?' His niceness is making me feel tearful again. 'But . . . I thought you wanted to have sex.'

'Libby. I may have done some depraved things in my time. But I've never had sex with a crying woman. Well,'

– he thinks about this for a moment – 'not one who was crying because she was *upset*. I have had the occasional instance, halfway through the act, where women just break down and sob in sheer awe. A bit like when you see the Grand Canyon for the first time, or Victoria Falls.'

I laugh. It's shaky, but it's a laugh.

He gets to his feet and holds out a hand. 'So, come on, darling. Let's get that kettle on. If you're really lucky, I might even be able to unearth a Jaffa cake or two. And we can have a bit of a chat.'

'About what to do about Olly?' I gulp.

'Well, let's not push it. But I'll happily talk a load of crap to you all night to keep your mind off what to do about Olly . . .? And if you've a better offer than that tonight, sweetheart, I don't know what it is.'

Chapter 17

So I ended up spending the night at Dillon's.

It was well after two in the morning by the time we'd finished our endless pots of tea and seen off more than one packet of Jaffa cakes, so it didn't make sense to head home at that hour. And while we drank tea, and ate biscuits, he kept me expertly distracted with amusing anecdotes about rehab, and about his family ... oh, and then we spent a good hour or two cosily settled in front of property websites on his iPad, at first trawling through to find a suitable new place for him to move to (a clean break from his old surroundings, as advised by his therapist), and then gorging ourselves on ever-more ludicrous fantasy houses, from twelve-bedroom townhouses in Knightsbridge to sprawling country piles where Dillon can cast himself as some sort of lord of the manor. By the end of the night, he'd 'decided' on a thousand-acre estate, complete with Palladian mansion, in rural Wiltshire, for the bargain price of sixteen million quid.

'Well, if you won't succumb to my advances, Libby,' he said, 'I may as well devote myself to the rural life. Breed horses. Shear sheep. Husband chickens. Or, if all that proves a bit too much like hard work, I could just drive around my land in a muddy Land Rover, making eyes at comely peasant girls and inviting them back to the nearest haystack for a good old-fashioned romp.'

Which made me ask if his impression of English country life had been *entirely* formed by sneaking glimpses of someone's mum's Mills and Boon collection during his impressionable years. Which led to a discussion of our respective teenage years, which led – somehow – to him bringing up the very thing he'd sworn he wasn't going to bring up: Olly.

'Look,' Dillon said, as he put on the kettle for the final time, and dug deep into the packet of Jaffa cakes for the last two, 'I know it's weirded you out, finding out this thing about your oldest friend being in love with you since you were both in short trousers. Or whenever it was you first met. But all I'll say on the subject, my dearest Fire Girl, is this: if you really are tired of feeling . . . what was the word you used earlier? *Peripheral?* Well, if you're really tired of that, then you could probably do a hell of a lot worse than to think about giving Olly Walker what he's always wanted. Because I don't think you've ever been remotely peripheral to him. The wanker,' he added, unable to prevent himself.

And about half an hour later, we went to sleep. Me in his big bed, and him downstairs on the sofa.

He was lovely.

He *is* lovely. Screwed-up, and unpredictable, and way more pleased with himself than anyone deserves to be, yes. But lovely.

If it weren't for the fact that getting back into a relationship with him would be like a chicken (one of the one's he's planning on husbanding, perhaps) getting into a relationship with a particularly dangerous fox, I'd probably do it like a shot.

Oh, and then there's the Olly thing, obviously.

Which, now that it's a brand-new day, and the shock of it all has subsided, is starting to seem . . .

Who am I kidding? It's not starting to seem any different at all. Not yet.

If anything, the brand-new day has just made the whole thing seem even more huge and impossible.

Because now that I'm out and about in the world again, jostling my way back home on the tube and inhaling the noxious fumes of Colliers Wood High Street, it's actually feeling *real*.

And ever since I woke up this morning (to diabolical coffee and badly singed toast; Dillon may be adorable but he's a shocking cook), I haven't been able to stop playing everything over in my mind.

Re-playing it, more accurately: replaying moment after moment in Olly's company these past seventeen years:

the first time we met, in the inauspicious surroundings of the top tier at the New Wimbledon Theatre; the first time we went out for the evening, with Nora, when they both talked nineteen to the dozen about their plans for their futures and I sat there, revelling, for once, in finding people who seemed to really like me; the first time we went out for an evening *without* Nora, to see *Bringing Up Baby* (my choice) at the Prince Charles cinema in Leicester Square, followed by *The Mummy Returns* (his choice) at the Odeon around the corner; the time when I surprised him with a homemade cake the day he graduated from catering college, and then had to spend the next three days hanging out with him at his student digs because I'd accidentally used seriously out-of-date eggs in the cake and given him a nasty dose of food poisoning . . .

All these times, and he was harbouring this burning desire for me all along? While I teased him about his taste in films, and proffered toxic baking?

And then there are all the more recent times, after we'd left behind those easy teenage years, and made our way into adulthood. The dinners he's cooked for me, while we sat around his kitchen table, putting the world to rights. The practical help he's always been there to offer, from lugging my furniture up endless flights of stairs when I moved into my flat, to hanging on the end of the phone to the British Embassy in Washington for hours, trying to work out if it might be possible to fly me home (with a ticket he was going to pay for) from hurricane-hit Miami. Coming all the way up to Scotland with me, at a time when he's been busier than he's ever been in his life, to offer me moral support at Dad's wedding.

I mean, here I was thinking he was doing all these things in the spirit of a big brother. It's a total head-spin to realize he was doing them in the spirit of someone with distinctly un-brotherly thoughts instead.

Such a head-spin that I can't even begin to work out how, in the light of all this brand-new knowledge, I feel about him.

Though there is one thing that keeps popping into my head. One more thing that I'm replaying even more obsessively than all the memories I've just told you about.

That kiss, in Paris. That lovely kiss, so comfortable and natural and – more surprisingly – heart-stoppingly erotic. Our Mistaken Thing, which we've never spoken about, never even alluded to, ever since.

Which might not, it appears, have been quite such a Mistaken Thing after all.

I stop in at the little coffee takeout place right outside the tube stop for a decent-ish coffee to clear my head, and I'm just approaching my building when I see a by-now familiar-looking motorbike pulling up on the pavement outside.

It's Tash, with the tiny figure of Nora riding pillion.

I'd forgotten that Nora said she was going to come

over and pick up Grandmother's veil before she heads to Gatwick.

While I'd actually like nothing more, right now, than to sit down and have the biggest heart-to-heart with Nora that I've ever had, it's not going to be quite as easy with Tash present at the same time.

Especially not if Tash really is on the verge of something with Olly, the way it looked last night.

'Nora!' I say, trying to sound normal, as she gets off the back of the bike and pulls off her helmet. 'Sorry, I was just . . . grabbing a coffee.' I think this is enough of an explanation; I don't need to add that the main reason I'm grabbing a coffee is because I was on my way back from the tube station, having just been served a spectacularly undrinkable one by Dillon, at his flat.

'So, did you stay over at Dillon's last night?' Nora demands.

Which pretty much undoes my attempt to keep the whole staying-over-at-Dillon's thing on the down-low.

'Mmmm, coffee,' says Tash, who's just taken off her own helmet, and looks as if she wishes she'd left it on. She gets off the bike. 'I might go and grab myself one of those,' she adds, in her nice, helpful, spectacularly irritating oil-on-troubled-waters way. 'Keep me fresh for the ride out to Gatwick. Anything for you, Nor?'

'No. Actually, yes. I'll have a black coffee.'

'Decaf?'

'No,' Nora practically barks. 'Regular.'

'Right,' Tash says. 'It's just that, strictly speaking, you have already had a coffee this morning, and from the point of view of a neo-natologist—'

'Tash, please, just get me a bloody coffee.' Nora looks a bit desperate. 'I've only drunk one small coffee a day for weeks. I haven't let so much as a millilitre of alcohol past my lips. I'm avoiding my usual lunch of Pret sushi like it's radioactive waste. Can I just have a day where I drink a solitary extra coffee without feeling like I'm drip-feeding my unborn child nothing but McDonald's chicken nuggets and crack cocaine?'

Tash looks marginally peeved, but she hides it well. 'One regular black coffee, coming up,' she says, before adding, meaningfully, 'It'll probably take me a few minutes.'

'I think she's giving us a bit of privacy,' I say, as Tash sets off, long legs striding as purposefully along Colliers Wood High Street as if she were setting off from base camp on K2.

'Yes. Because she knows how pissed off I am with you.'

'How pissed off *you* are with *me?*'

'*Dillon*, Libby. *Dillon*. And you didn't even *say* anything.'

So Olly's obviously told her, by now, about the video footage.

I can feel my hackles rising, defensively.

'OK, well, if we're talking about people not saying anything about really important stuff . . .'

'Can we leave the baby out of it?' she asks, putting a hand on her stomach. 'I've already explained why I didn't tell you over the phone.'

'I'm not talking about the baby.' I take a deep breath. 'I'm talking about your brother.'

Just for a moment, Nora's eyes widen.

Then she says, too casually, 'Jack?'

'Yes, Nora. Jack's the brother I'm talking about. The forty-three-year-old with the wife and three children in Andover, who I haven't seen hide nor hair of since your parents' ruby wedding anniversary party eight years ago.'

'So, Olly, then?'

'Yes. Olly, then.'

We stand in silence for a moment, a Mexican standoff on Colliers Wood High Street.

Because Nora knows what I'm talking about; the expression on her face tells me that she's worked out the reason for the expression on *my* face. You can't be best friends for seventeen years without developing that kind of emotional shorthand somewhere along the way.

'All this time,' I say, being the first to back down from our standoff, 'and you never found the right moment to say anything?'

'Libby . . .'

'All those nights out, and hungover Sundays in, and the holidays in Greece, and Ibiza, and St Tropez, and backpacking in Vietnam, and that week you took off work to look after me when I had shingles . . .' I make myself stop just randomly listing all the occasions, big and small, that we've spent time together over the past two decades, because we'll be here long after Tash comes back with those coffees otherwise. 'And then I ended up learning that Olly's in love with me from *Dillon O'Hara*, of all people?'

'Dillon told you?' Nora looks astonished. 'When you were with him last night?'

'Yes, look, just for the record, I wasn't *with* Dillon last night. And I only left with him because—'

'He shouldn't have even been there,' Nora says, abruptly. 'Not on Olly's big night.'

'Yes. I know that. You can thank Bogdan for that.'

'OK, but Bogdan didn't leave with him, did he? And Bogdan didn't break my brother's heart by getting back together with Dillon and leaving him to find out from your sister, of all people.'

'How the hell was I supposed to know I was breaking his heart?' I demand, raising my voice for the first time in this conversation, 'when even my best friend didn't think to mention that her brother felt that way about me?'

'All right. Maybe I should have said something. But you should have noticed, Libby. It was staring you in the bloody face! You just weren't paying attention.'

OK, now I want this to stop. It's in danger of getting out of hand, things being said that can't be unsaid.

But Nora clearly doesn't feel this way. Maybe it's hormones; maybe it's just the result of years of frustration building up in her. Whatever the reason, she's not stopping.

'I mean, you've always ignored the fact that he worshipped the ground you walked on. You're always looking for something shiny, and new, and better. It's like you don't think Olly is good enough for you, or something . . .'

'Are you kidding?' I stare at her. 'I've never thought Olly wasn't good enough for me! If anything, the reason I've not noticed is because I've always assumed he was *far too* good for me!'

'He's not far too good for you: you're fucking *perfect* for each other. And just when he'd finally decided he couldn't carry on like this, you choose the moment to stamp all over his heart by parading Dillon O'Hara around the place!'

'Will you listen to yourself for a moment? It's not like I *cheated* on Olly, or anything! And as for him finally deciding he was going to say something, well, if it really was that big a moment for him, why the hell did he back away so easily at the last moment? Take my name off the restaurant? Start making doe-eyes at Tash?'

'Because when he heard about you and Dillon getting back together, he finally realized.'

'Finally realized *what?*'

'That there's always going to be a Dillon. That you're addicted to the romance. Hooked on the fairy-tale ending.'

The words *fairy tale* make me think, quite suddenly, of Marilyn.

But I'm not as lost as her, am I? Not quite so obsessed with escaping reality?

'That what he has to offer you,' Nora goes on, 'is never going to be able to outweigh that.'

'But that's . . . ridiculous. How could he even know, if he never tried?'

Nora doesn't answer this. She's looking upset as she says, 'You didn't see him right before the party, Libby. When he told me you'd started seeing Dillon again. He was broken. And it takes quite a lot to break Olly.'

This hurts so much that I say, harshly, 'He didn't look all that broken when he was cosying up to Tash a couple of hours later.'

'Oh, Libby. Come on. A drowning man will reach out to grab anything he thinks is going to keep him afloat. Besides, Tash is a breath of fresh air. She'd be good for him, after all this time. He needs to stop putting his life on hold for you, and move on. He needs a girlfriend . . . actually, no, not my brother: he needs a *wife*. And children, and a life . . . A life that doesn't just revolve around waiting for you to stop messing around with whatever dream hunk you've set your sights on, and notice the man who's always – *always* – been there for you.'

I can see Tash coming back along the street towards us with two cups of coffee.

Which is both bad timing (because I don't want her

walking in on a very private quarrel) and great timing (because I want an end to this very private quarrel).

'I'll go and get the veil,' I mumble, turning on my heel and heading for the door, 'if you even still want it, that is.'

'Well, of course I want it,' Nora says, in a hopeless sort of voice, with a hint of tears behind it. 'You're still *family*, for God's sake, Libby.'

I ignore this, because it's giving me a lump in my own throat, and set off up the stairs to my flat while they wait with their coffee on the street below.

When I open my door, I can see immediately that there isn't any sign of Marilyn: mink-clad, pink-clad, or otherwise.

There is only the very, very faintest lingering whiff of Chanel No. 5.

Just when I could have really done with having Marilyn around. Just when I would have appreciated her take, however left-field, or pre-feminist, or just plain kooky, on the brand-new situation with Olly. Just when I really needed a friend.

But there's no time to stand around here feeling sorry for myself, because I need to take Grandmother's veil down to Nora, so that she and Tash can ride off on that motorbike together and get her to her flight on time.

I go to the drawers beneath my wardrobe, where I put the veil after I brought it back from Dad's wedding, and lift it out. It's still packed in its flat box, carefully folded in its layers of tissue, so – for ease of transport in Nora's large rucksack – I take it out of the box, still in the tissue, and then head off down the stairs again to hand it over.

Nora, when I open the door on to the street, is looking a bit tearful. She and Tash have already got back on the bike, and they're both sipping their coffee in silence.

'Here.' I walk up to them and hold out the tissue-wrapped veil. 'Have a look, if you like.'

Nora peels back a section of the tissue to reveal the ivory lace loveliness within.

'Oh, Libby,' she says, in a wobbly voice.

'It's even nicer than that when you fold it all out.'

She hands her coffee to Tash – who places it, and her own, ready for travel in the rather nifty cup-holder either side of the handlebars – and then turns round so her rucksack is facing me.

'I think it's best if you put it in. I don't want to damage it in any way. I mean, it might get a bit crumpled in there . . .'

'Crumpled isn't a problem. You can get the crumples out with a delicate steam when you get home.'

Then I busy myself opening up her backpack, folding the veil down inside, and then zipping the backpack up as far as it will go: there's a final inch of zip that won't close, because it's full to bursting, but the veil is safely packed down in there nevertheless.

'It'll look great on you, Nora,' I say, sounding

awkwardly polite. 'But obviously, you know, let me know if you'd like me to make anything special for you to wear with it . . . a simple little tiara, or some special jewelled grips, or something . . .'

'I will. Thank you, Libby.' She turns, briefly, and squeezes my hand, which is still on top of her backpack. 'I'll . . . well, I'll call you when I get home, shall I?'

'Only when you get the chance.'

'Of course.'

And then Tash turns on the engine, and she and Nora both put on their helmets, and a moment later the bike pulls off, slowly, into the traffic.

It's about two seconds later that I realize: I still seem to be holding Grandmother's veil, which is unravelling from inside the backpack at an alarming speed.

Except that I'm *not* holding it – I mean, it's not in my hands – so I don't understand . . .

Oh, God. Marilyn's bracelet.

The lace is caught on Marilyn's bracelet.

Just as I have time to think that *all Marilyn Monroe-related jewellery should come with some sort of health warning*, I realize that there's a second problem: the other end of the veil is still inside Nora's bag.

I don't know if the intricate, fine-threaded lace is caught on something else at that end – the zip, perhaps, or a brush or comb inside the bag itself – but there's no time to discover this one way or the other, because if I don't want Grandmother's precious, priceless veil to end up in two tattered pieces, I need to start jogging.

'Nora!' I yell, as I start to jog and then, pretty quickly, to *run*, at a fair old pace, along the pavement behind them. 'Tash!'

But with their helmets on, and with the rumble of traffic on the High Street, they obviously can't hear me.

Thank God, the bike is only doing about six or seven miles an hour right now, because Tash is trundling at a relatively slow pace – slow for a bike, that is; it's *bloody* fast for me – in the clogged-up traffic of the High Street. If I can't get to her before the traffic eases, and she speeds up, I'm either going to have to turn into a human version of the Roadrunner (legs cycling wildly and reaching a land-speed record that would astound my old gym teachers and anyone who's ever known me) just to keep a crucial degree of slack in the veil, or I'm going to risk horrible injury as the bike speeds off, taking half of Grandmother's veil and – possibly – my arm with it.

Oddly enough, the thing that's concerning me more than hideous arm-wrenched-from-socket injury is the *half of Grandmother's veil* aspect.

I can't let it rip into two, complete with my arm on one end or not. Not only because it's a family heirloom. Not only because it's so very beautiful. Not only because I'm slightly scared of Grandmother's reaction when she finds out. But for another reason that I'm in too much of a blind panic to explain right now . . . It's something to do with me and Olly, and what he said Grandmother

told him about me wearing it to marry him one day . . .
Something to do with that expression on his face, when
he came across me trying the veil on in my hotel room,
and pulled it back, and looked down at me.

It is, I think, the feeling that if this lace is irreparably
damaged, we will be, too.

It's a very, very unhelpful moment for this realization:
that I'm just as hopelessly in love with Olly as he is –
was – with me.

Because I'm already seriously out of puff, and – oh,
shit – the traffic is easing, slightly, and Tash is starting
to speed up . . .

'Nora!' I yowl, again. 'Tash! Stop!'

Now I can see passers-by, making their way to the
tube or waiting for buses, staring at me, looking like
some sort of demented bridesmaid to a biker. But some
of them are cottoning on surprisingly fast because they're
starting to yell out to the motorbike, too: 'Hey, slow
down!' I hear one smart-looking woman shriek in Tash's
direction. 'You've got some sort of runaway bride behind
you!' A couple of car drivers, alert to their surroundings,
even seem to have noticed there's something going on,
and are hooting their horns.

It's no good. The bike is still moving, and I'm still
running behind it, as fast as my legs can possibly carry
me, stumbling in my strappy sandals and halter-neck
sundress . . .

. . . and then one of those very heels catches in a

small pothole, and I'm not running any more. I'm falling, falling forwards, and the bike ahead is keeping up its same speed . . . I feel, mercifully, Marilyn's bracelet pinging off rather than my arm coming off at the shoulder (I hope, even in all the confusion, I'd still be able to tell the difference), and I just have time to see Grandmother's veil, still intact, swooshing off on the back of the bike as my head thuds on to the pavement, just outside the tube station.

Chapter 18

The first thing I say when I come round is, 'Olly.'

I know this, because a paramedic who doesn't look a bit like Olly (being small, and blonde, and – crucially – female) peers carefully into my face and says, 'Hello, there. No, I'm not Olly. Can you tell me your name?'

'Libby . . .'

'Hi, Libby. So, you've had a bit of an accident . . . nasty combination of motorbike and wedding veil, from what a few people who witnessed it have been telling me . . . do you know the day of the week?'

'Monday,' I say, because this is the first day of the week that comes into my head, and because the other days of the week are eluding me just now.

'Um, OK . . .' She doesn't sound quite as convinced. 'Well, don't worry, Libby, we're getting you straight to St George's. Now, this Olly . . . Is he your husband? Boyfriend?'

'No,' I hear myself say. 'He's neither. Though he probably should have been, by now. And if he isn't, it's all my fault.'

'Right . . .' She shines a light into my eyes before asking, 'So is this Olly the person you'd like us to contact? Is there anyone else?'

I shake my head. Or rather, I try to: I seem to have been attached to a stretcher, with some sort of brace either side of my head, to keep it snugly in an immobile position.

'There's no one else,' I say. 'And now, there never will be. If I can't have Olly, I don't want anyone.'

'OK!' she says, brightly, in the tone of voice of an emergency medicine professional whose concern for my physical wellbeing is quite a lot higher than her interest in my love life. 'So nobody else you'd like us to get in touch with? Someone you might want to come and meet us at the hospital?'

'No.' I can feel a big, hot tear spilling out of the side of one eye. 'There's only Olly. He's the only person I'd ever want with me in a situation like this. But he's gone. Gone forever. Along with Marilyn.'

'So Olly and Marilyn were the ones on the bike?'

'No, that was Tash and Nora. Olly will be at the restaurant. And Marilyn Monroe . . . well, up until last night she was in my flat, but she's not there any more . . .'

The paramedic's eyes widen, just for a second. Then she says, in an even brighter and breezier tone, 'Well! Let's get you to the hospital nice and fast, shall we? You can tell the doctors all about . . . er . . . Marilyn Monroe being in your flat when we get there.'

358

'They won't believe me,' I mumble. 'About Marilyn Monroe, or Audrey Hepburn . . .'

And then I think I must pass out again, because things are going all cartoon-wobbly, and the noise of the traffic on the High Street is reverberating through my head like a powerful bass-line.

*

The first thing I say when I come round for the second time is, 'Olly.'

This time, though, it's quite a lot more accurate. Because Olly is, indeed, right here in front of me.

He's gazing deep into my eyes, and when he sees mine open and look at him he smiles.

'Hi,' he says.

'Hi,' I say, as I smile back at him.

So here we are. Just the two of us. Alone together, finally, in this brave new world we're now inhabiting, where he loves me, and I love him, and there are no secrets between us any more. It's a *wonderful* world, to appropriate the classic song. All right, there may not actually be any trees of green, or red roses . . . we are, in fact, sitting in the middle of what looks a lot like a hospital cubicle, with synthetic curtains the colour of Dettol and a scary-looking machine attached to my arm that emits a bleep every few seconds . . . but I don't think Louis Armstrong would have had quite as much of a hit if he'd sung about that . . .

'Welcome back,' Olly adds.

He looks, I can't help but notice, absolutely exhausted.

'Thanks,' I say. 'But you know, Olly, I haven't really been anywhere. I mean, I'm sure it's felt like that at times, what with me being so unreliable, and never there when you . . .'

'Libby.' He leans forward, so that his arms are resting on his knees, and his face is even closer to mine. So close, in fact, that if I didn't have this terrible headache when I so much as move my head a single millimetre, I could lean a little way forward myself, and put my lips close to his, and . . . 'Don't you remember the accident this morning?'

Accident . . . ?

Hang on.

The motorbike . . . the traffic lights . . . Grandmother's veil . . .

'Oh, God. How bad is it?'

'Well, it could have been much, much worse, just remember that.'

'Olly. Tell me. I can handle it.'

'Libby, don't worry! You're going to be fine, OK? The medics are looking after you really well. It's just a nasty concussion – you've been pretty out of it for a few hours – and quite a bit of bruising . . .'

'Not me! Grandmother's veil!'

'Your grandmother's *veil?*' His eyebrows, above those knackered-looking eyes, rise sharply upwards. '*That's* what you're worried about?'

'Yes . . . I was holding it when I fell . . . it was stuck on my bracelet . . .' Which is the first moment that it occurs to me: Marilyn's bracelet. Another priceless sentimental object that will be lost forever, thanks to this stupid accident.

'Ah. That explains things a bit more. Nobody could understand, from what the witnesses told the ambulance crew, why you weren't just letting go of the veil . . . anyway, as far as I know, the veil's all right. Nora and Tash noticed it was billowing around behind them just as they reached the A3.'

'Oh, thank God.'

'But honestly, Libby, and I know that veil must mean a lot to you; you really should be more concerned for your own health, and not the health of a pretty piece of lace!' He takes one of my hands. 'I don't want to lose you to a crazy accident like that, OK?'

I love the way my hand feels in his. I mean, I *love* it. When I think of all the times our hands must have touched before, and yet I never felt this wonderful, warm, tingling sensation . . . And Olly looks so handsome. Tired, and bleary-eyed, but incredibly, startlingly handsome . . .

'Oh, Olly,' I begin. 'You're never going to lose me. I just wish it hadn't taken me so long to—'

'Shit!' he suddenly says, pulling his hand away from mine.

Which wasn't . . . *quite* the reaction I was hoping for.

'I promised I'd let Nora know as soon as you woke up and started talking,' he goes on, reaching into his back pocket for his phone. 'She'll want to come right away.'

'But isn't she on a plane right now?' I don't really have much idea of the timescale we're dealing with here, but Olly did say I'd been out of it for a few hours. 'Or back in Glasgow already?'

'Are you kidding? She wasn't going to get on a plane when she knew something had happened to you! They turned straight around and got back to you just before the ambulance drove off. Tash has been looking after Nora over at the restaurant all afternoon. They can be here in fifteen minutes.' Olly produces his phone. 'I'll just give them a quick call,' he adds, pressing his screen and lifting it to his ear before I can say anything else. 'Hi,' he says, a moment later. 'Yeah, it's me . . .'

Something about his voice, which has suddenly gone incredibly soft, and his face, which has suddenly gone even softer, makes me realize he's not talking to Nora.

It's Tash on the other end of that phone, I'm sure of it.

'No, you can tell her to stop stressing. Libby's awake . . . yeah, and talking . . . I know . . . exactly . . . I am, too . . .'

He's smiling, now, as he talks: that fuzzy-edged one, where his eyes crinkle a little bit at the sides; the one he gives when he isn't so much finding something funny as just feeling incredibly relaxed and happy.

It's a smile I only usually see him give when he's with me.

'. . . yeah, if she's feeling up to it . . .' He stops talking into the phone for a second, glances up at me, and says, 'It's OK with you, isn't it, Lib?

'What's OK with me?'

'If Tash and Nora head over to the hospital? I mean, I don't know how many visitors you're allowed, but even if they can only pop their heads in . . .'

'Yes, yes, of course. It would be lovely to see . . . er . . . them.'

'Yeah, Libby says she'd love to see you,' says Olly, as he returns to the phone. He listens to whatever's being said on the other end for a moment, and then, lowering his voice just a little bit more, says, 'Absolutely . . . sorry it's not exactly going to be as salubrious as I'd planned . . . it'll still be on me, though . . . hey, who says that's not a proper first date? OK . . . OK . . . see you soon . . . bye.'

He shoves his phone back into his pocket, not quite meeting my eye for a moment.

'So,' I say, in a voice that may not sound completely normal (OK, that sounds a bit strangulated), but which, thank God, could probably be explained by the whole recent-head-trauma thing, 'you and Tash . . .'

'Yes. Well, maybe.' Olly is turning slightly pink in the cheeks. 'I mean, we had this fantastic night last night, and we'd agreed to go out for a coffee together today, until . . . well . . .' He gestures at the Dettol-coloured curtains and the bleeping machine attached to my arm. '. . . all this happened.'

'I'm really sorry,' I mumble.

'Libby, don't be ridiculous! It's not like you had a nasty freak accident on purpose just to prevent me meeting Tash for a proper first date.'

'No. God. I would never do that.' I clear my throat. 'So . . . you really like her.'

'Well, yeah. I mean, obviously it would be a bit long-distance, and both of us work crazy hours . . . but if you let things like that get in the way, you'd end up alone forever, wouldn't you?'

'Yes. You would.'

'But yes, I do really like her. She's terrific. Don't you think so?'

I wonder, briefly, if it's at all possible that head injury can do any damage to other important parts of your body, too. Because it feels, quite palpably, as if my heart has just split into several pieces.

Something I might ask a doctor about, when one of them turns up in a few minutes.

'Lib? Are you OK? You look a bit worse all of a sudden. Do you need me to call a nurse? I'm sure one of them will be along any minute, now you're awake . . .'

'No, I'm fine. I was just . . . yes.'

'Yes?'

'Yes,' I swallow, hard, 'I think that Tash is terrific.'

Because she is, let's face it. She might be A Bit Much, but she *is* terrific. She'll make Olly very happy. And Olly's happiness is the most important thing to me.

It's just acutely, exquisitely painful that I'm not the one who'll make him happy.

'That's . . . I'm really glad to hear that, Libby.' He looks, if anything, more relieved than he did when I opened my eyes a few minutes ago. 'I mean, obviously Tash and Nora are already friends, but it's good to hear my other favourite little sister gives this whole thing her seal of approval, too . . . You know what,' he adds, quite suddenly getting to his feet with a look of alarm, presumably because I'm looking even worse now, 'I think I *will* just go and find a nurse, actually, just to see if there's anything . . .'

He stops, because the Dettol-coloured curtain has just been flung open, dramatically, and Cass and Mum appear on the other side of it.

'Oh, thank God!' Mum shrieks, as soon as she sees that I've got my eyes open and I'm talking to Olly. 'She's come back to us!'

Which makes it sound more like I'm one of those amazing patients who lie in a coma for fifteen years and then suddenly sit up and ask what's for breakfast than a person who's been concussed and dozing in a hospital bed for the morning. But I suspect this is exactly what Mum *wants* to make it sound like: the drama of hearing that there's been an accident and rushing to hospital will be a little bit tarnished for her now that I appear, undramatically, to be awake and chatting after only a few hours.

Oh, God: and talking of drama . . .

'You've not got your camera crew here, have you?' I ask Cass, as she strides into the cubicle in front of Mum.

'Don't be ridiculous,' she says, leaning down to give me a brief but rather fierce hug. 'What kind of sister do you take me for?'

A split second later, she goes on, 'I mean, we've left them out in the hospital grounds filming exterior shots. I would never *bring them in* to film you, Lib.'

A split second later, she goes on, again, 'I mean, unless you were *happy* to go on camera and talk about what happened . . .?'

'I'm not,' I tell her, patting her hand, which she's left lingering on my shoulder, as if she doesn't quite want to take it away yet. 'But I appreciate you asking.'

'Oh, Cass, how could she *possibly* go on camera, with her face all horribly mangled like that?' Mum says.

'My face is *horribly mangled*?' I gasp.

'Mum, for fuck's sake!' Cass glowers at her. 'No, Libby, it's not horribly mangled at all. I mean, obviously if you actually *needed* your face for any reason – if those exact same injuries had happened to me, for example – it would be a disaster, because you wouldn't be able to work for weeks, until all the swelling and the bruising had healed—'

366

'Honestly,' Olly interjects, shooting a reassuring look over Cass's head at me, 'it's not that bad. You just look a bit sore.'

'Exactly,' Cass says. 'I mean, it's not all that much worse than that time you accidentally hit yourself in the eye with a cocktail shaker.'

'*You* hit me in the eye with a cocktail shaker,' I tell her.

'Oh, yeah.' Cass grins at me, looking – and this is a seriously rare event in the life of Cassidy Kennedy, I can assure you – a tiny bit sheepish. 'I did, didn't I? Oh, well, at least I'm completely dissolved of any responsibility for this one. Now,' she goes on, before anyone can point out that it's *absolved* and not *dissolved*, 'have they told you when you're getting out of here yet? Because if you're not in overnight, I need to call my cleaner and see if she can go round to my flat and put some fresh sheets on the spare bed . . .'

'Cassidy, don't be ridiculous,' Mum says. 'Libby's not staying with you. I'll have her to stay at mine.'

Which is really, astonishingly nice of Mum.

Until she adds, 'You're *far* too busy with filming, Cass, to have an invalid around cramping your style. Besides,' she goes on, with one of her favourite dramatic sighs, 'I am The Mother, after all. People would be accusing me of a dereliction of duty if I wasn't the one to take her in.'

'OK,' I say, 'I'm not a pile of laundry. I don't need to be *taken in* anywhere.'

'Actually, you might,' says Olly. 'If they let you out today, you'll need to have someone with you at all times for the next twenty-four hours. Because of the concussion thing.'

'Oh, well, that definitely rules you out then,' Mum tells Cass. 'You said you had a Brazilian wax booked tomorrow at ten.'

'Mum,' says Cass. 'I'll cancel the fucking Brazilian wax.'

I stare at Cass.

'You're my fucking *sister*,' she adds, to me, with a swoosh of her hair. 'You matter more than a *Brazilian*.'

As far as sisterly declarations of love go, this is pretty much the pinnacle.

All right, it may not come wrapped in hearts and flowers, and there may not be Disney violins swelling in the background. But still. Cass would be prepared to cancel one of her grooming treatments for me. It's incredibly touching.

'Honestly, neither of you need to worry about it at all,' Olly is saying, decisively. 'Libby can come and stay with me. In fact, I insist upon it.'

My heart flutters, just for a moment, at this rather thrilling display of manliness. Not to mention the image of Olly carrying me up the stairs in his flat and tucking me tenderly into bed . . . until it occurs to me. Tash is staying there, too.

And the thought of trying to recuperate in one

bedroom while Olly and Tash get up to God knows what in the other . . .

'I mean, Nora might still have to head home tomorrow, because of work, but Tash is staying until at least Monday,' he goes on. 'So I don't think there's a better place for you to be. Even if I'm stuck at the restaurant, Tash could look after you at mine—'

'No!' I practically yelp. 'I mean, I hugely appreciate all your offers for me to come and stay,' I go on. And I really mean it. Even Mum's offer, which – although she did still manage to make it sound as though she'd be doing it to help out Cass rather than me – I actually think is just as genuine and open-hearted as Cass and Olly's. (It's just that Mum doesn't, with the best will in the world, have all that open a heart.) 'But can we at least find out if I'm even allowed out of here tonight before—'

'Too right you'll need to wait and see if you'll be allowed out,' interrupts a woman in nurse's uniform, walking into the cubicle and glancing around, disap-provingly, at all the people in it. 'Hi,' she adds to me, coming up to the bed and giving me a brisk wave before turning to check the scary-looking machine I'm plugged into. 'I'm Esther. Nice to see you properly awake. How are you feeling?'

'Fine,' I say, 'bit of a headache. That's all.'

Because I don't think she'll be all that interested to hear that alongside this headache, I'm actually nursing a much more serious ache: one that springs from the horrible realization that I've screwed up my one chance at Happy Ever After.

'All the more reason to get a bit of rest before Dr Regan comes round.' Esther shoots Mum, Cass and Olly the sort of look that suggests she's not accustomed to being disobeyed. 'There's a decent enough coffee bar at the front of the Grosvenor Wing,' she says. 'Only a five-minute walk away. I can wholeheartedly recommend the lemon drizzle cake.'

Which they take as the signal it's quite clearly meant to be that they're being told, in no uncertain terms, to bugger off. Mum and Cass, being Mum and Cass, do so with a bit of harrumphing and outraged hair-swooshing, respectively, but Olly seems amenable enough, simply pausing at the edge of my bed for a moment to say, quietly, 'Seriously, Lib. Come and stay at mine. After all, what's the point of a best friend if they don't look after you in the aftermath of a one-in-a-billion veil-versus-Yamaha snarl-up?'

I know what he's doing, with that lovely smile of his, and that casual mention of us being best friends. He's letting me know that our quarrel last night is all water under the bridge. That not even Dillon can come between us.

I give him a much-less-lovely, watery-feeling smile of my own, and watch him as he follows Mum and Cass out of the cubicle.

'I wish,' observes Esther, a moment later, '*all* best friends looked like that.'

370

'Sorry?'

'Him. Your friend. The gorgeous one.' She tweaks my sheets, rendering them perfectly neat in an instant. 'Single, by any chance?'

I have to say, I'm getting heartily sick of all these women suddenly coming out of the woodwork to point out how attractive they find Olly: Dad's new step-daughter at the wedding; this nurse; Tash, obviously . . . where the hell have they all *been* for the last seventeen years? I mean, if just one person had pointed out to me that Olly really is a bit of a dish, I might have stopped looking at him as Just Olly and seen him, instead, the way I now see him: as Hot Olly. Perfect Olly. Love Of My Life Olly.

'Not really,' I manage to reply. 'He's . . . just started seeing someone.'

'Ah, well. All the good ones are always taken, aren't they?' Esther turns to head out of my cubicle herself. 'I'll have an auxiliary bring some water, and press the button if you need anything else, but you should close your eyes now and try and get some rest before the neurologist arrives. Lucky though you are to have hot friends and concerned family flapping around you like mother hens, you need peace and quiet right now.'

'I'm not that lucky.'

She lets out a snort. 'I see patients come in here after accidents way more serious than yours, undergo trau-matic emergency surgery, and leave here a week later

371

without having had a single visitor. You had people flocking in here fifteen minutes after you arrived. Trust me,' she finishes, as she steps out of the cubicle and pulls the curtains shut behind her, 'you're lucky.'

This puts things in some perspective, obviously.

And it *is* lovely – not to mention surprising – that I'm in the position of fielding three separate offers of assistance.

It's just that none of that feels like it matters right now.

I close my eyes, ignoring the dull thud-thud-thud at the front of my head, and try to concentrate on doing what Nurse Esther told me to do – get some rest – without allowing Olly to pop up into my thoughts every other second. Olly gazing down at me as I opened my eyes; Olly on the phone to Tash; Olly calling me, effectively, his little sister . . .

'Is she asleep?'

This is a whispered voice, from down at the end of my bed.

'I don't know . . . she *looks* asleep . . . gee, that hospital robe does nothing for her, poor thing.'

'To be fair, darling, I don't think that hospital robe would do anything for anyone. That awful green, and that *fabric* . . .!'

'Should we put her in something a bit more flattering, do you think? I'd be perfectly happy to lend her this mink stole, but she's awful funny about fur, did you ever notice?'

'I can't say I did notice, darling, but then I'm afraid I'm not awfully keen on fur myself.'

'Oh, *honey*. Say, you're not Canadian, too, are you?'

I don't actually need to open my eyes to know that this is Audrey Hepburn and Marilyn Monroe talking.

But I open them anyway.

And I'm right: they're both standing at the foot of my bed. Audrey is in her classic black Tiffany's cocktail dress, tiara in her beehived hair and cigarette holder in her gloved hand, and Marilyn is (barely) wearing that astonishing nude-effect sparkly dress from *Some Like It Hot*, with yet another dead furry animal slung around her sequinned shoulders.

It's a bit of a shock to see them out in the real world like this. *Both* of them, standing next to each other, gazing down at me like two exceptionally glamorous guardian angels.

'Honey!' gasps Marilyn.

'Darling,' says Audrey.

But this makes no sense. How are they doing this: appearing here, in St George's hospital, miles away from . . .

'The sofa,' I mumble.

The two of them blink at me and then – glancing sideways – blink at each other.

'Is she calling *me* a sofa?' Audrey whispers at Marilyn.

'Oh, honey, no, I don't think that for a second! If she's calling either of us a sofa, it's much more likely to be me.'

'Darling, don't put yourself down – your figure is simply stunning!'

'That's real sweet of you to say so, honey!' Marilyn beams at Audrey. 'Though I always wondered what it would be like to be a dainty little thing, like you.'

'You're not missing much, darling, I promise you that! It can be the most awful trial finding things that fit, and don't make me look like a dreadful old ironing board . . .'

'Oh, honey, if you're worried about looking a little flat-chested, you should just do what I do, and—'

'Don't tell her to stuff her bra with pantyhose!' I yelp. 'Please!'

They both look back at me, rather startled.

'I'm just saying,' I go on, 'that this is *Audrey Hepburn* you're talking to.'

'Well, honey, I know *that*.' Marilyn looks faintly peeved. 'We've been getting to know each other over a few cocktails.'

'You know, darling,' Audrey leans forward to announce to me, 'Marilyn makes the most divine Manhattan I've ever tasted.'

Which I assume she's only saying because she's, well, Audrey, and utterly delightful about everything . . . but I can't be so sure about this a moment later, when Marilyn produces a cocktail shaker from beneath her mink stole, and Audrey's beautiful, feline eyes light up.

'Darling!' she says, excitedly. 'You must have read my mind! I'm gasping!'

'Well, then bottoms up!' Marilyn says, opening the cocktail shaker, pouring some of the contents into the lid and handing it over to Audrey to drink from. 'You go first, honey,' she says. 'I'll only end up getting lipstick all over it.'

'Oh, well, I won't say no to that,' says Audrey, perching on the edge of my bed to take a sip. 'Heavenly! Now, darling, you wouldn't happen to have a cigarette lighter, by any chance? I find it awfully hard to drink a Manhattan and *not* smoke a cigarette at the same time.'

'You can't *smoke!*' I hiss at her. 'This is a hospital!'

'Darling, if it's a hospital, I'm quite sure everybody in here must be smoking! Hospitals are ghastly places to be, and smoking's just about the only thing that could possibly make it bearable.'

'Well, that and a delicious Manhattan,' Marilyn adds, giving both of us a wink.

'Yes, look, you shouldn't really be drinking, either . . . in fact, you shouldn't actually be here at all,' I say. 'Not to mention that I don't even know *how* you're here. I mean, I thought it was all to do with the sofa being enchanted, but . . .'

'Honey,' Marilyn whispers to Audrey, 'she's talking about that sofa again. Do you think she's got some kind of a complex about it?'

'I don't have a complex about the sofa!'

'I mean,' Marilyn is continuing, 'I've seen a lot of

shrinks, and they've told me I have complexes about all kinds of things, but I never knew you could have a complex about a sofa.'

'Mmm, I don't know . . . she *has* had a bit of a nasty bump to the head, the poor darling,' Audrey says, 'so maybe that's why she keeps talking about the soft furnishings . . . head injuries can make you say and do all kinds of peculiar things, after all.'

Which is when the penny drops. My head injury. That must be why I'm seeing them here, out of the confines of my flat for once. And *together.* This time it's not so much magic as concussion.

It's a huge relief and a bit of a disappointment at the same time.

'Oooh, maybe we could find that handsome doctor and ask!' Marilyn's eyes gleam with excitement. 'The one that just left here a few minutes ago!'

'That wasn't a doctor,' I say. 'That was Olly.'

'Olly . . . Olly . . .' Marilyn frowns, trying to remember if she's heard the name before. 'Say, that wasn't the guy you always used to talk about when we lived together, was it? The one who kept mistaking you for some kind of cookie? The one you went blonde for?'

'No, look, I didn't go blonde for anyone,' I begin. (Though I'm actually starting to doubt that. Because the more I think about it, the more I suspect I was subconsciously trying to look more like Tash, when I suspected Olly was starting to like her.)

376

'Olly?' Audrey interrupts. 'I thought the name of the man you liked so much was Dillon?'

'No. I mean, yes. It was Dillon. But that was just because I didn't realize that . . .' My voice catches at the back of my throat. '. . . that Olly was the one all along.'

There's a short silence.

Then Marilyn leans over the foot of the bed, ample cleavage practically spilling out of her sequinned bodice, and says, in her breathy little-girl voice, to Audrey, 'I don't remember anyone called Olly.'

'Me neither,' Audrey says. 'I'm not sure she ever mentioned him to me. He must be new on the scene . . .'

'No! That's the whole point. He isn't new on the scene. He's *old* on the scene. And the only reason I never mentioned him,' I add, despairingly, 'is because he was always *there*. Always around. So I didn't really notice him until . . . well, until he fell for someone else. And now it's too late.'

'Oh, honey!' Marilyn sits down on the other side of the bed and generously extends her mink to mop away the tears that have started to come down my cheeks. I'm so grateful for the kind gesture that I don't even bat the horrible thing away. 'Don't cry! He's not worth it.'

'But that's just it,' I gulp. 'Olly *is* worth it. He's the best man I've ever met. He's kind, and funny, and good-looking – nobody ever pointed out to me that he was good-looking! – and he's been there for me through thick and thin since I was thirteen years old. He's my soulmate. Or rather, he *was* my soulmate.'

'Well, if he's really your soulmate, darling, then you have absolutely nothing to worry about.' Audrey glances over at Marilyn. 'Isn't that right, darling?'

'Sure it is! You just need to hang tight, honey,' Marilyn tells me. 'Wait until he realizes he just can't live without you!'

'And then,' Audrey adds, in a faraway voice, 'he'll sweep you up into his arms, and place a kiss on your lips, and—'

'Can we please,' I interrupt, 'stop with the fairy-tale endings? I wouldn't be in this mess in the first place if I didn't get so caught up in bloody fairy tales! Peddled,' I add, unfairly, as I use Marilyn's mink to scrub my tears dry again, 'by the likes of you!'

'Oh, now, that's rather unjust, darling.' Audrey gives me a disappointed frown.

'Besides,' Marilyn says, 'fairy tales *can* come true!'

'No, they bloody can't! Not in real life. In the movies, sure – you meet the handsome hero, and he falls in love with you, and you float off into the sunset together . . .'

'Honey! That's exactly the plot of this new movie I'm shooting!' Marilyn announces, to me and Audrey. 'With Tony Curtis! Now, *there's* a handsome man, and no mistake. Oooh, and he's single, too—'

'But it doesn't work that way outside the silver screen,' I go on, before Marilyn can offer to set me up with Tony

Curtis or something. 'In the real world, you can't see the wood for the trees. In the real world, you spend the next thirty years of your life alone while you watch another woman lead the life you should have had, with the man you can't get over. But that wouldn't make for a very entertaining movie.'

'What wouldn't make for a very entertaining movie?' says a familiar voice, as a rose bush on legs walks into my cubicle.

For a split second I think this is another concussive hallucination, until I realize that it's Dillon, coming into my cubicle behind the most enormous bouquet of roses in existence.

And Marilyn and Audrey have both vanished, instantly – or rather, I assume, gone back into the battered parts of my brain that projected them here in the first place.

'Because if you're talking about the movie I shot with Martin Scorsese last summer,' Dillon is continuing, 'you're wrong, plain wrong, I can tell you. All right, I haven't seen the finished version yet and, knowing Mr Scorsese's standards, there's a very good chance that my scenes are going to end up on the cutting-room floor . . .'

'This is not going to be happening,' says Bogdan, who's sidling in behind Dillon – or as much of a sidle as you can do if you're the size of Bogdan. 'No movie director worth his pepper is going to be cutting you out of film.'

'His salt,' I tell Dillon, who's just popped his head out from behind the roses to give Bogdan a confused look.

'And what are you doing here? I'm not meant to be having visitors.'

'Ah, yes, the nurse in charge made that very clear . . . but I happen to be pretty good with nurses,' Dillon says, with a grin, 'and then there was merriment aplenty at the nurses' station about this being the biggest rose bouquet any of them had ever seen . . .'

'Is true,' Bogdan adds, peering around the bouquet himself to give me a rather fierce stare. 'Is this not most impressive bunch of roses you are ever seeing in your life, Libby? Is it not kind of Dillon to be getting these for you?'

'Er . . . very kind, yes, but—'

'And all you had to do to get them,' Dillon interrupts, 'was involve yourself in a horrific road-traffic accident that could have got you killed.' He puts the bouquet down, precariously, on the floor beside my bed, then sits down on the bed himself, exactly where Marilyn Monroe was just sitting. (Sorry: exactly where I *imagined* Marilyn Monroe was just sitting.) 'For fuck's sake,' he goes on, looking deep into my eyes without the slightest hint of his usual cheeky-chappie irony or humour. 'What in the name of Christ were you playing at, Libby?'

'I'm not *quite* sure what makes you think I deliberately set out to achieve a nasty concussion and a face that my own mother has just described as *horribly mangled* . . .'

'It's not horribly mangled. It's just a bit battered. And you still look gorgeous to me.' Dillon reaches for one of

380

my hands. 'But seriously, Lib, can you be a bit more careful, please? When Bogdan called me to say you'd had an accident, my blood turned to ice in my veins, I can tell you that.'

'Well, that was nice of Bogdan to call you,' I say, giving Bogdan a look over Dillon's shoulder that is intended to let him know I've sussed exactly why he did this: because he'll use *any* excuse to contact Dillon, frankly. 'And I'm sorry I gave you a scare.'

'Well, you fucking should be. Now, deep personal regrets aside,' – he picks up my hand and gives it a swift, rather tender kiss – 'how are you feeling?'

'I'm all right. My head hurts. And obviously there's that whole battered-face thing I've got going on . . .'

'But nothing more serious than that, right? I mean, you're not still seeing stars?'

'Er, well, that might depend on your definition of *seeing stars*,' I mumble, before adding, 'No. There's a neurologist coming round later, but it sounds like I might even be allowed out of hospital today.'

'Excellent. Then you can come and stay with me until you're completely recovered.'

'Oh, Dillon.' I'm even more touched by this than I was by Cass's offer, and Nurse Esther's comment about how lucky I am is ringing more true than ever. 'That's really sweet of you.'

'Is not just sweet,' Bogdan looms over my bed to tell me. 'Is gesture of true gentleman.'

'Yes, thank you, Bogdan, I know that.'

'Is beyond and above call of duty.'

'Agreed,' I tell Bogdan, firmly, before looking at Dillon again. 'But I can't take you up on it, Dillon. You don't need me hanging around your flat, cramping your style.'

'On the contrary. It's exactly what I need. And anyway,' he adds, with a grin, 'if it all gets a bit much, I'll just call up a nursing agency and get them to send over a couple of nurses. One to take care of you, and one hot one to take care of me.'

'What was it Bogdan was just saying about you being a true gentleman?' I ask.

Before Dillon can reply, the cubicle curtain tweaks open, to reveal Nurse Esther, looking distinctly less brusque and tetchy than she was when she was chucking Mum, Cass and Olly out to the coffee shop.

'Ever so sorry to bother you, Mr O'Hara,' she says, sunnily, 'but there are a couple of teenage girls who came in a few hours ago with some nasty burns from a séance gone wrong . . . it would really cheer them up if you'd pop in and say hello to them, take a few pictures . . .?'

'Well, I don't know about that . . . I'd have to put in a call to my agent, and my manager . . .'

'Oh! In that case, please don't worry about it, Mr O'Hara, I'm terribly sorry to have—'

'I'm messing with you,' Dillon says, getting to his feet and throwing one of his wickedly charming smiles in Nurse Esther's direction. 'Couldn't be happier to come

and say hi. You'll be all right,' he adds, to me, 'while I'm
gone for a few minutes?'

'In a fully staffed ward at a major hospital? I think
I'll survive, Dillon, thank you.'

He gives my hand a squeeze, then follows a dazzled-
looking Nurse Esther out of the cubicle, leaving me
alone with Bogdan.

It's Bogdan's turn to sit, heavily, on the edge of my
bed. He gazes, mournfully, at me.

'Am being seriously concerned for your welfare, Libby.'

'Well, that's nice of you to say, Bogdan, but honestly,
I'm fine.'

'Am not talking about head injury. Though obviously
you are being my best friend, Libby, so am not wanting
you to be in agonizing pain or imminent danger of death,
or any such thing.'

'Oh, Bogdan.' It's the first time he's ever called me his
best friend. 'That's—'

'Am talking about why in the name of God you are
turning down the advancing of Dillon O'Hara! And do
not be trying to tell me that is anything to do with
altered mental state after accident, Libby. He is telling
me that you have turned him down last night.'

'Yes. All right. I did.' I look at him, hard. 'Did he tell
you why?'

'There is no possible reason that I can possibly be
accepting for—'

'I found out about Olly being in love with me.'

383

Bogdan says nothing for a moment.

'Even this,' he says sorrowfully, when he does speak, 'is not good enough reason to be rejecting Dillon O'Hara.'

I give up.

'All right, yes,' he goes on, 'Olly is being in the love with you. I am apologizing for not giving you this information, but am assuming you must be aware already.'

'I wasn't aware already. Apparently I really am that stupid.'

'But he is moving on, Libby. Are you not seeing him with this Tash last night? He is all under her.'

'All *over* her,' I correct him. (At least, I hope it's a correction.) 'I know. I know he's moving on.'

'Then is no problem with you to be moving on, too. With Dillon.'

'I'm not in love with Dillon.'

Bogdan shrugs. 'I am not in love with your ex-boyfriend Adam Rosenfeld. This does not mean I am not going on the date with him tomorrow night.'

'Bogdan, for crying out loud! He has a boyfriend!'

'Is open relationship.'

'Says Adam, no doubt? The high grandmaster of truth and honesty? Because I tell you right now, Bogdan, if Benjamin Milne ends up blaming me in any way for this liaison between you and his partner, and decides not to invest in me . . .'

'Is no chance that this is happening. He is already

planning on the investment. Adam is telling me last night. The pillow talk, if you are knowing what this is.'

'Yes, Bogdan, I know what pillow talk is . . . but did Adam really say that Ben's planning to invest in me? I mean, I haven't even sent over my business plan or anything yet.' Not to mention the fact – it just occurs to me – that I've missed the deadline, given that it's already Saturday afternoon and I'm lying in a hospital bed with concussion.

'Apparently he is really liking your stuff. And he is a person who is following his guttural instincts.'

'His gut instincts?'

'Yes. He has told Adam he is putting aside forty million pounds for initial investment . . .'

'*Forty million quid?*' I gasp, the blood suddenly pumping so hard in my aching head that I think I'm about to have a seizure.

'Oh. Maybe not million. Am always getting confused with the English numbers. Am thinking now that was forty *thousand* pounds. Is that sounding more likely?'

'Yes, that sounds quite a lot more likely, Bogdan.'

Though still astounding, to be honest. I mean, forty thousand pounds' investment in Libby Goes To Hollywood is pretty much beyond my wildest dreams. It'll give me the chance to hire a proper web designer for my website; maybe even to hire a tiny studio where I can have more space and more equipment . . .

'So I would not be worrying, Libby. There is nothing

that will be changing Ben's mind. You can be relaxing. You have made it. Is good,' he adds, 'to be achieving major success in the professional life when you are making the ear of the pig when it comes to the personal life.'

And he's right: not just about me making a pig's ear of my personal life, but about it being nice to have a huge professional achievement, at least, to reflect on. Because if it really is true that Benjamin Milne has decided to invest forty grand in me, that's *huge*.

'Is exactly,' he goes on, 'what am saying to Miss Marilyn Monroe when am making the conversations with her.'

'Bogdan!' I stare at him. 'You didn't tell her she made a pig's ear of her personal life, did you?'

'Of course am not doing this, Libby. Are you thinking am insensitive idiot? Oh, this is reminding me.' He starts to reach into the small carrier bag he's been holding. 'Am dropping into your flat on way to hospital to pick up any essentials am thinking you might be needing for overnight – hair straighteners, de-frizzing spray, the deep intensive conditioner I am recommending to you last time we are passing Aveda salon . . .'

It seems like Bogdan has the same view of hospital essentials as my sister does.

'Because seriously, Libby, there is no reason to be having terrible hair just because you are in serious road-traffic accident . . .'

'Actually, I think of *all* the times it would be under-standable to have terrible hair—'

'And anyway, while am in your flat, am seeing this left on top of television.'

He pulls out, from the carrier, the tiny glass vial of Chanel No. 5 that Marilyn spritzed me with the night she gave me all her advice on how to Marilyn-ify myself.

'Am thinking is not sort of thing you are owning yourself. Am thinking is something that is being left for you.'

I take the bottle from him and gaze down at it. The bright neon hospital lights glitter and gleam off its faceted sides and for a moment – just for a moment – I almost imagine I see Marilyn's face glittering and gleaming out at me, too.

And then I have no time to imagine anything any more, because I can suddenly hear Nora's anxious voice out in the ward behind the curtains of my cubicle.

'Sorry, I know you wouldn't normally let a friend in to see someone, but I really, really need to see if she's all right . . . and actually, she's not my friend, she's more like my sister . . .'

I feel such an immense weight off my bruised shoulders that it's all I can do not to jump out of the bed and run out there to greet her.

But obviously I'm still hooked up to the scary machine, for one thing, and I wouldn't like to encounter the wrath of any of the nurses, for another.

So I prod Bogdan in the ribs.

'Can you go and tell her I'm in here?' I ask. 'And that I'm absolutely desperate to see her?'

Because it's true what Nurse Esther said: I *am* lucky. I have, despite myself, the best friends in the entire world.

And I'm going to need them, let's face it, if I'm going to get over Olly.

As Bogdan gets up and pops his head out of the cubicle, I take the lid off the glass perfume bottle, hold it to my wrist and give it a little spray. I bring my wrist up to my nose and inhale.

It's like having one of those friends, Marilyn Monroe, here with me once more. Which is nice, apart from anything else, because I have a suspicion that this was her parting gift, and that – head injuries and concussion-related sightings aside – I'm never going to see her again.

Then I fold my hand around the little glass perfume bottle and hold it, very tightly, beneath the bed covers, as Nora comes hurrying through the Dettol-coloured curtains towards me.

She's holding Grandmother's veil, with Marilyn's rhine-stone bracelet still dangling off the end of it.

I can see a small rip, just on the hem where the bracelet is hanging.

But apart from that, it's still, somehow, undamaged.

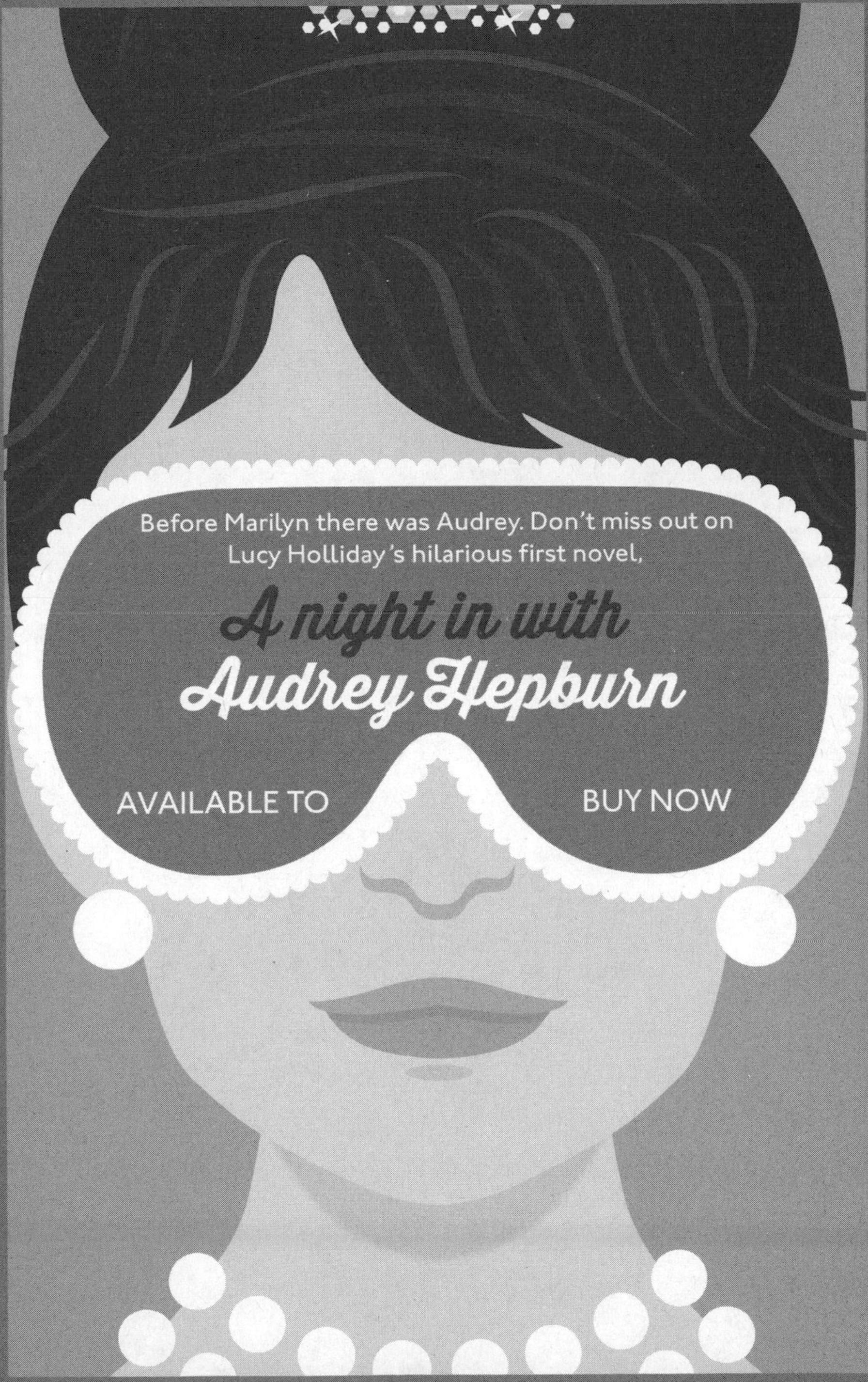
Before Marilyn there was Audrey. Don't miss out on
Lucy Holliday's hilarious first novel,
A night in with
Audrey Hepburn
AVAILABLE TO
BUY NOW

And the adventures continue for Libby in

A night in with
Grace Kelly

COMING IN   2016